POWER
MULTIPLIED

POWER MULTIPLIED

*The novel of a woman, a whale,
an alien child in peril*

CATHY PARKER

ACKNOWLEDGMENTS

Many thanks to my editor Jennifer Caven and to Joan Dempsey for her thoughtful preliminary comments; to Steve White for catching a catastrophic goof and giving me such excellent advice; to Dr. John Frank Hurdle for his medical input; and to my friends Peggy Buchanon, Deb Dearinger, Mavis Hunter and Renee Wanager for their unerring support.

For John, Cindy, Claudia, and Kim
For Mauyak, and
For beluga whales, mastiffs, and little black cats everywhere

PART ONE

STRUCTURAL FAILURE

CHAPTER ONE

SHANNON KENDRICKS SUDDENLY LOST SIGHT of the green-black waters of the Alaskan Sea. She saw nothing except black emptiness. On her lips she faintly tasted the salty sea, and she smelled a hint of repulsive, metallic blood. Fainter still, she heard the echo of frantic screams.

A premonition. A disaster would strike, strike soon, and strike here. The certainty of it chilled her to the bone, despite her heavy T-shirt and even heavier old cardigan.

She'd never before experienced such a foreboding of catastrophe—although she'd become good at a milder version of predicting the future: she could tell when someone would soon knock on her door, and when the phone was about ring. Those intuitions hadn't ever been wrong. Perhaps this new premonition resembled those, but on a much grander and more terrifying scale.

Her past predictions always affected her personally and happened shortly after the warning, so terrible tragedy would probably hit her and everyone around her any time now, inflicting immeasurable damage.

But *did* these strange and frightening impressions accurately predict her future? She had no reason to believe her mind had suddenly blanked out of reality and into nightmare mode; she'd taken no drugs, consumed no alcohol. Lately.

She didn't experience hallucinations. In fact, the last time she even *thought* she had fallen prey to hallucinations, the— *oh no. No, no, and no!* Surely not an alien visitation again. Shannon buried that thought deep in her mind, hopefully never to be revisited.

Okay, her mind checked out as sound, and capable of the forewarning. But seriously, *could* a disaster happen here? Shannon looked around. She stood in the Dickson Marine Mammal Research Center Underwater Complex, the UC for short, twenty-six feet below the sea. The UC consisted of a giant wheel with an outer and inner ring, connected, like the spokes of a wheel, by eight viewing corridors that radiated out from a central hub of research labs. At the point where the outer ring bordered the solid rock of the shoreline, elevators led up to the Dickson's landside buildings. Sure, tons of water pressed down on the UC, but the best engineers Dickson money could buy had sworn that not even a hurricane or an accidental collision by a ship could damage the structure.

Bright underwater lights reached out in every direction, yet revealed nothing alarming to Shannon's watchful eye, nothing that could cause the disaster Shannon expected to arrive any minute. But her vision told her that when it arrived, it would endanger, or end, dozens of lives. It would shatter the Underwater Complex like a heavy boot on thin ice.

Shannon should alert security, but what would she say? That a cataclysmic event would hit the UC, but she had no idea exactly what would happen or when? Security would simply ignore her until she could give them something concrete.

She closed her eyes and tried to recapture the salty sea, the blood, the tortured cries, hoping a fuller image would form.

Nothing.

As if she didn't already have enough to worry about with Juneau missing.

Today Juneau, a snow-white beluga whale and Shannon's research partner, had set out on her very first day of freedom from the steel-and-concrete sea pen that extended from the shore in a great semicircle around the UC. She'd lived in captivity for ten long years at the SeaQuarium in Ocean City, California, in a pool that the designers had declared generous compared to other captive whale pools, but compared to the whole northern Pacific Ocean, *um, no.*

The Dickson had set her free today at last. And then she had disappeared.

Shannon whipped her radio off her belt.

"Hey, Steve. Shannon here. Have you spotted Juneau on your monitors by any chance?"

"Why hello, Shannon. What's it been? Let me check my log. Wow, seven minutes since you last asked. I've been up here looking for her nonstop and chewing my hangnails, thanks to you. And no, nothing. Nada. She's definitely MIA."

"Are you sure?" Shannon said. Steve's throat rumbled and Shannon broke in. Steve had done his part. "Sorry, of course you're sure. And I'm not spooked. Maybe I'm a little spooked. Okay, I'm major spooked, Steve. And do not, I repeat, do not log that statement. Please."

"I've got your back. But look, you should call this in. You'll find yourself in the deepest shit if anything has happened to Juneau, and Moon finds out you didn't sound the alarm. They just beefed up the rescue forces, so now we have more assets on the ground, or more accurately, more bodies and boats in the water, for stuff just like this. Use 'em."

Indeed, Dr. Moon, the Director of the Dickson, would rain fresh hell down upon her if anything had happened to Juneau. Fortunately for Shannon, just this afternoon he had traveled down to the Dickson's main facility in Ocean City because of a major fire in the main lecture hall there. She'd gained some time to bring her errant beluga home before he caught wind of Juneau's absence.

"Yeah, I heard about the new troops," Shannon said, not really listening. "Let's give it fifteen more minutes. If I can't find her, I'll call it in. Let me know if you spot her. And thanks."

Steve clucked into the radio and said, "Okay, it's your funeral. And if I know Moon, we're talking cremation."

"Um, Steve, one more thing. Nothing else on the monitors looks . . . I don't know, suspicious, worrisome, out of the ordinary?"

"Like what?"

"Storm coming? Ship near the perimeter? A kraken? Some other giant monster from the deep, anything like that?"

"Nope, everything's calm and routine, and I'd likely have dozed off by now if I didn't have your calls to look forward to every few minutes."

"Okay, thanks. But keep your eye out, Steve. Something's brewing. I can feel it."

"Will do. Over and out."

Shannon pulled her long, thick, silver-blond braid over her shoulder and ran her fingers through the tip again and again as she tried once more to reach out to Juneau. She and Juneau enjoyed a telepathic link, thanks to an alien encounter five years earlier, which no one at the Dickson knew about. She used it now. Again.

Where have you gone? Can I help you?

She waited.

Nothing.

Juneau *always* responded. The fact that she hadn't done so for hours now meant that something was not right. Yet, because of the telepathic link, she'd know if Juneau had suffered an injury, or had become trapped and needed her help. And she knew that if she called in Juneau's AWOL status, research vessels would go out after her, intending to net her and bring her back. Shannon would not allow that. The biologists from the SeaQuarium had netted Juneau when they first captured her as an adolescent. They'd done enough damage. No more.

Slipping her pale green cell phone out of her pale green sweater pocket, Shannon dialed her friend and research teammate, Dakota Quartermark.

"You again?" Dakota said before Shannon could take a breath to speak. "She isn't back then, sweet cakes? I still think it's too soon to worry. I mean, she's tasting total freedom, out of the pen, or should I say penitentiary, for the first time, practically, since babyhood. Sure, the pen is a step up from that miserable little zoo pool she used to call home, but give me a break, a chance to flex that beautiful fluke for miles and miles? She needed this, Shan. She flat out freaking deserved it. Let her enjoy it."

Shannon tried again.

"But she's trained. She—"

"Shan, baby, you are definitely exhibiting mother beluga behavior here. But you didn't give birth to her. She will not swim alongside your belly forever. Get over it."

"But I—"

"Cut the apron strings, kid. And trust her. She'll be back in her own time. Everybody knows she's bonded with you. Now go away. I'm working. Eat a candy bar. Wash it down with a chocolate shake, like you always do. You'll feel better."

"Okay. And thanks. I—"

The buzz of the dial tone interrupted her. She looked at the receiver, shook her head, clicked off, and peered out into the dark waters, her hands fiddling with her braid.

Where are you?

Suddenly, as before, the image of salt water, blood, and screaming smacked her hard, but with greater urgency, like the wail of a disaster siren. To keep herself from collapsing to the floor, she gripped the handrail that ran the length of Corridor Seven.

Checking the crowd down the five-hundred-foot, tubed corridor, she spotted maybe ten tourists and a few researchers. More would be lingering in the other corridors. And in the central hub, rising three stories, housing lecture rooms, offices and research laboratories? Fortunately, at this time of day, ten past six in the evening, probably only a few scholarly types. But only the people up in the Visitor's Center, the living quarters, and the infirmary—all above ground on the inhospitable rocky coast—only they would completely escape a true collapse of the UC.

She must do something, but without anything concrete to tell security, frustration overwhelmed her.

Do you know anything, Juneau? Are you staying away because disaster is about to strike?

Exactly eleven minutes later, Juneau contacted her. As Shannon struggled to suss out more of an impression of the salty, bloody event to come, Juneau's telepathic image hit her with the shock and power of a sonar blast.

CHAPTER TWO

JUNEAU'S IMAGE, IMBUED WITH WILD URGENCY: Shannon running hard for the nearest elevator that could take her to solid ground. The enormous undersea complex cracking and splintering, followed by explosive thunder as the UC collapsed inward; the sea, the relentless, bitterly cold and salty sea, rushing in, drowning everyone who couldn't make it out.

Shannon didn't question the beluga for an instant. If Juneau told her the UC would break apart, then it would break. The sheer force of Juneau's message galvanized every muscle in her body. She touched her braid once for luck, then flipped it back over her shoulder, threw her clipboard to the floor, screamed "Run!" and took off, hell bent for leather.

The Dickson didn't close until nine on these glorious long-lit Alaskan summer evenings. As she ran, Shannon checked her watch: only 6:25. Even so, most of the visitors would have headed out for dinner by now. She hoped. Further along the corridor, she spotted Todd Zimmerman, fellow Dickson researcher and friend, with two guests. She stopped and grabbed Todd's elbow.

"Get the hell out, Todd. Structural damage. She's coming apart. Water's coming in." When the threesome only gawked at her, she paused and screamed, "And I mean *now!* Get these people moving."

With a tiny hop, Todd went into action and started moving his people. Shannon raced ahead. At the first intersection where visitors and staff could cut through the inner ring to the other concourses, she stopped.

Think.

Shannon couldn't warn everyone herself; she needed security's intercom system. She snapped her radio off her belt and pressed a new code.

"Security here."

Shannon, both panicked and winded, hurried into her words. "Hi, I need to warn—" but in the next instant she gulped in a large breath and choked.

Wait. What? Even in her current adrenaline-pumped state, her mind froze at the sound of those two words on the radio. She'd just heard the one voice she never expected. The one voice that could make her forget impending disasters and missing whales and everything else. That deep, calm voice with the slight, unidentifiable foreign accent and Old World formality she could listen to for hours. Her heart skipped a beat.

"Luke?"

"Yes, Luke Quintana. Shannon?"

"What?—why?—I—never mind." He should be down in Ocean City enforcing the law, not here in Alaska. She took a deep breath. "We have a major emergency. The underwater complex will collapse at any moment. You must make a public announcement and move everybody out now. And send some wheelchairs and people down here for the disabled. No time to explain."

Shannon heard a short muffled conversation.

"Shannon Kendricks? The Project Juneau operative? Jenkins here."

Shitsky. Rod Jenkins. Second in command of security. This would not go well.

"Rod. Luke told you what we have to do, right?"

"What's the source of your information, Kendricks? We haven't heard anything from anyone else. What's happened on Concourse Seven?"

"Nothing's happened yet, but we're running out of time. Get everyone out. People could die, Rod. This will be bad. Make the damn announcement."

"Not a chance, Kendricks, I'm not causing a panic on your say-so, no matter how much of a big shot you think you are around here. So get your butt up here and tell me what the hell's going on."

Triple shitsky. Once again Rod's giant ego was rearing its ugly head. He'd been offended since the day Moon prioritized the Juneau Project, he was offended by Shannon on general principles, and overall, he'd always been offended by the world.

Shannon pounded the nearest window wall, wishing it were Jenkins's bald, sunburned head under her fist. Wishing she had Thor's hammer for the pounding.

She took a deep breath. "Put Luke back on, would you, Rod?" she said as sweetly as she could muster.

Luke's voice returned. "This is Luke. If I'm not mistaken, we're exactly where we left off, Ms. Kendricks," Luke said. "You, in the middle of a crisis, and I, terribly afraid to ask what the crisis is."

Juneau, disaster, and now Luke. For sure *triple shitsky*. "Juneau imaged me that the UC will collapse. You've got to get the people out. Tell Jenkins, oh, I don't know, anything. Uh . . . tell Jenkins I saw an unattended, suspicious backpack at the end of Concourse Seven. If it's a bomb and it blows, it'll take out Seven, and will cause a chain reaction in the connecting tubes that'll take out the rest. He'll have to evacuate, right?"

Luke's voice became more serious. "Slow down, Shannon. Be calm. There's a backpack?"

"No, there is no backpack!" Shannon's raised voice reverberated down the concourse. Heads turned her way.

After a short pause, Luke said quietly, "But when he finds no backpack down there?"

"Luke, are you not listening? The UC is about to explode. There won't be any 'down there' down here anymore."

Shannon hung up, took a deep breath, and commanded her legs to pound forward.

White noise crackled over the public service system and Luke's voice followed—that welcome voice, authoritative, softly spoken, no hurry in it. Everyone would listen. No one would panic. But they would move with his command.

"Attention. This is security. All personnel and visitors in the Underwater Complex shall proceed immediately and in an orderly but timely manner to the nearest elevator and return to the Visitor's Center on the mainland. This is not a drill. I repeat. . . ."

Shannon ceased to listen, stopping each time she overtook hesitant souls to urge them again to run. Run!

As Shannon pushed on, odd thought-bits filtered through her mind. Her life did not flash before her eyes. No, she found her childhood, her career as an attorney, her life before Juneau and Luke and the aliens in most respects not worth remembering.

Luke. How had he popped up here? To know he was standing right up in the security center, so close, and she might never have the chance to look into his face again, to touch his cheek. . . .

Getting tired. Her legs dragged along, as if someone had attached an octopus to each one. She halted, breathed in long and deep, then took off again with grim determination. She *would* look into Luke's deep, dark eyes one more time; she *would.*

Hold up. Shannon halted abruptly, and took stock of her surroundings. Nothing had happened. Nothing looked about to happen. Had Juneau misunderstood the situation? Had Shannon caused this panic and mass exodus for nothing? How totally humiliating. She'd crawl under her bed among the dust bunnies and hide for the next half century if—

A thudding boom shook the floor. A crackle, followed by a thousand crackles more. The ear-splitting burst of the breaking corridor.

Up and down the concourse, people screamed. Those involuntary, gut-felt bellows of fear that restrained folks think they'll never be able to belt out, even when they need to. But then the world crashes in on them, and they find that terror yanks those screams right out of their mouths.

The flood of thundering water smashed through the top of the walkway, not behind Shannon as she expected, but in front of her horrified eyes, down near the elevators. At first, the hole in the concourse ceiling, about the size of a bicycle wheel, brought the water through like an overflowing stream, but that soon changed.

CHAPTER THREE

CUT OFF FROM THE ELEVATORS built into the coastal cliff, Shannon spun, breathing hard. She reached the connecting passage to Concourse Six and stopped to catch her breath. She looked toward the breach. The bicycle *wheel*-sized hole had become a *bicycle*-sized hole, but if she pushed herself, she had a fighting chance to reach the Concourse Six elevators before Seven's demise caused the inevitable collapse of Six.

"Get over to Concourse Six," she screamed to the people farther back along the corridor. She checked them briefly for familiar faces.

Yes, there.

With a sinking heart, Shannon recognized the woman she'd seen earlier with Todd: thick glasses, perhaps seventy-five, portly, a cane and an obvious limp, her face glazed with fear and glossy with tears. Todd remained at the woman's side, his arm circling her waist for support.

At their pace, they would never make it.

Shannon sighed. She must help them, even if it meant . . . She loped their way.

But never reached them. She heard the sounds of the concourse ceiling breaking up completely. Turning toward the sound, she stared, terrified, as water poured in like an ever-increasing, raging river, obliterating carpet and the discreet inset fluorescent lighting, inking out the very walls of the corridor.

She turned back and ran toward Todd. She'd made it to within a few yards of her friend when the wall of water, filled with roiling thermoplastic remnants of the broken concourse, caught up with her. The ominous rumble of it overtook her like a train speeding down a tunnel and overrode all other sound. At that moment, her eyes met Todd's, and he lifted his impossibly red, caterpillar eyebrows, as if to say, hey, I'll miss my Gina and the twins, but what you gonna do? Shannon gave a slight nod as she picked up the image of his family, as clear in her mind as in Todd's.

Dive now! Juneau interrupted her with a more urgent image.

Though Shannon saw only carpet in front of her, she gulped a lungful of air and dove without hesitation. She never hit the floor. The angle of her dive saved her from a broken back when the shockingly freezing water struck like a tsunami.

Debris and a stubborn piece of the concourse that had twisted inward but refused to rip free slowed the wave just enough to save Shannon from the full force of impact. The roiling sea spun her like a jelly bean in a clothes dryer. Sounds became muffled, echoing, as if from somewhere far off. Bits of the broken UC struck her, cut her, pushed her along. One big section of railing knocked the side of her head. A piece of the concourse flooring slammed hard against her left arm, causing an electric, sickening jolt.

The turbulence tugged her farther and farther from Corridor Seven until the waters calmed.

So cold. Frigid. Her jeans and oversized sweater weighed her down. *Get rid of them.* She shook off her flats, wriggled out of the jeans and pulled off the sweater and her bulky shirt, her injured left arm screaming in resistance.

No air.

Bad. Very bad.

Don't panic. Think.

Juneau? Can you help me?

The images came: *Juneau, fluke pumping, swimming her way.* Shannon couldn't wait. Her lungs burned.

She would die now.

The image of Shannon's grandmother, a tall, spare Norwegian, flickered into life, sparkling and spirited. Shannon made it a habit to sling her curses at the Norse gods in fond tribute to her grandmother, who'd passed down a considerable store of grit and determination to Shannon. She reached for that strength now. Her grandmother's ice blue eyes stared at her, intense and piercing. *You have not died,* those eyes seemed to say. *Not yet.*

Right. Don't give up. Fight.

Another image from the whale: *Shannon kicking and clawing her way up to the surface of the sea.*

Shannon whipped her head in every direction. Darkness. *Confusing.* The roiling water had somersaulted her so many times.

Which way to the surface?

Juneau's image: *Shannon's head pointed toward the surface.*

Somehow Juneau sensed Shannon's orientation. Probably echolocation, but how she could use it in this turbulent mess, Shannon didn't know.

Shannon kicked as if demons nipped at her heels, but one of her ankles wouldn't flex. It dangled uselessly. Her good arm punched up, fist clenched, then thrust down in a wide arc. She quickly tired. The burn in her lungs, the screaming need to open her mouth, the instinct to breathe, tormented her beyond her ability to endure. She pushed upward until she had nothing left. Soon she'd open her mouth, she'd breathe in the sea. She'd—

Despite her panicked desperation, Shannon registered a great cracking and whooshing as Concourse Six flew apart and continued the chain reaction that would obliterate the entire Underwater Complex. The collapse sent a powerful upward surge her way.

Sweet mother of Thor, thank you for small favors.

Her good arm, now spent, hung at her side. Her good leg could only kick like soft kelp waving in the shallows, moving with the upflow.

Every alarm system in Shannon's body screamed for her to take a breath, *take a breath.* A whimper sounded in the water. Her own desperate cry.

But . . . What—?

Clicks, crackles, a high-pitched whistle. Juneau? No. Her imagination.

No help coming. One more push. Push for the surface.

Blackness darker than the sea around her seeped into her mind.

Luke. She never told him she loved him.

Her mouth opened. Water rushed into her lungs.

A last impression, a brush of rubbery skin beneath her rapidly numbing arm. And then, nothing.

CHAPTER FOUR

SHANNON'S HEAD BOUNCED, her cheek hitting something slippery and hard.

That hurt. Shannon cast about her mind for an explanation of the painful thump. Couldn't think of one. Couldn't think much at all, really.

She rested for a moment, not worrying about thinking.

She stirred. *She ought to figure out her situation.*

Okay, open the eyes. Get some input. In her head, she gave the signal to her eyelids. *Open.* She waited.

Nada. Brain link to eyelids apparently not online. *Fine.* She kept them closed.

What else could she learn?

One: She was lying on her stomach with her left cheek resting on a smooth surface. Sand?

Two: the air smelled of brine, birds, the vegetation of the sea.

Three: she was listening to the slap of waves.

Maybe the incoming tide was pushing her along, then bouncing her head on the wet, hard, compact ground when the tide receded. Yes, maybe on a beach.

Four through fifteen: Cold. Very cold. Not in California then.

Why was she here? She struggled to remember. *Groggy . . . can't recall . . .* She pushed her mind harder for any inkling.

Nope.

So sluggish. Her brain had powered down to dim, as weak as a flashlight about to go dark.

A nagging message, just beyond her grasp, warned her that something important had happened and she should try to remember.

So sleepy. So cold. Her brain had turned into a cold snowball in an ice box in Antarctica . . . or even Alaska, like—

Oh.

Unwelcome memories rushed through her mind—the ominous crack in the UC ceiling, the ear-splitting roar of a murderous tide, painful blows—probably giving her some broken bones—the icy shock of the Alaskan Sea.

Right.

Now she remembered the pain.

She inventoried her body parts. Each and every one of them hurt like hell. And every bounce brought new anguish. The aching, pulsing, stinging cuts and bruises she'd sustained during the collapse now tortured every inch of her skin. Her puffy eyes stung; her salt-laden eyelashes accounted for the clamped-closed eyelids. Even her bones felt brittle and thin, as if they would implode, just like the UC. Her left arm screamed its objections to the slightest movement. And her chest felt as if a sharpish object was slowly slicing through her, chin to stomach.

No wonder she'd put off bringing the brain back online. Dumb and numb, that was the ticket.

She tried to clear her parched throat, but the action morphed quickly into a cough followed by the retching of a throat's-measure of salt water. Another cough. A cupful of sea spurting from her lips. More wrenching coughs convinced Shannon her ribs absolutely would break apart if she hacked one more time.

However. Better out her mouth than sitting in her lungs and stomach. She breathed in slowly, mindful of the protesting ribs.

Air in the lungs. Cool, fresh, wonderful air.

At least the groggy mind sludge, the heave-up of sea spit, even the insistent pain, all meant she hadn't died alone in the black suffocating depths.

A surprise, to be alive.

She welcomed the pain for a moment, because she could still sense it. She could still breathe. She would survive to keep her Juneau free from captivity. And Luke? She'd . . . she'd . . . okay, she didn't know what would happen when she saw Luke, but at least she'd last long enough that something would happen.

Perhaps.

To survive, she'd need to sit up and rescue herself here in a minute.

In a minute. . . .

* * *

She lay prone and still, bobbing, able to summon neither the will nor the strength to make any move.

The seconds passed. The terrible memories circled in her mind, a never-ending journey on a nightmare Möbius band. The echo of screams. Had Shannon screamed? Probably.

She remembered the elderly woman with Todd. A tiny detail of the terrified tourist drifted into Shannon's mind. A pale hand, blue veins rising to the surface, skin translucent, gripping Todd's arm, a bent finger on that hand, a bulging knuckle on that finger, swollen and red with arthritis. It must have pained her terribly. Perhaps not anymore.

She remembered Todd, with death-accepting resignation haunting his eyes, his family haunting his heart. Shannon's tears welled in her puffy, scratchy eyes.

Her thoughts drifted. Where *in Odin's eye* was she, anyway? Time to find out. Shannon lifted her head. Her neck, weak and shooting excruciating arrows of protest into her head, gave her only a grudging inch.

She cracked open her salt-encrusted eyes. She should rub that stuff off. But she'd need energy for that. Plus it hurt to move. She let it go. The bright light on the horizon blinded her at first. As her vision cleared, she blinked. And blinked again. She lowered her head and closed her eyes.

Hallucination.

Had to be.

No way she could be lying *here*.

* * *

Some minutes later, after a little nap, she returned to her train of thought.

No way she could be lying here, because it . . . it appeared she'd somehow ended her struggle to escape from the bottom of the sea sprawled on Juneau's rubbery, white back.

Couldn't be.

If she believed her eyes, which she didn't, the whale had pretty much lined Shannon up along her back to keep Shannon's head and body above the waves as much as possible. And Juneau was adjusting herself carefully and continually so Shannon would stay that way. Good thing too; otherwise, in these frigid waters, Shannon would already be dead of hypothermia.

A sensory memory flash. Before she'd passed out: the familiar beluga clicks, the sense of sliding rubber. Could Juneau have pushed her to the surface when she could hold her breath no longer?

People had spun tales of whale and dolphin rescues ever since ancient times. *But this?* Seriously? When they'd just given Juneau the freedom to explore the whole ocean? Floating calmly for who knew how long, while adjusting in the waves to keep Shannon from slipping back into the sea? *Uh, no.*

She had to give props to her imagination, though. This was hands down Shannon's best, most cosmic example of wishful thinking ever. She remembered something smacking her head. Could be a concussion.

So, where was she really? Some little outcropping of pale rocks more likely.

She slid her bruise-tender right arm back and forth an inch or two. *Loki's curse,* even that hurt. The surface felt smooth and rubbery, like a beluga. Not rough and rocky. She peered through slitted eyes. A few slight yellow cracks on whitish skin—just as a beluga in the wild would develop, just as she'd begun to see on Juneau once the whale had left behind the rubbing edges of the SeaQuarium pools for the smooth, circular, metal sea pen.

Directly under her she could see a dorsal fin, which was only a gentle ridge on a beluga, not really a fin at all. And not a knife, cutting her lengthwise as she'd imagined from the pain in her torso. If she craned her neck, which, okay, she could manage one time, and one time only, she could even glimpse a blow hole. Beyond that, the whale's melon, right where it should be, like a lovely bulbous forehead. If she concentrated—and didn't *that* make her head buzz—she could hear the steady whale breaths, the familiar and comforting sound of the muscular blow hole ring opening and closing with each puff.

She hadn't imagined it! Juneau had come to her rescue.

Shannon had often gone swimming with Juneau in the water at the SeaQuarium, but no one had ridden the whales. Ever. She'd never even contemplated climbing on Juneau's back. Yet here she lay, and at Juneau's election.

Holy Odin. Bobbing along on Juneau. The best rescue ever.

Weak as a baby bird, hurting like a tomato at the bottom of a barrel of rocks, cold as a frozen fish stick, she savored the joy of this moment. Saved from the sea by a beluga whale. Her own wild, freedom-seeking Juneau.

You're not hurt? she imaged the whale.

Juneau imaged back a perfectly healthy, happy picture of herself.

At that, the kinks in Shannon's shoulders, which had knotted when Juneau first went missing, gently relaxed.

Exhausted, in a world of hurt, she thanked Juneau again for her rescue by using the fingernails on her right hand—or rather, the pitiful nubs that passed for her fingernails—to feebly scratch along Juneau's side. Belugas always loved a nice rub.

Just then, another bounce from the sea waves brought an especially brutal stab of pain to her midriff, a reminder that she still hadn't picked herself up and self-rescued. The cold-driven stupor gripping her mind would kill her if she didn't act soon.

In a minute.

She promptly drifted off again.

* * *

Shannon stirred awake. She'd been sleeping. A dangerous sign. She moved the toes of her right foot, barely, to rub Juneau's back. The effort did not impress.

Hypothermia.

Even as the word forced her to focus on the threat to her battered body, Shannon's hands and legs started to shiver violently. She turned her right hand over for a look at her fingers. Blue on the tips. Palm, the color of skim milk. *Big trouble.*

World of trouble. Shannon needed help and she needed it soon.

Despite the hurt in every cubic inch of her body, sleepiness crept back over her. No other sound broke the quiet wash of waves around her except the occasional cry of a seagull.

So tired, want to sleep, want to just let go. . . .

No! Snap out of it.

Perhaps if she could get a strong enough grasp on Juneau's dorsal ridge, the beluga could swim for the dock. She tried scooting down far enough to position her hand in front of her over the ridge.

Try slowly moving forward, Juneau.

Juneau swam a few feet.

No good. Water covered Juneau's back, Shannon's right hand didn't have the strength to hold on, her left hand didn't function, and the ridge didn't extend quite high enough for her to grip well. She almost slipped off the beluga altogether.

She let her cheek fall to the beluga's back. She would rest a second and then she'd try grasping Juneau's broad sides with her legs. As weak and cold as her legs felt, she didn't hold out much hope, but she'd try. She remained quiet for a moment, gathering her strength. Then slowly she slid her legs down Juneau's sides. Her feet hit the water and she braced for the stinging cold of the Alaskan Sea. She felt nothing at all.

Not good.

Her left arm, the one that had been tormenting her with stabbing pain ever since she first awakened, now felt as numb as her feet. A long gash along the inner side of her right arm, which appeared to have bled extensively but had now stopped, ached a great deal. So, not numb; she could still use it. She slid her right hand close to her chest and used it to push herself up. A little scooting of the rear end, and she had achieved a sitting position, facing Juneau's fluke.

Hah! She'd half saved herself.

She looked around, expecting to see the shore in one direction or the other. The UC didn't reach so far into the ocean that land disappeared from view.

But when Shannon gazed about, she saw nothing but ocean. She must have drifted out to sea in the—*what? hours?*—that she'd remained unconscious. She looked for the sun. Yes, it hovered closer to the horizon than she would expect for an early summer evening. It might be nine o'clock or so by now. And not a single piece of floating debris from the UC dotted the water around her.

Even from her new sitting position she doubted she could manage to hold on tightly enough for Juneau to try swimming for land. She didn't dare slip into the water to hold onto a fin. The cold would kill her.

Sitting, staring at the horizon, her thoughts scattered. The water mesmerized. Soon she forgot the puzzle she needed to solve.

* * *

Her mind drifted, nothing but a black screen. An idea filtered slowly through the darkness. Shannon sought the essence of the aliens who had visited to her mind, deep within her own subconscious, the essence that was more than memory, less than the living creatures. And the essence of her friends who had visited her mind were here, too; the essence her mind shows to her as piles of colorful powder. She was thinking now of Luke, and yes, *there*, she saw in her mind his deep forest green essence. She saw herself gently running her fingers through that essence.

"Luke," she whispered, "Luke, I'm here. I'm in trouble. Find me."

The whisper died, and slowly her mind darkened again.

* * *

A voice rang out in the sea-washed quiet, startling Shannon into a spasm.

"Shannon! Thank God." Luke's usually gentle voice sounded harsh with strain, but she'd recognize that voice anytime, anywhere.

Had she imagined it?

Shannon turned her head with great care and turned in the direction of the sound. *Odin's eye*! She *did* hear a real voice. And the voice *did* belong to Luke. A cabin cruiser sped her way, Luke leaning forward near the bow, a bullhorn in his hand. Same tall and sturdy frame. Same unruly black hair, tousled by the wind. Same neat bushy mustache, deep dark eyes, long thick eyelashes. Strong face. Looking less confident than usual at the moment.

The boat, aptly name *Rescuer One*, slowed as it came closer, when the pilot saw that Shannon hadn't climbed onto floating debris to save herself, as he'd no doubt assumed. He cut the motor. *Rescuer One* drifted to within a few yards of the whale. But the pilot hesitated to inch the boat any closer. The stern of the boat came to rest near Juneau's tail fluke.

Shannon rubbed her right palm along Juneau's back. Her braid dangled from her left shoulder, brushing the beluga's back. *Steady,* she imaged, *they'll try to stay away from you. But dive if you need to.*

The beluga held her position, although she must have been eager to put more space between herself and *Rescuer One.*

Easy. It's all right.

"Easy," Luke said, now standing at the back of the boat. Shannon couldn't tell if he meant her, the whale, or the guy at the wheel of *Rescuer One.* "Can you reach my hand, Shannon?"

"Uh, um, not sure . . . try. . . ." Her tongue felt as thick as an ox's. She attempted to lean forward, her good hand outstretched. *Dizzy, so weak.*

She couldn't reach him. Not even close. Have to move. *Go for it.* She wobbled onto her knees, but her good hand slipped on Juneau's rubbery back, and she almost slid into the drink.

"Never mind. You stay still," Luke said, raising his hand, palm out, to signal Shannon to stay put. "I'll move to where I can help you. I'll . . . I'll . . . whatever."

He opened a small gate, climbed down the two-step ladder, and turned to face the whale. After a moment's pause, he pulled off his boots and tossed them back into the boat, along with his jacket. Taking a deep breath, he slipped into the frigid water.

"Don't get in this freezing—" Shannon protested, seconds too late.

Luke put his hands on Juneau's fluke and began to work his way along her side. He stroked her back, and murmured to calm her, as he quickly slid toward Shannon. The whale heard very little of his voice, the range being low for belugas, but the strokes and Luke's gentle way—these she understood. She stilled.

Juneau? You're okay?

The whale sent along a reassuring affirmative.

Shannon inched her left leg all the way over to the same side of the whale as her right leg, intending to slide into the water just as Luke reached her. But the movement caused Shannon's vision to darken. *Her ankle*—something was very wrong with it. Dots swam across her vision. In another moment she'd pass out. Tears formed in the salty edges of her eyes. *Too much.* She cried out as she scrambled unsuccessfully to slide her leg back over the whale to where it had been before.

Juneau flinched, Shannon lurched, and she slipped all the way into the water. She gasped at the sudden icy plunge as her head sank beneath the waves.

Luke lunged the last few inches toward her. His closest arm encircled her waist just as she slipped below the surface of the water.

"Another few minutes, *cara*," he whispered to her, lifting her head and cradling it to his chest. "Hold on another few minutes. I've got you." Luke studied her for just a moment, frowned slightly in a way that didn't reassure, and gently began to maneuver along Juneau's side toward the boat.

Warm hands reached for her as Luke lifted her up along the ladder on the back of the boat. Luke climbed out immediately behind her, took a blanket from one of the crew members, wrapped her, sausage-like, and then scooped up the sausage and carried it down into the cabin.

Odin's eye. Shannon Kendricks had spent a lifetime proving she could do it all herself, and every time she ran into this man, he ended up carrying her here and there like a tall stalk of corn.

"Juneau?" Shannon said, trying to peer out the cabin as Luke deposited her on a cushion-covered bench.

One of the crew—it sounded like Savannah from the scuba diving team—called down to her. "No worries, sugar. She's swimming right alongside us, calm as a child with a sweet potato pie."

Shannon messaged her admiration to Juneau as buzzing filled her ears, like a helicopter or pterodactyl or . . . she let it go because there stood Luke, right in front of her, all six feet four inches of him.

Luke. He gently removed the dripping blanket they'd given her when she came aboard, toweled her off, and added another blanket, one that had been warming near a heater vent in the floor. She watched him as she absentmindedly ran her hand down her braid. When he tucked her into the toasty, warm blanket, she became momentarily distracted by the wonderful heat that radiated through her limbs. She closed her eyes and sank into the warmth. Soon she had recovered enough to wonder how in the world this California police officer, her former love, had turned up in the security office here in Alaska just when she needed him most.

CHAPTER FIVE

WHEN THE VENT-HEATED BLANKET LOST ITS WARMTH, Luke tucked her into a battery-heated wrap that brought the color back to her fingers and toes, her nose and lips. He handed her a mug of hot herbal tea, which she pulled into one shaking hand and moved close to her lips.

"Thanks, Luke," she croaked hoarsely.

Holding his hands over her hand to steady her, he said, "Don't try to talk, cara. Just rest."

The dimly lit cabin, crowded with life jackets, tarps, rope, blankets, packets of bandages, and boxes of medicines and ointments, smelled vaguely of antiseptic. Shannon had always hated the smell. But of course, she *had* been rescued by a rescue ship; she couldn't really complain.

She focused on Luke's large square hands covering her own. Warm. Steady. *She wouldn't object if he wanted to leave them with her all the way back to the marina.*

Unfortunately, he stepped away, taking those wonderful strong hands with him, to pull on a dry sweatshirt and pair of sweat pants, grab a chair, and place it by her side. He sat and smiled at her. Lifting a long, wet, silver-blond strand of hair that had loosened from her braid off her cheek and out of her eyes, he said, "It's good to be here with you again." His eyes darkened and his voice sounded uncharacteristically unsteady as he added, "I thought I'd lost you."

Then he cocked his head slightly.

"You want to know something odd? The crew had given up searching for you in this area, didn't figure you could have drifted this far west of the UC. We were going to leave to search further south. But then I heard you whisper my name. And I knew I had to follow your whisper to you. So I did."

And then Shannon remembered. She *had* whispered to Luke from deep within her mind. And he had come.

For a brief moment Shannon forgot the cuts and bruises, the throbbing in her head, the sharp pain that gripped her when she breathed deeply, when she moved her left arm, when her ankle twitched. She forgot the thick fog that had frosted her brain like ice on a pond, her urgent need to pour calories into her alien-induced energy-hungry system. She forgot the horror of what had just happened to the UC. For a moment nothing existed but Luke's warm eyes and the gentle brush of his hand along her face.

For a moment.

In the next instant, Shannon found herself fighting a blackness that lurked at the edges of her vision and threatened to pull her under.

But before she could close her eyes, she must learn about the UC victims.

"The people," *Odin's eye*—her voice sounded even more unsteady than his. She cleared her throat. "The people in the UC. Did most of them—did they get out?"

Luke, who had been studying her face with a scowl, as if he sensed the blackness threatening her, blinked and looked away. "I don't know many details. Rod pulled you up on his monitor after you switched your radio off. We saw the ceiling collapse. Spotted the ocean washing you away." He stared at the floor.

"I couldn't get to the dock right away because of the crowd rushing from the elevators, and then some badly injured people surfaced near the shore and needed our help. It took too long, much too long, before I could make it to the docks and talk this crew—" he nodded toward the deck above them, "into the search. By then we couldn't see any sign of you. We haven't seen anyone else on the water, either. I wouldn't even have spotted you if you hadn't been sitting up."

Shannon lowered her tea cup to her lap. Her face must have betrayed how much it hurt her to learn they hadn't spotted other survivors on the water. He added quickly, "Hey, the crew will go back out after they drop us off. Every other available boat is already searching. The townies showed up with anything that floats. If you made it out, other people did. They'll find them."

So many people. Tears welled up and rolled down Shannon's cheeks. Usually she would have fought them back or brushed them away or thrown a towel over her head. But not today. Not now.

Luke grabbed a napkin and softly dabbed at her wet face. "Drink some more tea, cara; you must warm up."

Drink her tea. She hurt everywhere, and one of her arms didn't work. No way could she lift the mug again.

Noting her hesitation, Luke guided the cup to her lips, and urged her to try a sip with a nod of his head and an encouraging lift of those bushy eyebrows. She managed to down only a fraction of it before shaking her head. "That's all I can handle. Thanks. It helps. And thank you for getting a crew out looking for me. I don't think I would have lasted much longer."

The crew had tactfully remained aboveboard to allow Shannon some rest. Luke slid the pillows onto the floor that had propped up Shannon, and he slipped behind her to cradle her in his arms, whispering only once, "Cara." He inhaled the scent of her, nodded his head, followed by a sigh and silence.

Shannon registered Luke's sigh as the boat droned toward shore; he'd undoubtedly noticed that she hadn't lost her exotic scent—spicy, tropical, mysterious. She radiated the perfume naturally all the time now, during any conditions—even, it seemed, after an ice bath in the sea. After five years, the scent still hadn't faded. Despite her protests, her friends always assumed she wore an expensive perfume, one which she didn't care to share with them. But she couldn't share it, because her first close encounter with the little alien child Essi had left her covered in the scent of Essi's Riverworld. And it never left.

Her mind drifted in and out, as it had before the crew rescued her . . . The scent had attracted Luke to her in the beginning. She sometimes wondered if he would have cared so much for her without it. She'd asked herself that question only a thousand times or so. . . .

* * *

Shannon remained content to rest in Luke's arms in the darkened cabin, could have stayed there for hours, even though her pain had not subsided—a fact she'd neglected to mention to anyone—and her body was still battling the dangerous effects of hypothermia. She hovered on the edge of consciousness. Still. Luke's arms. A little pain, shock, and potential coma meant very little in comparison.

But only minutes passed before Savannah ducked her head through the hatch to announce their return to the Dickson dock. Fortunately, the UC did not connect to the dock, which hugged the shoreline north of Juneau's sea pen and Dickson's landside buildings. The collapse had caused no damage here.

Luke lifted her like a delicate blown-glass figurine, as if she might shatter—actually, the way her body screamed, perhaps she would. He carried her up to the deck, and then to a waiting stretcher. Of course he did.

Now they'd haul her up to the—*Oh, no, no, no!* Not the— "I'm feeling better already," Shannon lied, her feeble, pitiful voice unconvincing, even to her own ears. "No need to send me off to the infirmary. Really."

The Dickson staff, richly funded and with enthusiastic ideals, would never scrimp on a medical facility. As a result, the research center boasted a small, fully outfitted hospital, which it modestly labeled the infirmary. It catered to Dickson visitors; the extensive research, services, and maintenance staff; and even townspeople from the nearby isolated community.

Shannon hated hospitals. Always had, always would. Hated the smell of bleach over decay, the dreary walls and waiting room chairs, the uncomfortable beds in unfamiliar rooms. She'd been forced to escape from one in Ocean City to save Juneau. She'd nearly died in one after the alien troubles. She'd almost rather take her chances with the open sea than return to a hospital.

But her protests fell on deaf ears. The Dickson physician and paramedics who met *Rescuer One* at the dock, aided and abetted by Luke, bound her in a tight bundle on the stretcher and bore her to the infirmary straightaway.

Her head buzzed, and the blackness edging her vision expanded, as if she were receding slowly down a dark tunnel. The light faded to a pinpoint.

* * *

Shannon stands on a cold and windy outcropping of rock. The sea is behind her. She can hear waves crashing into rocks far below. But she doesn't turn to gaze at what must surely be a breathtaking view. Her eyes are fixed on a large creature crumpled on the ground in front of her.

Dead, deformed beyond recognition, a mass of blood and pus.

She glances up. Other forms like the one at her feet dot the landscape. Nothing stirs. Nothing appears to be alive.

This is her fault, she thinks—although she doesn't know how or why that could be true. But it is—all her fault. She could have helped Roebor—but who is Roebor?—remove the virus from Earth—she could have helped him save this world. But she failed.

* * *

Shannon rose rapidly from blackness to a view of recessed fluorescent ceiling lighting. She gasped as she took a moment to regain her bearings. Had another premonition just hit her full force? Great gods, she hoped not. Surely that kind of hell couldn't await her.

But if it were a dream, what did it mean? Where had it come from? She had no idea. She shook her head slightly to put it out of her mind.

Turning her head a fraction, she saw Luke striding along beside one of the infirmary physicians, Dr. James Copper. Luke bent the doc's ear with great passion. From the vibrations beneath her, Shannon could tell she'd entered the infirmary, and infirmary staff had transferred her to a gurney and now pushed her along toward her infirmary fate.

Copper . . . Competent enough . . . Shannon had met him twice when she'd ventured into his realm, once wheeling in a worker with a back sprain, and once supporting a tourist tottering with a dizzy spell. Medium height, compact guy, muscular, never smiled, never a friendly wave or nod.

Shannon's good hand fisted. For some reason, Copper made her very, very uneasy. She'd picked up a perplexing vibe from him the first time she met him. When she picked up the same vibe the second time, she'd been sorely tempted to use her talents to learn what the good doctor hid in his domed noggin covered with thinning gray-brown hair.

She had refrained. But she might rethink that, if her uneasiness continued, even though she worked hard to honor people's privacy.

At the moment, Shannon could just glimpse Copper's growing frown and the two vertical lines deepening between his eyebrows. Luke might be pushing the envelope.

What envelope could Luke possibly push? She'd made it back alive. More or less. Shannon's mind couldn't seem to concentrate on their conversation.

Focus.

"—so you may think she is suffering only from a severe case of hypothermia that you can treat in a straightforward way, and it may be," Luke said, "but I just ask that you assign a nurse to watch her. She . . . she burns energy more quickly than we do. She may eat like a horse, but I can tell she hasn't gained a pound since I last saw her, so her exposure could—"

Eat like a horse? She ate like a bird. Okay, maybe like a horse. But people shouldn't blabber it around.

"She developed a serious metabolic problem five years ago," Luke continued. "It nearly killed her. It's stabilized, now that. . . ."

Now that the aliens have left, Shannon finished the thought. *Stepped right into that one, Luke.*

"It has stabilized now that she's past the crisis, but her metabolism still runs much higher than average."

"Yeah, I've seen her metabolism at work," Copper said. "She shovels it in like a sumo wrestler. I don't know how she affords to eat."

Not like a sumo wrestler. For Odinssake. A pro football player, okay, she could see that, but a sumo wrestler? Surely not.

And why would he monitor her eating habits anyway? Despite Shannon's hurting head, a warning pricked her senses from a place deep in her subconscious, and for reasons unknown, a shiver ran down her already frozen spine.

Noticing that Shannon had rejoined the living, Copper said, "And as for you, Ms. Kendricks, bet your bottom dollar it would've gone better for you if you'd kept your clothes on."

"Have to disagree with you, Jim," Luke said mildly. "I saw her dragged out into the sea. She was wearing one of those oversized sweaters and a bulky shirt. She'd never have made it to the surface in those clothes." Copper's frown lines increased. Perhaps he didn't like to be contradicted.

So there, you jerk.

"Look, Luke," Copper said, reverting to Luke's earlier argument, "She'll be on an IV drip, and we'll monitor her. The staff at the central nurses' station will know if any metabolism-related problems arise. Beyond that, I don't have the staff to assign her a personal attendant. We're stretched to the limit with the injured. I mean, the Dickson's rolling in the green stuff, but that doesn't help me because medical staff doesn't grow on trees out here. When she's stabilized, you can sit with her, or you can find one of the research team members to do it. That's it. Someone will notify you when you can visit her. Now if you'll excuse me, I have some broken bones to set."

Wait. Broken bones?

Luke slowed to a stop and faded from Shannon's upturned eyes, even when she craned her neck to look back, which reminded her not to crane her neck: *Ow.*

The nurses fussed over her, placing her with care into a hospital bed with a new, recently warmed blanket, attaching intravenous bags of several varieties, as well as monitoring attachments for heart, blood pressure, temperature. Hopefully one of those bags contained a powerful painkiller. The smallest noise jarred her head and hurt her eardrums; the smallest movement hurt her entire body, most particularly her left arm and her left ankle.

. . . . Feeling woozy here.

Her eyes closed. Sounds receded.

* * *

A dreamless black sleep let loose its hold on her. She rose to the surface and opened her eyes. Darkness saturated the room except for a soft bed light above her head. She examined her pale blue hospital gown dotted with round, little, dark blue whales lined up in rows. Turning her head carefully to the left, she observed that no one occupied the adjacent bed. She rested her eyes.

The infirmary staff members went about their jobs quietly. She could hear people passing in the hall, an occasional word, and a few times the intercom calling for a certain doctor or reciting a code number.

Dr. Copper would probably visit her soon. Sometimes Shannon wished she weren't so honorable with her psychic skills. If she had no scruples, she would burrow right into

Copper's head to scope out what gave her the shivers every time she looked at him. And she would scope out Luke's mind, too, while she was at it, learn why he'd shown up here. It would be so much simpler and quicker to go to the source, to not wait for tedious conversations, evasions, lies, distractions, and omissions. But, oh no, Shannon Kendricks had to go all ethical and stay out of people's images and emotions, meaning she had to fight the temptation to pry every day, everywhere, with everyone, just like Sisyphus rolling that stone uphill over and over and over. It wore her down.

With time, she'd learned to contain her curiosity—and her temper. Usually. Or at least often. But if Luke returned to her life, and she found herself yearning to read the secret answers to burning questions about *him*? Would she be able to resist the temptation to peek inside his head, even she knew it would destroy the trust between them? *Could* she resist?

This depressing line of thinking reminded her of why she'd let the relationship sputter out these last five years. It had all seemed so hopeless.

Tears rolled out from under the lightly closed lids of her eyes like little soldiers creeping out of the trenches. She couldn't muster the strength to lift her hand and wipe them away.

Her hand . . . She looked at her left hand. No wonder she couldn't lift it. Her fingers and thumb now peeked out of a cast resting on her chest that stretched from her palm through an L-shaped bend in her elbow to her upper arm. Broken. Probably in more than one place.

Wait a minute. This cast was made of plaster. Nobody wore plaster casts anymore; now doctors used fiberglass. What the heck? She checked herself for other bits of plaster. *Loki's curse.* Her ankle too.

She looked at her other arm. *No cast.* Various tubes ran from a taped patch. Her index finger sported a monitor clip.

What else? She shifted. The ribs still screamed; she could feel the tape—Copper had tightly wrapped her broken ribs. Bandages here and there covered her deeper cuts. When she lifted her eyebrows she could feel a long thick strip of gauze on her forehead. Bruises large and small covered much of her skin not hidden by her hospital gown and casts.

She did not present a pretty sight tonight.

As she began to doze off again, the terrifying, ominous sound of that first crack in the UC echoed in her ear, the image of roaring black sea water tumbling toward her filled her mind again. She flinched.

An unthinkable, impossible disaster. *What had caused it?* Shannon reached out with her mind.

Juneau? You don't have any idea what happened to break up the UC, do you? Maybe she'd seen an object or movement from outside the complex that Shannon had missed as she ran along its corridors.

No, that's crazy. How could Juneau know? She—

But Juneau did know part of the story. The images flew into Shannon's mind. She bolted upright in her bed, pain ignored, her eyes wide.

What?

Shannon's monitors shrieked into the nighttime quiet at the Dickson Research Institute Infirmary as her heart rate and blood pressure soared.

45

CHAPTER SIX

TWO NURSES, ONE A PLEASANT, YOUNG FEMALE OFFENSIVE LINEMAN named Ivy, one a small, dark, middle-aged man called Shed, rushed to Shannon's bedside to discover what had sent Shannon's vital signs skyrocketing. But they couldn't figure out any external cause for Shannon's emotional explosion, naturally.

As Shed made notations on Shannon's computer chart, and the giantess Ivy changed one of Shannon's intravenous bags, Shannon tried to concentrate on recontacting Juneau but found she needed quiet. After her vitals had settled to the normal range, and the nurses continued to fuss, she told them that she had awakened from a nightmare, screaming and sweating. "The UC explosion, you see," she said, and nodded at them solemnly. All she really needed, she explained, was to fall back asleep, and she'd be fine.

Relatively speaking.

Ah, they had replied and, having checked her intravenous bags, needles, tubes, and blankets, having lifted some welcome water to her lips, having soothed her hand and patted her shoulder, they left her in peace once more.

Peace also being a relative term.

Shannon sat up in her bed, back rigid with tension. The image that came in from Juneau —*impossible. No way. Out of the question.*

But the image of Salesti appeared again—the tiny, fuzzy, kitten-like, hummingbird-like being from Riverworld, who'd left for home with the little alien child Essi after the alien problems had all been sorted out five years earlier. Mysterious Salesti, in whom Shannon had sensed immense hidden power, unfathomed depths. Salesti, neither male nor female, but simply "it."

When Salesti and little Essi had first come from the planet they called Selador, with the River Selador serving as its lifeblood, Salesti had called the planet *Riverworld* for Shannon's better understanding, and the Selador River, simply *the River.* Shannon still thought of the planet that way. Salesti and its kind lived there, as did little Essi and the other Seladorans.

Juneau had imaged to Shannon that Salesti had returned to planet Earth and *that* explained Juneau's disappearance.

Juneau had gone AWOL to answer Salesti's request to retrieve the little fuzzball. Salesti, like all the creatures from its world, could exist on Earth only by occupying the mind of an Earth creature. So, when it had plummeted through a portal to Earth, of necessity, it had quickly inhabited the mind of the nearest living creature. If it hadn't found any creatures within easy reach, its molecules would have scattered: Every jump to Earth risked death.

The little fuzzball had taken up residence in the head of a small hermit crab off the coast of Canada, not far south of their position here at the Dickson in Alaska.

Salesti had the power to enter people's minds, and if it did so, it could then communicate over distances with those it knew. Salesti could project images and emotions, even language, to Juneau, to Luke, and to Shannon.

Once Salesti had settled in the crab, it waited until Juneau left her pen for her free swim, and then reached out to her. Juneau, who knew Salesti well from its earlier visit, swiftly swam down to Canada, located Salesti, and swallowed the hermit crab, thus handily effecting Salesti's transfer from crab to Juneau's mind. Then Juneau sped back with Salesti on board, in the nick of time to rescue Shannon. The whale, with the alien on board, was currently swimming quietly along the outer perimeter of the damaged sea pen.

Shannon, though as weak as Superman caught in kryptonite, as fuzzy as cotton batting, remained bolt upright in her bed. Salesti could have asked Shannon to retrieve it as easily as Juneau, but Shannon suspected that the tiny hummingbird-kitten wanted its presence on Earth to be a fait accompli by the time Shannon learned of its arrival.

And she harbored a pretty strong suspicion into whose mind Salesti would want to jump next.

Even though Shannon loved the little Seladoran, she wanted Salesti's company in *her* head about as much as she wanted to take up permanent residence in this hospital bed. Memories from five years earlier came flooding back—all the terror, the pain, the heartbreak, the struggle to stay alive. She couldn't face that again, not a fraction of it.

Nonetheless, inhaling sharply, Shannon said, "Hi, Salesti. I've missed you." And it was true.

ssalesti misses shannon too. salesti hopes shannon learns to cast her colors in many ways now.

Interesting non sequitur. "No, Salesti, since your departure, I've tried never to cast my colors to do searches for people, never to read people's emotions and images, and certainly never to flow to their minds as you gave me the power to do. And I haven't taken anybody along with me to people's minds like the Seladorans and I can do, either. I didn't want to have anything to do with the skills you gave me. So. I haven't learned anything new either."

but shannon can cast far. cast colors for objects and people. cast colors in water. cast colors in minds. use colors to hear. use colors to move air and objects in minds. shannon learns. must learn.

"Shannon won't learn, Salesti. Shannon—I—don't think it's right to use such power. And I think it's dangerous."

shannon learns. shannon must.

This subject arose out of the blue for a reason. Shannon wasn't sure she wanted to find out Salesti's reasons.

Fortunately, the little fuzzball decided to shift the subject. *salesti thinks often of shannon.*

At least not many people, if any, could say that an alien thought of them with warmest regards while away traveling the universe. And, *thank Odin,* Shannon's ear registered only the most flagrant of Salesti's whispered *ssss* hisses now. Its English seemed to be improving.

"Why couldn't you or Juneau tell me Juneau had gone to pick you up? I nearly lost my mind worrying about her."

Salesti answered that it feared Shannon wouldn't free Juneau from the sea pen if she knew the whale would rescue it and take it on board.

"Ah. Well played, Salesti." Better to ask for forgiveness than permission, Riverworld style. Points for honesty, anyway.

Would Shannon have refused to free Juneau for this little mission? She collapsed back and stared at the ceiling. A close question, really.

On the one hand, to host another creature drained tremendous amounts of energy. Shannon should know; her various visitors five years earlier had almost cost her her life, and she still suffered from an accelerated metabolism. It wasn't fair to expect Juneau to sacrifice that kind of energy, endangering her life, just when she'd won her freedom.

And if Salesti never boarded Juneau, she also wouldn't make any future transfers from Juneau to any other earth creatures—for example, whale to human Travelodge Shannon Kendricks.

Plus, anything could have happened to Juneau racing down the coast in unfamiliar water like that. The beluga knew nothing of entanglement in fishing nets, of ship propellers that could maim or kill, of attacks by giant squid. Okay, maybe not giant squid, but still. Dangers abounded.

And finally, Shannon further darkly feared that another world crisis might be the reason Salesti had journeyed to Earth, and that it would expect Shannon to solve said crisis. How Shannon had been elected Guardian of the Planet she had no idea, but that seemed to be Salesti's take on matters. That's what had happened last time around.

So yes, plenty of reasons existed for securing Juneau safely inside the sea pen until Salesti gave up and headed back to Riverworld.

On the other hand, that same dark suspicion that a crisis was looming worried Shannon. If a world threat really did exist, under normal circumstances Shannon could hardly refuse to help. However, she would have to recuse herself from world crisis intervention this time around. She couldn't save the world with a broken arm, a broken ankle, broken ribs, a concussion, cuts, bruises, and hypothermia.

So that settled that.

"You do realize, Salesti, that I am out of the running for whatever mission you hope to talk me into. I'm incapacitated and in the hospital. I'm sure you can find somebody competent."

Salesti imaged her little Persian cat mooshed-in face with a sad frown on it.

essi drops to earth, flees to ocean city to look for shannon. Odin's eye! Essi?

Essi had returned to Earth too? Essi, the orphaned, curly-haired little alien child who'd fallen into Shannon's mind five years earlier in a fateful accident. Essi, with her musical humming so calming she could lull an attacking shark to sleep. Sweet little Essi.

Shannon squeezed her eyes shut and counted to ten. Where Essi came, trouble often followed. And sure enough:

essi carries a rare virus new to earth. virus harmless to essi and seladorans, but if virus escapes from essi here, virus causes death in all people on earth.

A rare lethal virus. *Bingo*, world crisis. And of course, Salesti had come here to chat with Shannon about it.

"But Essi's here in some kind of ethereal form, right? In a host's mind? How could she carry a virus?"

like people of shannon, essi made of very small parts. held together by positive and negative forces that cannot be seen. virus so small, virus remains trapped by same positive and negative fields that hold essi together.

A virus which was, like, the size of an atom, or smaller. Shannon couldn't fathom that. "What kind of virus? Like ebola?"

Salesti was quiet for a moment. *fever, weakness, insides liquify, blood out eyes, nose, mouth, skin pores even.*

Like ebola then. Only worse. *Not good.* Shannon's dream of the horribly deformed bodies flashed in her mind. She knew of the virus in the dream: was it premonition of a disaster striking or somehow a warning of how terrible it would be if Essi failed?

"So you need to take Essi home again, right? And somebody can deal with the virus there? You don't need me then." She hoped it was that simple.

The image of the morose catlike face returned.

if earth host of essi dies while essi inside, essi dies too. if essi dies, force fields holding her together vanish and tiny parts of her body escape into air—"

"Along with the virus. I take it this virus will kill in its airborne form?"

yes.

"And you want me to find Essi down in Ocean City to make sure she stays alive."

yes. shannon and salesti find essi and extract virus.

"*Extract* the virus? Why? How?"

roebor needs virus. he extracts.

"Roebor? Who *in Loki's name* is Roebor?" Shannon paused. She'd heard that name before, in that frightening dream she'd experienced when the medics had carried her into the infirmary.

creature from another world, world shannon might call fireworld. roebor searches for rare virus. finds only essi carries. roebor . . . Salesti hesitated so long before continuing that Shannon began to think the little alien had finished. But then Salesti said, *when roebor falls to earth, roebor breaks underwater building shannon in.*

CHAPTER SEVEN

"THIS ALIEN ROEBOR SMASHED THE UC?" *Thanks a lot, Roebor.*

"But he'd have to pass through the portal as an ethereal creature, right? How could he harm a solid structure?"

oh no, shannon, roebor travels from fireworld to earth whole. roebor not ethereal, roebor very solid. not like essi and salesti.

Solid? Guess so. Solid enough to put the total kibosh on the unbreakable UC. "How big is this Roebor, anyway?"

big as building on earth. and roebor shoots into water from portal very quickly.

Again, judging from the damage he'd done, Shannon wouldn't disagree.

"Did he . . . did he survive?" Probably not. Surely not. After hitting the complex that hard? Of course not. If he swam off, he must have almost immediately cratered.

oh yes, shannon. roebor feels very fine. roebor waits to go with shannon and juneau and salesti to find essi.

"Waiting? Waiting where? He can't be seen, Salesti, or he'll get us all in deep trouble. Did he hide in the forest somewhere?"

roebor walks the land, swims the sea, flies the sky, but now he floats far out in the ocean so no one sees roebor.

The giant could walk, swim, *and* fly? Talented.

"Why didn't he wait for you on Riverworld?"

must take virus home quickest way. virus cure for a deadly disease on fireworld.

"The virus that kills on Earth will save on FireWorld? Strange."

people of roebor die even now. another reason roebor, juneau, shannon, and salesti must hurry.

So now the fate of a *second* world fell on Shannon's bruised and bleeding shoulders. Splendid.

Sidestepping Salesti's insistence on including Shannon in her plans, she said, "But why does he have to accompany us . . . you, I mean? Accompany you? Can't he just walk swim fly around, hiding while you bring Essi up here?"

roebor removes virus from essi safely and quickly so no longer threat to earth. do as soon as possible for sake of creatures of earth. shannon, roebor, and salesti must all go together. no time to waste.

Shannon postponed the inevitable confrontation over what had begun to sound suspiciously like involuntary enlistment. "I never caught sight of him when he crashed in. What does he look like?" Shannon asked. "Anything like the last batch of aliens?" Shannon hoped *to Odin* not. They were an ugly and terrifying pair. "Or like Essi's people?" That would be much more pleasant. "Or you? Only much, much bigger?" Shannon wasn't sure whether a house-sized Salesti would be cute or frightening as hell.

Salesti's soft tinkling laugh echoed in Shannon's head. She'd missed that laugh.

very different, shannon. very different. shannon be surprised.

"Can you show me how it happened? Did a ball of lightning strike, like when Essi came to me?"

Salesti sent the images.

Shannon saw the UC from perhaps 300 feet away, as if she were scuba diving, viewing it from the side.

. . . .All seems quiet, the ocean a charcoal emptiness, the complex a lonely curve of light shining bravely within it. Out of nowhere, as if conjured by magic, a ball of pale blue lightning explodes into view above Concourse Seven, as large as a superstore. Blinding, crackling swirls of hot silver-white fire vibrate within. . . .

As Shannon gawked at the image, she caught a new scent. Not the spicy, exotic perfume that she'd inhaled the first time Essi's lighting had shaken her like dice in a gambler's fist and left her unconscious. This scent smelled subtly smoky. With hints of cedar. And aromas again indefinable and mysterious, warm and sharp. Shannon sensed ferocity in this aroma.

But this new lightning had not wrapped around the UC, or anything else as far as Shannon could see, in the way that Essi's lightning had captured Shannon and Juneau in its electrifying grip. *Thank Odin* for that.

. . . .The lightning ball fades . . . fades . . . and blinks out. At that very moment, flung from the lightning ball's core, propelled by some energy force within the lightning—a shimmering form. A . . . what, exactly? A dragon-like thing? Shannon

squinted at the image. No, not a dragon exactly . . . Bestla, mother of Odin. Her mouth gaped open; she shut it.

Catlike. Every aspect long, long, long. Dark blue and angular. Panther-shaped head, only sharper. Large, slanted triangular eyes flashing silvery pale blue. Canines the size of samurai swords. Gills slicing down its thick neck. Long legs, long body. Long sharp claws. Covered not with scales, but metallic-like, Prussian blue fur. Wings, oh yeah, great, long, gently curving wings. Whipping panther tail. Fire-breathing. Pale, blue luminescent fire. A dragonpanther.

A massive, beautiful beast. One that could also breathe underwater. Salesti had said he stood as tall as a building. Shannon agreed. Twenty feet tall, she guessed, and she'd estimate him at about fifty feet long, counting the tail.

yes, dragonpanther, as shannon calls, of fireworld beautiful. salesti not wishes for dragonpanthers to die without vaccine. roebor visits riverworld many times searching for virus.

Oh fine, why didn't Salesti go right ahead and douse Shannon with guilt, like a full faucet on a sponge?

And what's worse, Salesti's tactics were working.

"Roebor visited your world? Must've made quite an impression."

The tinkling laugh again. *oh yes, shannon, quite impression.*

Salesti's images continued, showing Shannon what happened after Roebor broke onto the scene above the UC.

. . . .The power of the energy that bursts from the pale blue light hurls the dragonpanther toward the UC, his cumbersome

body twisting, powerful wings spread wide, tail extended, but unable to stop.

He crashes down onto Concourse Seven and the complex's disintegration begins. The dragonpanther stills for a moment as if dazed, then shakes his great blue head, recovers in an instant, and swims away, quickly and capably, disappearing into the darkness. . . .

Shannon, mesmerized, failed to blink as the bizarre scene unfolded. The image ended. She bit her lip. "He must've been hurt pretty badly by that."

not hurt much. roebor strong. and also, shannon, one other thing.

"Do I want to know?" she asked.

salesti thinks shannon not wants to know.

And yet more images immediately arrived. Shannon sighed.

The new images began just after the UC had imploded.

Twisted, mangled metal sinks to the bottom of the sea, and pieces of it dangle precipitously from parts of the structure still attached to solid rock at the shoreline. Debris of every size and shape sinks with the metal. Other, lighter objects float toward the surface. . . .

Shannon's heart constricted. The beautiful complex, the research labs in the central hub, all wiped out in minutes. Unknown numbers of people dead or injured.

Salesti imaged again: *Out of nowhere, a ball of pale blue lightning appears for the second time, precisely where the first lightning ball disappeared. This ball expels another shape, which proves to be a dragonpanther similar to the first, although, to Shannon's eye, less magnificent. Instead of Prussian blue, its fur reflects a dull metallic bronze. Smaller than Roebor, its wings look boxier, less sleek. Shorter tail; its ears lay flatter to its head. But the same pale blue fire shoots from its mouth and burns behind its eyes.*

This one, too, rolls and twists from the lightning ball, knocking debris away as it goes, but since the UC has been destroyed by Roebor, this one encounters no serious resistance until it hits the ocean bottom, where it skids ten or fifteen feet on its side, then lifts off to swim directly south.

"So who's that?"

salesti not knows. shannon asks roebor.

"Yeah, close communications with dragonpanthers can be your job."

job of shannon

Shannon shifted her aching body and let that argument go. Apparently nobody would be trying to contact the big boy.

"How did you know the details of Roebor's unfortunate entrance to Earth in the first place? Where were you?"

The tinkling laughter came again. *juneau and salesti close enough for salesti to see.*

So now Shannon knew what had happened. Who else knew? Everyone at the Dickson would be reviewing video to determine what had decimated the UC. *Not good.*

salesti and shannon go to ocean city. now.

Hell in a hand basket. The last thing Shannon needed was another extraterrestrial adventure. She lived a regular life now. Or mostly regular. She did have her extra skills. And Juneau. But no aliens.

No, she'd been there, done that. Ixnay on the alien thing.

"I'm in the infirmary, here, Salesti. Did you get that part? Uh, gravely ill." Shannon crumpled back against her pillow for emphasis. "Gravely. Won't be up for a while. You'll have to press on without me."

Changing the subject, Shannon asked quickly, "And anyway, why did Essi pick Earth to run to?" A moment passed. "Wait, I don't need the details, I don't want the details, I refuse to know the details, don't even tell me anything. Since I'm too sick to help. So. Best of luck."

Shannon sank back on her pillow. Then she sat back up.

"No wait, actually, I do want to know if Essi is okay. I really have missed her, too. Not to change the subject."

Okay, trying desperately to change the subject. But it was true that she loved the cherubic, humming child Essi, despite the complications that always seemed to follow in her innocent little wake, like sharks after fish bait. It would be great to hold her close once again. To have her aboard Shannon's mind for a little while—*for a very, very little while. And—*

salesti not knows how essi does. salesti knows only that essi carries virus.

Ouch. The teeny tiny slap in the face.

salesti requires help of shannon. As if she hadn't heard a word Shannon said about grave illness and so forth.

But of course Salesti required her help. The denizens of Riverworld had left her in peace for five whole years. Probably thought she was straining at the bit to charge out and expose herself to disaster and death once again to clear up these little mishaps in the universal realm.

and shannon requires help of salesti, because shannon and salesti must repair damage to underwater building.

Well, ka-boom; something interesting Shannon hadn't expected from Salesti; a bribe: if Shannon helped Salesti find Essi and the virus, then Salesti would somehow help Shannon rebuild the UC. Tempting. Except how could they possibly accomplish the rebuild? They'd only need a billion dollars.

Shannon sighed yet again. A deep, deep sigh. She drummed her fingers on her bedcover. She studied the ceiling. A small, perfect spider web clung to the high corner of her room above a sink and a bar of wall lights. The spider had absented itself. Shannon wasn't a fan of spiders.

The little alien child Essi was hiding down in Ocean City all alone—although not quite alone, since she had boarded the mind of some creature, human or otherwise. But she could be lost. Lonely. Probably afraid. Shannon's gut tightened. Add a couple alien dragonpanthers swimming somewhere out in the deep looking for Essi. A viral death bomb waiting to explode. She couldn't turn her back on that. Shannon's resolve to stay well clear of this galactic disaster weakened with each tick of the clock.

Yet, she couldn't handle a burning batch of cookies in her current condition, so how could she go out and save a couple of worlds?

The familiar haze at her door, swirling a rainbow of colors—cobalt blue, forest green, lavender, white, pale yellow, iridescent black, rose red, midnight purple—heralded someone's arrival and abruptly arrested Shannon's train of thought.

goodbye for now shannon. Salesti disappeared from Shannon's mind.

* * *

Nurses Ivy and Shed rushed into her hospital room. They chattered as they came in about patients who'd just been rescued from a pocket of debris uncovered where Concourse Seven had collapsed. Shannon caught the image from Shed of structural wreckage crushed together in a way that preserved an air pocket. The air bubble had allowed four people to stay alive until rescuers could reach them. *Thank Odin.*

Now, however, the nurses descended on Shannon in response to an alert they'd received at the central desk that her intravenous drips had both emptied. Shannon had been so caught up in her exchange with Salesti she had registered only vaguely that she was no longer benefiting from the pain-dulling effect of the morphine or the nourishment and electrolytes of the glucose fluid. Her body had become even weaker than before; the dizziness had returned along with a monster headache.

Ivy muttered that the bags couldn't possibly have emptied so quickly, but she went about the business of replacing them, and Shed, joined in short order by Dr. Copper, hovered over her bed, poked, and frowned.

Shannon noticed that Shed took the opportunity to lean in and sniff her scent. She watched his pupils enlarge and his eyebrows go up. But, to his credit, he stayed mum.

"You adjusted the drips to take in the drugs more rapidly. Do you know how stupid that was? With the morphine pouring into your system that fast, and you in the shape you're in, I'm surprised you're not dead or dying," Copper said. "It's a waste of money to even treat you."

"I didn't adjust anything. Look at me; I'm totally incapacitated here," Shannon said, her voice rasping loudly with indignation.

Copper glanced down at his earlier handiwork. Cast on one arm, other arm burdened with the needles and tubes taped to it. Shannon watched as he shrugged with his right shoulder, and the thin curve of his lips puckered up; yeah, he knew the truth when he looked right at it. "Maybe you asked someone else to do it."

"No visitors have been allowed into her room, Doctor," said a third nurse who'd just entered, Illiana, according to her name tag, as she plumped Shannon's pillow behind her head.

Yeah she doesn't like you either, jerk. Shannon glanced over to the door. The colorful haze. Someone else would soon arrive.

Luke slipped in but judiciously remained quietly against the wall, his dark eyes intent and focused on Shannon, bushy eyebrows lowered, one of his hands rubbing, in his accustomed way, the perpetual dark shadow on his chin.

Shannon pulled her braid around with her right hand and tugged on it.

So now what's he thinking? Shannon, the crisis magnet? Shannon, always too close to the edge of life, too dangerous to love? She would not pry into his emotions, his images. She absolutely would not.

Maybe a peek.

No, no, and end of conversation, no.

"My metabolism spikes dangerously sometimes, Dr. Copper. It doesn't surprise me that I've burned through the drugs and the glucose. Nobody's messed with the bags. Ask Luke. He knows about my medical issues." Copper's head snapped toward Luke, whose hands rose in front of his chest as if to ward off the doctor's gathering rebuke.

"I told you," he said.

"You sure you didn't sneak in here and tamper with the drips?" Copper kept at it. "Pay somebody on staff to do it?"

Luke turned his palms up to protest his innocence. "I have been sitting out front by the nurses' station like a good boy, Doctor," Luke said.

"That's right, Dr. Copper. I staffed central after you settled Ms. Kendricks in. He stayed right there making small talk with me." Illiana radiated a huge smile Luke's way.

Shannon's big, round, sea lettuce green eyes narrowed.

Woman, get your smile off that man. And don't you dare smile back, Luke. Do not do it.

Luke smiled at the nurse, giving her a slight nod of thanks for the backup.

Shannon's head dropped back as she exhaled in resignation. Luke couldn't help himself. Too friendly, too nice, too much of an eyeful, he attracted women like sunflowers attracted bees. He didn't even have to try. She took a closer look at the nurse. Young, raven-haired, petite. Pretty enough. Shannon might not like her very well.

"Who the hell came in here, then?" Copper asked.

"Nobody," Shannon said again. "Hey, I have a question for you, too. Why did you use plaster for my casts instead of fiberglass?"

"Funny story," Copper said, forgetting his accusations for the moment. "You know we had a mass influx of casualties from the UC collapse."

Yes, that's hilarious, right off the bat.

"So we had a big unanticipated run on our fiberglass supplies. More broken bones than we had good product to cover."

Funnier by the minute.

"Some time back, when we started seeing the villagers here, the local doc, in appreciation, donated most of his supplies to us, and retired to the Baja in Mexico, and don't I wish I could join him. His stuff was really dated, I mean ancient, and I'm surprised no one tossed it out a long time ago. But fortunately for you, his plaster for casts came in handy." He tapped her arm cast. "This is fine; just don't get it wet."

The medical staff finished securing her new drips and settling her back in, and departed. Copper looked back at her as if daring her to tamper with the drips again.

"May I stay for a while?" Luke asked as Copper brushed by.

"She's still weak. Half an hour. Then out."

Shannon pondered Luke's calm face as he slid the visitors' slate gray, microplush chair toward the edge of her bed. *Should she tell him Salesti and Essi had returned? Did she dare bring him into this new mess?* Luke had been involved with the alien troubles last time. He knew about Shannon's telepathy and the two aliens. Their presence on Earth might be enough to drive him screaming back down to the lower forty-eight, even without a single word about the new feature attraction, a couple of big, colorful, flying swimming walking dragonpanthers.

And if Luke did exit stage left, would Shannon be relieved or hurt?

She sighed as her fingers played with the edge of her sheet. Both, of course.

She couldn't decide whether to tell him. She couldn't think. She needed quiet. Too much had happened too quickly. And admit it. The escape from the UC collapse into the Alaskan Sea had left her physically fragile. In fact, her protests to Salesti about her grave status didn't land as far from the mark as Shannon wished they did.

Shannon focused on the heart monitor to avoid looking at Luke—but as she watched, the monitor showed her heart rate quiver, quiver, spike, and then—

—flatline.

Hey what—

The alarm shrieked.

"Jesus," shouted Luke, leaping to his feet, his chair crashing over behind him. Copper rushed back in and pulled the defibrillator off the wall. . . .

A black, black universe swallowed Shannon whole.

CHAPTER EIGHT

NOT GOOD. NOT AT ALL GOOD.

Falling through the inky infinite. And if she hit bottom, she'd never recover; she sensed it in the depth of her fall, she heard it in the wailing rush of air past her ears. Death stalked her here; she could feel it, like an eager predator. If she continued to fall, she'd never again lay eyes on Juneau, Salesti, Luke. Her cat Narci. She'd never find Essi. The virus might wipe out her world. The dragonpanther Roebor might discover no antidote for FireWorld.

But how could she stop her fall? Nothing to grab, nothing to hold on to. Ideas fell away from her even as she formed them.

Falling, only the screaming rush of falling.

By all the heroes of Valhalla, Shannon Kendricks, think. Think and hold on to the thought.

An idea formed and she clamped onto it like a lion on an antelope, and, like a lion, she held on until the idea stilled and she could take it in.

The living essence. The life-energy left behind when her friends had departed from her mind five years earlier. Not as real as the living creatures, but more real than mere memories.

Much more. Her mind presented the living essence existing in her head to her as powder, so that she could comprehend it.

Focus. Find the living powder.

As if the thought itself controlled her unconscious plummet—and perhaps it did—Shannon's dizzying free fall slowed until she drifted gently down, landing like a feather on soft welcoming pillows of brilliantly colored life-energy: Shannon's own blue, her friend Becky's tint of summer sky, Essi's familiar, shimmery, thrumming lavender, Juneau's brilliant white, young victim David's palest yellow, the raven's iridescent night hue, her dog Indy's deepest purple, Salesti's glowing rose red.

And here, the deep forest green. Shannon stopped to touch it. Her fingers sifted softly through the powder, she smelled its fragrance. Luke. He, too, had forayed briefly into her mind five years earlier. She didn't visit his essence often . . . Recently, yes, for something she couldn't quite remember . . . She didn't visit because its presence complicated her relationship with him even more than it already was: a strange sort of theft of something valuable that he hadn't meant for her to keep.

However. A matter for another moment. Now she must focus on escaping from this infernal darkness, on finding her way back to the living world.

Shannon drew from the living essence pulsing with the energy of her alien and human friends, her special dog, the uninvited bird. Her mind began to tingle as that essence flowed through her. Images of each alien, human, dog, and bird swirled in her memory. Warming. Strengthening.

Living powder. Life-giving.

She began to float again, up and up, toward a distant paleness, like the horizon just before dawn.

And she knew she would survive.

* * *

"No way." Shannon had just returned to consciousness. Her coma had lasted for an entire day. She had no memory of anything except the falling, the powder, the fight to find her way back.

After the alien business, Shannon didn't believe anything could still shock her. But the news Kota had just imparted had given her a jolt.

"I had *cardiopulmonary bypass surgery* after I passed out? You're joking," Shannon said. "My heart could power a locomotive."

"Of course it could, sweetums," her friend and fellow researcher Dakota Quartermark said, pulling at the tips of her short pink hair to make sure the crest stood arrayed in a sharp triangle as intended. She had tugged one of the soft gray visitor's chairs to Shannon's bed and tucked her short legs under her. "But your ticker didn't cause the problem. Your icy condition and your extreme need to burn energy took you down, baby. Serious shock. We thought we'd lost you. So they needed to remove your blood and warm it up in a hurry. You managed to freak out Copper when you flatlined. In his esteemed view, he had your case of hypothermia well under control. I am pleased."

"You cotton-candy-haired wench. I'm glad my near-death experience provided some entertainment for you. Any time."

Shannon delivered this jibe as she always did with Kota, completely in fun.

Kota pulled her vape out of her backpack, fired it up, and inhaled. "Sweetcheeks, I must protest your sarcasm. We all freaked out, of course, the research staff, that yummy security guard who's been hanging around your bed all beagle-eyed, even Moon got agitated down in California. We were scared, for real." Her face had grown solemn as she spoke, but now she broke out in a grin. "Still. If it had to happen, it's grand that it unsettled Copper, am I right?"

"Well." Shannon's lips slipped into a smile. "Maybe."

Interesting that Kota disliked Copper even more than Shannon did. Or seemed to. Shannon would ask her about it sometime.

"I like the smell of your vape juice. What's it called?"

"Twin Mint. Anyway, Copper whispered to one of the nurses that he'd never seen a metabolism like yours. Hypercharged, he said—I happened to be accidentally listening in at the time."

"Accidentally."

"Do you impugn me, sweetie pie?"

"Of course I do."

Dakota shrugged. "Fair enough. So you're hypercharged. I guess I now know why you have chocolate ice cream sundaes and brownies for breakfast with your eggs and bacon and hash browns and biscuits with gravy—and still manage to look like a cover girl."

"Mm," Shannon said, still mulling over the shocker that she'd undergone heart bypass surgery, *for Odin's sake,* and wanting to shift her friend's attention from her metabolism to anything else. "Hey, do you have time to brush out my braid for me and redo it?"

"Sure." Kota dove into her backpack and came out with a brush. As she unwound Shannon's plait, she said, "And don't think I've forgotten that day at the Dickson in Ocean City when you miraculously pulled Juneau out of her coma, my little Popsicle stick. You looked like death frozen over when we pushed and pulled you out of the water that day too—getting to be a habit, isn't it?—until you went upstairs and started eating everything that hadn't already gone into someone's mouth. In fact, didn't you stick your fingers *in* Moon's mouth to pry out the last chocolate éclair before the party ended?

"A lie, I tell you; a terrible lie. I only plucked a crème puff off his lips, never a single éclair."

Kota grinned. "No wonder Copper's never seen anything like you." Dakota studied Shannon's pale face and waited.

She wants revelations. Sorry, Kota, I can't.

Silence.

Kota puffed on her vape and pursed her lips. "But, okay, let's just say your more interesting characteristics can wait for another time."

Another time or never. Back in Ocean City, when Juneau, Essi, and Salesti had sheltered in Shannon's mind, their presence had forced Shannon's metabolism to speed up to full tilt. She'd fought a losing battle to eat enough to sustain them and keep herself alive. She'd hoped that when she finally sent the aliens home—those who were still alive—and Juneau returned to her own body, she'd likewise return to her normal, quite acceptable self.

Didn't happen. Although she had recovered from the skeletal featherweight she'd become during the alien crisis, and had stabilized at merely thinnish, she ate like a—okay, *Luke*—like a horse, but never picked up poundage.

Shannon hadn't counted on the living powder, the real bits of her visitors that Juneau, Essi, Salesti, all of her friends, had left behind. The living essence, too, required energy. Not as much as her former guests, *thanks be to Odin*, but she still must stoke the fires. Not that she complained, given that the powder had just saved her from perpetual coma at best, perpetual death at worst.

But that history belonged only to her, and to Luke because he'd lived through it. And her doctor, Julia Bennett, who'd saved her life. Shannon scratched the back of her hand where it met the cast. That was probably two too many people in the know already. She wasn't adding Kota.

And now her powder-driven metabolism plus her adventure at sea had thrown her into heart bypass surgery. *Just great.*

"I can't be lying around here recovering now. The Dickson must be a royal mess. I want to help, Kota. And has anyone checked on Juneau? And who survived? Did the staff all make it out?"

"With those casts, babes, there's not a lot of recovery work you can do. You can help by taking it easy and giving us all one less thing to worry about," Dakota said, finishing up the newly woven braid, and curling her hand around the loose fingers at the end of Shannon's arm cast for a moment. "As for Juneau, why don't you contact her and find out for yourself how she is?" Dakota asked, casually laying her elbows on Shannon's sheets and blinking innocently into Shannon's eyes.

No dice, my friend.

Shannon's research partner had dropped hints on other occasions that she suspected Juneau and Shannon communicated in ways as yet unexplained. But Shannon hadn't revealed her link with the whale.

After a moment of pointed silence, Dakota huffed and frowned.

"I suppose this also means you won't tell me how you knew in advance that a frigging bomb blast would hit the UC?"

Shannon tipped her head and raised her eyebrows at her friend, making a clueless "What, me?" face. Then she relented a fraction. "I had some kind of, I don't know, premonition, I guess, about it. I don't know why. I've never experienced anything like it before. Magnetic particles gathering in the air, or whatever." *All true. Some truth to it. Okay. Not exactly full disclosure. Sorry, Kota.*

Dakota nodded. "Thanks for nothing," she said, but without a trace of anger. "How about that heavenly perfume you wear then? Are you ready to share where you buy it? Come on, throw me a bone here. And when did you put it on? You don't have the bottle here."

Shannon regarded her friend. "How do you know I don't have it here?"

"Oops busted. I caught a whiff of it practically the moment they brought you in from the deep. I knew the ocean would've washed it off you, so I may have, um, looked in your cabinet drawers here."

"Kota!"

"Oh, I just wanted to try it on. See if it smells the same on me as it does on you. You can't blame a girl for trying."

"Yes, yes, I can blame you." *And were you just looking for perfume or snooping in general?*

Now, why had that suspicion entered her head? Snooping didn't seem like something Kota would do.

"Okay. I apologize." Then Kota brightened. "Todd's just down the hall. You know Todd. He hardly ever talks, and when he does, it's like he's shooting a word or two out of a cannon. Good luck trying to decipher what he's saying. But you should hear him now; a regular Clarence Darrow. He's telling everyone how you ran back to help Ellen Flynn and him, and that's why the collapse washed you away. He ended up in a sort of tent of debris with an air pocket, and came out with broken bones and such, but he's alive. His family will fly up tomorrow."

Shannon smiled. "I'm so glad. And this woman, Ellen Flynn?"

Kota nodded. "Older lady. She survived too. Researcher from Woods Hole. But she was injured badly. Serious leg and hip fractures. Internal injuries. Concussion. Air-Evac flew her down to Anchorage. Anyway, Todd has been tagging you all over social media as the heroine in this disaster. For calling in the warning in time to save a lot of lives, and then for trying to help him and the others. Everyone wants to hug you and give you smoochie kiss kisses—" at which point Kota planted a slobbery and noisy kiss upon Shannon's warm cheek—"except Rod Jenkins, of course, who hates anybody who isn't Rod Jenkins. Jealous as hell. But word's out that if he'd had his way, lots more people would've died. Good thing your not-so-secret admirer overrode him and moved people out."

"Yeah, let's forget the smoochies to my noble cheek. Save them for survivors of this train wreck."

"Fat chance now, sweet potato. That ship has sailed." She puffed on her vape and fell silent.

After a few minutes she asked, "Do you really want the details about who didn't make it? Why don't we wait for a better time, when you're stronger."

"No good time ever comes for that kind of news. Might as well be now."

Although she hoped for the best, Shannon's shoulders tensed, her good hand fisted, her left hand in the cast being good for only about a quarter fist, and she braced for bad news. Shannon's hand clenched and unclenched with each name on the list of the dead that Kota delivered. Thirty-two deaths; of those, thirteen staffers. Shannon knew eleven of them well. Jerry, with those size fifteen feet everyone always kidded him about. Ann, beautiful Ann, with skin like a delicate white rose petal but a mind like a steel trap. That kid from Kentucky, Ross, a high school summer student, so eager, so earnest, who gave Shannon a high five every time they passed in the halls. . . .

So terrible. So much death. Too much for a heart to bear. Her lips trembled, and her eyes clouded. She squeezed them shut.

Dakota, who'd been watching her face closely, scooted her chair nearer to Shannon in an instant and gave her an awkward hug. She vaped silently for a moment, regarding her friend.

"Okay. Enough for now, sweetie."

"The collapse: do they—" Shannon gulped. "Did they figure out what happened?"

"Yes and no. They captured the moment of the implosion on video. A huge ball of eerie blue light appeared above the UC, I mean *big*, and then the ball of light, like, spewed out a large dark object, which smashed right into Concourse Seven. But then the whole monitoring system, everything, went black. No more video. Nobody knows why. Nobody knows what caused that ball of light. And we haven't located the dark object, in pieces or otherwise." She snapped her fingers. "Vanished just like that."

* * *

Let me guess. You know precisely why the video went down, am I right, Salesti?

Tinkling laughter seemed to echo through the room. At the sound, Shannon glanced sharply at Dakota. But her friend remained intent on her story. No sign she'd heard anything out of the ordinary. Only Shannon could hear the little creature.

And here's the sixty-four-thousand-dollar question: "Did they identify the dark thing on the video?"

Dakota slowly shook her head. "Not so far. It happened so fast, with that blistering light and water waves and such. Moon says he's not holding out much hope, but they've sent the sequence down to Seattle to some special government unit that specializes in photographic enhancement and recognition, just in case. The feds, apparently, think this might have been a terrorist attack. They're bringing their own snoops up here to look around, and I hear some naval carriers, maybe even a submarine, are converging on the area. Moon just *loves* that idea."

Loki's luck. Just what she didn't need. An alien dragonpanther or two lurking in the deep, and in wanders a fleet of sonar-pinging ships and subs.

Are you listening to this, Salesti?

yes, came the whisper back.

"Submarines? You're kidding. Can't Moon stop it? And why would terrorists target this remote facility doing harmless marine research, anyway? Seems a bit of a stretch. A bit unreasonable." *Yes, and the invasion of an infected alien and a pair of dragonpanthers was no stretch at all and very reasonable.*

Dakota shook her head, "Moon tried to make the feds back off. No luck." She stopped talking and a slight flush blossomed on her throat and then disappeared.

Shannon noticed. Kota wasn't telling her everything, and it was making her friend blush. Shannon cocked her head.

What in the world could her friend Kota possibly be hiding? Hopefully, she wasn't in any kind of trouble.

Shannon would be there to help if Kota landed in the soup.

As Shannon marshaled the energy to press Kota to spill her secrets, her pink-haired friend snapped her fingers. "Hey, how could I forget? We haven't talked about Juneau rescuing your skinny little ass. Can you believe that? Sweet mama, I wish I'd been the one out whale riding, but oh, no, I had the thrill of evacuating the sound lab, abandoning my efforts to coordinate Jacob's new algorithms with our local recordings of whale and dolphin communications, and I escaped all safe and dry. Fortunately, a lot of us were working near the specimen room, so we grabbed two pails each and took whatever marine life we could scoop out. So, while *you* were enjoying yourself cavorting around with Juneau, I was sweating and grunting hauling jellyfish and sea anemone into the cafeteria."

"*Odin's eye,* I never even thought about the aquarium tanks. Poor little seawater things. I wonder if any of the ones you didn't rescue escaped into the sea."

Dakota shrugged. "We can hope." Then she lit up again at another new thought and grinned at her friend. "Oh, and if you're not fond of your recently-elevated status to cheek-smoochie hero, wait 'til you hear about your movie star exposure. And I use the term 'exposure' without reservation."

Shannon frowned at her friend. "Exactly *what* movie star exposure?"

"So Moon assigned someone on board *Rescuer One* to capture everything he could related to the disaster. Including your rescue. On video. You can imagine the viewership potential. She framed her hands around an invisible headline. 'Drowning woman rescued by whale, floats on its back until help arrives.' Moon has sold the video to news outlets around the world. Bringing in buckets of money to the Dickson. You're an international star, whale woman. A rather naked star, I might add, but a star. Maybe they'll make a movie. Can I play myself? Or Lady Gaga would be my next pick to play me."

"No, no, and no," Shannon said, wishing she could simultaneously cover her face, wring her hands, and throw Thor's hammer at Moon, but the IV drip lines and plaster cast had pinned her down. "And don't call me naked. I had on my underthings."

Kota's eyes squeezed shut in mirth. "Such as they were. We could get Scarlet Johansson for you."

"Stop that. You're telling me they videoed me four-fifths drowned, blue, waterlogged, shriveled, and wrinkly, in my bra and undies?" And Moon had sold tickets to the show. Good thing the proceeds would help save the Dickson. "*Odin's eye.*"

"Your impotent Norse gods can't help you now, sweet Shanny, not in the face of powers like Instagram and the BBC. And look on the bright side. You, thin and fit, do present well in dishabille. Add to that—the salt water acted like a natural hair volumizer for you. And frozen bluish skin coordinates well with your silver-blond hair and huge green eyes, so no worries. You looked great hypothermic."

When Shannon continued to flash uncomfortable looks at her, Dakota added, "Also, the camerawoman recorded lots of lovely footage of Juneau holding steady while you were rescued, close-ups and so forth, and of your other hero, the security guy, hitting the water to bring you in. When he wrapped that big blanket around you and carried you below deck, you looked like a modest, half-dead mermaid rescued from the sea." Kota clasped her hands together over her heart. "Very romantic."

Shannon laughed at her friend's antics, despite her extreme embarrassment. "I just hope my fame lasts no more than its allotted fifteen minutes. Juneau, though, I hope she becomes even more fabulously famous than she already is. She deserves it. I take it somebody has connected the dots that she could only save my sorry butt because we set her free?"

"Moon jumped all over that. I still can't believe it: our own sweet Shanny rescued by a whale," said Dakota. She looked at her cell phone and rose from her chair. "And on that high note, I must be off. I have a late shift today. We're scuba diving around the clock to help clear debris. Just to make sure the wreckage didn't bury anyone else alive." With one last nervous pat of her pink triangular hair peak, she tucked her vape back in her backpack, and, her eyes wandering to the floor, she added, "Admin people have let it be known unofficially that a battle is raging even as we speak among the Dickson board members about whether to rebuild. Insurance and such. Hey, let me dim the lights for you on my way out." With that, Dakota breezed out the door.

"Thanks for visiting. Appreciate it," Shannon called after her, Kota waving in reply.

Not rebuild? The board of directors couldn't abandon the facility, the Juneau Project, the other research. They just couldn't. What would happen to Juneau? What would happen to Shannon's dream that Juneau could swim free and return to the Dickson with other belugas, that people would visit to watch the returning whales in the undersea viewing complex? That all cetaceans could be free, but cared for and cherished, that the Dickson could operate successfully?

Her spirits plummeted. Her head began to ache again.

* * *

"Ms. Kendricks."

Her head jerked up. James Copper stood in the hall light at her doorway, his face in shadow.

She hadn't been paying attention, or she would have seen the multicolored haze that had formed before he arrived.

"You startled me, Dr. Copper."

"How do you feel?" he asked, moving into the room.

Shannon's unease grew.

"How do I feel? Oh, as if the UC had collapsed, thrown me around like a beer can in a hurricane, as if the ocean had chipped me to icy bits, as if a bad neighbor had wandered into my garage and borrowed my blood without telling me. Why do you ask?"

Copper didn't so much as crack a smile as he reviewed Shannon's chart on the computer in the corner of the room.

ask copper when shannon leaves, Salesti said.

When she heard the little alien, Shannon jerked again, startled. She didn't know Salesti was tuning in.   W h e n Salesti connected with her, it could hear everything that Shannon could hear.

"So, doc, how long before I can get out of here and help with the clean up?" Shannon asked.

"With that arm and ankle? You'd be useless on clean up. I'm not going to clear you for duty, so if you don't have any sick leave, that's your problem."

Great bedside manner, jocko.

"As for moving out of the infirmary and back to your apartment, depends on you. For this particular surgery? Because we only required the operation to warm your blood, barring complications, we might send you home in a couple more days, if you're up to it, then bed rest in your quarters for at least another week. Unless your extraordinary metabolism complicates matters. I assume you've had that condition since birth?"

The question sounded innocuous, the kind a doctor might ask when encountering an anomaly like Shannon. But Copper still didn't sit right with her. She didn't like him questioning her. She didn't like answering. This was intuition on her part; but since the arrival of her special talents, she trusted her intuition.

"No, no," she said. "Happened during a lightning strike about five years ago. Quite a bad time I had. Almost died. Recovered. Left me with the high metabolic rate. Has its good points. I can indulge my chocoholic tendencies. Has its bad points. I sometimes require heart bypass surgery." *All true. Only a few tiny omissions.*

"Yes. Lesson learned there. We'll monitor you closely. Feed you well. All the chocolate you want. If you eat your veggies."

Ha, ha. What a card. Shannon didn't crack a smile either.

As Copper checked Shannon's monitors, her pupils, her lacerations, the tissue around her casts, he regarded her with a clinical kind of curiosity. Like a bug under a microscope. *Just finish and get out, you creep.*

"You have quite the connection with whales. Never saw a whale actually rescue a human before. Did you train her for that?"

Tempting. But she shouldn't lie. Very much. "No, we never trained her for rescue operations. I guess she just wanted to, so she did. The behavior isn't unlike the way a mother beluga brings her newborn baby up to the surface to take its first breath. Perhaps that's where the instinct came from," Shannon said.

Copper nodded. Then, without warning, his comments took a left turn. "Nobody seems to know how you were able to warn us about the UC collapse in advance. Moon will interrogate you about that, I suspect. The feds, too. The damage here must be in the hundred millions."

Interrogate? A strong word. Shannon squirmed. She could evade the questions of her easygoing friend Dakota. But Moon? The government, *for Odinssake? What should she say? What could she say?* Perhaps the truth. Or some of it. A kernel.

Okay, here's a kernel. "Juneau warned me. That is," Shannon added, each word tumbling onto the last, as Copper continued to study her, "she came close to the Plexiglas, exhibiting anxious behaviors, and I watched her jaws clap, clear signs of trouble. I trust her. So I ran to the security phone, and I used it." *And once again, the full Pinocchio.*

Oh crap. The video feed. Juneau wouldn't have appeared in it. Hopefully Copper wouldn't check.

"Mm-hm." Copper scribbled some notes on Shannon's charts and left without another word.

Mm-hm. Did he mean "mm-hm, that makes sense"? Or "mm-hm, what a load of b.s."?

Mm-hm indeed. She'd have to do better than that when Moon turned his shrewd, intelligent eyes on her. And the feds! What if they thought she'd communicated with terrorists about the collapse? *Mother of Odin—*

—Just then that familiar tug pulled her gaze toward her hospital door, where her multicolored haze swirled. A visitor.

Luke knocked and entered, a vase of deep purple and white irises in his hand.

Shannon's wrinkled brow smoothed and she grinned. "Beautiful. Thanks. Where did you find these, up here where the growing season lasts about fifteen minutes?"

"Oh, a greenhouse in town," he said, rubbing his five o'clock shadowy chin. "So. Heart surgery. You all right?"

"Good, good, all things considered."

"You had me worried. Just like old times."

An awkward silence followed.

They'd lost the knack of talking to each other. Five years without a face-to-face conversation between two people would do that.

"So," she finally said, "what in Valhalla brings you up here to the Dickson, Luke, out in the boonies of Alaska? Last I knew you worked for the Ocean City police force."

Don't say it. Do not mention her.

She said it.

"... And dating that vet Margie what's-her-name."

Yes, brilliant. Bring that up. Now would be the perfect time. Shannon, girl with the maturity of an eleven-year-old.

"I noticed you recognized my voice over the security phone," Luke said.

What? Was he engaged in a different conversation in a parallel universe? So what if she could recognize his voice even if she only heard one syllable of one word, like a listener correctly guessing the song when the D.J. played only the first note. So what?

"Yes, I did. But that doesn't answer my question." There. Very mature.

"Recognized it after five years."

Parallel universe. "Yes, I recognized your voice after five years. But why did I hear your voice, Luke? Why did you show up here, after . . . after so long? And why now?"

"Recognized it on a crackling line."

Her smile, generated by the sight of the man and his bouquet of flowers, faded as his grin widened. "It didn't crackle *that* much," she said. "So why did you come? Not that I'm not glad to see you, because I am. Really glad."

"If you're glad to see me, why are you acting like you don't want me here?"

Shannon fell silent. Of course she wanted him there. But she didn't want Luke to get the faintest whiff of Salesti's visit and all the trouble that went with it.

Seeing that Shannon wasn't going to answer, Luke shrugged and told her precisely why he was there. "Salesti asked me to come," he said.

CHAPTER NINE

"WHAT?" SHANNON'S VOICE ROSE A HALF OCTAVE as she grabbed her braid and held on tightly. She'd figured out some likely reasons for Luke's sudden appearance at the Dickson. But an invitation from *Salesti*? Never entered her mind. Totally out of the question. No way.

"Why would Salesti. . . ? Why would you. . . ?" Shannon half-asked; the words fell uselessly from her shocked brain to her stuttering lips and out into the air, like water spilled onto the desert sand. She tried again. "What. . . ?"

No good. Babbling achieved nothing. She closed her mouth.

Breathe deeply. Steady. Calm. Try again.

"Have a seat." She gestured to the chair Dakota had vacated. "So, Salesti sent a message to you—you!—down in Ocean City," Shannon said, her words slowing and lowering as they forced their way past her disbelief. "Why?"

"Why does that surprise you? I did my part last time you needed help. Salesti thought you might need help again. And Lithuania."

"Lithuania what?"

"My location when Salesti contacted me."

Lithuania? No. She would not be distracted. *Don't ask him. Do not ask.*

Hell. "Why were you in Lithuania?"

"Hadn't ever been."

Shouldn't have asked.

"Salesti went to Lithuania?"

"No. She contacted me from somewhere on the coast here," Luke said. "I may have misunderstood, but I think she said she'd boarded a crab."

That much lined up.

"But why would Salesti say I'd need your help? I mean, I did, obviously. Need your help. But. . . ."

"Not an inkling."

Yeah, sometimes she loved the brief, calm, steady way Luke talked, so direct, so bare bones. Sometimes not.

Did he know about Essi and the virus? The dragonpanthers?

"Tell me everything Salesti said."

Luke shrugged. "Not much. Said you would need me. So I came."

You would need me, so I came. See now, that's when Shannon liked concise conversation with Luke.

"So maybe," he continued, "Salesti wanted me here to pluck you off your beluga before you died of hypothermia," he said.

"Um." He didn't know the rest. *She would tell him nothing. Let him go back to Lithuania and wherever else he'd never been.* Last time around, events had deteriorated so quickly, so disastrously. Luke would not thrill to the news of a second incursion of other-worlders. *Don't make him have to choose to stay or go.*

"Yeah, probably so. Mission accomplished." Shannon saluted. "And I never had a good chance to thank you, by the way, so thanks. Really. I mean it. You did save my frozen butt."

He smiled and looked at his hands.

That overwhelming urge to tell this man everything flooded her again.

Don't do it, just don't.

Oh, hell's bells. "But, uh, also perhaps Salesti's call to you involved Essi's return to Earth. MIA down in Ocean City. With a lethal virus. Also the unidentified object that blasted into the Underwater Complex—" Shannon stopped.

Luke had just pushed his chair a foot backward. He probably didn't even realize he'd done it. Right. Too much information.

"Well, hey, never mind," she said. "That's Salesti–Shannon stuff. Um, underwater matters." Shannon waved her hands vaguely in his direction. "Underwater UC explosion problem." Shannon pretended to cough. *No need to dredge up all the pertinent details.*

"Essi and a lethal virus. Underwater matters," he said.

"Anyway, job well done. You can head back to Lithuania. Nothing's likely to go wrong now that you've done your part."

"Yes. It will." He wiped his hand across his stubbled chin. "You are involved. Essi is involved. Everything will go wrong. Very wrong. Inevitably."

He slid his chair another few inches backward.

Silence returned to the room. The wall clock ticked. The irises, still in their green foil cone, seemed to wilt even as Shannon watched them. Light filtered listlessly through the window, as gray as the day beyond.

"So why Lithuania, really, besides that you've never been?" Shannon asked, filling the void.

"As for underwater matters, I scuba dive," he said, as if Lithuania had never been spoken of, as if the previous conversation had never lapsed. "Have for years. Instructor-qualified."

Very difficult to move this man off topic.

"Yes, but . . . but—"

"The unidentified object that destroyed the UC," Luke prompted. "What do you and Salesti know about it?"

"Yes, the unidentified object." Shannon tapped her fingers on her bed sheet, a staccato rhythm to match her racing mind. He'd taken on more than his fair share of the fight last time around. She couldn't ask him to take on a dangerous virus and a couple of dragonpanthers.

Still, a trust issue between them had arisen five years before. She had almost lost Luke when he discovered she'd stretched the truth with him about her true reasons for going to a casino, trying to win the money for Juneau's freedom. Sure, she'd only fudged because she didn't think he'd believe that an alien child had come along and given her an extra skill set. But Shannon had promised herself then that she'd never withhold the truth from him even if it involved insane things that normal people would never believe. If she could possibly help it.

Yes, it had been a bad idea to involve him then, just as it would be a bad idea to involve him now. And yet Salesti had already pulled him in. He deserved to know the facts. To make his own decisions.

And then Shannon would find some way to keep him out of it.

Deep breath. "Dragonpanthers," she said. "Aliens. I mean, of course they're aliens, since Earth doesn't have...." Her eyes held fast to the off-white sheet over her chest as she added in a swift stream of words, "So we need to collect Essi, who carries a deadly virus lethal to mankind. One of the dragonpanthers wants the virus for an antidote. We don't know yet what the other one wants."

Luke nodded. Rubbed the stubble on his chin. "More aliens."

For one moment, it felt as if the room had frozen, as deeply as the glaciers to the north and east of the Dickson. All the warmth that had flooded Shannon when Luke walked into the room vanished, a tiny flame snuffed out by the fingers of an ice giant. Neither of them moved. Neither spoke. Shannon lifted her eyes. Luke gazed out Shannon's window at a view of granite sky and cement buildings.

"I still haven't recovered from the last alien incursion, cara," he said softly. He stood, his hands hanging at his side.

Good. Exactly what she'd wanted. Exactly.

Deep within her, in a secret, well-guarded place where she'd hidden her most fragile emotions, she broke apart. She registered it, as if seeing, but not hearing, an avalanche from a great distance off.

Even so. *Be the ice-encrusted rock. Send him on his way. Keep him safe.*

She nodded, kept her mouth closed and her eyes wide open, because if she blinked, the tears welling in the rims would trickle down her cheeks. Luke, moving with the long lean muscles he maintained in such fine tune, turned and disappeared out the door.

Loki's luck. Why must aliens choose to poke around in *her* life? If her arms weren't otherwise occupied with a cast, needles, and tape, she'd have thrown something. Many things. Then kicked them around the room. Then stomped on them. Then—

shannon? Salesti's voice whispered in her mind, its voice not as cheery as usual.

"I'm here," Shannon said.

salesti sorry.

"Aren't we all? So tell me, small one, why *in Odin's name*, must *I* be the one to fix these little glitches involving planet Earth?"

Salesti emitted a motor-like squeaky chirp. Like a purr and a hummingbird buzz interwoven. This time it failed to dent the black and weighty mood that had settled on Shannon like an anvil as Luke departed.

CHAPTER TEN

THE DRAGONPANTHER CAME FROM A WORLD SALESTI CALLED THE FIREWORLD for Shannon's benefit, because a water-like liquid covered ninety percent of the planet, and the surface of that entire expanse of liquid sea burned with pale, silver-blue fire, Salesti explained.

This narration didn't promise to answer why Salesti had pegged Shannon for alien duty. Perhaps Luke and Salesti lived in the same alternate universe where different conversations were happening, or maybe Shannon wasn't the only one around here trying to change the subject all the time.

Still. The FireWorld sounded interesting. She didn't interrupt.

The dragonpanthers lived on the islands of FireWorld, high on craggy hills dotted with networks of vast caves, which the creatures called home. Below the hills, lush, dense forests sheltered a host of other species, and at the lowest land point, thick swamps gave way to the seas.

Nothing human-like lived on the FireWorld. Except, Salesti said, the dragonpanthers.

"Stop. Did you just call the dragonpanthers 'human-like'?"

brains like brain of shannon. only bigger. science like science of people of shannon.

"Science? What do you mean?"

example, roebor finding antidote for disease on fireworld.

Oh. Of course. Shannon had skipped right over that indication of sophistication. But a dragon couldn't be doing scientific research, surely.

shannon unfair to roebor. Salesti sounded deeply disappointed.

Fair point. What did Shannon know about dragonpanthers? "Look, sorry, Salesti, but does Roebor even have fingers? Opposable thumbs? Computers? You understand what I'm saying?"

yesss.

"Yes, you understand what I'm saying?"

yesss, fingers, thumbs, computers.

Seriously. Okay then. Shannon needed to wash some dragon preconceptions right out of her hair. Although she still had trouble reconciling what she'd seen of Roebor and FireWorld with scientific inquiry.

Shannon changed the subject. "Salesti, do I call Roebor a 'he,' or a 'she,' or an 'it'?"

Salesti obliged with a clear and detailed image. *roebor male. shannon pays attention, shannon can tell.*

Shannon paid attention. Yes, she could tell. Most definitely male. Most definitely.

She removed her gaze and focused on Roebor's eyes, which glowed like nothing on Earth, blazing from the creature's head without pupil, without iris.

Even as she stared at Roebor's eyes in fascination, Shannon's own eyelids drooped, her chin began to sink. *Damn meds.* Check that; she needed, and therefore loved the meds right now, but the sleepiness she could do without. She opened her eyes very wide and willed them to stay open, giving her head a shake.

"He can see out of those eyes?"

as well as eagle.

As captivating as Salesti's image had proven, and despite Shannon's best efforts, her mind drifted away from Roebor. . . .

. . . .far away, someone hums, cries, in ineffable sadness . . . Essi? . . . Shannon flies, gliding through the black void with great skin-covered wings . . . Where has the little alien child gone?. . . . Have to find her . . . But no matter how swiftly Shannon flies, no matter how determined her rhythmic advance, Essi's cry remains far, far away.

* * *

Shannon jerked awake. "Sorry, Salesti. I'm very tired. Just tell me one thing. How can Roebor and the other dragonpanther breathe here?

fireworld air much like earth air. same with riverworld. this allows roebor and salesti to visit earth.

"Lucky." Or not, depending on whether a person was Shannon, who sometimes felt quite *unlucky* that Earth attracted these visitors.

"How did he happen to burst out of the portal on top of the Underwater Complex? Last time, uncommonly bad luck put me in the wrong place at the wrong time, right? So I became the most convenient host for Essi when she popped out of the portal. Surely I do not suffer a curse so rotten that I just happened to be standing under a portal again?"

oh, no, shannon, portal roebor takes from fireworld seeks shannon. shannon's gift to attract portals.

"*Gift?* No thank you. I don't want a gift like that. Forget it. Return to sender. Seriously, how do I get rid of this so-called gift?"

salesti fears shannon keeps gift if she likes or not. sorry. and other portal, riverworld portal, follows shannon always, always close by. nice for seladorans going home.

Odin's eye. "A portal to another world follows me around? That's impossible. And creepy."

possible.

"But if that's right, shouldn't Essi be up here and not down in Ocean City?"

one permanent portal over ocean city now.

"What? Why?"

salesti makes during last visit. for emergencies. very good one.

"Emergencies? What emergencies?"

emergencies where earth needs salesti right away.

So this was a two-way street. Shannon could ask Salesti for help if she needed to. Something to remember. "But why not use my portal?" My portal. *Did she really just ask that question?*

portal of shannon not always works.

"Why not?"

Salesti shrugged. *universe harsh.*

Not comforting. "So when you came here, if the portal didn't work, what could have happened?"

The little creature shrugged again. *end of salesti.*

Could she just go screaming into the night now? A portal following *her*? And a temperamental one at that. A portal in Ocean City by *Salesti's design*? *Odin's eye.* She didn't want a portal, or rather two portals, spewing alien children and dragons like a bubble gum machine. She wanted the portals to leave her alone.

This was all too much. Too much. She felt sick.

Shannon's stomach lurched. Foul-tasting, burning bile erupted like a sudden shot from Mt. St. Helens, and spread rapidly like lava down her hospital gown.

She rang for the nurse.

* * *

Freshly decked out in a new hospital gown, this one solid government green, Shannon reached out for Salesti. Salesti remained silent. Apparently it had thought better of elaborating on the matter of a portal that tagged along at Shannon's heels like a playful puppy.

"Salesti. You can finish your story. I won't throw up or scream or go insane. I'm calm now. Fairly calm. Okay, I'm not calm, but I'm too worn out to get upset. So speak on."

Haze filled Shannon's door.

A knock. Luke popped his head around the door. His eyes scanned the room.

"Oh. I thought I heard you talking to someone. I didn't wish to interrupt."

"Did I talk out loud? Didn't even realize." Shannon wiped one hand across her forehead, wincing when her wrist stung where the IV needle penetrated her skin. Oh yeah, they had told her not to move it. "Nobody's here. I'm talking to Salesti." She raised her voice. "Or *trying* to talk to her."

"Hell of a fighter, Salesti. For a little flyspeck," he said, undoubtedly thinking back to the good old alien-fighting days. Luke's hands moved back and forth along his belt. "I wanted to say that I have reconsidered. I'm with you." With that, Luke's head vanished back around the door and the door swung closed.

Shannon stared at the empty doorway for a moment. *Just like that?*

"Wait. Luke, come back here. You can't just—" But of course he just did. Leave. Without talking it through.

His return would do him harm; she knew it would. Yet, she didn't think she possessed the strength to turn him away.

"Are you back, Salesti?"

yes.

"So every time the good folk of Riverworld shoot down to Earth, they'll end up my problem?"

salesti hopes visits rare.

"Yeah, every five years so far. Not that rare. But why me, *for Odinssake*? With billions of people to choose from, why would the portal attach itself to me? Can't we reattach it to somebody else?" She could think of a few lowlifes she'd like to stick with this awesome privilege. Good old Rod Jenkins for one.

complica—

Shannon held up her good hand as if to push the words away, even though the little creature didn't have a clue what she was doing, since it was miles away. Ow. That stung. Stupid needles.

"Don't say it, Salesti." Her hand dropped back to the bed. "All right. I'm too tired to push it. But we have not finished with this topic, I promise you that." Complete bluster, of course. Salesti could be finished with any topic it wished at any time. Not much Shannon could do about it.

"But one more thing, if I'm such a portal magnet, why did Essi choose Ocean City?"

essi panics, essi takes wrong portal.

"But then how did you know which portal to use?"

salesti knows which is which. essi jumps first, looks at which portal after.

"Yeah, that's Essi."

Shannon could ask a million more questions. But no. She didn't have it in her. "Sorry, Salesti. We've officially hit info overload. Let's leave it for now. I can't do anything about anything until they let me out of here anyway. We'll wait to learn how tomorrow shapes up. Okay, my friend and tiny thorn in my side?"

The tinkling laughter surrounded Shannon again. *shannon so funny. salesti thorn. salesti likes to be thorn. shannon be rose. tiny rose rests now.*

The room fell into silence. Shannon's body relaxed. Her mind floated in the darkness behind her eyes. Better. Images of Salesti, dragonpanthers, and Essi faded and disappeared. She slept.

* * *

She awoke from a heavy slumber with the big question on her tongue. Without even opening her eyes, Shannon said, "But, Salesti, we both know you're the powerful one. Why do you need me?"

Laughter like water over stones.

shannon more powerful than shannon knows.

Before Salesti could say more, an abrasive voice interrupted.

"What did you say? Are you talking to me?"

Shannon opened her eyes to find Dr. Copper's cool, gray, bespectacled eyes four inches from her nose. She emitted an involuntary squeak.

He jumped back. Cardinal-colored blotches appeared on his neck, as if dripped on him by an invisible syringe.

Embarrassed, you frog? Serves you right.

"What were you doing?" Shannon asked, hastily sitting up.

Copper glanced down at the clipboard in his hand as if he had written the answer there, and then looked up at Shannon. "You mumbled some words. I thought it might be important. That is, I thought it might relate to your medical condition. I was also trying to place that perfume you're wearing. Very unusual. Probably very expensive. But why you think you need it in here is beyond me."

Yeah, you were spying. But why? "I must have been talking in my sleep, that's all. Stuff left over from the explosion, Juneau, the operation, all that. I used to sleepwalk too. Not so much anymore." She kept a close eye on his reaction. Did he believe her?

A slight downward tug at the corners of his mouth, a moment too long before he blinked. No, he suspected her of lying. Which she had. But then, so had he.

Who was this guy, really?

CHAPTER ELEVEN

COPPER'S WEIRD BEHAVIOR CALLED FOR EXTREME MEASURES. Shannon gathered her multicolored haze and, with no misgivings—hardly any—cast out for the doctor's images, his emotions.

. . . .Her medical record, her face staring at him, the hall to which he wanted to escape, intense embarrassment mingled with anger and distrust. He—

Before she could learn more, he turned and strode out the door without another word, and she lost her concentration.

Shannon's lips tightened. She needed more time in his head. But first, she needed a fresh, renewed head of her own. This one throbbed and pained her to such a degree she could hardly read her own thoughts, let alone Copper's. Fatigue settled on her like soft snow that fell and fell, burying her deeper with every minute that passed.

* * *

When Shannon next opened her eyes, Dakota was sitting by her side, calmly vaping and texting.

"Hey, sweet cakes. Thought you might sleep right on through until we finished rebuilding the observation decks. Slacker. You feeling any better?"

Shannon, still groggy, tried to sit up. "Ouch. Can you crank the bed up a bit, Kota? Thanks for coming. Another nice vape flavor. What's this one called? How long have I been asleep?"

"Key Lime Cookie, and let's see. . . ." Dakota began counting on her fingers. "To recap: July first, Monday morning, four-fifths-drowned, deep frozen, and dramatically rescued, an immediate worldwide phenom."

Shannon winced.

"Monday night. Heart surgery." Another finger went down. "Tuesday, wakey wakey, fireside chats with me, with Copper, poor child, and with the luscious Luke—I introduced myself to him last night." Finger down. "Now it's Wednesday." She pulled out her phone and glanced at the time. "Eight fif-ty-five. Gotta say, lollypop, you've been pretty much resting on your thin, yet sweetly brainy laurels since Monday."

Yes, well, Salesti hoped to get Shannon up off her resting laurels soon enough.

"Wednesday night, wow. I can't keep track." Shannon shifted her good arm as she sat up. "Hey, look at that—the IV needles have disappeared. That must mean real food will appear at some point. Let's call the nurse." She lifted her now-free hand to brush her greasy hair from her forehead. Moving without the needles; much better.

If only her thinking would improve as easily. Her metab-olism was playing havoc with her concussion, for one thing.

"I feel more cotton-headed than—" Shannon had almost said "than when aliens invade your mind." *Bad bad bad.* "More cottony than uh—" Before Shannon could think of a substitute, Dakota, never at a loss for words, finished the thought.

"—more cottony than too much weed on top of too much whiskey. I hear you," Dakota said as she walked into the bathroom to adjust her pink spiky hair triangle.

Weed and whiskey? Shannon shuddered.

While Dakota fussed with her hair in the mirror, her back to Shannon, Shannon said, "You know, Kota, I don't trust Dr. Copper. I'm getting a strong vibe that he's not what he claims to be. Do you think you could snoop around a little? Find out what other people are saying about him. Talk to him, try to catch him out?"

Dakota, despite her free spirit, her pink hair, and her goofy behavior, had shown skills as one crackerjack researcher and observer. Since she also loved adventure, this request should suit her perfectly.

And yet, as Shannon watched Dakota's expression in the bathroom mirror, anger flashed across her face so quickly Shannon would've missed it if she hadn't been looking right at Kota's mirrored image.

A facade of false serenity replaced the displeasure a millisecond later, and Dakota turned from the mirror and came back from the bathroom.

Shannon looked quickly down at her arm cast. *Kota?* Shannon hovered dangerously close to tears. *What had brought that fury on?*

"'Catch him out' on like what?"

"I . . . I think he's spying on me for some reason."

"For some reason?" Dakota said. "The reason is the bond between you and Juneau, obviously. Duh. We all know you two have secrets."

If that's supposed to be my cue to open up, you can forget it now, girlfriend. "No, I don't. And might you satisfy your inquisitive instincts by finding out about *his* secrets instead?"

"Will do, cookieface. Let's see. I know he's obsessed with money. It's practically all he talks about. I know he's sadistic and arrogant. And that he's definitely breeding bats in the belfry. But everybody knows those things. So I don't know what you hope I can find out. Oh, I hope he's not KGB. They're vicious."

"He's not KGB. They don't exist anymore. But I suppose you're right. He might be trying to find out about the bond between Juneau and me." *Or about Shannon's limited psychic powers, or what had really happened to her friend Becky down in California. The list went on and on.*

"Yeah, wouldn't we all like to find out more about the bond between you and Juneau, shug," Dakota said. When Shannon started to protest, she added, "But I mean like a competitor or someone who wants to steal Juneau for nefarious purposes."

"Exactly." *A competitor or someone who wants Juneau for nefarious purposes. Well said, Kota.*

"Okay, honeybee, I'm on board."

Shannon and her friend mulled over what they knew of Copper. In the early stages of Project Juneau, Copper headed a medical team that had been very fond of testing the resiliency and resourcefulness of the research staff who would spend time underwater in the dark, turbulent waters off the coast. Shannon and Dakota had endured their fair share of such resiliency exercises, and often voiced the opinion that the line between physical capacity testing and torture appeared to be very fine. Very fine indeed. They'd formed the impression that Copper regarded them as little more than lab rats and, as to his little lab rats, he harbored a very hard heart.

They had also decided he was one wheel short of a wagon. Something that made normal people *normal* definitely was missing there.

Yet Copper did possess excellent medical knowledge, and the other doctors and staff spoke highly of his surgical skill. So, whatever his deficiencies, whatever else he might have up his white hospital sleeve, he hadn't faked his medical credentials.

"Okay, so I'll be Matahari," Kota said, as they finished up their plotting against Copper. "I'll buy a trench coat, of course, and a fedora. Do you think I can get by without the French cigarette in the cigarette holder, sugarplum? Go with the vape instead?"

Shannon laughed. "Ow, it hurts when I laugh. Quit making me," Shannon said. But she continued to chuckle—softly, with due attention to her ribcage. "No trench coat, and the fedora would ruin your pink hair triangle"

"Oh, I never thought of that. Right. The fedora is out. Maybe one of those mysterious hoods that falls forward over my face so I can't be seen. Loose enough to maintain the pink triangle, do you think?"

Shannon laughed again. "Ow. No hood either. Just your regular clothes. They're irregular enough," she said, as Kota pouted and threw a magazine at her.

Yet even as she laughed, Shannon sensed a falseness now overshadowing their banter, that a darkness shaded their friendship.

She should never have brought up the topic of Copper. She needed to change the subject. "Hey, have you heard anything new about whether we'll keep the Dickson research going up here?"

Kota leaned in closer to Shannon and said in a near whisper, "You gotta give Moon credit. While he's down in Ocean City at the Dickson's main facility fighting for the rebuild, he has quietly given the go-ahead to start construction."

Already crews had begun a hastily-built improvised area above water for both viewing and ocean work, later to be replaced with a longer-term and sturdier facility, which would, in stage three, theoretically give way to the new and improved completely rebuilt Underwater Complex.

"We have operating funds still flowing now, but who knows what will happen down the road, so he wants to be ahead of the game if he wins the day for us. If the board decides against the rebuild, though, and they catch him spending unauthorized money, he'll be in the hottest of water for spending money on the site."

"Are we going to keep doing the scientific work too?"

Dakota confirmed that their research work would indeed proceed until somebody ordered them to stop. They were still using the boats for research, too. The work wouldn't match the quality of research achieved here pre-bust-up. But it beat shutting down.

"One hitch, though," Dakota said after a pause, and with an uncharacteristic uneasiness. "The one project that Moon wants to move back down to Ocean City right away is, uh. . . ."

"Seriously?" Shannon could fill in the blank on that one easily enough. "Juneau and I have to go back? What, to the SeaQuarium at the zoo? Or the Dickson pool? They can't do that to her."

"I don't know where they mean to send her. I've only heard that she must go back down to Ocean City with you as soon as you can manage it."

"I'd rather she took off and never came back," Shannon said.

"But then you'd never touch her lovely face again. You can't mean it."

"Oh yeah, I do. She hated it in the pools."

Dakota brushed her hand restlessly back and forth on Shannon's sheet next to her leg. "But she won't run away, right? I mean she's bonded to you and the research team now." She cocked her head at Shannon and squinted. "Or do you know something the rest of us don't?"

Yes, indeed, my friend, I know many things you can't even imagine. And wouldn't believe if I told you. But until I can figure out what's going on with you, you will learn nothing from me.

"No," Shannon said. "I only know that her freedom means everything to her."

"Shanny, sweetums. You know the rumors."

"What rumors? I don't know about any rumors. Unless you mean the rumor that you and Rod Jenkins secretly married in Vegas last Christmas," Shannon said, repeating an old joke between them.

"We did, sweet pea," Kota said without missing a beat, "and I'm now carrying his bald little mustachioed girl-child." Dakota regarded her a moment and shook her head slowly back and forth. "You probably haven't heard the rumors about you, you clueless naïf. I hear on the grapevine that you possess telepathic skills, you and Juneau."

Shannon blinked at her. They all suspected the truth, or some version of it?

"Oh." She tried to laugh as if the notion struck her as too absurd, but a choke emerged from her throat instead. She waived her hand airily. "Ridiculous of course. It's all training."

* * *

Thinking of Juneau made Shannon want to contact her. Contrary to her denial to Kota just a moment before, Shannon reached out with her tired, foggy mind, casting her colors, concentrating on the white beluga living essence that Juneau had left behind. With this to guide and connect her, she searched for the whale.

Juneau?

The whale's anxiety about Shannon came to her first. Shannon sent along an image, showing Juneau Shannon's hospital room, a sense of Shannon's eagerness to join her, a sense of Shannon's well being. *I'm fine, Juneau. A bit banged up, but fine.* She was not fine, but Juneau didn't need to know that.

Juneau conveyed an image. A Prussian blue dragonpanther, lying on a rocky outcropping high enough to reach above all but the most vicious of storm-driven waves.

Roebor. His head rested on his paws, his eyes closed. Sleeping.

Salesti?

salesti here with juneau. juneau well. roebor well. salesti and juneau remain here for now.

A hand waived in Shannon's face, breaking her concentration.

* * *

"Ship to shore. Hello? Anybody home?"

"Sorry, my mind latched onto Juneau for a moment," Shannon said. "You know what? I need to talk to Moon. He's still down at the Dickson in Ocean City?"

"Look, that's exactly what I mean, what you just did. Blanking out. I'm just saying that *if* you somehow did communicate with Juneau, in some way the rest of us can't—but I'm not saying you do, but if you did, and *if* someone saw you blink out, off in a trance, like just now, and if you snapped out of the trance, mentioning Juneau ate salmon for dinner or whatever, what do you think people would believe? Some people, who were not quite so much your friends as me, if they thought that you had psychic powers, might envision dollar signs, military uses, captive whale and captive woman trained in spy combat, shit like that. So. I'm just saying. Sometimes you're a tad obvious. Not that I'm saying."

"What did you say?" Shannon asked, trying for a smile.

But she understood. Kota made a good point, and it wasn't funny: Shannon must take care as to how and when she communicated with Juneau. And what else had Kota implied? Had she mentioned military uses and captive whales because she knew of some concrete plan involving Juneau, or had she merely spilled out whatever words flitted into her mind, like typical out-there Kota? It sounded to Shannon like Kota was attempting to warn her without coming right out and saying who might be after her. Shannon's hand clenched. The room seemed to grow yet darker.

"I hear you, Kota. Thanks for looking out for us."

"No problemo. Now. Let's wash this oily, droopy, salt-infested mess sitting on your head."

* * *

Before Kota could wash Shannon's hair, however, Copper returned.

Had he overheard Dakota's rambling warning? And did he believe these rumors about a psychic connection between Shannon and Juneau? Her jaw clenched. Her headache had returned, killing her chance to get into his mind; she just couldn't concentrate.

Kota filled Shannon's water glass and handed it to her. She gave Shannon a gentle hug and said, "Gotta go. The internet awaits. But I won't forget the, uh, research you gave me, cupcake. And I'll be back to help you with your hair."

After the usual ritual of checking the computer for Shannon's history since his last visit, and looking her over himself, Copper folded his arms across his chest and said, "Now that you're awake, I'll have a food tray sent in. The nurses can read on your chart that you're to have as much as you like, so don't be shy about asking. I'm a little hesitant about letting you go home, but everything looks pretty good. And home is only a few hundred yards away, after all. It's not like you'll need to pay for an ambulance. Let's see how you do with real food and how you sleep tonight. If all goes well, I'll discharge you tomorrow afternoon.

"Thanks. I cannot tell you how happy those words make me."

"What, that you can eat all you like?"

A regular stand-up comedian. "No, that I can get out of here." Shannon hesitated. "Can I ask you, have we accounted for everybody now?"

Copper pushed his glasses up his nose. "Not visitors—it's hard to determine who might have been here. But staff, yes. The seven previously unaccounted for all ended up here in the infirmary, some hurt quite badly, others with minor injuries."

Copper's foot began to tap repeatedly against her bed leg, jarring her slightly with each tap, his frown tightened; his own words had made him angry for some reason. Shannon pulled her braid around and fingered the tip with her right hand. She studied his eyebrows pushed down low over his eyes, his forehead a mass of wrinkles. This grim face had appeared as he talked about the injured staffers—as if he resented having to take care of the patients. Like he didn't want to be bothered with them. But that couldn't be right. Surely.

"Sorry. I . . . I know that's a lot of work for you."

"Yes." Copper bit out sharply, then seemed to realize what he was doing. The jarring foot-tapping stopped. "But none of it's your fault. I'll go order up that tray."

* * *

As Wednesday night ticked on toward midnight, Shannon dozed off and on. Lights in the hallways remained bright, but she could hear the rustling of nurses' uniforms as they began clicking off the lights in individual rooms.

The nurses had fed Shannon well. Shed, the small, dark man who'd worked with Shannon's depleted IV bags, had even baked her a double batch of chocolate chip cookies. Which lasted until just after eleven that night.

Steve, her friend from the comm center, had brought her laptop by. Before the UC collapse, she'd left it in her little cubbyhole in the library complex, which sat on high ground, *Odin be praised.* She pulled up her email. Friends checking in, the usual junk mail. Nothing from Moon.

It had not been lost on Shannon that the order for her to take Juneau to Ocean City provided the perfect opportunity for her to find Essi. Time to email him then, one-handed and all. If Moon planned to require her to take Juneau down to Ocean City, Shannon might as well shape the narrative.

> Dr. Moon: heard you are fighting the good
> fight to rebuild the Dickson up here. Hope

the effort goes well. I'm still in the infirmary but plan to go home tomorrow. Someone probably told you I went into shock and they did a pulmonary bypass. But I'm recovering nicely. From the reports I've received, Juneau escaped the implosion and has encountered no problems.

I learned today that you may want to move Juneau and me back down to Ocean City. If so, let me know ASAP so that I can make plans.

I feel quite comfortable with her in the open water now. I think she and I should travel down along the Canadian coast. Much less stressful for her than air transport. And cheaper. Shall I make arrangements for one of the boats here? Or would you rather take care of the boat? If we must come down, I'd like to set off as soon as I possibly can so that we can get back to work!

p.s. I think I'll have to sue you over the video of me being rescued. Just kidding.

Shannon began to answer her messages but hadn't made much of a dent when Moon replied.

Shannon. Very good to hear you are doing well. The news that you underwent bypass surgery shocked us all. You must not push yourself too hard until you fully recover.

We are all in mourning here at the terrible loss of life. This circumstance has compelled some of our directors to insist the entire Alaskan Center be closed and all operations moved back to California. I continue, as you say, to fight the good fight. I will tell you the truth: at the moment I am fighting the losing fight.

I regret that I did not have a chance to talk to you myself before you learned of your re-assignment to Ocean City. I would have explained that one reason and one reason only led to this decision: the video you amusingly refer to in your correspondence resulted in an outpouring of sympathy for the whale, for you, and for the project. Simply put, I need you here to encourage a further groundswell of good will and the donations that naturally follow.

Like you, I am eager for your return to work. However, risks attach to a sea journey down the coast. I must evaluate further. I will let you know my decision soon.

Keep well.

p.s. You must prepare yourself for the very real possibility that the SeaQuarium, which has continued to be our willing partner in the Juneau Project, will require Juneau's permanent return to captivity if we must cancel the Project.

CHAPTER TWELVE

SHANNON SNAPPED HER LAPTOP SHUT ON MOON'S WARNING. If her laptop weren't so bulky and heavy to lift and heave with one hand, she would have flung it across the room. Damn dragonpanther, busting up the UC and ruining everything for Juneau. Well, the good folks at the SeaQuarium could "require" Juneau's return all they liked; they would not place her in captivity again if Shannon had anything to do with it. If the Dickson decided not to rebuild, then Juneau would disappear.

Along with Shannon's heart.

* * *

Shannon slept late again Thursday and awoke to a lunch of fried chicken, mashed potatoes, cornbread, a vegetable salad, a fruit salad, peas, a quinoa-edamame-red pepper casserole, a chocolate shake, a piece of apple pie, and a crème-filled doughnut chaser. She made sure all the evidence had been swept away before Copper's afternoon rounds; no reason to invite rude remarks.

But apparently someone had reported her culinary intake. As he entered the room, he said, "I hear you're back to your usual high standards for sheer quantity of calories. I'll have to make sure the lunchroom doubles their usual supply order today. Our accountant will have to struggle to stay within budget."

Stop. Please. Your sense of humor is killing me. And not in a good way.

"I'm glad to be eating real food again," Shannon said with a bit of an edge, and left it at that.

"Blood work looks good, vitals are good. How do you feel?"

"Super, doc. Ready to check out and head back to quarters." *Super* overstated her health condition slightly. Overstated it quite a bit. Okay, substantially. But she'd suffered the infirmary too long already. She wanted out. She'd tell him she felt good enough run a team in the Iditarod, if that's what it took.

"All right. I'll release you. The paperwork will take a while. Plan on later this afternoon. You will sit in a wheelchair to ride to your apartment. That's not a walking cast on your ankle."

Q Block contained the staff's living quarters. Happily, enclosed walkways connected all the on-land blocks to make passage from any one point to any other point at the Dickson easy and pleasant. Staff could get from the Underwater Complex to the Visitor's Center to the cafeteria to their own sweet beds without sticking a toe out in harsh weather.

Shannon failed to mention to Copper that she planned to cruise down to California in a few days. For reasons she still could not articulate, her intuition told her he should not learn of it.

* * *

Salesti didn't check in throughout the rest of the afternoon, giving Shannon time to stew over impending events. Earlier, she'd considered asking for leave to fly down and look for Essi, but if Moon gave the go-ahead for her and Juneau to travel down to California along the coast, she wouldn't need to fly.

And, although she had no desire to get mixed up in alien business again, how hard would it be, really, this time? It sounded like a simple, straightforward, completely safe mission, right? Not like the struggles she'd gone through last time. She could handle it, even in her current condition.

Paperwork appeared at four that afternoon, and not long after, Luke also appeared pushing a wheelchair and carrying Shannon's backpack. He held it up: "Real clothes, unless you've grown so fond of the hospital gown you'd like to make it your go-to evening wear?"

"You are a life saver," Shannon said, reaching for her crutches to swing to the bathroom.

Uh-oh. She'd have to go with one crutch; no way to use a crutch with the arm in a cast. Never mind. She could do it one-crutched.

She shut the bathroom door and changed into a pair of black sweat pants flexible enough to slide over her ankle cast, and a loose, deep green sweatshirt with sleeves wide enough to work over her arm cast. She flipped her braid over her shoulder and frowned at her reflection in the mirror. The pale woman staring back at her looked awful, with deep, purple shadows under her eyes, a large bandage across her forehead, and a bluish-brown bruise spanning her entire right cheek. *Oh well*; she shrugged. No beauty pageants this week.

"We can just put the backpack on the seat of the wheelchair. I'm using the crutch," Shannon said. She planned to swing along with the crutch as long as her strength held out, and then five steps more. Copper would *not* dictate whether she sat in the wheelchair.

Luke watched her carefully, ready to catch her if she stumbled. But he did not protest.

* * *

A half hour later, Shannon had gritted her way through the walk that normally took ten minutes, and hopped to her front door, only to discover she had no keys. She'd forgotten to ask Kota to bring them to the infirmary. She sagged against the wheelchair.

"Need help?"

Luke reached out and gently wrapped two arms around her. He turned her to face him and leaned her against the wall by her door like a beam he'd propped up while he reached for his hammer to nail her down.

She hated these casts.

"I don't have my key."

"Do you have one hidden on your balcony, like everybody else living here?"

"Of course not. I wouldn't be that obvious."

He gazed steadily at her.

She tried for defiant, but she blinked first.

"Under the gargoyle. The one on the left."

"Be right back."

The key also fit the balcony door, and in a matter of minutes, he'd admitted her to her own apartment, guided her to her big, old, overstuffed navy blue couch, and eased her onto it, as if she were the stranger and he the host.

That burned.

He straightened up from tucking her favorite pale green afghan over her and surveyed her living room, which opened into the kitchen. His eye moved to the hall that extended to her bathroom and one and only bedroom.

Odin's eye. She'd left her bedroom in a seriously disheveled state back on the morning of Juneau's big day. She could *not* let Luke get an eyeful of that mess.

"The bedroom's off limits. I mean, not that we'd go into my bedroom. Or, I mean, not that I thought you wanted us to go into the bedroom." Shannon bit her tongue. *Fool.* "I need to clean up before anyone sees the bed, that's all. The room, I mean, before anyone sees the room."

Why did she say "bed"? She hadn't fixated on that bed. Okay, she might be thinking about the bed. But she didn't want him to think she was thinking about the bed.

Luke sank down into Shannon's large, comfy navy blue reading chair and regarded her silently.

"Is Narcissus here?" he asked after a moment.

Shannon nodded. "When I'm not home, Narci usually spends her time tucked into a ball on my bed."

In a voice that said he'd rather do anything but, he said, "Do you want me to check on her?"

Still not over having spent time in Narci's mind. Poor Luke.

"No, no. Nothing's wrong with her hearing," Shannon said. "She'll show herself as soon as she figures out who belongs to the deep voice, since she's shy with strangers. It may take her a minute to remember you."

As if on cue, the black cat with the big sapphire saucers for eyes rounded the bedroom door and padded at a silent run down the hall carpet, straight to Luke. She rubbed along the legs of his black security uniform, then sat on the foot of his boot and gazed up at him.

"Obviously she remembers you."

"Hey kitten," he said as he gingerly lifted her up and cradled her in his arms, "She feels a little skinnier than the last time I held her." She licked him once on the end of his nose, climbed up on his shoulder, and wrapped herself around his neck, her thin front legs stretching comfortably down his shoulder.

"I can't let her outside here. Too many predators. She's not used it. So no muscles."

"And also the calories burn off quickly, do they not? Like with you? In addition to me, the raven spent some time in her head, as I recall, and Salesti, so her metabolism remains elevated also?"

"She does burn off more calories than a normal cat, but luckily she didn't host any of you long enough for the metabolism to seriously overwhelm her love of all things that come in a cat food can."

Ten minutes later, Narci climbed down Luke's arm to the chair, to the carpet, and jumped onto the couch. She purred loudly and kneaded Shannon's lap before curling up half on, half off her legs. While Shannon had been languishing in the infirmary, Dakota had stopped by to feed Narci and keep her water bowl full, but the sociable, black feline had clearly missed Shannon; she gazed up with wide, unblinking blue eyes as if she didn't intend to turn Shannon loose any time soon.

A silence followed. The easy rhythm of conversation Luke and Shannon once knew still eluded them. Maybe for good.

Shannon's chest constricted.

"Thanks again for helping me get home," she said at last. "You want to stay for a minute? I have diet soda and cold water in the fridge, and I think I have leftover pasta and chocolate cake too. Help yourself to anything you find."

"I'd be delighted. Come along with me, Narci. If we eat, you may eat as well."

Shannon heard him rummaging in the kitchen cupboards, a cat food can popping open, and Narci, as she landed on the kitchen counter to oversee her food prep, then jumped to the floor and padded to her food bowl. The refrigerator door opened, items clinked as they came out, the microwave rumbled, the tang of pasta sauce permeated the air, and soon Luke returned with a thirty-two-ounce mug of Diet Dr. Pepper, lots of ice, just the way Shannon liked it; a glass of water for himself; and a portion of chocolate cake for Shannon that would normally satisfy four people. He'd located the leftover lasagna, and he served her a heaping dish, then lowered himself into his chair to eat his.

"Thanks. I needed this," she said, swallowing a super-sized bite of cake.

"So I see," he said.

After a time of companionable eating, Luke said, "Do we have a plan regarding Essi and her virus?"

"Don't you have to work?" Shannon asked, still not committed to throwing Luke back into these alien matters.

"No. Why? Oh, did you think I hired on here?" Luke said, wiping a trace of lasagna off his mustache. "No, I went to the security center to visit an old friend I trained with at Quantico. Sam Bendixen. Great guy. I've been helping out here since the disaster, but strictly voluntarily. Sam lent me this uniform. It doesn't fit any current staff."

Shannon nodded. Bendixen headed up security. She'd never met him. The uniform fit Luke well; few security personnel up here would be as tall as he was, or as fit.

"He'd just left the security center to check on a shipment when you radioed in your warning. You sounded rattled. That man Jenkins was acting hostile. So I intervened."

"About which I am so glad. But I'm surprised Rod let you on the radio."

Luke shrugged. "He's a coward at heart. I told him he could take it up with Bendixen if he had a problem with it." Luke shook his head at the memory. "He folded. So, no, I don't have to work."

"You're still on the police force in Ocean City then?"

"Yes. I took a six-month administrative leave. On the fifth anniversary of Essi's arrival, somebody over at the *Tide Tribune* dredged up the murder, the shootings, the whole story—the official version. Including my breach of several major police protocols. This stirred up some resentment against me again in the chief's office due to the negative press. My supervisor, Lieutenant Chen—you remember him—wanted me out of sight for a while until things cooled down."

Shannon dipped her face low to hide her dismay. She'd nearly managed to get Luke fired five years earlier, and he was still suffering the ramifications. Another reason to keep him out of anything going on in Ocean City this time around.

"When's your leave up?"

"Not for another month."

"So you were vacationing in Lithuania."

"Yes. Some of my mother's people came from that country."

"That's where your very slight but very sweet accent comes from, then."

"My Lithuanian grandmother lives with my parents, and my mother lived in Lithuania for much of her life, so we all spoke it as I grew up. Along with Spanish for my Aunt Maria, who also lived with us."

Shannon scooted up straighter on the couch. "I'd like to meet them some time. Anyway, Moon has ordered Juneau and me to go back down to Ocean City for publicity and fundraising."

"That's bad news. I thought they planned to continue the various research projects up here."

"Yes, everybody but us. And just before you came to help me home from the infirmary, Moon called. He's agreed that I can take Juneau down the coast."

"I'm surprised he bought into that."

"Me too. But he decided it would be just as safe, less expensive, and easier to arrange than having her flown in. She came back to the Dickson from her free run after the UC went down to save my scrawny neck—that convinced him she could do it."

"Still, Juneau is a pretty valuable asset."

"True. I guess he's swamped down there with everything going on, the fire, the UC collapse, directors up in arms, possible litigation, and so forth, so he didn't think it through with his usual caution. And I expect he'll put out some PR about her trip too. About how great she's doing, how well the research money has been spent, all that."

"I see. You are being very calm about her return to captivity in Ocean City. Was it your idea to cruise the coast? Do I smell a double cross in the making?"

Surprise flicked through Shannon's mind; Luke knew her better than she'd thought. "Yes it was, and yes you do. She can't go back to the SeaQuarium right now, because the SQ has just successfully integrated a new beluga with the four already there. So Moon plans to put her back in the pool at the Dickson. But I'm not asking Juneau go back into a pool. Ever. She can't do well in the California ocean, either—not part of a beluga's normal range—so I'll turn her loose up here and go on down the coast without her."

"Are you sure she'll be safe at sea?"

"No—it makes me sick just thinking about it, but it's her choice. I imaged her. She would never choose to go back to a pool, now that she's tasted open water. At least she's vaccinated against wild species diseases." Shannon blew her nose and brushed some tears away. "I wish I could leave her right here near the Dickson, because she knows the area, but ships and submarines are investigating the disaster and looking for terrorists here. I'm afraid they'll find her and turn her over to Moon."

"Moon will have your hide when she goes missing."

"I hope to avoid premature death by a little creative storytelling."

"Lying."

"Not lying exactly." *Okay, lying.* "I'm going to take the boat and Juneau far enough away from here to clear her of the ships and subs coming in to search, and then I'll turn her loose and cruise on down the coast as if she's still with the boat."

"Won't the crew notice?"

"Ah. For one thing, if you still want to have anything to do with this venture, the safest part would be helping me get the boat down to Ocean City. So you would be crew."

"Fine by me."

"Thanks. I appreciate it. So then her official disappearance will occur down in the more heavily traveled shipping lanes. I can blame her mysterious disappearance on those mammoth cargo vessels coming across the Pacific."

"I see. Moon doesn't blame you; he blames the ships that in general do cause whales problems."

"Right. As he should." Shannon winked at him.

"But doesn't that mean that Salesti will have to move from the crab into your mind to go to Ocean City to find Essi?"

Shannon's smile faded. "Yes, she's already moved into Juneau's head, and when we leave Juneau farther down the coast, Salesti will come with me, but hopefully not for long."

Luke rubbed his stubble. "No good, Shannon. Salesti will take you down, just like Essi and Juneau did before. Your system couldn't handle them when you were healthy. Now you're depleted. Don't do it."

"Essi has holed up in the head of some land creature in Ocean City, so Salesti has to come on board at some point to help me find her. And I should be able to finish the task easily this time, so I won't need to keep Salesti on board long enough to cause much damage."

Luke shook his head. "I don't like it. I have a feeling I'll be able to say 'I told you so,' but if you're dead when I say it, I won't get much pleasure out of it."

"I'll be fine, really." *For a while, anyway. For long enough. Okay, maybe not fine, but I'll live. I should live. Probably.*

"No, you won't be fine." He sat in a frown of silence for a minute. "When do we leave?"

"Moon suggested the day after tomorrow. I think I'll be feeling better by then, and in the meantime we can provision the boat."

"Who did Moon choose to accompany us?"

Shannon hesitated yet again. "You understand that once we get to the alien part, you can bow out gracefully at any time, right?"

"Somebody will have to pick up the pieces when this whole endeavor falls apart," Luke said. "I nominate me."

Shannon nodded, both happy and unhappy at the prospect of Luke's company. "The boat Moon assigned to us, the *Seatation,* sleeps four. Moon had planned to assign Chance Kopalaoillai to pilot us, but I may have mentioned that you're trained as a navigator."

"A navigator."

"Yes. He remembers you, by the way, from before. You made a very good impression. So he okayed Dakota and you, and I'm supposed to look for a fourth."

"I *can* navigate, as it happens. I say we skip the fourth and use the space for extra provisions. You'll eat a ton with Salesti on board."

"My thinking exactly."

"Why don't you rest up, then, and I'll go down to the *Seatation* and look her over. And start rounding up supplies."

* * *

With Luke gone, Shannon closed her eyes. Just as she began to drift off, her doorbell rang. The door immediately opened, and Dakota yelled, "Shanny, you awake?" Kota's face, topped by her signature pink triangle of hair, peeked around the corner from the front hall. Seeing Shannon on the couch, she bounced into the living room and plopped down where Luke had just been sitting, throwing one leg over the plump armrest and taking out her vape.

"I just got the memo from Moon that I'm coming with you down to Ocean City. How fun! I can't wait. When do we sail? Who else will crew? Will we go formal for dinner? Evening gowns and tuxes? Shall I rush out and buy a steamer trunk? Tell all, my little crumpet."

Shannon waited patiently for an opening. "Leaving the day after tomorrow. Just you, me and Luke. Are you mad at me for asking Moon to name you to the crew?"

"Are you kidding? Let's see, cruise down some of the most beautiful coastline in the world to warm weather, or spend my days dragging disaster-related flotsam and jetsam out of the dark, cold sea? Let me think. I know it's counterintuitive, but . . . I pick fun company, sunshine, and warmer waters." She took a puff on her vape.

Shannon said, "Oh, and it's fine for you to vape on deck, but will you try not to vape in the cabin. I've been getting really bad headaches since the UC collapse. Promise?"

"Sure. The weather should be pretty good. No reason I can't vape up on the bow, which is my favorite place on a boat."

"Thanks. Will you bring some of that peach flavored juice? Love the smell."

"Will do. But don't you mind that Moon plans to force Juneau back into the pool?"

The assurance rose to Shannon's lips that Juneau would definitely *not* wind up anywhere near a pool. Then the image of Kota's reflection in the bathroom in Shannon's infirmary room flashed in her mind: Kota's face stone-cold raging when Shannon told her she harbored suspicions about Copper. Shannon hesitated. For reasons she couldn't yet name, she elected not to explain that Juneau would never make it as far as Ocean City.

Instead, she said, "I don't have a choice. Moon wants her in Ocean City for publicity purposes, so we can raise the money to rebuild here." *There.* True so far as it went. Kind of true. Okay, not true; Shannon damn well did have a choice, and she would choose Juneau's freedom every time.

Kota departed after another hour of friendly chatter, and left Shannon even drowsier than before. She snuggled further into the couch. She pulled her blanket up to her neck with her good hand. Narci stirred on her legs, waking long enough to lick her paws and rub them over her ears, before settling down again.

* * *

Just as she slipped into a calm dream of ocean waves lapping against a boat, Salesti called out to her.

salesti tells shannon what salesti learns from roebor about second dragonpanther.

Without opening her eyes, Shannon drowsily murmured, "Okay, Salesti, who is it, and what does it want?"

dragonpanther named tidak. tidak no friend to roebor. tidak and roebor compete as scientists. also compete to determine who leads island of roebor. tidak wishes to reach virus first, beat roebor to antidote, but tidak ruthless, roebor says tidak plan—end life of essi, turn virus loose on earth, let virus spread, take diseased specimen with many virus cells to fireworld.

Salesti continued on for several minutes more.

"Odin's eye. Why wouldn't this Tidak just take Essi back to his world to extract the virus in a lab?"

roebor says tidak only knows how to extract virus when many virus cells present. essi not has many virus cells. only one.

"Then how does Roebor plan to do it?"

roebor knows better way. roebor extracts virus from essi without ending life of essi. without turning virus loose on earth. roebor better scientist.

"Where's Tidak now?"

on way to ocean city.

"Loki's curse. So we have to find Essi before he does. One thing in our favor; he's a tad conspicuous. He can't avoid being seen on land, and as soon as someone does spot him, everyone will be after him. So he'll have to stay hidden."

bad news, shannon. toss on board with tidak.

"Toss, as in Essi's friend from Riverworld?"

yes, same. and with toss on board, tidak has ability to jump to land creature. tidak likely will board human.

"So a big nothing in our favor."

big nothing, Salesti agreed. *salesti now knows essi drops to earth to flee tidak because essi knows shannon will protect her.*

Shannon winced. That stung. Shannon didn't feel strong enough to protect a lady bug. "Why did Essi have to run? Couldn't you protect Essi from Tidak on Riverworld?"

salesti away on important matters. salesti very sad salesti not protects essi.

Away on important matters? The little hummingbird-kitten? Interesting. "Don't be sad. We'll handle this. But if Tidak has already left for Ocean City, we'd better get moving."

Shannon grabbed her cell phone and dialed.

"Luke? The situation just heated up. It turns out the second dragonpanther, Tidak, has been in some sort of twisted competition with Roebor all his life and Tidak never won. His father treated him horribly about it. Tidak came to hate Roebor. So the whole Must Beat Roebor thing has become an obsession for him. He wants to lead the people that Roebor leads now, and he'll never achieve it unless he gets to the virus first and beats Roebor back to FireWorld with it."

"So an alien with an inferiority complex?"

"Exactly. But here's the kicker: he doesn't care if he has to kill Essi to get the virus, and he doesn't care if he sets the virus loose on earth and it starts a pandemic. A pandemic would actually make it easier for him to retrieve an infected creature. Which Roebor doesn't need because he can extract the single virus from Essi. But with an infected creature, Tidak has plenty of virus cells to experiment with to make the vaccine they need on his world.

"So how does this affect our plans?"

"We have to find Essi before he does. Can we leave tomorrow?"

CHAPTER THIRTEEN

AFTER EXPLAINING THE LATEST PROBLEM TO LUKE and then calling Kota to update the departure plan, Shannon sank back on her couch once again and contemplated the ceiling.

Stupid arm. Stupid ankle. She felt as useless as hairspray on a bald man. Luke and Kota would have to ready the boat and gather the necessities, including a large store of groceries, without her help. About the need for a food stash, Luke had spoken the truth; when Salesti boarded her mind, she would start eating like . . . well, like a whale. No offense to Juneau.

So. Tidak had rushed off after little Essi. Developments had turned negative already. Of course they had.

She breathed deeply and slowly, trying to calm her mind. To sleep. To let the anxiety go for one evening. . . .

Suddenly new unfamiliar images entered her mind.

I must go with you.

"What—?"

Shannon looked down the couch at her cat, who stared back at her unblinking.

"Narcissus?"

I must go, the cat imaged.

Sure, Shannon had touched Narci's mind back during the alien troubles so that she could transfer Luke to the cat. Salesti too. Apparently some kind of connection existed. Yet Narci had chosen not to use it until now.

Five years of silence. How very like her aloof little cat to keep her thoughts to herself.

"Do you mean you want to travel on the boat?"

I must. Must go.

"No way. You wouldn't like rocking on a little boat on the water, dipping up and down. And where would I put your kitty litter?"

Must.

"Why?"

You will need me.

"No, I won't need you for onboarding the aliens. I know you took some of my guests on board last time when they became too energy-draining for me, but I shouldn't need help this time. And, even if I do, you're too small. Desperation drove me to it last time, Narci, and you happened to be there for me. But you got really sick, same as me. I thought I would lose you. We can't go through that again."

Dakota instead?

"No, I don't want Dakota to know anything about Essi and Salesti." A shadow crossed Shannon's mind. She didn't want Dakota to learn about Shannon's onboarding ability or about her connection with Juneau, either. But Shannon didn't know exactly *why* she so clearly didn't want Dakota to know. She mulled that over. *Should* she include Kota in her plans? Kota would certainly be a stronger host in a crisis than her little eight-pound cat . . . But no, absolutely not. Shannon didn't trust her.

She had grown wary of her best friend at the Dickson. *How sad.*

Luke instead? the cat imaged.

"He almost swam all the way back to Ocean City when he heard the simple outline of this little adventure. He'd never willingly invite anyone on board. And I can't push him or I'll lose him. Do you understand any of that, Narci?"

Yes. So. I must go. Besides, I will be too lonely if you leave me, the cat imaged.

Shannon struggled with that thought for a moment.

Oh *for Odinssake.* It would seem Narci must go with them.

"Are you sure, Narci?"

I am sure.

"Okay then. But you will take on boarders only as a last resort, understood?"

Shannon shivered suddenly. Narci faded from her sight. Shannon could see only darkness. In that moment, she heard the cat purr, followed by a soft swish, a sound she recognizes immediately: the flow of an entity's essence into a mind. The absolute certainty that circumstances would in fact force her little feline to take on a boarder passed over her as clearly as if someone had whispered it in her ear.

Then the sound of Narci's weak meows rose in her ears. It was the sound of pain, of exhaustion.

Narcissus would not fare well as a result of the boarding.

Her vision returned. She pulled her braid around and rubbed the tip for a moment. Then she looked at it as if she had no idea why she held it in her hand, and flipped it back over her shoulder.

She shook her head, her lips pressed firmly together. This mission to rescue little Essi would in no way proceed flawlessly.

CHAPTER FOURTEEN

SHANNON SCOURED HER KITCHEN for a late dinner, pulling together three peanut butter sandwiches, a large cabbage salad, four apples, an orange, a plate of leftover eggplant *parmigiana,* and two chocolate bars with almonds: gearing up for Salesti's arrival. Then she loaded the usable remnants of her kitchen cupboards into a box, along with Narci's cat food and dishes.

Using her crutch to reach her bedroom, she intended to pack her duffel. But, lying on her bed to rest just for a moment, thinking she really did feel too awful to be entertaining aliens, she fell soundly to sleep, Narci curled snugly into her side.

* * *

Excitement to be underway roused her early the next morning. She looked forward to days at sea: to catch up with Luke, to figure out the meaning of that angry look by Kota at the mention of Copper, and to connect with Juneau before they parted company, perhaps for the last time.

* * *

The Dickson marina maintenance staff had come to prep the boat for a voyage and were gone on Friday morning before Luke arrived to load their provisions on the *Seatation*. When he came to fetch Shannon, she helped him stow her duffel and bags in his hybrid Ford Expedition for the short trip to the modest marina.

Luke studied the pile of Shannon's gear. "Why am I looking at this kitty litter box?" Luke asked, standing in front of rear cargo bay.

"Because we will be extremely sorry if Narci doesn't have it when she has to pee," Shannon said.

Silence.

"Narci?"

"Yes." Glancing around for passersby who might overhear, she added, "She insists."

"She insists."

Luke said nothing, but he placed the litter box on the gravel parking strip and folded his arms across his chest, a broad chest, Shannon noted. "She could go overboard with any unexpected lurch. She'll get seasick and throw up. She'll drive us all crazy, bouncing around the cabin at night."

"Oh, thanks for reminding me. We need to make a quick stop at the commissary so I can refill my meds and the vet called in some motion sickness pills for Narci."

Luke resumed placing Shannon's gear in the van but left the kitty litter where it sat. "Why would Narci insist on coming?"

Making one more sweep of the area for eavesdroppers, Shannon said quietly, "Because we may need her for onboarding." As Luke started to protest, she hurried on. "She's in her carrier, which I haven't brought out yet. Ask her yourself if she wants to go."

Luke's hands shot up in front of him, warding Shannon off. "No thank you. The next time I converse with Narci will be never, I hope. I can't change your mind?"

"No choice. Can you trust me on that?" Shannon hadn't discussed her ongoing spate of premonitions with Luke yet, but decided this wasn't the right time.

He sighed and picked up the litter box and tucked it next to the duffels.

They finished loading up and drove in silence to the commissary. When Luke switched off the van, he said, "Narci talks to you?"

"It seems she *can* image and emote to me. But she has had nothing to say until yesterday."

"Ah."

Three hours later, they'd found a place to stow everything, and they had prepped the boat to depart. They could leave any time—except that Kota had not yet presented herself. Shannon had called her cell several times, to no avail.

At last Kota arrived, unloading her Kia and breezing in as if nothing were amiss, saying, "Ship ahoy. Raise the gangplank, hoist the mainsail. Let's get this barge underway."

From her perch on the cushions lining the stern bench, Shannon watched, her foot propped up, as Luke helped Kota bring her gear on board. As carefree as Kota's words sounded, as wide as the grin she sported was, Shannon nonetheless noted two bright red dots in the middle of each cheek, sweat on her flannel, long-sleeved, pink plaid shirt, and a nervous glance back toward the parking lot next to the dock. The lot consisted of four rows of parking spots. Only a few vehicles sat on the gravel today, one of them a black sedan with extra dark windshields idling in the last row at the far end from the *Seatation*. Shannon couldn't tell with her naked eye whether anyone was sitting inside. Casting her colors, she reached into the car. Yes, she sensed someone in the driver's seat, relaxed but alert, motionless.

Watching them.

As Luke finished preparing the boat to move out, Shannon kept her eye on the car. The occupant did not move.

Could be nothing. Could be something.

* * *

Shannon had piloted plenty of short sea excursions, both as a college student and after she'd arrived in Alaska. The Dickson's skilled captains had taught many willing members of the research teams to navigate along the coast in the institute's small cruisers and runners. She could at last prove useful. She zipped up her jacket against the cool summer breeze on the water, took the helm, and steered the boat south, balancing her cast and foot lightly on the deck as she steered from the captain's chair.

Kota, on the other hand, professed to possessing no boating skills whatsoever.

"I can watch for pirates and your larger objects like islands or oil tankers. Hand out cold beer at appropriate intervals.

Throw the life preserver if Narcissus falls into the drink. But that's about it."

Kota had purloined some hydrophonic gear that had been salvaged from her lab and planned to troll for whale and dolphin sounds, then record and study them. She soon had assembled her equipment and claimed what would become her favorite perch in relative isolation on the bow of the boat, wearing headphones to listen to the sounds of the deep.

After an hour or so, Luke volunteered to take a turn at the wheel so that Shannon could prop her ailing ankle on the bench cushions. She watched her friend on the bow. The image of Kota's face in the bathroom mirror rose unbidden to her thoughts again. Shannon squinted more closely at her.

Wait a sec. Were her lips moving?

But so what if they moved? She'd probably found a radio station within range and was rapping along to a song. Shannon turned to gaze at the mountains on the coast, green trees rising steeply to bare gray rock, to towering, snowy white peaks. Unlikely she could get reception. Maybe Kota had brought a little CD player with her. Shannon pulled her braid around and fiddled with the tip.

As she continued to gaze Kota's way, the hairs on the back of her neck rose up. Shannon had no idea why.

Juneau swam alongside the boat just then, keeping up with no apparent strain. Her ceaseless laps around the inside perimeter of the sea pen were paying off. She imaged her greeting.

Shannon imaged, *Getting tired? I don't want to push you today. You're not used to long distances yet. And you have a guest on board sapping your energy.*

Juneau imaged herself falling behind to rest, then catching up.

Yeah, I know it feels good to stretch and swim full out, but you're not in shape to do much of that yet. Plus, it's dangerous for you to fall very far behind us with submarines and other navy boats lurking about. So. We'll stop early. Have you fed yet?

The whale had transitioned surprisingly quickly from the thawed herring and mackerel she'd eaten at the SeaQuarium to live fish she caught herself, first in the pen at the Dickson and now at sea.

Juneau sent her a negatory.

Go hunt, then. How about you, Salesti? Doing okay?

salesti good. juneau good company.

Juneau's white form disappeared beneath the waves.

Shannon kept a careful eye on the whale and checked in with her every few minutes for the first few hours of cruising, not wanting to lose track of her even for a moment. But no mishaps occurred, and all remained well. Shannon soon relaxed and checked in with the whale telepathically only every hour or so, learning each time that her plump friend and visitor Salesti were faring quite well.

Narci had also settled in well. No hacking up of hairballs on Luke's bunk, no peeing in Kota's duffel. She had staked out the galley countertop as her own special observation post when it was not in use, and if Luke or Kota objected, they didn't say.

* * *

The cruiser pulled into a small bay to anchor for the first night.

Luke stood on the port side trying his luck at hooking a flounder or halibut beneath the *Seatation*, promising Shannon the next turn at the one fishing pole they'd brought. Kota had carefully packed her hydrophonic gear for the night, having reported the presence of two small orca pods, a large pod of humpbacks, a fin whale, and a harbor porpoise. She sprawled on the dining room bench preparing to paint her toenails the same pink as her hair. Shannon joined her, wrapping herself in a blanket on her bed.

The two of them carried on a halfhearted conversation for a bit, but Shannon had exhausted her thin reserves of energy, and Kota acted strangely subdued, unlike her usual buoyant self.

After a time, Kota decided to start some dinner, with or without Luke's fish, and Shannon picked up her paperback, but she still lingered on the page she'd started an hour earlier. *Couldn't concentrate.*

"I'm kind of in the mood for tunes," Shannon said, remembering Kota's moving lips up on the bow earlier. "Did you bring a radio or do you have a good play list on your phone or anything?"

Kota flipped the hash browns frying on the stove. "No, sorry, sweet thing, but I didn't even bring my cell phone, what with the bad reception out here. Didn't even think about a CD player. My bad."

So, moving lips but no music. And she hadn't brought her cell phone? Who didn't bring their cell phones everywhere? A hundred to one, Kota had just lied to her face. Shannon should cast her colors. Circumstances justified it, right? Friendship be damned, right? Privacy be damned.

Oh hell. She couldn't do it, she—

Kota scooped up one of the meatless burgers she'd fried, popped it in a bun, dished on the hash browns, added an apple and some carrot sticks and made her way above deck to give the plate to Luke.

Shannon recalled Kota's rifling of her drawers at the infirmary. Maybe Shannon could snoop the same old-fashioned way. She slipped from her rear bunk and up to the fore bunk where Kota slept. Her duffel sat on top of her blankets, half zipped. Shannon quickly stuck her hand down the sides, feeling for something other than clothes, although she didn't know what.

Nothing on that side. Try the other.

Got to hurry.

Suddenly her hand thumped into a familiar object—Kota's cell phone; *the cell phone Kota had just claimed she hadn't brought.* Shannon felt suddenly cold.

Moving quickly, she pressed her hand along the front of the duffel. Soon her fingers grasped the handle of a—*seriously Kota?*

Shannon had found a gun. She drew her hand back as if it had been stung.

She heard Kota's voice getting louder, talking to Luke as she stepped back down into the cabin.

Shannon stood and hopped over to the galley.

"I was going to help myself. Okay with you?" she said.

* * *

After she ate, Shannon climbed back on deck.

"Where's tomorrow's dinner?" she asked Luke.

"Up in the pantry over the refrigerator," he said. "Not so much as a bite."

She sat down next to him. A heavy mist drifted above the calm water. The lights on the boat couldn't penetrate the mist more than a few meters in any direction. Nothing moved within the white swirls. She heard the lonely cry of a sea gull. The world had become a dark shell enclosing an empty white cloud.

Surreal.

Which seemed fitting. A couple days earlier, she'd been enjoying a near-perfect life. Working with Juneau every day or cruising with the research team, on the lookout for whales and dolphins. Relaxing with Kota or Todd or a group of her friends. Hiking in the high country. Visiting town.

And now? Her life, too, looked like a surreal, white cloud: filled with the unknown, the unseen.

Kota worried her; that gun worried her. Sure, things could happen out here that might require a gun. Luke carried one; Shannon had seen it more than once. But Kota had told her early in their friendship that she couldn't abide firearms. That sentiment fit so nicely with Kota's whole laid-back personality that Shannon had never questioned her words. She questioned them now. And why would Kota lie about her cell phone?

Shannon closed her eyes. She'd never been a worrier; she preferred to take things as they came. She breathed deeply, trying to simply let it all go.

Perhaps she'd encounter no trouble on this trip at all.

The white mist she was gazing at suddenly turned black. The sound of a motorboat buzzed in her ears; she heard the splash of an object hitting the water. In the next instant, she was swimming under water, awkwardly, in her dry suit, she was sure of it, although she still saw only blackness. She felt unbearable pain in her ankle, the awkward movement of her arm in its cast as she tried to gain forward momentum against the water. Suddenly the beautiful hues of her colors as she cast them pierced her dark vision—and then the darkness lifted as suddenly as it had descended.

Strange how many premonitions she was experiencing ever since the collapse of the UC. Maybe the knock on the head she'd taken from the swirling debris accounted for them.

In any event, no way should she be swimming underwater with a plaster cast.

Oh, there would be trouble on this trip; that was certain.

TROUBLED WATERS

CHAPTER FIFTEEN

THE FIRST OF THE TROUBLES ARRIVED IN THE FORM OF A NAVY SHIP bearing down on them that very next afternoon.

Shortly after one o'clock, Luke took the helm. Shannon sat nearby, holding a plate of sandwiches in her lap, munching on one, keeping track of their heading and progress more by honing in on Juneau than by reading the compass at the center of the steering box. She also kept her eye on the fish finder, in the event any cetaceans, dragonpanthers, or other interesting underwater species came close enough to register.

Kota had returned to the bow of the boat with her equipment, a pair of binoculars, a cup of coffee, and a large bag of Cheetos, and settled in to scan the horizon for signs of steam puffs or fins that would signal whales or dolphins, even as her hydrophone scanned below the surface of the sea for sounds of them. At least Shannon hoped that's what she was doing. No helpful premonitions had appeared on that score.

"Hey, you guys. Look over there to the southwest. A big ship just appeared, and it looks like it's heading straight for us," Kota called from her perch in front.

Odin's eye. The navy, probably, because of the loopy theory that terrorists had bombed the Underwater Complex.

Shannon and Luke had earlier studied the charts and decided the waters in an area that they'd reach later today would be cold enough for Juneau, but far enough from the research center for her safety. And now along came the navy to complicate things. But if the *Seatation* could slip past the ship, and if the ship would continue on its merry way to the wreckage of the Dickson, all should be well.

"Why isn't it changing course to bypass us?" Shannon asked, as Kota climbed down the short ladder from the side deck to land next to them.

"Maybe they want to uncover our secret ISIS cell. Locate our stash of explosives and machine guns. Hand-held missile launchers," Luke said.

"Or," Kota said, "Moon might have contacted them, to let them know they would encounter us on their way north."

"Either way, if they board, it's okay," Shannon said, "They might wonder about the amount of food we brought, but maybe they'll think we're just rank beginners at boating. Let them search her stem to stern. Whatever the stem is."

"Um, Shan, sweetheart? I don't think it's such a good idea for them to search the boat," Kota said.

Luke and Shannon turned to stare at her. She offered nothing more for a moment, but had the good grace to blush.

Under their unrelenting stares, she finally said, "drugs."

"What?" Shannon said.

"What?" Luke said. "Are you crazy?"

"Well, I haven't been vaping in the cabin, so I needed something to relax me," Kota said.

Bogus. Shannon sensed the lie. She began to speak, but Luke spoke first.

Looking murderous, he gritted his teeth and said, "I will keep the *Seatation* horizontal to the ship's approach. You go find your stash, all of it, and attach something to weight it down. The portal in the head—the bathroom—opens outward from the top. It's on the far side of the boat from the ship. Drop your stash overboard from there. Hurry!"

Kota scrambled down into the cabin. The look Luke threw at Dakota's disappearing back could have melted all the ice in Antarctica.

Had Shannon invited along a friend who would sink Luke into even deeper trouble with the law? If the feds busted him on a drug charge, he'd never get another law enforcement job. He'd never forgive her. She'd never forgive herself.

Shannon's vision darkened. *What, again?* The smell of an opened beer can filled her nose, followed by the sounds of a portal opening and the splash of a small object hitting the water. Shannon blinked. Her vision had returned.

Without hesitating to think about it, Shannon followed Kota down to the cabin. As Kota quickly prepared her drug bundle to throw overboard, Shannon grabbed a six-pack from their ice chest, plucked a beer out, opened it, and placed it on the counter. Then she said, "I'll go to the head to get the portal open for you." She hid the five pack behind her back as Kota glanced briefly up, nodded, and went back to wrapping her stash. Then Shannon turned, hurried into the head, opened the portal, and tossed out the five-pack.

A few seconds later, Kota appeared with her stash. Shannon inched out past Kota so she could maneuver into the small space.

"Sorry, Luke, I didn't know," Shannon said, back on deck, watching the advancing ship. Okay, she'd always suspected Kota kept a modest marijuana stash at her apartment. A lot of the staffers did. Isolated location, the need to decompress from a hard day. It happened. And they could legally purchase the weed right down in Washington. But why hadn't they smelled the distinctive odor of the weed in the little cabin?

Luke lifted his broad shoulders as he took in a big breath and let it out slowly, his shoulders subsiding in sync. "Why don't you go back and make sure she dumps every particle, and quickly. The boat will arrive in a few minutes."

* * *

Shannon watched through her binoculars with her friends, as a small, swift boat set out from the platinum-colored naval vessel looming in the near distance, like a dark bird darting from a solid rain cloud. A man and woman in crisp white uniforms and blue rain jackets studied the *Seatation* through their own binoculars, watching her watching them. Also on board, two divers in black dry suits and scuba gear sat with their backs to the water on the side of the speedboat. As they neared the *Seatation*, they flipped over backward into the water.

"Uh-oh," Kota murmured.

"Luke's been slowly moving forward, so we're not above the spot where you threw your stash overboard." Shannon said. "Stay calm."

Dakota grabbed her pink triangular hair wedge and yanked. "Sweeties. Don't kid yourselves. These guys know all the tricks in the book. Of drug runners *and* terrorists trying to get rid of evidence. We'll be here for a long time while they search the whole damn area. I wouldn't be surprised if they arrested us and netted Juneau once they find my stash."

Shannon shifted uneasily against the boat rail, her braid bouncing on her back. Her friend sounded quite knowledgeable about such searches. Yet Kota had told her she'd gone the strict academic route right through her post-doc research, and then hired on with the Dickson. *What kind of past had her friend hidden from her?*

As Shannon considered Kota's words, a flash of intuition struck Shannon with crystal clarity, as if Kota had opened her mouth and confessed. *Kota had set them up.* She'd set the drug trap to get them arrested. And Juneau netted.

Juneau! Listen to me. Did you watch the package fall from the boat a few minutes ago? Shannon carefully imaged the packet that Kota had thrown over.

Yes.

And the pack of beer? Shannon sent a clear image of the difference.

Yes.

Are the divers anywhere near the package?

No.

Can you grab it and run without them seeing you?

Yes.

Do it. Now. Not the beer, just the package. Drop it far, far away. And stay out there for now. Thank you, Juneau.

Salesti asked, *shannon, what goes on?*

I can't explain now. Just get far away from us where you'll be safe.

"You *did* just have marijuana, right?" Shannon asked Kota.

Kota shook her head briefly back and forth. "Um. Meth."

"What?" Luke and Shannon said in unison. Shannon wanted to say more, but Luke grabbed her arm quietly and nodded toward the approaching skiff. Its passengers might be able to hear them soon, even over the sound of the skiff's outboard motor.

The two naval officers boarded the *Seatation*, their words and demeanor as crisp as their uniforms. They both carried firearms. They all trundled down to the cabin, where Dakota, Shannon, and Luke provided their driver's licenses, water safety and navigation training certificates, and the *Seatation's* paperwork. Then the three of them sat, crowded together on one of the benches that served as seating for the dining table. Luke leaned back against the wall calmly, but Shannon spotted tiny beads of perspiration on his forehead. Kota fidgeted with her hands. Shannon fought an overwhelming urge to grab those hands and hold them still. Instead she opened her eyes wide and looked as innocent as she could.

The two officers remained standing over Shannon and her friends, the man with hands on his hips, the woman opening a notebook, pen poised.

"What are you three doing out here? You have quite a stock of rations."

Shannon spoke up. "We're from the Dickson Marine Mammal Research Center, Alaska Division, north of here, not too far from Yakatut. We're taking a beluga whale down to Ocean City in northern California. She's a research project at the Dickson, but when our Underwater Complex collapsed, we had to move her. You, uh, you may have heard about that."

"Yes. She's with this boat then?"

"She's gone off hunting. We might not spot her again until tomorrow." Shannon glanced casually at Luke. He knew a lie when he heard one.

He'd been looking at her as she spoke, and lifted both eyebrows in surprise, but as quickly as the surprise crossed his face, it vanished. Shannon smiled brightly and studied the two officers. Judging from their expressions, they hadn't spotted Luke's momentary surprise.

"She moved well out of range of her tracking device a while ago, so I can't even track her right now." Shannon added this bit of misinformation for the benefit of Kota, who merely continued to follow the conversation as if Shannon's baloney could actually be the case.

Light gleamed suddenly in the female officer's eyes. She looked up from her notebook. Shannon squinted—her name tag read "Ens. Shaw."

"I recognize you," Ensign Shaw said. "I thought I recognized your, uh. . . ."

Yeah, we don't need to hear what you recognized from Moon's X-rated video.

"Recognized your name. You're the one the dolphin recently rescued; you ended up floating on his back until a rescue crew came for you. Damnedest thing."

"Yes," Shannon said. "A whale. A beluga whale. Damnedest thing. Anyway, we stocked up so we could stay at sea long enough to make sure Juneau—that's her name—has plenty to eat before we get further south where the water warms up and her usual food sources become scarcer. We also want her strong for the final push because the waters to the south fall outside her territory, and we must get her to her Dickson pool by moving through the last leg as quickly as possible."

Too much, too much. Stop blathering.

Narci seized the moment to leap down from Shannon's berth where she'd been sleeping, patter over to the male officer, and rub along his crisp white slacks, leaving a stripe of black fur.

"Is that a cat? Why the bloody hell would you bring a cat on this little boat?" the officer said. He was, according to his name tag, Lt. Hughes.

"Yes. Yes, good eyes, she is a cat. Her name is Narci. She catches rats.

The lieutenant did not crack a smile.

Shannon tried again. "She's . . . uh, our good luck charm."

"You have a black cat for your good luck charm. Narci—is that short for Narcotics?"

"Hah," Shannon laughed, limply, falsely. "No, that would be Narco. Her name is short for Narcissus."

Lieutenant Hughes apparently decided the preliminaries had ended. He abruptly changed course.

"We spotted one of you throwing an object overboard. What did you toss, and why did you discard it?"

Kota started to speak. "Yeah, that—"

"Was me," Shannon said, talking over her friend. "Oops, busted," she laughed weakly. "I popped a beer out of a six-pack, and I'd just given the helm to Luke, and . . . and . . . and I accidentally dropped the whole rest of the pack into the drink when I went to set it down—it's this darn cast. So awkward." She held up her plastered arm helpfully.

Luke coughed suddenly into his hand. Kota, whose mouth had remained open when Shannon interrupted her, and whose mouth had stayed open while Shannon talked, snapped her lips together.

"A six-pack of beer," Hughes said.

"Right. One missing, of course, the one I pulled out."

Hughes frowned at her, shook his head slowly, his arms tightened further across his chest. He wasn't buying it. Shaw scribbled feverishly in her notebook. No one spoke.

"What did you do with the beer you pulled out? Overboard too, I presume?"

Witty. Almost as funny as Copper.

"No, no," she said and nodded toward the kitchen counter. "Right there."

The officer glanced at it for a few seconds, then said, "We have a guest on board who had his binoculars trained directly on the boat from the minute we spotted you. He says he saw a packet go over. Looked like drugs to him."

Kota and her buddies had *set a trap.* No one on the ship could have seen either *Kota* or *Shannon* drop anything from the port side of the boat.

"Yeah, he's wrong. And, Ensign Hughes—"

"That's Lieutenant, Ms. Kendricks."

"Oh sorry, yes, Lieutenant Hughes and Lieutenant Shaw, right."

Shaw did not look up from her notebook, but her mouth curved upward in a quiet smile.

"No. *Lieutenant* Hughes, *Ensign* Shaw."

"Right, right. Sorry. Anyway, I am trying to say, if you won't interrupt, that if you don't believe me, I think your men can find the beer pretty easily. Or I can find it, if they can't."

Dakota's mouth dropped open again. Luke, who'd turned to face Hughes again, turned once more toward Shannon. This time he mouthed the word "what?"

"What?" Hughes said.

"What?" Kota said.

"Shannon, I do not think—" Luke said.

"Yes, yes I can," Shannon said. She hoped. Salesti said she could. She'd better be able to find it, or this would end very badly. "Your divers can come along with me. I have a certain knack for locating items I watch drop in the water."

Pure drivel. Or not. *Salesti?*

yes, shannon casts colors.

Cast for an item in the water. *Loki be damned.*

Lieutenant Hughes looked slightly confused, but he leaned toward a microphone attached to his collar. "You boys find anything yet?"

Shannon could just hear the faint "negatory, Loot" in his earpiece.

He looked down at her. "What about your arm? You can't swim with a cast, can you?"

"I think I can pull my dry suit's sleeve over it."

"And that ankle cast?"

"Right, I'll lose it, naturally, since it will be soaked through. I'll have to cut it off when I get back. Small price to pay, forfeiting the cast, to show you that no drugs are involved here."

"Okay. If you think you can find the so-called five-pack, get your gear."

"Let's do it." Shannon said, as she rose from her seat and made for the stern to retrieve her scuba equipment.

"Lieutenant Hughes, perhaps you might return topside, and Ensign Shaw can remain here to make sure I don't stuff a five-pack into my dry suit."

CHAPTER SIXTEEN

AN HOUR LATER, A BRIGHT HEAD LAMP STRAPPED OVER HER SCUBA HOOD, weights in her belt to sink her to an appropriate depth, Shannon pushed backward off the stern ladder of the *Seatation*. Hitting the water played hell with her ribs, but she gritted her teeth and turned to face northwest. The two navy divers waited, treading water with flippered feet and chatting in low but cheerful voices.

Shannon figured the five-pack would float, but it would be easier for her to swim beneath the surface instead of trying to fight the waves. And just in case the pack didn't float, she'd see it anyway.

Was she nuts was she nuts was she nuts was she—
shannon casts the colors now, Salesti said.

Cast the colors. Well okay then. Shannon sank into the ocean depths. The bottom shallowed out in the area where Luke had positioned the boat. Although she found it awkward to swim one-handed, and with a flipper only on one foot, she proceeded about halfway between the surface and the rocky, kelp-covered floor of the sea, searching for the shape she fervently hoped to find, trying to ignore the pain in her ankle, her arm, her ribs.

She glanced back to orient herself to the *Seatation* and cast out through the water, with the idea of the five-pack fixed in her mind.

Casting in the water: a first. The haze spread out before her like the glow of high beam headlights on a rainy night, except that her glow shimmered, as if millions of tiny bits of silvery colors—purples, blues, greens, yellows, reds, iridescent black—sparkled in the light from an unknown source. Her head lamp interfered with her ability to follow the haze, though, so she reached up, fumbled along its rim, and shut it off.

A hand touched her side. One of the divers swam beside her, forming intricate hand signals. Shannon watched intently, but could not understand.

Forget that. She cast into his mind. Images of her with a broken light. Of the diver staying close to her so she could use his light.

Uh—no. Shannon shook her head back and forth, pointed to herself and formed her gloved fingers into the universal "okay" sign, and motioned him away from her.

He complied by maneuvering several feet to her left. The other diver swam a few feet to her right. A tad close for comfort, but given their high level of suspicion about this little road show, likely all she would get.

She faced forward again and her eyes adjusted. Yes, this would do. The haze shone in a clear cone, widening more and more the farther she cast.

This would be the first time she'd cast the colors under water; the first time she'd been busted for smuggling drugs. What a red letter day.

Shannon focused. She shut out all sense of the dark sea around her. The navy divers blinked out. The noise of her breathing through the scuba apparatus disappeared. In her empty, silent world, only the haze of colors existed.

As easily as she could step forward, as easily as she could take a deeper breath, she sent the haze out and out, wider and wider.

And then she spotted it, bobbing along in the waves, still almost a quarter mile away: a set of five beer cans bound within a web of plastic rings. One can missing. And no sign of Kota's drug packet.

Shannon rose to the surface, pretended to get her bearings, adjusted her course, and headed toward the modest prize like a child to its mother.

* * *

"Check it for a homing device," said the short, burly diver who'd boarded the *Seatation* with Shannon while the other diver clambered aboard the skiff.

He gestured toward Shannon as she slid off her scuba tank. "She zeroed in on this—" he raised the beer cans by the empty plastic ring hanging from his index finger, "—like she had a rope tied to it."

That burned. In a flash of anger Shannon stepped into the diver's face. Shoving her right ear against his nose, she said, "You see any receiving device in there? No?"

She turned abruptly, to show him her left ear. "Nada, am I right? How about this ear? How about in the hood? The gloves? The flipper? The weight belt? Anywhere on the scuba equipment? You want me to strip right here so you can make sure no device falls out when I take off the suit?" She grabbed the zipper resting under her chin and pulled down about six inches.

Just as Luke raised his hand as if to zip her right back up, Lieutenant Hughes lifted both his hands to stop her from any further unzipping. "Ensign Shaw will attend to that, Ms. Kendricks."

The ensign stood in the stairwell to the cabin. She motioned to Shannon. As Shannon passed Hughes, with the scuba diver well behind her, she winked at Luke.

His face remained a stone, an Easter Island statue.

Shannon turned as she reached Ensign Shaw and said to the assembled group, "I told you I had a knack for finding stuff I watch drop in the water. It's almost like, I don't know, a psychic gift. I haven't had much use for it, though. Sure came in handy today." She smiled the smile of prisoner who had just learned her DNA didn't match the murder weapon, and descended to the cabin.

As she shed her suit for the ensign's inspection, the shivers assaulted her.

So close to losing everything. The chance to help Roebor, to find Essi, to get the Dickson up and running. They could've gone to prison. For years. Decades even. And who knew what could've happened to Juneau, with Kota's weird talk of the navy netting her.

"You okay, Ms. Kendricks?" Shaw said as she searched inch by inch along the inner surfaces of the dry suit. "You look cold. Why don't you turn that heater on?"

"Yeah, think I will," Shannon said, setting the heater in motion, as she toweled off.

Her ankle cast had turned into a spongy mess. With Ensign Shaw's help, she found a sharp pair of scissors and cut it off. She examined her arm cast. Unfortunately, the pressure applied by the sleeve of the dry suit had collapsed the plaster around the top edge and all along her forearm. But, as it seemed dry enough, she left it alone.

"My apologies, ma'am," Shaw said. Shannon winced at that moniker. "I am required to perform a body search." Shannon winced again.

She squeezed her eyes tight closed; pain, fatigue, frustration, anger, the residual shakes from her earlier fear, embarrassment, all vying for top emotion.

The ensign worked efficiently and gently, though, and the inspection ended quickly.

"That's it. Go ahead and get dressed, Ms. Kendricks."

"It's Shannon. You have a first name?" Shannon quickly donned her black sweat pants, a short-sleeved lavender cotton turtle neck, and a large, warm, wool cardigan in various shades of violet.

"Alice," Ensign Shaw said, "but, sorry, unless we meet in San Fransisco for R&R, it's Ensign Shaw to you."

"Right. Ensign Alice Shaw. Got it," Shannon said, toweling her hair from scalp to waist. She'd have to ask Kota if she would braid it later.

When Ensign Alice Shaw had completed her notes on the search, and Shannon's shivers had subsided, Shannon grabbed a piece of angel food cake, and they climbed back to the deck where a second skiff now floated alongside. Only Lieutenant Hughes remained on the *Seatation*. At the all clear from Ensign Shaw, Lieutenant Hughes shook hands all around, and dispensed a parting lecture to Shannon about the dangers of drinking and piloting.

* * *

As Shannon stood with Luke and Kota watching the skiff head out, Luke turned to her.

"What were you thinking, offering to undress on the deck?" Luke asked Shannon.

"How did you know you would find a six-pack of beer floating around, cupcake?" Kota asked Shannon.

"I didn't think you'd mind me unzipping, after not calling, not visiting, not choosing me over Lithuania," Shannon said to Luke, and then wondered where these words had even come from. She felt sick; the search had wrung her out. "Anyway, I knew the lieutenant wouldn't go for it."

"And as for you, missy," Shannon said to Kota, "do you promise on your mother's grave that you will not bring any more drugs on board this boat?"

"My mother isn't dead, Shanny," Kota said.

"Oh. Then . . . then, break your promise and I'll put her in her grave," Shannon said, shaking her fist in a mock threat.

Luke said to Shannon, "You never heard of the sexual harassment scandals in the navy? Those men are notorious.

They loved seeing you unzip. And I didn't think you wanted me up in Alaska. You didn't call before I didn't call." He turned on Kota.

"And don't you ever again make me an accomplice to your illegal drug activities," Luke said. "Ever. Or I will keelhaul you off the back of this boat for shark bait."

"I told Lieutenant Hughes the truth about having a sixth sense for that kind of thing," Shannon told Kota, returning to Kota's earlier question. "More or less the truth. Kind of that."

"I'm sorry Luke. I didn't think we'd be stopped by the feds out here," Kota said. "I promise, never again."

"I didn't call because you deserved better," Shannon said to Luke. *Meaning someone without psychic talents, who didn't attract aliens.*

"I actually wouldn't mind that much if you offed my mother, Shanster. She out-witches the official Wicked Witch of the West. But I swear anyway, I've put the drugs behind me," Kota said. "And you never mentioned any sixth sense for finding things on the ocean floor before. But it's baloney anyway because I dropped a packet of drugs and you led them to a six-pack, which you described in detail and which hadn't even been in the salt water very long so what kind of sixth sense do you have? You possess a nose for abandoned Bud?" Kota asked.

"All right, I accept your apology. If you swear it will never happen again," Luke said to Kota.

"Right," Shannon said, echoing Luke's words while she squinted at Kota.

"Don't go all Clint Eastwood on me, Ms. Kendricks. You've got secrets a lot bigger than my little packet of meth. Like Luke here. You two used to be an *item* back in the Lower forty-eight? And now he shows up here the day the UC breaks like a tinker toy and you float off on the back of a whale? WTF?"

"No, I don't have a nose for sniffing out beer. I don't even like beer," Shannon said to Kota.

"Why not just tell her? You pretty much gave up the game with your six-pack trick," Luke said.

"Tell me what?" Kota asked.

"That's what I asked Luke, Kota, when he showed up, WTF? But I guess it was pretty much a coincidence," Shannon said.

Luke said, "And what do you mean, 'I deserved better?' Did I deserve for you to toss me out like an unmatched sock? You call that better?" Luke said.

"An unmatched. . .?" Shannon said.

"Okay, forget it. Don't tell me anything. You two dredge up all your old laundry and I'll just go up front and work on my log," Kota said.

She didn't move, however.

She expects me to tell her everything. Shannon opened her mouth. Then the image of Kota in the bathroom mirror flashed. The image of Kota throwing a packet of meth— *meth for Odinssake*—overboard in the shadow of a naval vessel. The words of Lieutenant Hughes . . . *We have a guest on board who had his binoculars trained directly on the boat from the minute we spotted you. He says he saw a packet go over. Looked like drugs to him* . . .The look of astonishment on Kota's face when the packet that the *guest on the ship* had spotted turned out to be a five-pack Shannon had dropped. Shannon closed her mouth.

Kota had set them up. If the packet had been found, they'd have been arrested. But why would she do that? Unless Kota and the "guest" on the ship wanted her and Luke out of the way.

And the most likely reason? Juneau.

CHAPTER SEVENTEEN

KOTA WOULD CONTINUE TO PRY unless Shannon gave her something. She placed her hand quietly on Luke's arm and said, "Here's what happened, Kota. When you went to wrap up your drug packet, I had the sudden urge to add some insurance, so I threw over the five-pack and kept my eye on the general vicinity where it went in. Given enough time, I was pretty sure I could come up with it because I knew the heading Luke had taken when he eased forward. But I can't tell you why they missed your drug packet. Maybe it drifted further west, and the divers just quit when my story panned out. Lucky we found the five-pack first, right?"

"Wow. Okay then. Fast thinking," Kota said.

"Are we finished?" Luke said. He snatched up Shannon's scuba gear and stomped down the steps to the cabin.

"Hey, somebody has to pilot the boat," Shannon called after him. "I have an ankle here that's broken and hurting like hell."

Luke's head popped up from the cabin. "Let me wrap your foot. Then I'm putting on a pair of headphones and listening to nueva canción tapes. Dakota can pilot."

"Nueva canción?" Shannon murmured.

"Yeah, it's like Peter, Paul and Mary meet Segovia," Kota mumbled back.

Thor could've struck Shannon with his hammer at the way Kota tossed that out, like, *hell, everybody knows that.* Shannon breathed in a lungful of air. If a person lifted that pink top knot on Kota's head and peeped underneath, they'd find a lot more than the loose screws Kota pretended to keep in there.

"But somebody has to steer. . . ." Shannon said to the spot Luke had vacated.

"That's okay," Kota said, taking the helm. "I'll drive, sweet potato."

Kota had forgotten her earlier insistence that she possessed no boating skills.

Things had certainly gone to hell in a hand basket. Shannon slid down the steps to the cabin on her keister, since the mere idea of hopping down to the cabin made her ankle and ribs cry out in protest. There Luke wrapped her ankle with an ace bandage as tightly as he could manage, and applied a fresh bandage to the stitched up gash on her forehead.

* * *

Juneau had returned, safe and sound. She trailed the boat as Shannon followed the chart, searching for the inlet where they planned to leave the whale while they headed south.

Luke appeared with two dinner plates of enchiladas, beans and Rice-a-Roni, apples grilled with oil and cinnamon, and a package of coconut-chocolate cookies. He smacked them down on cushioned seating beside Shannon and stalked back down to the cabin without a word, as Shannon's "thanks" died on her lips.

She eyed the plate. *Just in time.* Shannon's underwater adventure had caught up with her overactive metabolism. Misery wrapped her like a rope. The sway of the boat bounced her stomach up and down. The wind battered her ears until she could no longer concentrate on any other sound. Her head throbbed, and a high pitched buzz filled the background of her thoughts. She couldn't actually swear her neck still connected her head to her body. She grabbed a handful of cookies from the bag and stuffed them one by one into her mouth.

"Hey," said Kota, "I love Mexican. No fair that you got twice as much as me, Shan-Shan." *Kota was trying to wriggle back into her good graces.*

"You know my metabolism," Shannon said, a flatness in her voice that she hadn't meant to reveal.

"You're still mad about the drugs, Shanny? I'll make it up to you. I promise."

Shannon ate in silence. She swiftly cleaned every morsel off her plate, gobbled down all but two of the cookies, and assumed the helm so that Kota could eat.

After she'd eaten, Kota stood suddenly. "I think you and Luke have some unfinished business. I'll send him up."

"No wait—" But before Shannon could stop her, Kota gathered up their dinner dishes and slipped out of sight. Shannon studied the chart again and looked up.

There. The inlet they'd picked. Where Shannon would break with Juneau for the first time since she'd laid eyes on the beluga fifteen years earlier. Perhaps permanently. At the thought, a heaviness gripped her as if it would pull her down straight through the bottom of the boat.

Luke climbed on deck.

"I'm not feeling well, so I'm pulling into that inlet for the night." Shannon gave Luke a silent stare. He pulled the chart toward him and quickly recognized their location. He nodded.

"I required time in Ocean City alone, cara," he said quietly as the *Seatation* slowly puttered nearer to shore. "Time to process the aliens. The deaths. You. Everything we went through. Even after all this time, I'm not sure I've recovered or come to grips with it all. I still can't adjust to the unreal happenings that always seem to surround you."

Shannon wanted to continue this conversation, but she feared Kota would eavesdrop. She whispered back, "I'm afraid Kota will hear us. Let's talk later."

He nodded.

Shannon located a protected spot for the boat to anchor, and the two of them went about securing the boat for the night.

* * *

Dusk had come and gone, smothered by the dark of a starless night. Shannon checked her watch; almost ten o'clock already. She felt several cool raindrops and studied the sky. Looked like they might be in for some serious rain. But the raindrops petered out, so Shannon made herself comfortable on the deck bench to enjoy the gentle rocking of the boat, the lapping waves, the cool breeze.

Too tired to stay alert, too wound up to sleep. Hell of a thing.

Luke wandered below and took his paperback out of his pack, stretching out on his berth. Kota reappeared on deck for a while, and Shannon tried to make small talk with little success. Finally, she said, "I'm sorry Kota. I'm terrible company right now. You heard how things blew up with Luke this afternoon. Maybe after I clear up our relationship, I can deal with everything else."

Kota nodded, unfolded from the bench, stretched, and ambled off. "I'm going to work on the harbor porpoise sounds I recorded today, then."

As if nothing had happened at all.

Shannon stood, balanced on one leg, and stretched. *Odin's eye.* No way could she deal with relationship issues right now. Kota or Luke. They had a lethal virus to stop. Essi to find and send home. A research facility to help rebuild. And her energy had gone AWOL.

Shannon didn't turn as she heard Luke arrive at her back. A large cinnamon roll on a napkin slid into view on the work surface by the helm where she stood gazing aimlessly at the shoreline. Followed by a refill for her large mug of Diet Dr. Pepper.

"Thanks." Shannon didn't speak again. She opened her mouth three different times, but the brain supplied no words to issue out of it. Luke picked up the slack.

"Have you read Kota? Her feelings, her images?" Luke asked.

"No." Shannon said, mustering all the indignation she could. "I don't cast into the minds of anybody, if I can help it. Hardly anybody. But especially not you, not her. No, I won't do that."

"You should."

"No."

"Why do you trust her? How'd you meet her?"

"I don't trust her, but I met her at the Ocean City Dickson Center on the university campus. She was already working there when I came to visit Juneau after the lightning hit her."

Luke nodded. "Just after I met you."

"Yes. Here is the thing: She picked me up off the bottom of the pool when I sent Juneau back to her body. With Juneau lost to my mind, and me so very tired, Luke, that night in the pool I didn't care if I ever took another breath of air. So I almost didn't bother. Kota pulled me up off the bottom of the pool. She saved my life."

"You never told me. I thought you collapsed in the pool from the fatigue, from the toll taken by carrying Essi and Juneau, and the others in your head. Fighting the aliens and Old Salty. All of those things."

"Yes, all that took its toll. I didn't have any fight left. And when Juneau left my head . . . I'd grown so used to having her with me. I didn't want to tell you that I nearly called it quits. It didn't . . . I don't know, it didn't seem right to dump that on you."

"You could have told me anything, cara," Luke said in a soft, low voice.

"Right. But there it is. Kota pulled me up when I would've drowned. So I owe her."

Shannon felt a few more raindrops and wondered if more would fall this time.

A quiet sigh, so soft Shannon caught it only because she strained to hear his next words.

"I wish you had told me how . . . hard you took losing Juneau's spirit."

Shannon gazed out to where she figured the sky met the sea. No way to find that exact line in the dark; the inkiness had advanced rapidly once the sun set. Tears formed at the edge of her vision. "I'm not so great at sharing. And we didn't have much of an opportunity."

"Because I didn't visit you in the hospital when it was all over," Luke said.

"No, you didn't." Just like Luke, to zero in on the heart of the matter.

Silence wrapped itself around the boat. No sounds floated up the steps from the cabin. Neither Shannon nor Luke spoke. The steady lapping of waves against the bow only served to emphasize the quiet.

Bitter memories flooded Shannon. Until today she hadn't acknowledged the depth of the hurt caused by Luke's failure to reach out to her during her weeks in the hospital. But she was honest enough to form the rebuttal: *What could he have done, even if he'd come?*

Most of that time she'd remained deep in a state of unconsciousness, half sleep, half delirium, as her body stabilized calorie by calorie, as her organs responded one by one, as her mind moved farther from the horror of those last days before she and her friends defeated the aliens.

Still, she'd needed him.

Pitiful, that. Shannon hadn't needed anyone for most of her life. Not anyone.

She'd left him behind in Ocean City, telling herself they'd simply arrived at the end of their allotted time. Telling herself it would work out better for Luke that way.

An unpleasant insight hit her like a blast of stale air from a dysfunctional air conditioner. *She was afraid that if she loved Luke, she would lose her hard-won independence. And she took such pride in her independence. So proud she didn't want love to interfere.*

But she wanted to love him now. Nothing like a dip in the Alaskan Sea to clear the mind. If she hadn't left it too late.

Luke said after a long silence between them, "I'm here now. I will be here. Aliens or no aliens. Are you good with that?"

He had pledged to stay with her. She squeezed her eyes tightly closed. Thank Odin.

"I'm good." *But also furiously worried.*

"I'm good," she repeated.

"So why—" Luke began.

"So what if—" Shannon began.

shannon. listen.

"Wait—one second, Luke, Salesti's trying to reach me. It sounds stressed."

Shannon cocked her head in concentration. No sound broke the stillness beyond the slapping rhythm of the sea and the occasional patter of raindrops.

I don't hear anything. Talk to me, Salesti.

cast to hear sounds in water.

So she could do that. Another talent Salesti had mentioned, but Shannon hadn't tested. What a fascinating voyage of discovery this mission had become.

At any rate, she'd give it a try now.

She cast the colors. At first she only managed to *look* below the surface of the sea, the haze, a diaphanous swirl of color, once again acting as a floodlight, illuminating the dark reaches in front of the boat. She caught the occasional flash of a fish, little more.

listen, Salesti whispered to her.

Shannon imagined herself under the water, swimming with the light. She held her breath, as if even the sound of her own inhaling and exhaling might interfere with whatever Salesti urged her to hear.

Gradually she distinguished a rapid, repeated *whap, whap,* like the bent wing of a seagull against air, the long fin of a humpback whale against water. She peered ahead. Nothing.

The dragonpanther, salesti?

yes. beyond your eye but not your ear.

An occasional grunt punctuated the stroke of the dragonpanther's wings heading south toward them. A familiar infrequent ping overlaid the swimming sounds.

"Sounds like something's chasing Roebor, Salesti. What—"

A submarine. That's where she'd heard that ping before, in every submarine movie ever made. The telltale ping of a sub's sonar search.

"*Holy Odin*, Roebor's being chased by a sub," Shannon said, bursting the silence on the boat's deck.

CHAPTER EIGHTEEN

SHANNON GLANCED TOWARD THE CABIN. She'd blurted out the dragonpanther's plight too loudly. With any luck, Kota's headphones still adhered firmly to her ears as she continued her supposed porpoise study, blocking Shannon's outburst.

Luke stepped toward her. "Didn't you say he could fly? Why doesn't he fly out of the water?" he asked in a much quieter voice.

As if in rebuttal to any hope of Roebor taking to the air, the burr of a twin-engine plane sounded in the distance.

Shannon searched the sea for the sub with her silvery, multicolored floodlight and then cast her colors at the plane. She couldn't yet spot the dragonpanther, but the plane was heading north, straight at them. A sub *and* a plane. This could go very wrong.

Salesti, Roebor doesn't have many choices.

Her mind working rapidly—*thank Odin* for the mug of Diet Dr. Pepper chock full of caffeine. She continued, "He could surface and fly as high and as fast as he can away from that plane to land and hide."

"The plane may have floodlights," Luke said, touching Shannon's shoulder.

roebor weakens. no high flight.

At that moment, the dragonpanther appeared at the edge of Shannon's hazy spotlight underwater. *Weakens?* He was speeding straight for their boat like a bullet shot from a rifle.

"What's he doing?" Luke asked, as the noise of the plane increased. The twin propeller swooped in low toward the boat. Its floodlight bathed them in momentary, blinding white-gold, and then swept the quiet water in front of them as it continued its course north toward the dragonpanther and the sub.

The sub, which popped into the range of Shannon's underwater haze, was moving rapidly, not far behind the dragonpanther. Not far at all.

"He's swimming deep, coming our way," she told Luke. "Still ahead of the sub."

Shannon reached for Roebor with images.

"Roebor," Shannon quietly said aloud for Luke's benefit and simultaneously imaged, "I hope you can understand me, and if you do, push as hard as you can. You need to create some distance from the sub. Then shoot out of the water, fly low, straight for land. The plane has passed over you and hasn't turned yet. They shouldn't spot you against the dark water."

Luke said, "See that outcropping of rock just north of us? If he can stay out of the water until he reaches that, then sink back under, he may blend into the rock face."

Shannon passed along the new information. She concentrated on the view her haze gave her.

"He's doing it. He's doing it!" She said, grabbing Luke by his bicep—and taking just a fraction of a second to admire that hard muscle—"Increasing the distance from the sub. Tell me when the plane turns to make another pass."

Come on, you can do it.

"The plane has moved well up the coast. It will turn any minute," Luke said.

The extra distance Roebor had gained would have to do.

Now, Roebor, pull up out of the water now. Hurry!

As if Shannon's words pulled him by a rope, the dragon-panther's forward movement ceased in an instant and he shot at a right angle straight toward the surface of the sea.

"Wow, he's—"

Before Shannon could spit out the words, Roebor burst from the water and leveled out so quickly Shannon would have sworn he'd hit a solid ceiling at fifty feet.

"There he is," Luke said quietly. "My god, just look at him."

Luke, one hand on the port rail, touched Shannon's back with the other as she stood beside him. In a voice so low that Shannon heard him only because all her senses had heightened under a jolt of adrenaline, he said, "Better cook up a story for Kota."

"Let's pretend we see something else. Jump on the radio, try to contact the sub. Ask them if that—she held up her fingers in air quotes—'flying sub' belonged to us or the enemy." She grinned. "Or could it be a UFO?"

Luke's eyes sparked. He moved immediately to the comm device and began yelling like any unsuspecting boater who happened to witness a bizarre chase involving an unidentified flying object. But the sub didn't answer; the plane's pilot did. Shannon listened, admiring Luke's fabricated awe at that amazing sub that could fly. A tiny laugh escaped her. He lied almost as well as she did when circumstances were dire.

Wait. Her grin disappeared. *Not a good thing. Not good at all.*

Shannon caught a slight twinkling of silver-blue off to their right. *Uh-oh.* Roebor's beautiful coat shimmered in the moonlight. She'd didn't realize his metallic fur would look so florescent at night. Forget worrying about the floodlight. The men on the plane would spot him in the dark in a half second if they came close enough.

"Kota," she called down into the cabin. "Get the flare kit. Hurry."

"What? Why?" Kota asked, popping her head above the steps, her earphones around her neck.

"Please. I'll explain in a second," Shannon said.

As Kota headed back below, Luke said, "You see him?"

Shannon nodded.

"You neglected to mention he glitters in the dark," Luke said. "We'd better send one flare right away, then point the rest closer to the plane when it passes. Get them to veer off. We'll put the flares up between that creature's location and the plane until it flies farther away."

"Roebor," Shannon murmured. "He's a dragonpanther."

Kota hollered up from below. "I can't find them. What do you want them for?"

As Shannon started to speak, Luke broke in and told Kota, "A sub has entered the area as well as a search plane. We want them to know our location and that we're friendlies. I don't want anyone torpedoing us as terrorists. Do you?"

shannon. roebor tires. help roebor.

"Roebor needs help. I don't think he can make it to land," Shannon whispered to Luke as Kota searched frantically for the flares. She peered up at the approaching plane. "You have any idea how much longer the plane can stay in the air?" she asked Luke.

"Too long, if it—Roebor," he said, avoiding Shannon's gathering frown, "If Roebor has already run out of gas. I don't know where their flight originated, but I'm guessing Juneau. An Alaskan puddle jumper like that is designed for flights in and out of the hard-to-reach villages and resorts up here. He'll stay airborne for a while before he returns home."

"You're sure?"

Luke shrugged. "I have my pilot's license. I'm checked out in those." He nodded toward the seaplane, just as it blinded them again in brilliant light on its pass over the boat, still too far west to spot the dragonpanther.

"You have your . . . ?" Did she know nothing about this man?

Kota raced onto the deck. Luke grabbed the flare gun with a quick thanks and before Shannon could even react, he'd aimed one directly overhead and let it rip. Two more flares arced into the sky in quick succession, each designed to put a burst of light between the dragonpanther and the plane. At the same time, he resumed his conversation with the pilot, feigning fear that the sub would mistake the boat for whatever they were chasing. He nodded, listening patiently to the pilot's curses for endangering his night vision, and proceeded to apologize profusely. The seaplane moved on above the *Seatation*, veering slightly out to sea because of the flares, heading on south, giving no indication it had spotted Roebor.

Now that Kota had joined them, Shannon continued her images silently.

Roebor, if you can't make shore, fly to us now. We can only hope the sub thinks you're part of the boat.

dakota must not know, Salesti said. *dakota talks with human on underwater ship.*

Salesti's words slid into Shannon like a long, sharp blade. Her mind raced over the recent moments. Kota down below—doing what? Communicating with the sub?

"Shannon? What's happening? Talk to me," Kota said.

Shannon suddenly yanked Kota closer and shouted, "Look, look, out to the southwest, a huge . . . huge what? Floating on the water. Do you see it? Do you see it? Of course you see it, you're the best spotter at the Dickson. Quick Luke, tell the pilot, a big object, I don't know what, south by southwest. You see it too?"

Luke, ever the quick study, calmly replied, "I see it. It could be a boat, but it wasn't there a minute ago." He grabbed his binoculars. "Kota, get on the radio and tell the pilot where to look."

Okay, Roebor. You must land with perfect timing. When I tell you to drop to the water as close to us as you can, you drop. She watched as Roebor approached, his body looming larger and larger.

But drop carefully.

"Luke, we need to get even further out of the way of this search, whatever it is," Shannon said for Kota's benefit. "How close can you get to the shore? Maybe by those rocks?" She pointed at the outcropping Luke had spotted earlier.

By the light on his captain's table, he checked the chart depths. "I can pull right in next to them. Well out of the way of the search. Kota, can you make out the identity of that thing yet? And tell them we're getting out of the way, over by those rocks."

Kota paused in her conversation with the seaplane to say, "Too dark. Can't tell. But the plane will get a spotlight on it. They haven't identified it either."

At that moment, Narci chose to make her first appearance of the trip on the deck. She jumped up on the bench about a foot and a half from Kota.

Shannon aimed her haze at the sub again. It had shifted slightly to a heading more in line with the nonexistent object Shannon had fabricated, but its sonar wouldn't be fooled for long.

Luke raised the *Seatation's* two anchors and eased toward the shore. Fortunately, they'd nestled in to anchor for the night not far from their new destination.

Kota peered through her binoculars, still trying to spot what she never would.

Narci inched closer to Kota.

Roebor approached the boat from the direction of Kota's back.

Odin's eye! Up close and personal, Roebor looked like a Boeing 727.

The rain began to pick up. With a crack of thunder, the skies opened, and it began to pour. In a matter of minutes the storm had soaked them through.

Shannon grabbed Kota's arm once again and pointed at nothing. "It's flying now! Are you watching? What the heck could do that?" She gave Kota an excited shake for good measure, raindrops flying off her at every angle.

Lightning flashed not far the south of them, lighting up the night sky.

And now. Sink, Roebor. Right by the boat.

Shannon stumbled and fell into Kota, knocking the two of them against the rail just as Roebor's weight in the water rocked the *Seatation* hard. "Sorry. A gust of wind rocked the boat and caught me off guard," she said, raising her voice to be heard above the thundering rain. Kota stood and turned to complain, but just then Narci leaped up onto Kota's jacket front, and began to climb onto her shoulder to reach her head.

"Gah, get off, cat," Kota said, wiping rain out of her face and pushing Narci away—and over the side into the water, just as Shannon fell into Kota again, this time accidentally as she rushed to relieve Kota of the cat. The two actions together—Narci jumping Kota and Shannon bumping her— sent Kota over the side into the sea right behind the cat.

Shannon shrieked, and then shouted, "Luke, where's the fish net, Narci's in the water."

CHAPTER NINETEEN

KOTA SCREAMED, "NEVER MIND THE CAT, *I'M* IN THE WATER!"

Luke cut the engine, abandoned the wheel, and jumped to the starboard side deck to retrieve the net.

"Swim around to the ladder, Kota," Shannon said, throwing her a safety ring. Shannon's feet slipped on the wet surface of the deck as she limp-hopped as quickly as she could along the port-side deck searching for a glimpse of the cat, her ankle screaming its objections.

As Luke returned with the net, a very wet and angry Kota pulled herself up the ladder onto the deck. She stormed below to towel off and change into warm, dry clothes and her rain gear.

Shannon crisscrossed the water with her flashlight beam in a desperate search for Narci. Ten minutes passed. Twenty. Suddenly she cried out as she spotted the bedraggled black form in the downpour, paddling like a piston pump about ten feet from the boat.

Shannon said, "I'll net her."

Kota had just reappeared, her short hair already dry under her rain coat's hood.

"No, let me do it. I've got two good arms," she said. "Ugh, my ribs. I'll have a bruise right on the tattoo of my—"

"Hey," Shannon interrupted, having already had a close look at Kota's startling tats. "Yes, good, a little closer, Luke, very slowly; can you reach her, Kota?"

Kota dipped the large net into the lively black waters and came up with a sopping, sorry-looking bundle. Once they'd brought the cat back on board, Luke proceeded toward the rock outcropping, Roebor tucked close to their starboard side.

"Good job. You got her!" Shannon pulled the cat out of the net and took her below to warm her up.

As Shannon dried Narci in a thick purple towel, she silently asked the cat, *did you do that on purpose?*

The cat did not reply, but stepped away from the towel and licked her paw delicately. Shannon would have sworn she spotted a small smile playing around Narci's lips.

Shannon left the cat with a bowl of cat food warming by the heat vent and rejoined Luke and Kota above deck. She'd stripped out of her wet clothes and into her flannel black-and-blue plaid pajamas, and wore her rain pants and coat. "Go get dried off, Luke. I'll tell them I'm going to bring Juneau in close to the boat to help them keep her separate from the thing they're chasing," Shannon said. Juneau, in fact, still swam well north of them.

Kota had resumed her conversation with the seaplane, which had arrived back in the general vicinity of the nonexistent object. As they watched, it made one pass from south to north, well west of them, and then dipped its wings, flew northeast and kept going, no longer willing to fly in the storm.

Juneau, stay out at sea for now. You okay?

salesti and juneau okay, Salesti said.

If the sub saw more than just the Seatation's blip, fingers crossed, they'd think the whale accounted for the extra. Although the dragonpanther dwarfed the beluga.

As they approached the outcropping of rock, Shannon could tell that some of the boulders loomed as large as the boat. That would help disguise Roebor's shape.

"Did they find that thing?" Shannon shouted to Kota over the pelting rain.

"Don't think so. It must have flown away and they missed it." Kota lowered her binoculars. "Maybe terrorists did blow up the UC. The pilot said the sub had picked up another big and super fast sub out at sea, south of the Dickson and heading away. And if it could also fly? That's pretty advanced technology. Who could afford that around here, except some well-financed terrorist living off oil money?"

"Yeah who?" Shannon said. "Hey, I don't know about you, but that whole thing gave me the shakes. Want a beer?"

"Hell, yes," Kota said and started down to the cabin. Shannon casually moved between Kota and the starboard side where the dragonpanther floated, mostly submerged, with his head and back still visible above the water.

"Luke, you want one?" Shannon called out as she stepped down below deck behind Kota as she began to close the hatch again to keep out the rain and block Kota's view.

"Hell, yes," Luke said as the hatch tightened down.

* * *

Later Shannon returned to the deck to check for the plane and sub, and reported to the other two that the seaplane hadn't returned. The sub had headed west and later north.

Thank Odin. She let out a long, slow breath.

As the tension in Luke's shoulders and face relaxed as well, she nodded. *They'd come very close to dragonpanther disaster.*

After Luke had changed, he and Shannon went back up to the deck long enough to check the *Seatation's* two anchors, winching them tight to keep the boat clear of the rocks, and hoisted the buoys over the sides to protect the boat in case they drifted close enough for scrapes. And stole one more glance at the behemoth accompanying them.

* * *

Two hours later, the rain stopped. Shannon went back on deck to check on the dragonpanther. She peered at Roebor's dark form in the water.

A close call.

She let Roebor know the sub had moved off. He promptly sank to the rocky bottom. Exhaustion radiated from him like heat. *Poor guy.* Alone on an alien world, chased by bad guys, desperate for the antidote for his people. And Shannon thought she had it bad.

I wish no pity from a puny earththing. Leave me alone.

Shannon jerked her head toward the shape floating below. The dragonpanther had heard her thoughts. And answered them. *Grand.*

Puny earththing? *You understand my thoughts in English, not images and emotions?*

I have learned your language, just as Salesti has, although its English still sounds rudimentary. I sometimes think Salesti speaks in such broken English on purpose, to hide its true intellect. Essi, though, still requires your images and emotions; she doesn't speak English well.

You said you don't wish my pity, Roebor. I don't pity you. Believe me, to a puny earththing, it doesn't appear that a giant like you needs pity. I admire you for coming after the virus you need for the antidote. But I do empathize with your situation.

Did Shannon hear a soft, grudging acknowledgement?

And really? A puny earththing? Did we not just help you out of a jam?

Roebor grumbled low in his chest. Shannon watched the water vibrate in concentric circles.

I did not need help. I am Roebor, first of the Island of Swords, greatest warrior of the Sea of Storms Conflict, preeminent among the scientists of my time. And anyway, compared to me, are you not puny?

Well we all need help sometimes. Shannon laughed softly to herself, knowing only to well that five years earlier it was she who needed to hear that pearl of wisdom. *And I am not puny.*

Are puny.

Am not. You are huge.

Am not.

Are.

You are impossible to talk to. I am done.

Are too, Shannon said.

Luke joined her. "Shouldn't you get some rest?" he asked.

"Yes, I'm coming soon."

Luke nodded. "You need a chocolate bar. You're shaking. I'll get it," Luke said, as Shannon sank onto the stern bench, brushing a sheen of water to the deck.

So Kota was working with one of the sub's people, Salesti had said. Meaning maybe someone aboard the sub, just like the *guest* on the navy ship, meant to sideline Luke and Shannon and get their grubby hands on Juneau.

But fortunately the navy had interrupted those plans to chase down an unidentified swimming object. At any rate, Shannon didn't think a sub could capture Juneau. Perhaps the *guest* on the sub simply meant to make sure the whale hadn't veered from the route to Ocean City. Now that they thought they'd confirmed Juneau's itinerary, perhaps they'd move on north to their official business at the Dickson.

And hopefully, since the gambit with Kota's drug package had failed, whoever had orchestrated it would fear that another incident attempting to separate her from the whale might draw suspicion.

Shannon gave the skies and the sea one more hazy sweep of color and, satisfied that the pursuit had ended, she called Juneau in.

* * *

A half hour later the whale appeared behind the boat. Shannon hopped one-footed down from the deck onto the short ladder that attached to the stern to allow people in the water to access the boat. She continued her painful way down until her good foot felt the rung closest to the water. The beluga appeared beside her and raised her beautiful white head. Shannon wrapped the leg attached to her wounded ankle around the ladder rail and tucked her broken arm in close. She could just reach down far enough with her good hand—if she ignored her ribs—to scratch and rub Juneau's head, her sides, her pecs, her fluke, as they leaned into one another.

The occasional high wave washed over Shannon's boat shoe. The cold began to numb the fingers curled at the end of her cast. And the hand that Shannon used to rub her friend grew frigid, but still Shannon endured, spending these last moments interacting with the whale she loved so much.

Fifteen long years they'd been together now, first all the years Shannon had spent volunteering at the SeaQuarium, then the years they'd spent working as part of the Dickson Project to win her freedom.

She sent images, reminding Juneau of the dangers of the sea—ship propellers, ship speed, sharks, fishermen's nets, plastic, loose rope, everything she could think of. She imaged her plan—for Juneau to elude humans, ships, subs, and seaplanes until Shannon could call for her, which would be as soon as she could.

Shannon also sent emotions, her love for Juneau, her worry, her sadness that they must be apart for a while, her pride that Juneau had fared so well in her newfound freedom. Shannon had long ago ceased to try to sort the exotic, wild, unknowable emotions of the whale in return, but Juneau sent an image of herself coming to Shannon at a place in the middle of the ocean, coming to find her when she returned.

Shannon nodded

Salesti, time for you to flow to me. She closed her eyes . . . she traveled within her body toward her fingertips, then past her fingertips and into Juneau, and the little fuzzball Salesti appeared, glowing, buzzing happily, wings vibrating with hummingbird quickness, four little furry paws dangling. Shannon beckoned her to follow, and, hesitating just for a moment before leaving Juneau because she sensed the whale's watchful awareness, she waved one more good-bye, and then she and Salesti flowed back into Shannon's fingertips, traveling up to Shannon's mind, the place where Salesti could survive as long as Shannon survived.

Off you go, Juneau. Whenever you're ready.

Shannon reached out her hand one last time and rested it on the beluga's head. She stood and watched Juneau duck beneath the waves and disappear. For a time, she remained motionless, following the whale with her senses. Then she climbed carefully back to the deck.

* * *

Luke had gone below, but a candy bar rested on the stern bench. Shannon picked it up and sat down, heavily, to ease the pain everywhere in her body.

"I guess I should officially welcome you into my humble head, Sal—"

shannon must bring roebor on board, Salesti said, now firmly ensconced within Shannon's mind. *roebor too big, too strange to travel openly in this world.*

"You're just now noticing? But I am not bringing *him* on board. No way."

salesti thinks the ocean more deserted. salesti wrong. body of roebor hides here while roebor comes with salesti and shannon.

"I understand the logic, small one," Shannon said softly, "but I'm not sure I can handle another presence. You remember . . . near death by implosion, near death by drowning, near death by hypothermia, near death from shock. Busted ribs, broken arm, busted ankle, concussion, abrasions, and contusions. Plus, the ego on that guy could smother the city of Seattle. Let's leave Roebor here and bring Essi back to him.

roebor stops tidak. only way.

"You don't think we can stop Tidak ourselves?"

Salesti imaged the likeness of Tidak to Shannon again, emphasis on the fangs and claws.

"Gotcha," Shannon said. She leaned her head back against the polished railing that circled the the boat.

"Will his body die? Juneau nearly did, even on life support, when Essi brought her into my head."

I can hear you. I'm right here. The answer is no. If I were to board you, my autonomous nervous system works so well that my body could function without my consciousness for weeks of Earth time. If I were to board you. Which I won't. Earththings are too puny. Too alien. Too primitive.

"And that settles that," Shannon said.

Salesti dug in. *no. roebor boards shannon. too dangerous for roebor to swim, fly, walk.*

I am not boarding.

"I guess we'll just have to deal with this other dragonpanther, Tidak, ourselves," Shannon said.

At the mention of Tidak's name, a rumble erupted from Roebor.

tidak goes on board some land creature with help of toss, likely human, to find essi. shannon and salesti too weak to fight tidak. salesti explains already.

Shannon caught an underlying sharpness to Salesti's words. She'd never heard Salesti express anything approaching true irritation before. The little creature sounded deadly serious. Now Roebor was in for it.

roebor comes, Salesti added, for the dragonpanther's benefit.

I will not.

comes.

Will not.

comes.

Oh for Pete's sake. The dragonpanther would never win this one; the little dynamo Salesti had a will of iron. However, their arguing might drag on all night. Or rather, since her watch read almost three in the morning, it could drag on all day.

"Look, Roebor, I apologize for being a puny earththing, and nobody understands the alien creepy-jeebies like I do, believe me, but Salesti's right, don't you think? We really don't have a choice. You just stand out too much in this world because of your, your . . ." Shannon swallowed hard. "Your magnificence."

Magnificence? Too magnificent for Earth?

Shannon rubbed her hand on the back of her neck and pressed hard. *Okay, if that's what it takes; I can lay it on thick.* "We've got nothing like you here, nothing that even comes close. Nothing so grand, so fierce. Nothing with a coat that shimmers like yours. Nothing that can fly like you can, except some tiny creatures called birds that count for nothing compared to you. So. Of course you can't escape being followed, badgered, bothered, harassed, and haunted by too many odious puny earththings.

They would chase me again in the boat? In the airplane?

"The submarine and the seaplane. Yes, definitely. Chase you. And it's not so bad being in my head, right Salesti? You probably forget how puny I am, don't you, Salesti"

very nice in head of shannon. shannon not feels puny to salesti.

But that's because you're not—Never mind, Roebor said.

"So shall I climb down the ladder for you? If I touch you, I can lead you back. Salesti can flow down with me if you would feel better about it."

Did she really say that? *Invite* trouble like that? Yes, she did.

Very well then. I will allow it. But I will not like it.

Shannon bit back a choice response, climbed down to touch Roebor's back, brought him on board, and then limped down to her bunk, wrapped up in her quilt, and laid out, closing her eyes. She traveled to her Great Room to meet this new passenger.

CHAPTER TWENTY

FIVE YEARS EARLIER, after Shannon had first unwittingly taken little Essi aboard, she'd learned that she could imagine a place in her mind where Essi—and now other guests—could talk to her face to face. She would rest, close her eyes, and travel inward to this place, which she came to call her Great Room, because of the sense of never-ending space reaching far up above and far out around her. When she boarded the minds of others, she could find their Great Rooms as well.

The floor of Shannon's Great Room, deepest purple in color, felt soft to walk or sit upon. A lavender-tinted light permeated the very air of the room, and bright beams of the light cut across the space at odd angles. She entered now, and the welcoming calm surrounded her.

Compared to Salesti and Shannon, Roebor still looked like an airliner. She didn't much relish going anywhere near the giant creature, but as he had taken up space in her head, she should say hello.

Out of habit, Shannon held out her hand. "I'm Shannon, Roebor. I'm glad you're here." *He scared her shitless and she wanted him anywhere* but *here.*

Roebor glared down on her with fiery, pale blue eyes. If the fire in those eyes could burn, Shannon would be a pile of ash.

Why does your hand dangle in the air, puny earththing?

Shannon dropped her hand. "Here, a polite way to greet someone is to shake their hand."

Or she could use it to throttle him. Check that. With her tiny hands, she couldn't throttle Roebor's little toe.

Roebor raised his paw. *Do you see a hand here?*

Shannon studied his raised paw. "I suppose I see a paw. But only the size of your paw presents an issue. Your—we would call them toes here—your toes are very long, very finger-like. Much longer than I would have thought. If you were the right size, I think you could shake my hand. You could probably change size here. In fact, you could have given it some sort of effort even at your size."

At a slight sound like a spring being sprung, gigantic claws extended from each of Roebor's toes. *So long as I remembered to retract these,* he said, narrowing his eyes.

"Yeah, so long as. How well does your memory work, Roebor? Do you tend to forget things?" Shannon blinked innocently.

Roebor's head rose up. His eyes opened wide. It seemed he hadn't expected any sass from Shannon when he went all fierce. Hard to tell with a dragonpanther, but his lips seemed to curve upward like Narci's did when she felt in particularly good humor. However, he remained silent.

"Well, gotta get back, been fun, see you around," Shannon said, nodding at Salesti, who looked like a dust mote compared to Roebor. Shannon wondered if he could even see it.

* * *

The rest of the trip south passed uneventfully. Shannon engaged in a serious chat with Roebor and Salesti to explain that internal squabbling between them or with her would result in their immediate ejection into the ether, good-bye, gone forever, no more Salesti or Roebor, virus be damned. She needed peace and quiet, and would they please oblige and reside in silence? Which they said they would, and, for the most part, in fact, they did.

Other than staying off her broken ankle, sleeping, and stuffing her face with enough food for her body to survive Salesti's and Roebor's presence, keeping Kota in the dark about Juneau's absence proved Shannon's biggest challenge. She would wait until Luke engaged the pink-haired researcher in a friendly game of five card stud, and then announce her plans to go visit with the whale, so that Kota couldn't follow her. Or Kota would start a bacon and egg fry on the small galley stove top, and Luke would lean into the cabin from the deck and recount how he'd just spotted Juneau performing an awkward arc off the bow of the boat before disappearing again. Shannon would mention her pleasure that Juneau was succeeding in finding food on her own so well.

Kota appeared to buy into these tall tales; Shannon kept her fingers crossed. She still hated deceiving her friend, but after the drug bust stunt, she didn't see any way around it.

Yet a persistent worry poked at Shannon. *She and Luke had kept Kota from noticing Juneau's absence awfully easily.* At the Dickson, Kota enjoyed giving Juneau a good rub now and then, and often hung around to record her clicks and whistles.

If Shannon's suspicions about her were correct, maybe she'd distanced herself from Juneau because the whale was her kidnap target, and Kota didn't want to get too fond of her. If that were true, it had made Shannon's job much easier.

Or perhaps Kota already knew Luke and Shannon were pulling an elaborate hoax. Shannon watched her former friend for signs that the jig was up, but if Kota didn't believe Juneau was still following them toward Ocean City, her acting skills were good enough to send her to Broadway.

* * *

The day arrived on which Shannon planned to implement Juneau's fake disappearance. They'd just passed St. George Reef at the northern tip of California. Kota assumed her accustomed spot at the bow of the boat, headphones on, binoculars hanging from her neck, appearing to listen intently to her underwater hydrophone. Whether she actually was listening to the whales sing, Shannon no longer knew.

At noon Shannon made her way up to the bow and plunked down beside Dakota, who pushed her headphones back from her ears and onto her neck.

"Have you seen any sign of Juneau this morning? She usually checks in about ten or so, but I haven't spotted her. I'm started to get worried. So much more ship traffic runs through here than up in Alaska."

"Nope, I haven't seen her, sweet potato. Can't you tell where she is?"

"We've been through this, Kota. No, I can't."

"Hmm. Too bad. It would be so much cooler if you could just connect with her telepathically. Then you'd always know where she is."

Yeah, you would like me to confirm that, wouldn't you? Then you could use her to spy for Homeland Security or the navy or the CIA. Run covert missions into Russian naval bases. Plant a few bombs in Iranian ports. Not happening.

"Yes, so much cooler. Anyway, earlier this morning, around eight or so, I watched her swim up to some sea gulls floating on the water. I haven't seen her since. I've tried buzzing her transmitter, naturally, to signal her to return. Still nothing. I hope she didn't rub the transmitter off again." Shannon had, in fact, removed the transmitter herself days earlier.

"This reminds me of the day you spent worrying that she wouldn't come back from her first solo, but, bam! She reappeared just in time to save your little tush and provide you with a wonderful, if slightly frigid, photo op. Now quit worrying and let me get back to my work."

"Okay. But if she doesn't check in by two this afternoon, we're anchoring until she catches up with us." *Or not.*

"Fine by me, pumpkin," Kota said, and flipped her headphones back up over her ears.

*　*　*

"Calm down, cara. Panic will not help us find her," Luke said to Shannon in his best police officer de-escalation voice, placing his hand on her arm. She stood in the well of the boat staring off the stern through her binoculars. Kota stood by her side, picking at the desk charts.

"Don't tell me to calm down," Shannon said in an unsteady voice, brushing his hand off. "Juneau's missing. We haven't seen her all day. It's now four o'clock, eight hours since my last contact. If she could, she would've checked in by now."

Shannon didn't put a lot of stock in her acting ability, but she remembered only too well how petrified she'd been when she didn't hear from Juneau on the day of the UC collapse. She figured she was channeling her former angst fairly competently.

"You don't know that, Shanny," Kota said. "I mean, isn't it possible she didn't like these southern waters and just took off back north? It will take her a few days to reach the Dickson, but that might be where she's headed."

Ooo. Not bad, Kota. I can run with that.

"Oh, maybe you're right. We've traveled far south of her normal migration range for sure." She paused, pretending to think over the possibility. She wobbled a bit on her wrapped ankle and grabbed the railing with her good hand. "More big ships down here, with their underwater noise, and then if you add in her temper and her 'I'll do as I flippin' well please' attitude, I guess I can buy her simply packing it in, and heading back north. If she isn't hurt."

"She made it this far without mishap, so I vote either she simply wants to play for a while longer, and she will show up bright-eyed and bushy-tailed any minute now, or, as Kota said, she headed back to the Dickson," Luke said.

"Bright-eyed and bushy-tailed?" Shannon and Kota said in unison.

Luke ignored them and continued, "So our working hypothesis is that she returned to the Dickson. What do we do next?"

We beat a fast track to Ocean City and find Essi. "We call the staff at the Dickson, now that we have cell phone reception, and ask them to watch for her. Then, when I get to Ocean City, I'll need to go face the firing squad, a.k.a. Dr. Moon." *The first true thing she'd said about Juneau's absence.* She closed her eyes. No lie, that would turn into one ugly meeting. "But we should wait here for a while, right? To see if she shows up?"

Come on Luke, now you tell me we can't stay.

"We won't go ahead full throttle, and if Juneau swims this way, she'll be able to catch up or find the boat in Ocean City. She can recognize the boat, correct?"

"Yes, she zoomed right in on the *Seatation* all the way down the coast, so she should be able to find it at the marina. But—"

Shannon kept a casual eye on Kota. *Did she buy Shannon's angst?*

"I think Luke's right, sugar. She's trained to come in; she hasn't, so she's gone. Either gone for good, gone wild, gone girl, bye-bye birdie, more power to her, or gone back to the Dickson to help with underwater repairs. So I vote we press on until we're somewhere I can jump into a long, long, long, really long, hot shower in a nice hotel with room service," Kota said and trooped back down to the cabin.

Shannon and Luke looked at each other for a moment. "I believe our friend has had enough of the boating life," Luke said.

Shannon said nothing because she'd begun feeling dizzy about an hour earlier, and it had only become worse as they stood in the afternoon sun debating the fate of Juneau. The presence of Salesti and Roebor were taking their toll. She didn't need to fake her current distress; she felt distress all right; she'd only faked the source.

"Sorry, Luke, I really need to eat or I—"

And in the next instant, she fell backward, out cold.

* * *

When Shannon next opened her eyes, her head rested on her comfy pillow, and her right foot dangled off her bunk. On the little dining table, which displaced Luke's bed during the day, perched a tray laden with an odd assortment of goodies. A can of sardines. A box of cocoa crisps, no milk. Leftover pan-fried halibut. Oyster crackers. Other sundries. It appeared Luke had emptied the cupboards and tiny ice box, and laid out everything they hadn't already consumed. Logical, since they would need to clean out the boat when they reached Ocean City.

She sat up, reached for an apple and a granola bar, and glanced out the nearest porthole. Dark skies fighting bright artificial lights. *How long had she slept?*

She couldn't hear the engine's noise, couldn't smell its oily exhaust. The boat sat motionless on the water, rocking gently side to side. They'd docked in Ocean City. She'd slept a long time.

The breeze blew in from the cabin portholes, much warmer than the Alaskan breeze she'd become accustomed to. She took in a long, deep breath. And coughed. Ugh. Warmer but not as crystal pure as the air up north. Air pollution. A disturbing thing.

She's all right, then? Roebor said just then to Salesti.

shannon well, Salesti said.

"'Well' is a strong word for what I am, small one. I'm awake. Let's leave it at that."

"What?" Kota said, clambering down the steps.

"I said, 'Have we docked in Ocean City already? Has Juneau showed up?'"

"Yes to the first, no to the second. We just docked. That's probably what woke you up." She eyed the tray of food and snatched a package of Fritos, ripping it open and popping a handful in her mouth in one fluid motion. "Luke said your metabolism crashed again. So eat, already."

Kota gathered clothes strewn about the cabin to pack up her duffel, and Shannon opened a jar of crunchy peanut butter.

As Kota straightened up to arch her back and stretch, Shannon smoothed a few stray hairs from her braid away from her face, dug a knife into the peanut butter, brought out a fat glob, and began licking it off. "Listen, we didn't really talk about our plans for when we got here. I thought we'd have our hands full arranging to airlift Juneau into a truck tank to take her to the Dickson. But with no Juneau, I'm not sure if Moon has any other PR plans involving us."

"Involving you, you mean," Kota said, returning to her packing. "My scantily-clad bod did not appear on the evening news the day Juneau made like a life raft, sweetheart. I want nothing to do with anybody's PR plans, thank you. I've arranged for an Uber to take me up the hill to the Marriott with my cetacean recordings and my logs. I'm going to write a long report about the noise encounters along the coast, and I'm not coming out for a week. Tell Moon I fell overboard, and a great white made a feast of me, very sad, nothing left but my right shoe and my nose ring."

"But you'll come with me to talk to Moon tomorrow, to tell him Juneau went missing this morning, right? Please, please, please?"

You grovel, puny earththing. Stop it. I am shamed to watch it, said Roebor. *The pink one will not agree to accompany a coward.*

Kota dropped the pink polka dot shirt she'd been folding, stared at Shannon for a moment, and said, "Oh, all right, honey bunny. But only if I can stand behind you when Moon starts throwing sharp objects. Just ring the hotel when you want to go. Make it late afternoon. I'm sleeping in."

You see? Shannon asked Roebor.

I see many things. What am I supposed to look at? Roebor asked Salesti.

"Thanks. I'll owe you," Shannon said to Kota.

salesti thinks shannon means: does roebor see that groveling of shannon works?

No, I meant: do you see, Roebor, that she is coming with me? And I didn't grovel. I engaged in more of a . . . a high art form of communication between friends on Earth.

Groveled, said Roebor.

Did not grovel.

Groveled.

Did not.

Roebor growled.

Kota finished packing and hoisted her bags up and out to the deck. She turned and wrapped Shannon in a big good-bye bear hug. A week ago, the embrace would've meant the world to Shannon, a hug of comfort from her closest friend at the Dickson, as she secretly mourned for Juneau's absence, as her onboard guests sickened her, as she gathered all the reinforcements she could find for her meet-up with Moon tomorrow.

And yet, after this boat trip, Kota's hug would never comfort Shannon again.

***

Shannon's house had been shuttered for five years. She'd paid a neighbor to take care of the lawn and car, and check the interior now and then, but she hadn't remembered to call down and ask him to arrange for the electricity and water to be turned back on, and to find someone to polish away the dust and air the place out. Shannon could have camped out in the living room anyway, but, as Kota had said, the idea of a soft bed, a hot shower, and room service sounded much better. She'd tackle her house tomorrow; tonight she would go with a hotel.

First, however, she asked Luke, who'd volunteered to transport her, if he would stop at the hospital so she could ask for water-resistant fiberglass casts.

"Don't get water down inside the casts, though, Ms. Kendricks," the hospital resident who applied the casts instructed her. Those two large gashes on your arm inside the cast and that deep round cut on your ankle just below the cast line could easily get infected if they get wet. So here is waterproof tape to use on these plastic bags to keep them dry if you shower. Understand?"

"Perfectly."

Luke helped her into her hotel room with her duffel and the cat before taking off for his own house. As Shannon closed the door on Luke, her mind felt suddenly very sluggish. She called room service and ordered a generous dinner.

"That will be service for two, then, Ms. Kendricks?"

"Yeah, sure, why not. Dinner for two." *Me and me.*

"Salesti, we need to figure out how we can find Essi. What's your plan?"

shannon knows essi. what plan shannon has?

Indeed. What plan Shannon has? "My house? Essi's been in my head there. That's where she'll probably go. If she can find her way. Maybe I should've gone straight home after all. Tomorrow for sure. At least Tidak won't have any idea where Essi went, right, Salesti?"

tidak has no idea, Salesti said.

Roebor began, *Wait, Salesti may be incorr—*

Narci seized that moment to yowl her desire for release from her crate, so Shannon turned her attention to the cat.

Why, this looks like a miniature dragonpanther, as you call my kind, Roebor said. Shannon detected a tenderness in his voice for the first time since she'd met him. *But the dragonpanther has no wings. Poor little fellow.*

"Poor little girl, in this case, Roebor. On Earth we call her species 'cat.' And, correct, no wings. *Thank Odin* for small favors. Although I suppose wings would be helpful for cats trapped in trees. Or dumped in the Pacific Ocean in a rain storm. She's been on board the boat with us. Didn't you notice her on the trip down?"

Salesti's tinkling laughter followed. It said, *roebor pouts whole trip to ocean city. retreats deep in mind of shannon. not looks out from Shannon's eyes as salesti does.* She laughed again.

As always, its laughter lifted Shannon's spirits.

I do not pout, Roebor said. *I . . . meditate.*

"I'm sure you do," Shannon said. *No, he pouts.*

I heard that, Roebor said.

Narci jumped up on the motel bed where Shannon had flopped back, and climbed onto her chest, stepping carefully over her arm cast, purring loudly. Shannon stroked her gently. "Glad to be back on solid ground, sweetheart?" she asked the cat. "Tomorrow we'll go home finally."

I wish to smell her.

"What?"

I wish to smell the little dragonpanther.

"Oh, why not." Shannon buried her nose deep into the fur of her little black feline and breathed in deeply.

The cat smells like a dragonpanther. Her fur feels like dragonpanther fur. I shall consider her a miniature dragonpanther. I like her best of all earththings I have discovered. I wish to know her mind. Let her come on board with us.

"Oh no, no, no, no. No more onboarding, I can't handle more than you and Salesti right now. Plus you don't really want to know Narci's mind. It isn't like yours."

I wish her to board.

"Not happening, end of story. Now please keep it down so I can set up services for my house," Shannon said as she picked up her cell phone, "and then I want to rest until the food arrives."

Roebor rumbled his unhappiness. *I find the little dragonpanther more interesting than you, puny earththing, with no fur at all.*

Shannon paid him no attention, made her phone calls, and tried to doze off. But the prospect of facing Moon the next day gave her no rest.

CHAPTER TWENTY-ONE

LATE ON WEDNESDAY AFTERNOON, Shannon and Kota found themselves sitting on wooden chairs outside the door of Dr. Moon's office at the Dickson Research Center located at the university. The Dickson had long been one of the U's principal public partners. Kota had embraced the warmth of the California summer day with her wardrobe and lounged on her chair in her brightest, dark pink tank top and matching shorts, watching students pass by in the hall. Shannon had stopped at home and pulled out a slightly dusty purple-and-blue cotton dress and one comfortable blue sandal.

Although they'd passed hallways cordoned off with pylons and yellow tape, and walls of plastic strips blocked off the view beyond, the area that housed Dr. Moon's office showed few signs of the big fire that had torched the main lecture hall on the first floor.

The air smelled of smoke, and Shannon's eyes stung a bit, but otherwise, the outer administrative office looked just as it had when Shannon had perched here on the edge of her seat the very first time she'd met Dr. Moon and pitched her idea to free Juneau from captivity.

Inside Dr. Moon's office they could hear voices raised, one of them clearly Moon's. Shannon had never heard the man raise his voice; an icy chill usually suited his purposes better. The other voice sounded like that of Thomas Tremaine, Shannon's least favorite member of the research center's board of directors.

Now there was a man Shannon loved to hate. He had fought the Juneau Project and the Alaska Dickson facility all the way. And by riling up Moon now, he had just chalked up another black mark in her book. *Thanks a lot, Tremaine, working him over before I can break my bad news. Sure way to get me killed. And wouldn't that deeply satisfy your stunted ego.*

She glanced at the administrative secretary behind the counter in the outer office, who supported several other luminaries at the Dickson in addition to Moon. A middle-aged, efficient-looking man with a beard and a ponytail, wearing the rattiest orange-and-green plaid cotton shirt Shannon had ever seen, clacked away at a keyboard in front of a pair of interconnected computer monitors. After inviting them to be seated, he hadn't given the two women a second glance.

Shannon reached for her braid but then remembered that with no one to help her braid it, she'd had to wear her hair down today. Her palest blond-white hair floated down her back to her waist.

"Excuse me," Shannon said, rising, grasping her single crutch and hop-stepping up to the counter. "Do you know the current, ah, topic of conversation?" She pointed her thumb back over her shoulder toward Moon's office. "I'm just wondering if I'm supposed to be in there already."

"Dr. Moon said he would be with you as soon as he and Dr. Tremaine completed their meeting," said the man, his voice dripping with disinterest. He sported no name tag that Shannon could see.

She tucked her hair behind her right ear, frowning. "Okay, thanks, I just—"

At that moment, Tremaine burst from Moon's office, his face covered in an unpleasant red rash, saying, "—Board will never allow it. Period." He stopped when he reached Shannon standing directly in front of him at the receptionist's counter.

"You," he said.

"Dr. Tremaine, I believe," Shannon said, a smile plastered on her face. She held out her hand. "So good to see you again." *Not.*

Tremaine ignored Shannon's hand. Shannon let it fall to her side. *Creep.* Her smile remained pasted to her face.

"The Alaska facility would not exist but for you," he said. "If it never existed, the UC would never have collapsed. And yet no one sues *you*. Well, let me tell you this. Your research project has ended. Period. Over and done. We'll be lucky if the Dickson can avoid bankruptcy. You—"

"Ms. Kendricks. How good to see you alive and relatively healthy after all you've been through," Moon said, appearing at his office door. "Please enter. And Ms. Quartermark too. You have broken your arm and your foot, Shannon. I had not heard this. Please accept my condolences."

"Both are on the mend. Thanks for the kind words."

Moon beckoned Shannon and Kota through the door. Tremaine hesitated, as if he were contemplating following them back in. Moon shut the door gently in his face.

Hah! Take that, you platypus.

Moon's office looked just as Shannon remembered. You could see, smell, practically taste the powerful financial forces that swirled here. The Tudor furnishings, the old Dutch Masters and the Impressionists on the wall, some of them originals, the thick Burgundy carpet, all as Shannon remembered.

Moon ushered the two women to the conversational grouping of brand new camel leather furniture at the far end of his office. Shannon perched on the front edge of her seat, while Kota took the couch and threw her arms over the back as if she hadn't a care in the world. A tea set filled the small, glass-topped table top centered between the couch and chairs, and Moon went quietly about the business of pouring them each a cup. With that accomplished, he sat back and said, "Don't take what you heard from Dr. Tremaine too seriously. He counts for no more than one board member of twelve."

"We *will* rebuild then?" Shannon asked, leaning forward to spoon four more teaspoonfuls of sugar into her tea.

"It may be too early to say with certainty," Moon replied, eyeing the sugar bowl. "The matter of the lawsuits must be addressed, I'm afraid."

"You're talking to a former lawyer, Dr. Moon. If the families of people who died or were injured in the UC collapse sue the Dickson, the matter could be tied up in litigation for years. Surely we can't wait that long to rebuild."

A small smile creased Moon's face. "Perhaps I should have said we must address funding the portion of any settlement or liability judgment that will not be covered by insurance. Although the Dickson heavily insured the Alaska facility, our legal team warns us that it may not be enough. Our board wants to be sure that we have started a fund for the purpose of paying for the litigation, and any liability sums we may owe in the future."

Shannon nodded. She turned to Kota to check whether she wanted to ask anything, but Kota's eyes gazed in an unfocused way at a famous Monet reproduction across from her. The one with the irises. Shannon couldn't tell if she'd even heard Moon. Maybe the thwarted drug bust had not been totally bogus after all; maybe Kota had invented the trap based on some personal experience. *But* now, *Kota? Really?*

"At the same time," Moon continued, "the board wishes us to begin a separate fund to study the cause of the catastrophic failure of the UC and to determine whether such cause can be prevented in the future. This fund would also rebuild the facility, if feasible, and pay the new insurance premiums, which the insurance carrier tells us will be substantial."

The odds of another dragonpanther blundering into one of our facilities had to approach nil. Too bad she couldn't explain that to Moon.

I didn't blunder *into it; the explosive force of the energy vortex which encased me caused an exit trajectory over which I had no control,* Roebor said.

Fair enough, but not now, Roebor.

"Do they have a pretty good idea of the cause now?" Shannon asked. "I heard some kind of explosive force occurred, and the energy from it threw some debris at the UC. Right?"

Exactly—wait. Debris? I am not some debris. How dare you call me debris?

I want Moon to keep on thinking of the cause as debris and not a dragonpanther. Understand? And please be quiet. I can't concentrate.

The dragonpanther roared. *And if I do not wish to be quiet?*

Shannon involuntarily squeezed her eyes shut at the sound, her good hand flying to her ear.

Moon, who had heard nothing of the noises echoing in Shannon's head, half rose from his chair. "Ms. Kendricks. You are unwell. Do you wish me to summon help?"

"No, I'll be okay. Thanks, Dr. Moon. Just a flash of a headache. Left over from the explosion. No worries." The UC explosion had turned into a handy excuse for just about anything and everything.

Roebor, no more roaring while you live in my head. Or I won't be well enough to help you find the virus.

Roebor grumbled but remained quiet.

Moon sat back and nodded. "If you do not require assistance?" He paused a beat to give Shannon a chance to change her mind and then said, "We have the most peculiar video footage, that which you have referred to, in which a strange ball of energy does indeed seem to explode and send a large form into the UC. But what that ball of energy consisted of, why it happened to appear where it did, even the nature of the large form ejected from it—to date we have no answers. We cannot rule out another such occurrence until we know its nature."

"What if you never know the truth?" With any luck Moon never would.

Moon shrugged. "In that case some of our board members will interpret the uncertainty to mean we dare not try the project again; others on the board will conclude the explosion was a one-off, the chances of a repeat therefore miniscule."

"And you favor moving forward as if the destruction of the UC did, in fact, constitute a unique phenomenon, right?"

"Indeed. Although Tom Tremaine has stirred up some disagreement, I hope to fund the rebuild at the earliest possible moment."

"Two fund drives, then. Not easy," Shannon said.

"No, not easy." Moon placed his tea cup carefully on the tabletop. "But you and Juneau will help us with these tasks. I have scheduled almost six months worth of appearances for the two of you. The major networks will interview you, also NPR, BBC, National Geographic, and many others. You will also be speaking without the whale at various venues around the country. We have varied the exact topics of these appearances, each focusing on a slightly different aspect of the disaster or the whale species or Juneau in particular or your work with her. We have prepared scripts. The Dickson will pay all your expenses, of course. We are counting on you and Juneau to pull us out of the financial hole that threatens us.

Now you're in trouble, puny earththing.

You're one of the reasons I'm in trouble, so zip it.

Zip it? Zip what, Salesti, do you know?

salesti thinks shannon wishes roebor to zip lips of roebor to closed position so words not escape.

What? No one can tell Roebor to zip it. I am Roebor, leader. . . .

Shannon did her best to shut out his words. She slowly closed her eyes and sagged back into her chair. "Yes, um, there's one problem with your plan, though."

Moon stilled. Perhaps because he'd suffered through some of Shannon's "problems" five years earlier, or perhaps the look on Shannon's pale face caused the reaction, but whatever the reason, Moon soon jumped to the correct conclusion. He shook off his stillness, bolted from his chair, stood over Shannon, and said, "Please do not tell me the problem is Juneau." Yeah, that would be the icy chill voice. At least he didn't scream.

Slightly alarmed, Shannon put her good hand up in front of her as if to ward off the blow that would come when she next spoke. She took a deep breath and pressed on. "Juneau *is* the problem. I don't have her."

"What do you mean, you don't have her?"

Shannon peered over at Kota. *A little help here?* But Kota might as well have transported herself a thousand miles away. She had picked a magazine off a round table by the couch, and was now leafing casually through it less than two feet from Moon's glowering countenance.

"She's not in Ocean City," Shannon said. Then her words rushed out all at once: "She disappeared at sea on the way down." *True, if Shannon didn't count the teeny omission that she had engineered the disappearance.*

"What do you mean, she disappeared?"

"I mean she failed to return to the boat, failed to respond to her call signal, failed to show up at the marina when we arrived yesterday. I checked again this morning, and then right before we came here, and she still hasn't appeared. We think maybe, um, maybe she decided to return to the Alaska facility." *Also fairly true. Fairly.*

"What do you mean, she decided to return to the Alaska facility?"

And I thought the puny earththing burned the dimmest candle around. I believe we have a new contender, said Roebor.

Moon's repetitions probably meant he'd gone into shock. If so, Shannon couldn't blame him. Moon regarded Juneau as a multimillion-dollar asset, as well as the lynchpin in his plan to keep the Dickson afloat and the Alaska Project alive. To be fair, the whales and dolphins had always fascinated Moon, and he did care about Juneau for her own sake. But he still considered her an invaluable asset first and foremost.

"Juneau has always had a mind of her own. At the SeaQuarium, if she didn't want to perform behaviors, all the fish in the world wouldn't entice her to perform. If she didn't want you around, she'd spit water in your face. If she decided she'd had enough of performing, she'd leave right in the middle of a training session. That's just Juneau. So we figured, if she felt uncomfortable, she might just head back home."

"Home?"

"I mean, back to where she last felt safe, which would be the Dickson in Alaska.

She wanted to slap Moon in the face to get his brain working again. Of course *home* would be the Alaska Dickson. The SeaQuarium had never been home and never would be.

"I called up to the Dickson this morning and let them know to be on the lookout for her, but she won't arrive for a few days, if that's where she's going."

"You lost Juneau."

"Actually, I didn't lose her so much as she—"

"Do you realize what Tremaine will do with this information? He will kill the project. He will have my job. And yours. We will be done, Ms. Kendricks."

As if he'd just noticed that he was hovering over her, he turned in a daze and sat back down.

"Finished."

CHAPTER TWENTY-TWO

SHANNON'S FREE HAND GRASPED THE FINGERS of the hand in the cast and held tight.

Quick. Think of some story that can pull this disaster out of the dumpster.

"We'll have to say that, uh, that . . . that I *sent* her back up. That she had developed some sort of skin condition as we came farther south, and I didn't want to risk any further infection in these waters. That we knew the media would want to see her swimming free in the ocean, not stuck back in the pool where she started. If Tremaine wants my head because of it, fine, but if Juneau does return to the Alaska Dickson, it'll prove our point. That a whale can swim free and still return to base for care and observation."

Not bad, Roebor said.

—for a puny earththing, I know. Shannon said to him. *Might you just possibly call me Shannon, my actual name?*

I do not mean it as an insult anymore. I simply do not like this word Shannon. It has an unpleasant sound. I shall call you Daq.

Daq? Where did that come from? It's not my name. It makes no sense to call me that.

Daq is a pretty name. I shall call you by it.

Moon sat silently, elbows on the chair arms, tenting his fingers, bouncing them to touch and fly apart, touch and fly apart. . . .

"Perhaps. Perhaps Tremaine will believe this story. He will still want your head. But he will find himself in the lonely minority in that regard. And we can continue with some publicity events without her. Starting tomorrow."

Shannon poured herself another cup of tea; she didn't much want the drink, but she very much wanted the sugar she added by the teaspoon as Moon spoke.

"It will not be easy to reschedule her appearances. We will have to wait, for one thing, until we confirm that Juneau has returned to the Alaskan facility." He paused for a moment. "I do not want a dozen news agencies reviving the photos from the destruction of the UC, however. The whale will be transported here by military plane as soon as possible."

"But that—"

"If you will excuse me, I have phone calls to make," Moon said, brushing past them on his way to the large mahogany desk at the other end of the room, dismissing Shannon like a schoolchild.

Very humbling, Daq, said Roebor. She could have smacked him.

Her face flushed. She gulped down her tea in order to get the sugar into her system. Then she prodded Kota. "Wake up; we've been kicked out," she said under her breath.

* * *

From Dr. Moon's office, Kota drove Shannon to Dr. Bennett's office for medicine for her flagging health. Dr. Julia Bennett had learned all about Shannon's alien guests five years earlier, so Shannon could count on her for help now. And Shannon liked Dr. B., which couldn't be said about many doctors in Shannon's life.

Dr. B. sniffed at Shannon. "Still wearing the same scent. Fascinating." She also took a look at Shannon's newly-cast ankle and arm, and warned Shannon that her ankle would have to be re-broken in order to heal properly if she walked on it again before it had knitted. Shannon promised to stay off it this time, having not the slightest clue whether she'd be able to keep the promise.

She had arranged for the utilities to be turned on at her house, and, given her broken body parts, she'd also sprung for a cleaning service. Its staff had scrubbed and polished all afternoon, so that when Kota and she pulled up at the house with her duffle, the cat, and a car full of groceries, a blast of cool air, an aroma of lemon scent, and countertops clean to the touch awaited.

Home.

Shannon opened the crate door, and Narci scooted out, running up the stairs to reacquaint herself with her old haunts.

Aw, the little dragonpanther has run away. Where did she go? Will she stay safe in the upper regions?

safe, Salesti replied on Shannon's behalf.

As they brought in the groceries, Kota apologized again. "I *said* I screwed up, cookie. Okay, so I smoked a little too much marijuana and spaced out. Moon has always made me nervous. I can't face him if I'm in my right mind."

"Not much help? Not any help. I might as well have Ubered over to the U by myself. You know, I think we should be worried about how much of that stuff you're smoking. If you're stressed, maybe you need some counseling.

The life of a spy can stress a girl right out, am I right, Kota?

"Are you kidding? A counselor would have no idea what to do with me. But I promise to cut back. Let's get these groceries put away, and then I'm off to work some more on my research."

Research. Of course *you will work on your research. But will it concern porpoises or prying?*

"Are you sure you need to go? We can whip up some dinner, if you want to stay and visit," Shannon said half-heartedly.

To her relief Kota declined dinner, and after they'd shelved a very large quantity of food, Kota prepared to take off.

"You seem to be eating even more than you did up in Alaska, princess. What's going on?"

Oh nothing much. A couple of aliens sucking my energy away in order to stay alive, that's all.

"The metabolism has kicked into high gear again for some reason. Probably the whole hypothermia, shock, heart bypass, broken arm, broken foot, near arrest, Juneau disappearance scenario. I'll probably talk to Dr. B. about it again soon."

"I would say you'd better go back tomorrow, Chiquita. You don't look so hot. I shudder to think of the makeup job you'll need for the PR appearances Moon's lined up. Hours and hours."

Shannon grabbed the nearest object, a paper towel she'd used to wipe up some spilled cat food she'd spooned out for Narci, and flung it at Kota. "Stop! You mean creature."

Kota grabbed the paper towel out of mid-air and tossed it back at Shannon.

"Hey, no fair. I'm one-handed here. Not an even fight."

"You started it," Kota said, grinning.

Almost like old times.

Almost.

"But seriously," Kota said, "Go back to your doctor, Shan, and this time explain how bad things have become. No papering over the problem. If you need a ride, I'll take you. It's that or just take your bedroll and move into Safeway, preferably the candy aisle."

With that, Kota wrapped Shannon in another bear hug, then grabbed her back pack and headed for the door.

Such mixed signals. Friend or enemy? Roebor asked.

Friend or enemy? Shannon didn't even stop to think about her next move. She cast out to Kota's mind, searching for her emotions and images, translating them in her own mind into coherent thought. Perfect timing, too: a roiling cascade tumbled through Kota's mind.

Poor Shannon . . . Would Kota ever see her again?. . . Kota in the white lab coat of a researcher, then in a dark blue suit . . . skyscrapers . . . office complex . . . Homeland Security! . . . Kota in an office, nice digs.

Kota, of all people, a government bureaucrat, no pink hair, no pink anything.

Big conference room, meeting of suits and ties . . . Juneau in a coma at the Ocean City Dickson . . . Kota shakes Moon's hand.

HSD must have dropped her into position at the Dickson just in time to save Shannon's exhausted butt five years earlier.

Kota on a black throw-away cell phone, not her normal fuchsia one . . . Kota on the boat talking through a headset to a blond-haired man she called Kurt, Kurt with a crew cut, tall, muscular, dark glasses.

Oh brother, could he look any more cliché?

He stood peering through binoculars at them from the deck of the naval ship that had stopped them . . . Mortification that she'd failed to pull off the drug bust, so carefully planned, irritation that Jack, the agent planted on the sub, felt the need to keep tabs on the whale, as if she couldn't take care of that herself.

Guess again, Kota.

Relief, such relief, that Juneau would never qualify for the naval marine cetacean training program, no espionage, no bomb carrying for her . . . Shannon: her good friend; how did that happen, anyway? She couldn't afford to make friends on this assignment and yet she had, and then she'd almost succeeded in betraying Shanny . . . finish the report for HSD, return to her work at the HSD research lab, never do anything in the field again.

Shannon withdrew from Kota's mind.

So Homeland Security had recruited Kota from research work to turn into a spy? And she'd been tasked with capturing Juneau for a marine operation, but it had made her *happy* that Juneau had supposedly taken off in a huff, proving her too unpredictable for bomb duty? *Odin's eye.* The whole thing made Shannon's head hurt. Oh wait; it already hurt. But now it hurt worse.

I do not understand, Daq. I still do not know if Kota is a friend or enemy. On FireWorld, as you call it, I easily know which is which.

I guess she's both, Roebor. My very own frenemy.

She cannot be both. She must be one or the other. You have confused me.

So tempting to retort that she could confuse him with very little effort. Smack down! But she bit it back. One of them had to be the adult. So far, that wouldn't be him. Plus, he seemed to genuinely care who Shannon's friends and enemies were. She'd leave him be.

"Yeah, me too, Roebor—confused as hell."

Shannon wobbled with fatigue. She waved at Kota from her doorway, then beelined for the nearest chair.

* * *

Shannon sprawled in her wine-colored leather armchair for a time, running shaky fingers through her long loose hair, considering again how they'd missed disaster by inches out there on the high seas. Then she made for the kitchen to cook up a nice dinner and make further plans.

Bitter disappointment had greeted her when she arrived home first thing this morning, just briefly, to find out whether any stranger happened to be wandering around the premises with the alien child Essi on board. No such luck.

That would have been too easy, of course. Nothing came easily where Essi and Salesti were concerned.

And speaking of nothing coming easily, what about that disaster with Moon? She had hoped after the allegedly ill-fated trip down the coast, Moon would allow Juneau to roam the sea at the Alaska Dickson, not suffer a risky transport plane ride and a soul-killing long-term stint in the pool here. But if Juneau remained at large—because, really, nobody could stop her now—Tremaine would turn her absence against them, and try to scotch the whole project. A catastrophe for Moon and the Dickson. Zero sum solutions. No good.

As she placed the last item of her dinner, a pie that she'd just removed from the oven, on the kitchen table with her other menu items, and settled in to eat, a tap, tap, tapping sounded at the kitchen window. Shannon looked up sharply and peered out the window. Then she laughed.

"No way. You're still around after all this time?" She stood to get a better view of the fat, black raven sitting on her windowsill, a raven that had briefly resided in Shannon's mind. Shannon opened the back door and let the bird fly in. "You waited for me all this time, I guess I can say hello," Shannon told the bird. "But you can't stay, blackbird."

The bird fluttered around the kitchen and settled on Shannon's shoulder. The bird seemed content with its perch, and Shannon went back to work on her dinner, feeding the occasional bit to the bird. She had finished the last of her lasagna pan and opened a bag of marshmallows when her cell phone rang.

"Shannon? It's Luke. I think I have a lead on Essi or that other dragonpanther or both. I'll be over to pick you up in ten."

CHAPTER TWENTY-THREE

SHANNON, ON ONE CRUTCH, HURRIED QUICKLY—or as quickly as she could—outside to meet Luke, sending the raven off toward the pines behind Shannon's house.

"No way. That's not the same crow I found flying around your kitchen that time you almost died?"

"The very same. We've just enjoyed a little reunion. Tell me more about your lead on Essi."

"On my scanner I picked up word of an older guy, scuba diver, still in his wetsuit, following a young man, both weak-looking, staggering a bit, maybe drunk. That sound like a guy with a dragonpanther on board and another guy with Essi for company?"

"Yes! I hope Tidak hasn't killed the diver like the aliens. . . ."

"I remember. If he's as ruthless as Salesti says, he might have. If he sends his host's essence out into the air, that person dies, correct?"

"Right. Essi wouldn't do that, so if she's on board the young guy, she explained herself as best she could, which is not very well, and urged him to run. Have the police picked them up?"

"No. The two entered an apartment building. The squad car waited to see if they came back out. They didn't, so the officers figured they'd reached home, end of story."

"But he could have done anything to the younger one once they went into the building."

"The squad car reported pulling up to the young man and asking if he needed a lift, or if the old guy was bothering him, and he said no, so the squad car just followed a few blocks, until they disappeared inside the apartment building."

"So that's where we're going?"

"Almost there."

"Roebor, how do we handle Tidak?" Shannon said out loud so Luke could listen in.

"Wait," Luke said, "You took the dragonpanther on board too? When? Back the night he flew to us? You're kidding me. Shannon, you can't handle him, not after the beating you've taken the last few weeks."

I do not believe I care for this earththing, Daq. What do you call him?

"Luke."

"What?" Luke asked.

I do not like this name Luke *either. He shall be called Toran.*

"Why did you ask me 'what'?" Shannon asked Luke.

"Because you said 'Luke,' as if you planned to say something to me."

"Oh. No, I said 'Luke' to Roebor. He wanted to know your name. Which he doesn't like. He's rechristened you *Toran.*

And it's too late to offload Roebor. We left his body back up in Canada."

"His presence will kill you, Shannon. Surely you know that. And tell him I don't care for the name Roebor, either, so I'll call him Little Kitty. And forget 'Toran.' How does he like that?"

Little? I am not little. And what does a kitty look like?

Salesti, ever helpful, said, *kitty short word for kitten, means baby cat.*

Baby? I am no baby. Does he not remember I am grand in size both in this world and among my own kind? Does he not know I am full grown, a leader, a warrior, and a scientist? And what offends him about the name Toran? It is a strong name.

"Finding Essi should be pretty easy, so I won't have him on board long, Luke, and no, Roebor doesn't care for Little Kitty. And please don't call him that, because if I can hear you, he can hear you, and then I have to listen to him grouse about it. You, on the other hand, won't hear him call you anything. Sorry I mentioned it. Toran."

salesti believes toran makes joke to tease roebor. because you big, he calls you little. because you full grown, he calls you baby. salesti right, Daq?

"That's not funny," Luke said.

"Don't you start," Shannon said.

"Start what?" Luke asked.

"No, not you, sorry, I meant Salesti."

Yes, it is funny, Roebor said.

"It's funny that Salesti called me Daq?" Shannon asked Roebor.

"Daq? Roebor calls you Daq? Yes, that's funny," Luke said.

No, the name Daq is not funny. Toran said it was not funny that you called him Toran. I said it was funny.

shannon tells salesti do not start what, Daq?

"Call me Shannon, please, Salesti."

but roebor—

"Shannon," Shannon said. "On Earth, you two call me Shannon, please. On FireWorld, you can call me whatever you like."

The other two may call you Shannon, Roebor said. *But I shall call you Daq.*

Odin's eye. This conversation had spiraled way out of control. "Roebor. You never answered my question: how do we handle Tidak? Don't forget, he brought Toss along from Riverworld, which I don't even know how that happened, but we can't hurt Toss."

toss enters tidak to help essi flee, Salesti said.

"So Tidak came to Riverworld for the virus and that's why Essi ran to earth?"

Yes. Tidak—

Luke said, "And we have arrived." He pulled up in front of a long city block comprised of four rectangular, cream-colored buildings with brown trim, the paint beginning to chip and peel. Each identical, each four stories high. A double door stood at the end of each building.

Shannon reached for her car door. "I'll cast my colors. If Essi entered this place, I'll find her."

* * *

Two hours later Shannon had hop-walked on her crutch while casting the colors through all four floors of all four buildings, to be absolutely sure. She'd found no sign of Essi. She'd been certain that she'd find Essi in the young man's head. *Certain.* But if the guy lived behind one of these apartment doors, he didn't carry the alien child, or Shannon would have sensed Essi when she cast the colors from the hallway.

After the search, Luke took her to a drive-through to buy her a chocolate shake and a burger with fries. She gobbled them down, even though she'd eaten dinner just a few hours before. The second dinner didn't do much to re-energize her. She'd already lost the battle to replenish her energy faster than Salesti and Roebor drained it from her.

Five years earlier she'd been healthy and active when her alien visitors came on board: she barely managed to survive a week. This time, after everything that had happened, even with the extra rest and medical care she'd been enjoying, she doubted she could last four or five more days. She knew her body would shut down rapidly. It wouldn't take long for her die. *To die.*

She sprawled out now with her car seat back tilted almost flat like a bed, her eyes closed. She could feel Luke's eyes on her. Even so, she kept her eyes closed.

"I'm sorry the lead didn't pan out. I thought we'd found them; it seemed like such a good fit. I tired you for no reason," he said.

"No, we had to check it out. I thought we'd found them, too. And it may still be them; maybe they left the apartment. I think if I rest a minute, we can go on looking," she said, still without opening her eyes. "She has to be trying to find my house. Or—" Her eyes shot open. "Or, maybe she made it to the SeaQuarium. That's where she started out last time—and it was her departure point when she went back to Riverworld. It's close to the seashore; much easier for her to find than my house. Maybe she thinks I'll check there. Let's try it."

"But the SeaQuarium closed several hours ago."

"Yeah, I'll have to break in."

* * *

A half hour later, they had parked in the SeaQuarium staff lot, where the official vans with SQ logos stood silently waiting for the next educational trip to schools and libraries. A few scattered cars also dotted the lot. Luke parked in the shadow of one of the big vans and shut off the engine, but kept his hands locked on the steering wheel.

Shannon looked over at him. "What?"

"You do recall that I am still an officer of the law in this jurisdiction? That I almost lost my job the last time I bent the rules for you? That even now, five years later, I am persona non grata to some people in the mayor's office?"

"Right. Do you have a pair of lock cutters for that padlock on the gate? You stay in the car. It won't take me long to cast the colors for Essi. I can find her pretty quickly if she's here."

Luke gave his head a little shake. "See that squad car?" He pointed. "Somebody on the force moonlights as security here. As we speak, that officer is patrolling inside the fence, walking the perimeter and the pathways between exhibits.

What makes you think a person with Essi on board could avoid detection all this time? Or that you can?"

"Maybe she jumped from her original host to a zoo keeper in the Marine Mammal Center and from them to . . . to a beluga! That makes perfect sense."

"Perfect sense to you. But would little Essi think of that?"

"One way to find out. Do you have lock cutters or not?"

∗ ∗ ∗

Ten minutes later Shannon quietly made her way on her crutch down the hilly slope of the SeaQuarium, casting her colors, and doing her best to stay away from the pole lamps that dotted the pathways. No sign of the security guard. Nor of Essi.

She reached the Marine Mammal Center, and then the beluga enclosure. She couldn't reach the private area of the exhibit to approach the belugas without being seen, because the staff had locked the door from the public area to the fish house. The fish house, in turn, led to the private area.

Instead, she climbed over the railing that prevented spectators from trying to touch the belugas. She scrambled and slid down a ten-foot, gray concrete, angled wall to a path that encircled the pool, normally accessible to staff only. *Ouch. That hurt the poor ankle. If she kept this up, she'd break the cast again.* Crouching low, she grabbed the crutch in her good hand and limped to one of the platforms jutting out into the pool where trainers asked the belugas to go through their behaviors.

SeaQuarium visitors thought of the behaviors as "tricks," a part of the show, and it was true that staff couldn't resist asking the whales to perform some of their more spectacular behaviors for the crowds, like arcing out of the water in unison or sliding up onto the platform, flukes raised high behind them. But the behaviors weren't tricks for the amusement of spectators; the staff biologists had designed them all to aid with the evaluation and care of the whales.

Sometimes Shannon missed being a part of those "shows." But not often. Not since Essi had given her the gift to understand the emotions and images of her beloved Juneau, to understand how Juneau hated this place, how the tiny pool had slowly driven her mad.

Now she focused on the three whales that floated quietly, half asleep, in the main viewing area. She carefully avoided touching their wild thoughts. Her heart would break all over again to feel the same desperation that Juneau had known here. *Someday, soon,* she imaged to them, *you will all be free.*

She cast the colors. No Essi.

Five belugas should occupy the pool. Two more must be resting in the adjacent private pool, connected to the viewing pool by an open gate. That pool curved away out of sight behind a concrete wall made to look like rock. Shannon cast the colors again, concentrating on those two whales, even though she couldn't actually see their beautiful white forms.

No Essi.

As Shannon stood, deflated, shoulders stooped, already tired again, and not too happy about having to scramble back up the steep angled wall behind her, she heard someone whistling cheerfully as they made their way down the main path toward the Marine Mammal Center.

The security guard!

Shannon looked frantically for a hiding spot. Underwater wall lights cast the pool in a soft blue glow. One overhead light shone from the far side of the water, bathing the whole area in yellow—and brightly illuminating Shannon.

Beyond the far side of the pool stood another concrete wall, smooth, over fifteen feet high, that separated the beluga pools from the orca enclosure. No way could she climb over that.

No bulky equipment or machinery lined the path around the pool to provide Shannon with cover.

Nowhere to hide.

Anyone glancing into the enclosure would spot Shannon for sure. She had not choice but to slide as quietly as possible from the platform into the water.

Odin's eye. The cold enveloped her like an icy glove. Again. She felt immediately sick to her stomach. Making her way along the concrete wall, around to the gate between the pools as quickly as she could, she half-swam, half propelled herself along by pushing against the wall with her one good hand. Her braid trailed in the water behind her. The cold became unbearable. Energy drained from her like juice from a sieve. Her arm cast took on water, though she tried to keep it dry.

Three curious belugas stirred and swam her way. She didn't worry about them becoming aggressive except, per-haps, the big male. He might not like an unknown person in his pool with his females. In which case he might let her know she was unwelcome. With his teeth spaced farther apart than human teeth, and designed more for holding fish than tearing and ripping them, a bite from him wouldn't slice her up as a shark bite would, but the power in his jaw could hurt.

Hurry.

And here came big Sitka, the only male in the group, right on cue, to give Shannon a firm message about whose pool she had wandered into. Shannon gently pulled her legs out in front of her, bending her good leg so her foot tucked under, leaving her new fiberglass cast to greet the whale. Sitka placed his big mouth over the cast and clamped down. The cast broke. Sitka released her foot.

Odin's eye, that hurt. She continued on her way, the whale trailing her to see what she would do next.

She'd barely slipped on through the gate when she heard the whistling travel past the walrus and seal enclosures, and the Pacific white-sided dolphin pool to the beluga pool. The steps paused and the whistling stopped.

Her teeth chattering, her body shaking, Shannon didn't wait to find out what had caused the guard to pause; probably the unusual activity of the belugas, which now followed Shannon through the gate. She moved further out of sight along the wall between the pools.

"Where you going, kids?" The guard, a woman, said. She sounded vaguely curious. Not alarmed. Shannon knew that voice: Londy Taney. She used to be Luke's partner, and had drawn the assignment to guard Shannon on several occasions when Shannon first feared being murdered, and then when she fell under suspicion of committing murder. They'd become friends or at least friendly, and for one small moment Shannon almost called out to seek her help.

But no, Officer Taney couldn't overlook Shannon's breaking into the SeaQuarium and taking a swim with the belugas. Shannon held her breath.

Officer Taney paused a moment and then said to the belugas who had disappeared around the corner with Shannon, "Okay then. I guess I can take a hint. Later, dudes."

Once the officer's whistling faded, Shannon took off as quickly as she could across the pool to the steps on the far side that allowed staff biologists in wetsuits easy access to in-water training. She pulled herself clumsily onto the first of the steps with the quickly-fading remnants of her energy. Sitka had not followed her across the pool.

So cold, so damn cold.

Her fingers touched the rough concrete of the pool deck. Only a few more steps on her good hand and her knees, and her legs would be completely out of the water. She splashed as she climbed out.

Too much noise. But Shannon could do little to quiet her exit; her exhaustion and the numbness enveloping her limbs ruined any hope of a quiet ascent. Out of the water and completely spent, she stopped for a moment and lay, stomach down, exactly where her half crawl had deposited her.

She listened. The whistling had ceased, but now the officer was tapping a rhythm on the guard rail as she passed the orca enclosure.

Shannon struggled in and out of consciousness. She mustn't go under; if she lay here all night, she'd die. She needed dry clothes, food, heat. And when she went missing, Luke would come looking for her, once again breaking the law. If he didn't find her out on the pathways, he'd raise the alarm, and the police would be all over him. *Fight it. She must fight the need to close her eyes. Fight the blackness that pushed inward from the edges of her vision.*

salesti said, *stay awake, shannon. salesti and roebor talk to shannon. remember essi. remember the virus. salesti calls luke.*

"No, don't call Luke. I'll make it without him." Fat chance.

Come on, Daq, you may be puny, but you are strong of mind. Stand up. Get out to the path so Toran can locate you. Up you get.

Right. But no way could she stand up; she could muster no energy for that; she tried rising upright so that she could push forward on her knees. Blackness enveloped her and she almost fell. *Nope, nope, not working, too dizzy.* She lay back down.

Crawl on all fours then, Daq. It will suffice.

Shannon's whole body cried *no, let me be.* How could she crawl anyway, with only one good arm, and one caved-in, wet cast to contend with?

Well, they would have to do.

She'd leave the crutch behind; too much trouble. She emitted a tiny laugh: a single crutch lying beside the pool would cause an interesting furor in the morning when the staff arrived. Shannon wished she could be a fly on the wall.

But she was stonewalling; she must move.

Slowly, slowly she inched her legs up under her until she could pull herself onto her hands and knees. She placed her good arm in front of her, flat on the ground from hand to elbow. At the same time, she tested the same position for her left arm, conveniently already bent in half by the cast. *Hurt like bloody hell.* Tears streamed down her cheeks. She moved her good arm forward, brought the cast-enclosed arm up even with it, knees following.

Good arm, bad arm, knees, tears. Good arm, bad arm, knees. The blackness at the edge of her vision grew. She was sobbing now. Good arm, bad arm, knees.

good job shannon. keep going. for essi. for earth. for fireworld.

Effective. Well done, Daq.

Odin's eye. Deja vu all over again. She'd struggled from the pools to the Fish House for help five years earlier, after the lavender lightning that brought Essi had enveloped her and Juneau, leaving Juneau unconscious and drowning, and leaving Shannon physically wrecked.

Not a performance she'd hoped to repeat. But she'd made it then. She'd make it now.

Slowly she crawled forward to the Fish House door. She rose up on her knees, squeezed her eyes closed against the dizziness, and tested the door. Open. No need to lock it, since the fish house door to the pubic would be locked.

Open the door, back to hands and knees. Good arm, bad arm, knees, tears. Through the fish house to the door leading to the public pathway. Deadbolt. Turn lock. Through the door. On the path.

She'd made it. More tears.

But the effort had cost too much. Shannon collapsed. She rolled onto her right side so that she could cradle her broken arm against her. Her tears became sobs.

She had nothing left.

She lay curled on the concrete for what seemed like hours, but she knew only minutes had ticked by; how many she couldn't say. Her eyes closed, she listened for the guard. Her concentration wavered. She felt the warm night breeze off the ocean on her cheek, even here inside the SeaQuarium walls. She listened to the stirrings of the crows that haunted the trees on the slopes below the park grounds. The familiar tang of the chlorine-scented pools prickled her senses. The smell reminded her of back when, back when . . . back. . . .

"Cara. What in god's name?" Luke appeared, scooping her up in his arms. Again. *Odin's eye*, she'd always managed to be so competent and independent, except with *him*.

"Hiding," she murmured.

"Essi?"

She shook her head no, and the sobs began again.

"Guard?"

"She's on her way to the aquarium. It's Londy. We have time to get out," Shannon said faintly.

Luke rushed her up the path, out the gate, to his car. He helped her into the back seat where she could lie down. In his trunk he found an emergency blanket. It crinkled as he wrapped it around her and laid her on the back seat. He cranked up the car's heater to its highest setting. Then he broke the speed limit all the way to her home.

So, Luke had broken the law for her again. Breaking and entering at the SeaQuarium, now speeding well above the limit. Shannon couldn't keep screwing up his chances with his department. He was already dangerously close to losing his job.

Excellent effort, Daq. For a minute, I thought you would die and take us with you. But I am proud of you.

Sweet. High praise from the big guy.

And then Salesti said, *shannon, salesti knows what shannon must do to find essi.*

CHAPTER TWENTY-FOUR

"WHAT MUST I DO, Salesti? Clearly, the 'guess and go' method isn't working too well," Shannon said.

shannon visits essence in mind of shannon. shannon finds essence of independence. shannon shows essence of essi to independence. shannon casts wide, wider than shannon ever casts. casts all of ocean city with help of indy.

"Independence? What does my Indy have to do with this? Why do I want her essence?"

"What about Indy?" Luke asked.

Indy? Roebor asked.

"Salesti says I need to connect Indy's essence to Essi's essence, and together we can cast the whole city looking for Essi. Indy is my mastiff, Roebor. Or she used to be. She sacrificed herself to save my life five years ago."

"That confuses me on so many levels," Luke said as he pulled up in Shannon's driveway. "But right now, let's get you dried out, so as not to invite too many questions we cannot answer, and then you will go to the hospital. Give me your phone, I'm calling the doctor who took care of you last time this happened. Tell me where to find her number."

She pulled her cell phone out of her purse, ran through the contacts until she reached Dr. Bennett, and handed the phone over to Luke. He talked to Dr. B., who suggested they meet at her office in an hour.

When they reached Shannon's house, he said, "You stay put; I'm coming around."

No protest about being able to do everything herself tonight; she needed all the help she could get. Alternatively, she might just spend the night on the back seat of Luke's car because otherwise she'd have to move, and no part of her body wished to place itself in motion.

He circled around the front of his shiny, black Prius, opened her car door, and helped her to her feet. "Can you stand?"

"No," she said.

He wrapped one arm around her waist and gently pulled her good arm around his neck. As a result Shannon's feet, floating several inches off the pavement, had very little to do. She didn't complain.

* * *

"Again?" Dr. Bennett said, as she met Luke and Shannon at her darkened office door, keys in hand.

"Again," Shannon said.

"All right, we're going with completely waterproof this time."

Dr. Bennett took X-rays and recast her arm—on account of seepage that required new dressings for her arm wounds—and ankle—on account of the completely busted cast. She thoroughly examined Shannon, and confirmed what Shannon already knew: soon her body would shut down, because Salesti and Roebor required much too much energy, especially Roebor. Dr. Bennett gave her three to four days, unless she could offload her visitors, and even then she could die, if her body couldn't beat the damage already done.

Dr. B. didn't mince words. Shannon liked that about her.

Shannon's survival, Dr. B. continued, also depended on her taking on no more visitors.

"No more visitors," Shannon said. *Except Essi and Toss.*

"Is the little alien child there?" Dr. B. whispered near Shannon's ear so that her attending nurse, who'd also answered the late night call, would not hear.

"No, no, a different crowd this time. One I know will enchant you. The other, your reaction may be different."

Do not hurt the feelings of Salesti, Roebor said.

Shannon, despite her overwhelming fatigue, managed a small chuckle in unison with Salesti's tinkling laugh.

What? Roebor asked.

"What?" Dr. B. asked.

"Never mind, just the hysteria of a depleted mind."

* * *

Once home with a new crutch, thanks to Dr. B., and ensconced on her couch under her favorite blue-and-green blanket, Shannon asked Salesti to explain how it could possibly help to bring Indy's essence into the search. Even after all this time, thinking of Indy filled her heart with sorrow and longing for her brave mastiff. The thought of disturbing Indy's essence troubled her deeply.

sense of smell stays with her essence, Salesti explained. *shannon uses.*

"Come on, Salesti, that seems a little far fetched. Her olfactory glands haven't survived; her nose hasn't survived. So how could her sense of smell survive?"

shannon not knows what survives in essence of independence. salesti knows. sense of smell survives. not the whole dog lives within shannon but remember—more than the memory survives; shannon knows this. more than the memory.

"Okay. Say her sense of smell still attaches to her essence in my head. How does that help me?"

Luke entered the room with a tray of meat dishes, set them in front of Shannon, and mouthed, "Eat."

Shannon mouthed "thanks" back.

mind of shannon not very open tonight. poor shannon overwhelmed. how shannon uses essence simple. indy uses scent and helps show shannon essi.

"All right. Say that Indy's sense of smell has survived in her essence; say that Indy can hunt Essi down, why do I need Indy's help at all, if I can cast my colors as far as you say from right here in the comfort of my own living room? I really don't want to disturb her if I don't need to."

Salesti buzzed with impatience. *shannon too weak.*

For Luke's benefit, Shannon repeated Salesti's explanation, then said, "Let's give it a whirl, then. I'm not getting any younger here, folks. Or healthier."

"It can wait until tomorrow, cara. Right now you probably can't cast the colors any farther than you can cast me. Sleep first."

"Luke, the clock is ticking. I may not have many nights to accomplish everything we need to do. Why should I waste one on sleep?"

"Because you will fail if you don't rest. Would failure do Essi any good, you back in the hospital, unable to help her at all? Back me up here, Salesti."

Shannon heard buzzing and tinkling, although not a laughing sort of tinkling this time; more of a ruminating kind of tinkling.

hard choice luke gives salesti. yes, time for shannon runs out; shannon should not wait. but shannon stronger tomorrow than now. She hesitated for a moment. *salesti says sleep now, get stronger, up early tomorrow to cast.*

"She backs you up," Shannon said to Luke, and shrugged "Two against one. So I'm going to bed." She stirred, trying to stand, but her good leg wobbled and her head spun. Luke reached her side in a flash.

"I'll help you," he said, taking her firmly at the waist. "Why don't you ask Salesti if invoking Indy will drain you more quickly than if you let sleeping dogs lie?"

Shannon shook her head. "Waste of time. I don't really have any choice."

When they reached her bedroom, she pointed Luke toward her bed, which was the only destination she cared about, fell onto the soft covers, and slept a sleep deeper than midnight until almost six the next morning.

* * *

When she awoke, Luke had gone. He had, however, left a cardboard box full of edibles by her bed, a trick she'd developed last time around, so that she wouldn't awake to find herself too weak to climb out of bed and make it to the kitchen. It had happened.

She pulled on a new pair of dark green sweat pants and a green T-shirt that matched her dark, sea-lettuce-green eyes, sat down on the edge of the bed, and downed a quart of orange juice and a package of string cheese. Then she headed downstairs on her crutch to make breakfast.

After she'd squared herself and Narci away food-wise, she curled up in her favorite chair and said to Salesti, "Okay, let's do this thing." She waited for instructions.

salesti not tells shannon how, only that shannon must.

Odin's eye. Now what? Shannon laid her head back against her armchair's soft microfiber fabric, closed her eyes, and concentrated. She imagined that she floated forward, far inside her brain, toward a quiet room, because that's how she thought of the place deep in her subconscious where the essence of the others had been left behind, more than memories, less than whole beings. She entered the room, a large dark place with a ceiling so high she couldn't find it. The essence of Essi, Salesti, Juneau, Indy, Becky, the young man David, Luke, even the raven glowed softly in the darkness. She floated to the powder shining the deepest of midnight purple, her Independence, her Indy, her beloved and loyal friend.

It seemed sacrilegious to even touch it, as Salesti had directed. Tentatively, she reached out both her hands and lifted out a scoop of the powder-like substance, or at least her mind showed it to her as powder so she could comprehend it.

Shannon laughed quietly: here, at least, she still could use two hands. And two legs.

The powder radiated warmth. As she held it, she saw images of Indy, curled up on her kitchen floor. Loping around the back yard after a soccer ball, stretched full out on her half of Shannon's king size bed and taking up every inch of it, slurping a big tongue on Shannon's face and leaving a gooey residue behind. She could *feel* Indy, as if the dog were here right now in the essence room. Shannon looked down. An attentive translucent Indy sat at her feet.

The essence sifted silently through Shannon's fingers to float slowly back to join the rest. Indy faded from her view.

Indy, she breathed. She missed her so much.

Reaching out again, she brought powder to her face, smelled it. It smelled of green fields and store-bought treats, of wet dog fur and Indy's favorite dog bed. She rubbed a handful against her face and felt it stick, like butterfly wings, like pollen from yellow dandelions. She let her hands fall back over the rest of the essence to allow the powder to drift down.

That would have to do. She couldn't bear to lose any more of Indy's essence by disturbing it.

I want to view this place in Shannon's mind. Why can't you and I join her? Roebor asked Salesti.

some places not for roebor.

Will my essence be there too, when I am gone?

yes, essence of roebor there.

What color shall it be?

palest silver blue, the color of eyes of roebor, of fire of roebor.

And it will be available to Daq in times of need, as Indy's is?

yes, just so.

Hmm. I find this satisfactory.

Shannon floated from Indy over to Essi's powder, lavender and sparkling, from which arose a soft humming, so very like the little alien child. Again she leaned in, gently scooped up a handful of the powder-like substance, and brought it to her face. She inhaled it deeply.

The little girl appeared beside her, translucent like Indy, looking just as she did the first time Shannon caught sight of her. Her skin glistened silvery lavender even in the faint glow of the room. Her hair, the palest blond, the tint of the early evening moon, floated around her face. A tiny mouth below a tiny nose, between tiny ears. And those eyes. Those huge, innocent, silvery-green eyes, deep as cedar trees. Essi took Shannon's hand. The little lavender fingers snuggled warm and small and solid in Shannon's. Those enormous eyes regarded her with solemn trust.

Shannon remembered Essi curling up in her lap in the Great Room and hugging her around the waist when she'd returned from some task. Essi gazing solemnly up into Shannon's face with her round emerald eyes. Essi softly humming to calm Shannon and Juneau when they needed it. How Shannon had missed her when Salesti took her home.

But Essi hadn't been able to stay, of course. Her very presence over the course of a week had nearly killed Shannon.

Essi's essence smelled just as Shannon's perfume now smelled, since Essi had bestowed the scent on Shannon, but here, so close to Essi's powder, the scent was overpowering, in a glorious way, engulfing her in the mysterious, the other-worldly, the enticingly unknowable.

If only she could remain here, holding the child's hand, or the essence of it, anyway, for a few hours, a few days.

shannon cannot stay. shannon must find essi.

Reluctantly Shannon returned the powder to Essi's mound. She turned and floated out the door, out of her mind and up, until she opened her eyes and found herself staring eye-to-eye into Narci's big blue sapphires.

* * *

The cat silently perched on the arm of Shannon's chair, waiting patiently for Shannon to surface.

Shannon rubbed Narci's whiskers and under her chin.

"What's up kiddo?" she asked the cat. Narci put her paws up on the back of the chair and raised her head, staring at the front door.

Almost immediately Shannon's multicolored haze appeared, announcing the imminent arrival of some unknown person. The doorbell rang.

"You too, eh? You're even quicker than I am." Shannon said to the cat, as the doorbell rang, and she pulled herself from the comfort of the chair and grabbed her crutch.

Luke stood patiently dangling a bag of groceries in each hand. He thrust them forward.

"Daily food delivery," he said. "Have you found Essi yet?"

Shannon took the two bags in one hand and opened the door. "Thanks. I've been to visit Indy's essence and Essi's, and I'm about to cast the colors for her. Come on in."

"Here, give me those back, and I'll put them away. You go in the living room, and start casting."

"Thanks, Luke." Resettling under her blanket—it seemed so cold in the room for summertime—Shannon said, "No pointers for this part either, I suppose, Salesti?"

no pointers.

I have a pointer; wipe that dog smell off your face. It troubles me.

"Sorry, Roebor, no can do. I need it. Put on your big boy pants and suck it up."

Pants? I do not wear pants. I have no pants to put on. And why would I? The very notion makes me laugh. Shannon has lost traction, Salesti. Tell me again why we picked her for our vessel.

Salesti said, *earth people talk in metaphors. on fireworld dragonpanthers more straightforward. roebor learns or roebor remains confused. and shannon perhaps more thoughtful in choices of words.*

"All right, fair enough. My apologies, Roebor. I meant to say I require Indy's essence, so you will have to endure. I know you have it in you."

Yes of course I can endure. I can endure great pain and suffering. I can endure great hunger and thirst. I can en—"

"Exactly. So now, quiet, please, everybody, so I can concentrate."

Shannon cast the colors in her usual way, except the lavender, Essi's color, glimmered blindingly bright among the other colors. Shannon reached the end of the range she'd always assumed to be her limit. Then she redoubled her effort and cast farther and wider.

The colors and shapes within the room around her disappeared. Narci's form faded. Luke's clattering in the kitchen tapered into silence. Indy's form appeared again within her mind. Shannon joined her there. Ghost-Indy and Shannon searched along the trail of colors, searched everywhere. Indy sought Essi's scent. Back and forth she ran, searching for a trace, a hint of Essi's passage. Shannon followed the dog. Farther and farther they went, wider and longer their track expanded through the city. Soon they had covered every square mile within the city limits, and expanded out into the countryside. Indy searched, and—

There. Shannon's eyes opened wide. *Surely not.* Surely the child would not travel back to the place that still caused Shannon the worst nightmares of her life.

But she had. Essi must have hitched rides with hosts from the SeaQuarium out to the maintenance center, a long way west of the city along the shoreline. The place where a good friend had died, where her best friend had gone insane. The very thought of the maintenance center turned Shannon's stomach to a slab of lard, thick, oily, heavy, unpleasant. Now she would have to go back.

* * *

"But why would Essi go there? How could she find it? It sounds crazy," Luke said when she brought him up to speed.

"I've been trying to understand it too, Luke. It *does* seem crazy. She retained some vague idea of the place, I suppose, because she accompanied me there—you remember. Any of the truck drivers going out there from the SeaQuarium could've taken her. And maybe she went there because Tidak has no sense of places Essi might go, does he, Roebor?"

Tidak captured Essi. Did I not tell you? Then the Riverworld boy Toss helped her escape and Tidak in turn captured him, but Tidak could have interrogated Essi about Earth while he held her captive. Your home, the SeaQuarium, these he may have known because Essi would have touched upon them as he forced her to tell her story. This maintenance center, I do not know."

"*Now* you tell me. But why would he interrogate her about Earth?"

Ah. Roebor cleared his throat. *You see, if we cannot find the antidote for the disease that wipes out my people and all our food sources, we will need a new planet.*

Shannon grabbed her braid and held on tight. *Better get that damned virus-antidote to Roebor pronto.*

CHAPTER TWENTY-FIVE

SHANNON HELPED HERSELF to the rhubarb pie Luke had carried in and placed on the coffee table. While she tucked into it, she related the story of Essi and Tidak to Luke. "As soon as I'm finished," Shannon said in a muffled voice, her mouth full of pie, ""I'm going out to the maintenance center. With any luck, Tidak has no idea that's where she went."

Before she'd managed to work through even a quarter of the pie, haze appeared at the front door.

Shannon glanced over. "Somebody's coming," she said.

A few minutes later, someone knocked on the door. Luke gave her a quizzical look; she shrugged. "No idea. Kota maybe."

Luke pushed up off the couch and made for the door. He'd opened it only a few inches when someone on the other side kicked it hard. The door flew back, catching Luke by surprise and knocking him backward. A tall beefy man barged through, leaving the door open behind him.

The raven, Shannon saw, swooped in behind the intruder.

Roebor roared, and this time the roar passed Shannon's lips in a screaming rage.

"Tidak."

"Roebor—that's the human vessel you have chosen? A puny Earth woman? I will easily end your life, and hers."

Shannon—Roebor—growled low and long, her upper lip curling to reveal her teeth.

I claim the right to fight him, Daq. Turn your body over to me for this battle, or he will kill us all.

Shannon backed up toward the dining room, wincing on her overworked ankle, and talking fast. "Luke? That's Tidak. I'll let Roebor take the lead. Get a weapon. He means to kill us."

"First I want the Riverworld girl. Give her to me," Tidak said.

"I don't have her," Shannon said.

"Do not lie to me."

"She doesn't lie, Tidak," Roebor growled, the voice issuing from Shannon's mouth, and yet not hers. "We haven't yet laid eyes on her."

Look at that. Another clever prevaricator who could wrap a lie in the truth.

A bark of frustration escaped the man whom Tidak had displaced. "Where can she hide? I have searched the places she remembered in this city. She has vanished."

Good. He doesn't know about the maintenance center. Essi probably hadn't thought of it in a long time. Nothing but bad memories there. Or maybe she held it back on purpose once she'd given Tidak as much as she dared. Good girl, Essi.

As they spoke, Tidak stalked by Luke, who had hit the back of his head against the staircase when the door slammed into him, and who now pulled himself slowly to his feet.

Tidak kicked viciously, connecting a sharp cowboy boot to Luke's stomach. Luke buckled into a ball.

Shannon frantically surveyed the room for a weapon. The lamp on the end table by her chair lay closest to hand. She grabbed it and yanked the electric cord out of the wall. Raising it up, she wielded it like a baseball slugger, and backed toward the dining room.

"Over here, you coward. Pick on somebody standing up. Or do I scare you too much?" Shannon said, hoping Tidak possessed an ego the size of Roebor's.

Tidak screamed in outrage and leaped cleanly over the couch toward her.

Apparently he did.

Roebor said, almost gently, *My turn, Daq.* Shannon experienced the strangest sensation—that Roebor had quietly taken her shoulders and moved her behind him. Suddenly she became a spectator, at the forefront of everything that transpired, yet no longer in control.

Roebor hefted the lamp, as if to take measure of its weight and balance, and began to circle clockwise around Tidak. Without the crutch, her ankle screamed every time she put weight on her cast. But now her limp diminished.

Roebor ignored the pain better than Shannon.

Tidak turned to face him and attacked. Roebor stepped into the swing and brought the lamp around right into Tidak's face, as if he'd played baseball all his life. The lamp hit Tidak so hard that the wood base splintered and broke in two. Tidak stumbled back, and then fell to his knees.

Roebor immediately fisted Shannon's hand and swung it in an underhand upward arc into Tidak's nose.

Odin's eye, that hurt. Shannon shook her hand, trying to relieve the pain.

The force of the blow drove the bones of Tidak's nose inward into his brain, finishing him.

Luke, who hadn't seen the damage Roebor had caused, chose that exact moment to step up behind Tidak, and deliver a karate chop to the back of his neck.

"Luke, no!" Shannon said. She'd gone through this long ago: Tidak would seize the slightest human contact to escape the dying body of the poor man he'd invaded. He'd shoot through Luke's hand like a meteorite to his brain.

The unlucky person who'd been forced to host Tidak fell to the ground, limp and lifeless.

Luke rose to his full height and grinned with a sneer and a narrowing of his eyes, in a way that Luke had never done. "I could learn to like this body," Luke, but not Luke, said.

"Tidak," Roebor raged.

"Hide, Luke," Shannon screamed, "Find a secret vault deep in your own subconscious. Lock the door. Don't let him push you out."

Roebor wrested control again, picked up a dining room chair and said "Come on Tidak, let's finish this."

No, Roebor, Luke's in there; we can't hurt his body.

Tidak will hurt him, Shannon, count on it. Tidak controls the body now.

Okay. Think of the Luke-thing as Tidak, not Luke. Yet as long as Luke could still be alive, they could not destroy Luke's body.

Tidak started toward Shannon, but, at that moment, the raven, which had settled atop Shannon's bookcase and had quietly watched the encounter between the stranger and Shannon unfold, dove down on Tidak's head, claws digging at his scalp, then his eyes.

Tidak roared at the bird and swung his arms wildly, but the raven fluttered just beyond his reach, darting in to use his claws again each time Tidak left him an opening. Roebor advanced on Tidak while the bird kept him preoccupied. But Tidak had suffered enough at the hands of the bird and Roebor for the present. He fled out the front door.

* * *

The bird returned to the top of the bookcase and preened his feathers.

"Well done, raven. I'll have to give you a name if you keep this up." And then, to Roebor, Shannon said, "You almost had him. Good work."

Shannon slowly put the chair down and slid it into place neatly at the dining room table, then came back into the living room, and sat down heavily in her reading chair.

Luke.

Had he listened to her when Tidak invaded and fled to a safe refuge in his mind? Did Tidak surprise him before he could react, and push his consciousness out into the ether? Or were they locked in a life and death battle of the wills, each trying to eject the other, even now?

Luke. She'd meant for him to stay safe. Now look what she'd done. Shannon's stomach heaved, and she ejected the remains of her rhubarb pie onto the living room carpet.

She sank back in the chair. Even if he'd found a hiding place, the chances of his mind surviving intact after a cruel alien creature had taken the helm were slim; the tragic experiences of her friends had proven that much. And the longer Tidak controlled him, the smaller the likelihood Luke could recover. She brought her knees up to her chest and hugged them with her good arm. She began to rock herself. *She couldn't lose him. She couldn't.*

* * *

shannon: salesti and roebor and shannon must go. tidak learns from luke where essi hides. shannon and salesti and roebor reach essi first.

Essi. She'd find a way to get Luke back, she damn well would, but right now little Essi, virus and all, needed her help. Yet fatigue wrapped around her like tropical vines, tugging her down, holding her fast. Nothing sounded as good to her as curling up in her chair, pulling her blanket up to her chin, and sleeping.

Please, Daq. I know you feel the stress of our presence. When I took charge of your body, I sensed the extreme pressure Salesti and I have applied to your system, and I frankly do not know how you have managed to carry on. For my part in this, I apologize. But the Riverworld child depends on you. Earth and FireWorld depend on you. Can you find the strength to go forward one more time?

Huh. Who knew the dragonpanther could play nicely with others?

"Thank you, Roebor. I can try."

Shannon struggled up from her chair. "But I need to pack some food," she said, her body and her voice numb. She ignored her crutch. It was too late for her ankle now; if damage had been done by Roebor rushing around on her cast, so be it. She'd see to it later. Plus, she couldn't fuss with a crutch; she needed her one good hand free for packing, for carrying, and maybe for fighting Tidak. She limped up the stairs to change her clothes. Then she packed a knapsack with snacks, tucked Narci into her kennel—Shannon might need her little sapphire-eyed friend—and took first the cat and then the food to her car, which had been stored all this time in her garage.

* * *

Her neighbor had checked in periodically to start up her little VW bug; fingers crossed he'd done a good job. Shannon had sold the VW she'd driven five years earlier. She'd loved the thing; she'd owned it since her college days. But she associated too many bad, bad memories with it from the alien troubles. She had to let it go. She bought a new VW bug, which she simply called Bug, vowing never to get too attached to a car again, just in case she ever accumulated another set of memories she'd have to put behind her some day.

That day might be at hand.

She pressed the power button. The engine turned over without missing a beat.

Thank Odin.

Driving one-handed proved a frustrating challenge. First Shannon tried to wedge her cast in between her body and the steering wheel. It didn't fit. She slid the seat back; now her cast fit but the extended reach to the gas pedal and brake for her legs felt unfamiliar and uncomfortable, although she needed the room for her ankle cast in any event. *She'd just have to get used it.* Good thing she'd chosen an automatic transmission; she tucked her foot with the cast far over to the left out of the way.

Then she tried several methods of turning the steering wheel one-handed until she gained at least the illusion of added control. At last she'd bolstered her bravery enough to strike out for the SeaQuarium's maintenance facility over on the coast.

CHAPTER TWENTY-SIX

SHANNON KEPT AN EYE ON THE REARVIEW MIRROR to check whether she'd been followed by Tidak—she tried hard not to think of the body as Luke's. No sign of Luke's Prius appeared in her review mirror, even along the Old Coast Road, where she encountered only sparse traffic. Perhaps Tidak hadn't thought she'd leave as quickly as she did, or maybe Tidak had quickly stolen her destination from Luke's memory, and had already pulled ahead of them. Shannon wouldn't know until she reached the maintenance center.

A half hour later Shannon approached the facility. Now, where would Essi be hiding—or more accurately, in whom she would be hiding?

Essi could be on board someone who worked on the pumps that kept the water flowing from the ocean to the SeaQuarium pools, or the coolant equipment that lowered the water's temperature for the northern Pacific residents of the SeaQuarium. Might be riding on board a cat or dog. Probably not a truck driver who went out each day on various tasks—Essi wouldn't have risked that. A secretary. A janitor. The big boss. Who knew?

The final hill loomed in front of her. She'd soon have the answer. She crested the summit and searched immediately for Luke's Prius; no sign of it yet.

She drove cautiously down to the facility. As she approached, she avoided looking directly at the low aluminum-sided maintenance building. Her friend had died right at the single door facing the parking area. The gun. The blood. She remembered it all as clearly as she remembered the exact color of Luke's eyes.

The entrance gate stood open and welcoming. She pulled into the parking lot and parked, hiding in the shadow of a large SeaQuarium truck.

Time to cast her colors. The rainbow haze formed in front of her, stretching out to encompass the entire building, the silvery gleam of Essi's lavender blazing brightest.

"Come on, Essi, sweetheart. Salesti and I have come for you."

heeere. essssi heeere.

Is that her? Roebor asked.

yes, Salesti answered.

"Yes! I know her location. I'll have to go inside."

* * *

Shannon climbed from the Bug and hurried into the building in limp-walk fashion as fast as her ailing ankle allowed. She passed down the familiar long hall with doors on either side. Today, while some doors remained closed as before, most stood open, people inside clacking away at computer keypads, frowning down at documents, standing in front of file cabinets, sipping coffee.

She moved without hesitation down the hall, around the corner, to the lunch room. Several people glanced up from the round tables that occupied the greater part of the space and then looked back down at books they'd brought with them, or turned back to conversations they'd interrupted.

"She's in here," Shannon said under her breath, "Somewhere."

indy, whispered Salesti.

Why do you whisper, Salesti? whispered Roebor.

because shannon whispers, whispered Salesti.

But you don't need—

indy, indy with you, Salesti whispered.

Shannon visited the essence of her mastiff and beckoned her ghostly form. Immediately they picked up the spicy, exotic Riverworld scent of Essi up ahead. Casually strolling toward the refrigerator, and then beyond, Shannon peered at the counter space stretching along the wall.

A coffee maker. A microwave. A sink. No Essi. She should be here.

Cupboards. She opened each cupboard in turn. Nothing.

"Can I help you find something?"

Shannon turned to find a woman with messy, perm-fried, orange hair, a pair of bifocals perched on her nose, and a straw—a straw?—tucked behind her ear, staring at Shannon expectantly. "Boy, you look like you've been through hell," the woman added, gaping openly at Shannon's pale face, her arm and ankle casts, her bruises and bandages.

Most of Shannon's bruises had faded by that point, but several of the biggest and most insistent still dotted Shannon's skin in shades of an unfortunate greenish-brown. *Yes; yes she had been through hell.* Shannon ignored the comment and addressed the woman's offer of help.

"Oh, thanks. A friend of mine came in here when she visited somebody the other day and she thinks she lost her, uh, earring here. I happened to be in the vicinity." *In the vicinity? This place sat in the middle of nowhere, fool.* "So I said I'd drop by and look for it. I thought someone might've found it and stuck it in one of these cabinets. But no such luck."

"We have a lost and found box in that big metal cabinet in the back," the woman said, pointing an ink-stained index finger across her chest and back toward the far corner of the room. "Maybe it's there."

"Oh, great! Thanks."

As she turned to trudge to the back to make a perfunctory search for the nonexistent earring, Shannon heard Essi's soft hum. She squinted closely at the small gap between the refrigerator and the counter.

And there he sat on the floor, a little gray-brown creature, no bigger than a dormouse, with bright black eyes and a tiny whiskers twitching on a tiny face.

And, judging by the scent and the sound, with Essi on board.

Essi! Can you get the mouse to venture out? Will it bite if I pick it up?

yesss and no.

Hopefully that meant yes, the mouse will come out, and no, it won't bite. *Stay quiet for just a minute and I'll be right back.*

Shannon dutifully pawed through the lost and found box, noting an interesting paperback or two, a beautiful orange-and-white silk scarf, a toothbrush, a fork, a single argyle sock—*just one?*—and various other sundries. On her way back around the room, she took a paper cup from a stack next to the coffee machine as if to pour herself a cup, and allowed her purse to slip off her shoulder by the refrigerator.

Bending down to retrieve it, she placed the coffee cup on its side. *Hurry, Essi, into the cup.*

The mouse scurried into the cup and Shannon hoisted her purse's strap back on her shoulder while she gently turned the cup upward.

Shannon walked back out of the lunch room, down the hall, to the door of the building, trying desperately to push back a river-rush of horrible memories. She carefully peered through the window pane set in the door, searching for Luke's car. No sign of it. She cautiously opened the door and, still seeing nothing, she proceeded out of the building and back to her car.

"I must touch the mouse for you to come across, Essi, so let it know not to be afraid."

She crouched down by her driver's side door, unseen because of the truck parked beside her, and placed her index finger on the mouse.

The mouse screamed.

Honest to Odin, screamed. The cry sounded eerily human. Shannon shuddered.

"It's okay, little one," Shannon said, as Salesti helped Essi jet through her finger, up her arm, and into her mind, while Shannon's attention remained on the frightened mouse. "I won't hurt you."

Narci yowled from the passenger seat, clearly disagreeing with the sentiment.

"Yeah, don't mind her. Off you go now." The mouse hesitated a moment, ran under the adjacent truck, and turned its tiny head to look back at Shannon. Whether it meant to convey a tiny mouse thanks or didn't trust Shannon to actually let it go, Shannon couldn't say.

Shannon climbed into her VW and paused. Still no sign of Tidak. *Time for a quick reunion.* She closed her eyes and flowed into her Great Room.

To her surprise, Indy padded through the door behind her and flopped to the floor by her side. The dog still looked translucent, as if Shannon could pass her hand straight through her, unlike Salesti, who seemed as solid as a real humming bird-kitten would be. But then, Salesti was actually here in its ethereal form. Her Indy was not.

"Salesti? How can Indy show up here. She's . . . she's. . . ."

essence of indy here. not same as living Indy but more than a memory. in this room, indy real enough.

Shannon bent down and, seeing that her hand did not pass through the dog, she wrapped her arms around Indy, burying her face in the extra folds around her neck. "I've missed you, baby," she said.

A figure glided through the door of the Great Room. *Essi! At last.*

* * *

Come here little one, I can't wait to. . . Hold on—that's not. . . .

A young woman ran toward Shannon. A young woman with pale, moon-blond hair curling around her face and along her shoulders and back, with the largest forest green eyes in the world and the sweetest little nose and ears. Essi's hair and eyes and face and lavender skin.

But that couldn't be little Essi. Couldn't be.

The alien child had been four or five years old at most when Shannon last saw her five years earlier. That would make her nine or ten now. This young woman must be in her late teens or early twenties.

yes, essi, said Salesti as the little humming bird-kitten-alien joined Shannon in the Great Room.

"How can she be Essi?"

salesti forgets to mention? different planet in different solar system and different kind of people from earth. more time passes on riverworld than five years. and children grow older very fast on riverworld compared to people of shannon.

Huh. Made sense. Shannon had just always assumed. . . .

Essi stopped awkwardly a few feet from Shannon, waiting for her to overcome her shock, humming nervously. Shannon opened her arms wide. "Come on, Essi!"

Essi came, and Shannon hugged.

So good to have the little one in her arms again. Although "the little one" now almost equaled Shannon in height. No more curling up in Shannon's lap for little Essi.

Roebor stalked in, gigantic compared to the four already in the Great Room.

Essi shrieked and ran behind Shannon. As always, Essi's words were few.

afraid. send away.

Daq, why do you call this girl little Essi? *She is not little for a Seladoran. She is not a child either. Is this another example of human high humor?*

"It's okay, Essi. He's a friend. He's here to help you. He won't hurt you." Shannon made the introductions. "And no. No high humor here, Roebor. Essi was a little child the last time I saw her. She's grown much more than I ever dreamed possible."

Roebor sniffed. *Shannon should have scientifically calculated the woman's new age.*

Shannon ignored the jibe; in truth, she'd simply thought of Essi as she'd been the day Shannon met her, and that's probably the way she'd think of Essi ten years from now. But Essi had grown into a beautiful woman, at least by Earth standards. Probably by Riverworld standards too.

Essi turned to Salesti, who hovered near Shannon's shoulder.

toss?

ah. toss. roebor says toss fights dragonpanther named tidak on riverworld, to distract tidak so essi can escape. toss captured by tidak. salesti not knows condition of toss or if toss still lives.

Essi's hands flew to her face. Her beautiful, happy humming ceased. Toss had been Essi's slightly older friend and protector when they both became orphans as children. Apparently those feelings had remained, perhaps deepened.

Shannon pulled Essi into a close embrace. "We'll find him, Essi. We'll be able to rescue him from Tidak, right, Roebor?"

Salesti left Shannon's side and flew to perch on Essi shoulder, resting its small face against her neck.

Roebor watched Essi cry for a moment, studied the concern on Shannon's face, then nodded. *If Tidak still has Toss, we will return him to you. But I cannot promise the boy lives, or that he fares well. Tidak does not grant mercy.*

Essi buried her face in Shannon's shoulder. Shannon held her tight for a long moment.

tidak? Essi asked, looking at each of the others in turn. Three sets of eyes looked down.

"He's still looking for you," Shannon said after a moment. "But you have all of us now. He won't touch you, I can promise you that." *She would die first.*

"How have you been doing on Riverworld, Essi?" Shannon said, trying to distract the girl. "Is the planet on the mend?"

The same aliens that had threatened Earth had devastated Essi's planet, and many of her people had died.

A series of images flashed through Shannon's mind. *Rains . . . Selador, the great river that had dried to a trickle, slowly growing again . . . The survivors at last able to return to the ribbonlike form in which they dwelt in the water . . . Dozens of Seladorans, most of them children, tearing down the abominable temple the aliens had erected, using the stones to form new homes . . . Crops slowly beginning to grow again . . . Toss and Essi holding hands, changing to mist, then to the ribbons that flowed with the River. . . .*

"A lot of hard work, little one. Are you happy?"

Essi nodded and managed a smile. She sent a question of her own.

zhoo?

"Juneau's doing wonderfully." Shannon imaged the high-lights of all that had happened for Juneau and Shannon since little—since Essi had departed for home.

Essi nodded and clapped her hands as she watched the images unfold of Juneau swimming free in the ocean.

Roebor stretched and yawned. Essi, distracted, frowned and spoke to Salesti rapidly, emphatically, in a melodic rhythmic language that reminded Shannon of the sounds of water flowing softly over stones.

essi asks how roebor removes virus.

During the reminiscing, Roebor had laid down in a cat-like lounging position, back legs stretched out to the side, front legs tucked close to his chest with his head resting on them, his long tail wrapped around his body and curled at the end under his chin. Now he looked up, his eyes opening to reveal palest silver-blue fire.

"I believe I can extract the virus here on Earth while the girl remains in her current form. But we will need time and quiet. I recommend we not try the procedure at your house, Shannon, because Tidak will likely return. Where else can we go?"

"A motel," Shannon said, and started up the car.

* * *

The VW had only traveled a mile south of the maintenance center along Old Coast Road when Shannon noticed the skyline to the south taking on a brownish haze.

Uh-oh. This *was* California and it *was* summer time. But please, please, please, somebody tell her that dark sky did not mean smoke and smoke did not mean fire.

She turned on her radio.

"... Evacuate all properties west and south of the city limits. I repeat California Governor Matt Portman has declared a natural disaster, and local authorities have issued an order for the evacuation of all properties between the ocean and the city from as far south as the county line north to Jebson's Creek. The fire began near the Left Hand Campground and spread north rapidly along the coast. At this time authorities do not believe the fire threatens Ocean City itself, but that situation could change at any time. Please stay tuned to this station for ongoing updates. We take you now live to our reporter. ..."

West and south of the city. That would place the fire right square between Shannon and the city.

CHAPTER TWENTY-SEVEN

SHANNON FLICKED OFF THE RADIO and tried to remember the available routes for reaching town without running into the fire. *What available routes?* The Old Coast Road ended to the north at Twisted Pine Bay, just beyond the SeaQuarium maintenance center. Ocean City lay almost due east of her. She knew of no roads—paved, gravel, dirt, or otherwise—branching off Old Coast Road that could take her around north or east of the fire and over to the city. Old Coast Road, which she was now driving, ran south for another ten miles. There it bisected State Road 12, which led directly northeast to the city. If she continued south on Old Coast Road, she would likely run right into the fire.

Maybe a small road or two she didn't know about branched off Old Coast heading east before the SR 12 intersection.

Daq, a dragonpanther always notes the terrain in which he travels. Coming from the city, I observed a small lane only a quarter mile or so ahead of us to the east of the road. It appeared to be little more than a track for tire wheels and I cannot say where it leads. I observed no other pathway heading east.

"Good for you, Roebor. Let's go check it out." She stepped on the gas and plowed ahead.

Then she saw it: Luke's silver Prius, heading due north, straight at them.

*　*　*

"*Loki's luck,*" she said, and stomped on the accelerator. "Come on, baby, give me everything you've got."

Who is she talking to? asked Roebor.

to car, salesti thinks.

The car does not live. Does Daq think it can hear her? Roebor asked. *I am worried that the strain has affected her analytical skills.*

"Don't worry about my analytical skills, just keep your eye peeled for that turnoff."

An eye doesn't peel, what—

"*For the love of Loki,* Roebor! Watch for the turnout."

Her poor VW could once move at reasonable speeds on a good day; today would not be such a day. Apparently its long, idle wait for Shannon's return had, in fact, clogged up the works in some way. Shannon couldn't coax the speedometer much above fifty. At this rate, they would reach the turn Roebor had spotted before Tidak reached them, but the Prius would turn behind them, and catch up long before they reached Ocean City. If the fire didn't catch them first.

All right then. They'd get as far as they could, and if Tidak forced them to make a stand, they would stand.

Just before the next hill, do you see the turn?

"Got it," Shannon said. Curse her broken arm—she would need to slow down significantly for the one-handed turn, especially with Narci in her crate in the passenger seat. She gave a little mental shrug. Couldn't be helped.

She screeched through the turn as quickly as she dared, and stomped on the accelerator again. Thirty miles per hour, forty, fifty, fifty-two—and they were maxed out. Much too soon, she spotted the silver Prius in her rearview mirror as it rounded the turn on two wheels and roared after them.

They crested a steep incline. Not far ahead, another hill. A trough between. *Perfect.* Shannon started down into the trough and slowed, looking for a hiding spot—large boulders, a clump of trees, anything. Just off to the right, some brush. It didn't stand very high, but then neither did the Bug. She stopped just beyond the bushes, eyeing the terrain. The rough ground cover would kill the undercarriage of the Bug, but it was better than nothing. She backed and bumped and scraped into the sage, placing the brush between the Bug and the view of the oncoming Prius, which Shannon could just make out screaming over the top of the incline.

I fail to see what this maneuver will accomplish, Daq. Tidak will know we have hidden ourselves here as soon as he passes the hill ahead. If we try to go back, he will still catch us before we can reach safety. A foolish and useless tactic.

"And just when you'd started to grow on me. Please keep it down; I need to concentrate."

The Prius roared past. As soon as it cleared the next hill, Shannon lurched quickly onto the road and sped after it.

Wait. You will chase Tidak?

By the time the VW reached the top of the hill, the Prius had proceeded down the incline, and was currently in the process of backing sideways on the right side of the road in order to reverse course. Just as Roebor predicted, Tidak had realized he'd passed the Bug.

Perfect. Better than she'd hoped. Shannon had dreaded a head-on collision. But a glance-off T-bone? She could do that.

Shannon aimed at the Prius's front tire, slid the cat crate onto the floor, placed her arm in its cast in front of her head in crash position, tried hard not to look at Luke's body in the driver's seat, and slowed but did not stop. She swerved left at the last minute to soften the blow.

Impact came swiftly, abruptly, and painfully. Shannon's airbag deployed.

* * *

She immediately released her seatbelt and rolled out onto edge of the gravel road. Although she'd held her forehead tight against her arm and the steering wheel, when she tried to stand, the world would not remain still. She nearly toppled over.

Ignore it. Move!

Using her good hand to prop herself up on her car, she limped around the hood, over to Luke's driver's side. The first thing she saw caused her stomach to lurch. *Luke.* She swallowed the bile and willed herself forward, but the sight of Luke's body, pinned by his airbag, head back, blood pouring from a long gash in his forehead, nearly broke her.

She gathered her courage. She took a moment to press some paper towels she found in the glove compartment over his wound, and said, "Time to take the fight to Tidak."

salesti ready. roebor?

Ready.

essi?

A strong, determined hum rose in reply, but Shannon immediately objected.

"No, Essi should stay back. We don't want Tidak anywhere near her."

Shannon propped the driver's-side car door open, knelt, and arranged herself across the air bag, the steering wheel, and Luke's body. She placed her hand on Luke's neck. *If the essence of any of the others can help me, find me now. Juneau, Indy?*

She streamed her consciousness through her fingers into Luke's body, finding Luke's own Great Room, a light and airy place with a floor of white marble and sun yellow walls. A pale yellow light filtered down from somewhere high above. Roebor and Salesti followed.

Roebor towered over her, like a basketball player looming over a lawn gnome. Because Indy and Juneau were comprised only of the essence they had left behind in Shannon's mind, their images flickered, pale and transparent, unlike Salesti and Roebor's image, which appeared solid, vivid, and fierce. Even so, Juneau's ghostly form floated as if the room were filled with water, and as the whale approached Shannon, she rubbed along Shannon's arm. Indy stood foursquare in front of her. Just at that moment, the transparent essence of her Luke arrived. He'd spent time in her mind long ago, and the essence that still resided in her mind from that time had followed the others to stand shoulder to shoulder with Shannon.

Shannon spared a second for the mind-blowing idea that the ghost Luke was hovering here in Luke's mind, even though—Shannon hoped—the real Luke was also hiding somewhere here. The two might even meet face to face. *Huh.*

But Tidak cut short Shannon's bemusement by flying down from the darkness above and thundering to the ground before them. His massive bronze frame dwarfed everyone except Roebor.

"Now that I can compare you nose to nose, Roebor, you're definitely the bigger, better, more beautiful dragonpanther, no doubt about it," Shannon said. *Come on, Tidak, take the bait; get good and mad and make a mistake.*

True, Daq. I am bigger, better, more beautiful.

No, roared Tidak. *Bigger, yes, but better, no. More beautiful? Perhaps to a puny earththing, as if her opinion matters.*

Odin's eye. Him too?

Roebor moved forward until he stood toe to toe with his rival. They roared into each other's faces. Shannon winced at the deafening sound.

You always pushed us toward this point, Tidak, did you not? A fight to end it. You or me. You would never allow us to resolve our differences like two rational scientists.

You speak of the old argument—the dual natures of our species: the primitive, in close proximity to the intellectual, Tidak said. *You always believed we had mastered the primitive. Wishful thinking. Or a lie.*

Shannon listened, fascinated, her mouth open. *What in the name of Odin?* The dragonpanthers had paused on the brink of battle for a short philosophical discourse on the subject of their dual psyches?

I never believed it, Tidak continued. *Just look at the Annual Hunt. The Choosing of Mates. The Aerial Competitions. So yes, Roebor. I always intended for it to boil down to this. The fight to the death. Your death.*

Death? They fought to the death?

Tidak looked around. *This battlefield will do as well as any.*

CHAPTER TWENTY-EIGHT

"ROEBOR, HOW CAN WE HELP YOU?" Shannon asked quietly.

The dragonpanther, never taking his eyes off Tidak, shook his head. *I must fight this battle, Daq. Find Toran and Toss. Get them out.*

Without warning, Tidak sprang forward, aiming his great fangs at Roebor's neck. Roebor reared up, smacked at Tidak's head with his front paw, claws extended, and sunk his teeth into Tidak's bronze shoulder. Tidak roared in pain. The sound reverberated in the Great Room like a volcano erupting.

Shannon and the others fell back from the battle, cringing, the noise assaulting them like physical blows.

Roebor had not escaped the first attack unharmed. Although he diverted Tidak's aim for his neck, the fangs still found Roebor's thigh. Roebor took the bite silently. He shook the other dragonpanther off, and Tidak fell away from him.

Reluctantly, Shannon turned away from the battle.

"Salesti, I need images of Toss, emotions you've sensed from him, anything to help me cast the colors and find him in here."

In an instant, Essi materialized by her side, unable, as ever, to leave the important work to others.

Esssii will give, the girl said.

Essi took Shannon's hand, and a wealth of images flooded her. She still remembered the images of Toss that Essi had sent her as a child, but Toss, too, had grown—into a man, taller than Essi by several inches, with chestnut-colored hair, bleached by the sun to streaks of burnished copper. Another pair of impossibly large, round eyes, turquoise, tender but resolute, eyes that Shannon liked instantly. A slim build, but muscular. A ribbon of richest turquoise, too, when he misted from human form to River form. A gentle kiss on Essi's forehead. A squeeze of her hand. A hug from behind, both arms wrapped snugly around her to clasp at her waist, his chin resting on her head as they contemplated their beautiful moons.

"Okay, I think I can cast for him. Salesti, will you stay here and help Roebor if you can?"

Shannon wasn't sure she could cast the colors inside another person's head though Salesti promised she could; she'd never tried it. A first time for everything.

As the dragonpanthers roared and thrashed behind her, Shannon turned to the archway of the Great Room, stepped into the darkness beyond, and cast the colors throughout Luke's mind, the streak of polished turquoise gleaming strongest. Ghost Indy stood beside her; the dog barked once, and took off loping into the haze. Shannon followed. Suddenly she found herself in a maze, but not a maze of green hedges or bales of hay. Pulsing, impenetrable, red light formed the walls, floor, and ceiling of this maze.

Indy never hesitated, running just ahead of Shannon, passing by two openings, taking the third to the left, passing by four openings, taking the fifth to the right, and on and on, until suddenly the mastiff disappeared around a pulsing red wall. Shannon followed, Essi close on her heels—and saw the still form of the young man Toss, curled on his side on the throbbing blood-colored ground. Essi pushed past Shannon, and ran to kneel by his unmoving form. Shannon sank to her knees near his back. She felt his neck.

"He has a pulse, Essi. He's protecting himself, hiding away from Tidak's foreign and unsettling thoughts and emotions. She shook him gently by the shoulder. He didn't move. Essi took his hand and kissed it. Nothing.

"Let's get him up and out of here."

Juneau and Luke appeared rounding the corner of the maze. Juneau's ghostly essence might not support Toss, but she'd try it. "Need your help, Juneau. We're going to lay him over your back if we can. That's it. Essi, you go around to the other side and hold his hands, so he doesn't slip to this side. I'll try to keep his leg up against Juneau's side, so he doesn't fall toward you. Slowly, Juneau. Let's get him back over to my body."

"Let me take this side, Shannon," the ghost-Luke said, startling Shannon. "You conserve your energy." He hoisted one of Toss's legs up under his arm and matched his pace to Juneau's slow progress forward. Salesti joined them.

*shannon, not necessary that toss floats on back of juneau—*Salesti began, but seeing that the method they had employed was working fine, it said—*oh never mind.*

Down they flowed, out of Luke's head, back through Shannon's hand, and on through her body to the Great Room in her own head. They gently laid Toss's still-unconscious body on the floor, and Essi settled beside him.

"Salesti, can you do anything for him?" Shannon asked.

Salesti buzzed, and shook its tiny head. *mind of toss hurt by tidak. shannon lets toss try to heal.* It turned away from Essi's huddled form and said, *maybe heals, maybe not.*

Shannon nodded grimly. "Now let's find Luke." She glanced at the translucent image of Luke that had accompanied her from her own mind. "The other Luke, I mean, the real one. Or, not the real one, but the one my mind sees when I'm in Luke's head. Of course, my mind sees the essence of Luke, you, too, but you're . . . and he's. . . ." *Confusing as hell.*

Back over to Luke they went, and in Luke's Great Room they saw that the dragonpanthers had taken their fight to the unbroken heights. Shannon and her group stood watching in awe for a moment as the two creatures darted and swooped through the air, attacking and retreating, and then they pushed on, back into another segment of the red, nightmarish, pulsating maze. Given Luke's scent from ghost-Luke, at first Indy ran an unhesitating path, just as before. Shannon's haze followed, and Luke's forest green blazed as the boldest color in her stream of colors.

Suddenly Indy stopped. She looked left and right, sniffed the air, and then sniffed the ground. Cocked her head. Like the dog, Shannon stared around in confusion. The forest green in Shannon's haze simply vanished, right where they stood. Apparently, judging from Indy's behavior, his scent ended at that spot too. Juneau approached and rubbed her head against Shannon.

"Can you tell where Luke has gone, Juneau?"

The whale floated upward, her head turning, seeking with her echolocation, but imaged Shannon: *nothing.*

Tidak must have pushed him out, then. Shannon's heart constricted. Her thoughts stuck, as if trapped in bottomless quicksand: *he's gone. Gone. . . .*

She sank to her knees on the red pulsing ground, her braid brushing the floor. *Gone.* Her eyes closed slowly on a flood of tears. Ghosts Luke, Juneau, and Indy waited silently beside her.

* * *

Time passed. At length Shannon roused herself.

"We'd better go back and help Roebor. Indy, back to the Great Room and the dragonpanthers."

Indy shot off with Juneau, Luke, and Shannon close behind, and soon they'd taken a bewildering series of turns through the maze to the Great Room.

Just as they ran into the room, the two dragonpanthers crashed to the floor, locked in each other's grip, wings ripped and tattered, deep purple-red blood pouring from their wounds.

Shannon joined Salesti, who fluttered helplessly nearby, and surveyed the damage. Bloody, matted fur covered both dragonpanthers, making some injuries hard to see, but she could distinguish the worst of them.

Tidak had ripped Roebor's front right thigh in a long triangular gash, deep enough at the wide end to reveal torn muscle, thick skin, and flapping, matted fur. Another serious rip to his back just above his right back leg bled profusely. A bite mark had taken a small, deep chunk of skin on his shoulder near his throat: nearly a fatal strike. Tidak had scratched Roebor's face and chest, but the rest of the damage didn't appear to be as bad as those three wounds.

As terrible as Roebor looked, Tidak had taken the worst of it. Two giant parallel rips had opened his chest, which presented a mess of purple-red muscle, fat, fur, skin, and bone mixed together. Another great gash had removed his left eye and ripped the skin nearly off the left side of his face. One back leg dangled helplessly, broken in numerous places. Thick blood covered his entire left front thigh.

"Will their real bodies suffer these same wounds, Salesti?"

real bodies not suffer these injuries. easier for roebor and tidak to fight to death here, because though loser really dead, here and now, winner knows actual body of winner fine.

"All or nothing. Then it's worse here than a real battle, isn't it; Tidak would've surrendered by now, and Roebor would've accepted his surrender, if both of them knew these injuries would be inflicted on their real bodies."

Salesti buzzed in agreement.

yes, worse. pain of wounds real here. death to loser real.

"*Odin's eye.* We have to put a stop to it. Not you, Indy. I don't want the little bit of your essence I have left to get pushed out again. You stay. Good girl. You too, Juneau; you're too important to me."

salesti not important?

"Of course you are, small one. But somehow I don't think Roebor and Tidak are any danger to you at all."

Salesti eyed the gigantic forms that wrestled, snapping, biting, clawing, some five hundred feet away. *salesti and shannon cannot approach; salesti and shannon flattened.*

"True," Shannon said. "Help me think. My special skills might be able to separate them somehow."

Salesti looked at her, head cocked, buzzing hesitantly. *of course shannon separates. shannon knocks them both out.*

"What now? I can knock them out? How"

shannon sends wind. hit tidak and roebor like brick wall.

"Send *wind*? In here? Not possible."

The dragonpanthers rolled, separated briefly, then slammed together once again, each grappling to gain access to the neck of the other.

possible. but only possible if shannon inside a mind, like now, said Salesti.

"Quickly tell me what to do."

salesti expects shannon to practice some things on her own, the little hummingbird-kitten said, frowning in her Persian cat smooshed face way.

"Yeah, my apologies. But help me."

cast colors over great room. far, quick.

Shannon cast her swirling colorful mist, cast it with all the strength that the anger at Tidak, and the grief over Luke, and the fear for Roebor could lend to it, taking care to cast only in front of her, not behind where her friends hovered.

now shannon inhales haze. creates air current moving back to shannon with haze.

"You said I could do this, Salesti, but it's crazy. There's no air here."

no, not crazy. shannon inhales.

"Okay, stay behind me, all of you."

She concentrated. She inhaled. Her mind filled with haze.

Immediately a wind picked up, blowing hard, straight toward her, so strong she bent into it in order to keep her feet. Juneau appeared behind her, the whale's lovely melon forehead helping to steady her. Shannon's long hair, braided from a high ponytail, flew out behind her above the whale. Her eyes stung with the force of the wind.

now, shannon, think of wind, cast colors with all wind inside back at dragonpanthers.

"Here goes nothing," Shannon said, and cast haze and wind forward again, right at the dragonpanthers, clutched now in a death grip. She gathered the haze in her hands and aimed for the narrow open spot between their heads where they held each other slightly apart.

Shannon's wind hit them hard. They flew apart as if separated by great invisible hands. Shannon cast again. The wind threw each dragonpanther high into the air, then slammed him to the ground. Roebor lifted his head, checking on his enemy once, then lay still. Tidak never moved.

Spots formed before Shannon's eyes. *Dizzy.* The casting had required too much of her energy. *Odin's eye.* She couldn't pass out now. She must get to her body, back to the car, and to the food. She struggled over to the two inert forms, and fell to her knees in front of Roebor's huge head. She listened for his breath, which came in a hush, but steady and strong. She exhaled the breath she'd been holding.

Laying a hand on his cheek, she said, "If I hadn't intervened, Roebor, I know you would've wiped the floor with Tidak—which means I know you would have won handily. But we have to go."

Salesti flew over to Tidak, while ghost Indy, ghost Luke and ghost Juneau planted themselves between the vicious dragonpanther and Shannon.

"Salesti? How's Tidak?"

breathes. not awake. shannon now pushes tidak out into ether, gone forever?

Shannon hesitated. She had killed aliens before. Back when they had threatened everyone she loved. But she carried the burden of that killing with her even now, in a small, cold, empty place in her mind that would never be full and warm again.

"No," she said. "I'll construct some kind of jail in my head for him. Let Roebor take him back to FireWorld for whatever punishment he's due. Now. How *in Loki's name* do we get these two big brutes back to my mind?"

shannon makes them float.

"I can't make them float, what do you mean?"

salesti tried to tell you before with toss. like when juneau floats here. shannon sends images to roebor and tidak, tells dragonpanthers to float, and roebor and tidak will float. Shannon floats if shannon tells self to float.

"And this, too, only works if I am inside a mind, right?"

very good, shannon. this correct.

"And only if they are unconscious?"

no, conscious will work if they are willing.

She touched Roebor's head and imaged a feather. *You're a feather, big boy, a stiff feather as light as a breeze and I can carry you. Float now, float like a feather.*

She slid her hand under his head and lifted. The enormous dragonpanther rose up, his body ramrod straight, stretching far out in front of her, but as easy to carry as a long, long pencil. She maneuvered him to the side and walked over to Tidak to image the same. Ghost-Luke offered to pull Tidak back to Shannon's mind, while she ferried Roebor along.

In a matter of minutes they had all floated over to Shannon's hand, up her arm to her head.

* * *

She opened her eyes, took a deep breath, and pushed away from Luke's still form.

Luke.

Can't think about that now.

She closed her eyes again, and concentrated on her own Great Room, on binding Tidak in bandages, then in chains, then taking him to a prison in her mind that she created just for him, one that was as big as a gymnasium, but with bars covering all four walls, floor, and ceiling. Noncombustible.

Then she wrapped Roebor in bandages, too.

She checked in on Essi and Toss; the young man had regained consciousness, once they had captured and shackled Tidak. Salesti explained that he'd fled into the maze to hide and placed himself in that comatose state when they'd entered Luke's mind and had steadfastly remained there. Now that he had awakened, the damage inflicted by Tidak's vicious, twisted mind became apparent: as yet, he hadn't spoken a word. Salesti didn't know whether he ever would. But he recognized Essi without a doubt, and seemed at ease with Salesti and Shannon.

It was a start.

Shannon could do no more. She would faint any minute. She needed to eat and she needed to eat now. She regained full consciousness.

She stood, trembling for a minute against the door of Luke's car and looked down at Luke. Still unconscious. His condition seemed unchanged. She glanced around her. Her dizziness had caused the very air to look gray and spotty. She—

Oh hell. Dizziness had not caused the spots in front of her eyes: ash and smoke had. The fire. It had almost overtaken them.

CHAPTER TWENTY-NINE

AS THE ASH FLOATED AROUND HER, Shannon slowly and unsteadily made her way back to her car, which sat diagonally across the middle of the lane, where the impact of the collision had tossed it.

Food first, before anything. She opened the trunk and fished in the bags of groceries for anything easy and edible. She noticed her spare gas can had fallen over during the crash. The last thing she needed was for it to contaminate her groceries. She lifted it out and set it on the lane.

As she ate, she perched on the back bumper of the Bug and studied the sky to the south. The wind was blowing to the north. Not good. She couldn't yet spot any flame, but with this much smoke and soot in the air, fire couldn't be far off. With the fire heading north, she didn't dare go back to Old Coast Road and continue south to SR 12. She'd have to hope that this narrow road would take her to Ocean City.

If her car would start.

She'd eaten so much she should be re-energized, but she still felt extremely weak. She moved around to the passenger side, pulled out Narci's crate, and opened it. "I can't make it back with both dragonpanthers, Toss, Essi and Salesti on board, Narci. You'll have to take Salesti. That okay with you?" The cat rubbed against her hand and sat expectantly on the car seat. "Okay with you too, Salesti?"

okay with salesti.

Sending Salesti would help a little bit, and every bit counted, but it wouldn't be enough. Too bad Shannon couldn't send one of the dragonpanthers, too, but Narci couldn't support anything more than the little hummingbird-kitten. And even that little dynamo pushed the envelope. Shannon placed her hand on Narci's back and Salesti scooted over.

One more thing to do before they got moving, and it wouldn't be easy.

Shannon made her way back over to the Prius. Luke's head was still bleeding, but not as profusely as earlier. She felt for his pulse. Still breathing. It didn't matter whether Tidak had destroyed Luke's consciousness, or Luke had hidden so well she and Indy couldn't find him, or some other phenomenon accounted for his breathing—she would not let his breathing body burn in the Left Hand Campground fire. She unbuckled his belt, slid her good arm behind his back, hooked her hand under his arm and pulled him from the car. As his body cleared the Prius, Shannon lost her grip and Luke tumbled out onto the road.

"Sorry Luke." Tears of frustration formed in her eyes as she surveyed his inert body crumpled in the road. Slipping her cast completely out of her sling, from behind, she maneuvered her left arm under his left arm and her right under his right. With his head cradled against her chest, she backed over to the Bug's back seat, step by painful step. Her back ached, her left arm, the one with the cast, ached. Her ankle screamed. Although the distance between Luke's car door and the Bug's backseat could not have measured more than ten feet, she stopped to rest four times, and stopped once to eat half a box of donuts.

Minutes crept by. The temperature rose slowly as the heat of the fire advanced. Ash floated into her face, her mouth, her eyes. She cried out. She cried out in frustration. From the pain. From the effort. From the futility of trying to save a probably-dead man. But she would *not* leave Luke's breathing body behind.

Finally she reached the Bug's backseat. She half lifted, half shoved Luke into the car. Limping as quickly as she could on her injured ankle to the driver's seat, she threw herself in.

She tried to start the car; it wouldn't turn over. *Battery?* Indicator light registered okay. *Gas?* She checked her gas gauge; very low. She remembered her gas can; unless her neighbor had replenished it for her, it was awfully old gas. She'd have to hope her neighbor had gone the extra mile. She limped back around to the trunk, and took the can, with the funnel she kept taped to it, around to her gas tank.

As she unscrewed the cap, trying to hold the can with her fingers peeping from her cast, she lost her grip and dropped the can, right onto her ankle cast. *Ow ow ow.* She grabbed her braid and held tight until the pain receded. The gas sloshed out until Shannon scooped the can up and poured the rest of the gas into the tank. By the time she'd placed the gas can back in her trunk, she'd managed to get gasoline all over her hands. She'd even smeared a swatch of the smelly stuff on her face.

Using a hand towel that she kept on the front passenger side floor for small cleaning jobs, she wiped her cheek, both her good arm and her arm with the cast, and then her leg, ankle, and foot.

But what was this? As she wiped, gunk had come off her casts and stuck to the towel. She looked more closely at the casts; dents, smears, and even holes had appeared where she'd been rubbing the gas off. *But why?*

Oh.

The gas contained ten percent ethanol. A solvent. Just the thing for dissolving fiberglass.

Oh well. Too late now.

She turned her attention back to the car. Would the Bug's engine turn over? She gave it a try. *Yes,* bless the Bug's little gas-infused heart, not only did it start, but she also managed to slowly and awkwardly steer it into a forward-facing position next to the ditch where Luke's car rested. Her right front bumper, however, would never be the same. Several pieces of it fell off as she started forward.

The Bug took off east down the rough road that might or might not lead to Ocean City, racing against the advancing fire. Shannon peered out her smoky window. Off to the left of the road, a large concrete irrigation ditch appeared. Water! It contained water.

She spotted orange flames rising in the distance, moving north toward her. It appeared that for the moment, the main body of the fire remained further west, behind her, as it advanced north. She could make out isolated pockets of fire, though, almost due south of her, and even a few fire lines already burning in the road ahead. She pressed the gas pedal to the floor, but it didn't help; her Bug would not top twenty-nine miles per hour after the collision.

A few miles later, the road appeared to curve slightly northward; *good*. Now, if only the road would also continue east as far as the city, and if only the fire would slow, she might reach home in one piece. *If only.*

* * *

Shannon didn't understand quite how it happened, but suddenly, the heat in the car rose unbearably. The steering wheel became searing hot to the touch.

Shannon. We must abandon the car and immerse ourselves in the ditchwater. It offers the only hope now.

Shannon coughed. Her mind moved sluggishly. At first Roebor's words didn't register. Smoke billowed on the road up ahead. Flames flickered through the smoke on both sides of the road. Mesmerized, she continued to drive right at it.

Shannon!

shannon!

Juneau added a loud set of clicks and whistles.

Right. Right. Leave the car.

Concentrate. Take it one step at a time. She parked. She unbuckled. She slung her cross strap purse across her chest. She opened the car door. She moved to the back seat. She pulled Luke from the car, and freed Narci from her crate.

Leave Toran. Get to the water. Now.

"No, I can't leave him." She used the same method she'd used before to pull Luke backward over to the irrigation ditch, *so slow,* and then turned to allow his weight to slide him toward the water. She eased into the water behind him, and pulled him close, her purse crushed between their two bodies. She felt the warm ditch water seeping into the holes in her casts. She'd need her bandages changed again. If she escaped this fire.

She could hear the fire now, crackling, roaring. The air smelled like charred wood.

"Narci, come here," Shannon said, waving the cat into her arms as well, half tucked into her side, half propped on Luke's head, which Shannon held above the water.

Shannon floated to the other side of the ditch, a distance of maybe fifteen feet. *Thank Odin* the ditch carried a fair amount of water. From this vantage point she could watch the flames advancing, overtaking her Bug. *Her poor Bug!* "Sorry, Narci," she said, as she closed Luke's mouth and nose with the fingers of her right hand, and tucked the cat as tightly as she could under her cast on her left, took a huge gulp of air, and sank under the murky green water. As the cat struggled, digging her claws deeply into Shannon's side, Shannon looked up and saw orange flames flying over the ditch. The flames disappeared. She surfaced.

Another wave of fire approached. Again she grasped Luke and Narci, ducked beneath the water, and watched the fire roar over her head.

No more, please no more. Shannon wouldn't be able to hold Luke and the cat much longer. *Let it end.* But when she surfaced, yet another wave of fire had almost reached the ditch. She caught a quick glimpse of the Bug, burning brightly, the paint melted away to a dull gray. Along with burning Bug went Shannon's food. This time, when she submerged, she lost her hold on Narci, who struggled wildly, pushed free of Shannon, and disappeared.

Salesti?

safe. salesti and narci safe.

Shannon surfaced for the last time. No more flames had burned into their vicinity. She clambered part way up the bank, pulling Luke along as best she could. Sharp rocks and pebbles gouged her hands and arms. She crawled forward, an inch at a time. Part way would have to do; Shannon couldn't go any farther. She put her hand over Luke's mouth. *A faint breath; she detected a faint breath, didn't she?*

Shannon lay still for what seemed like a very long time. She continued to cough in the smoky air, but other than that, she didn't move; she couldn't move. Maybe she would lie there undiscovered, until her bones sank back into the ditch, erasing all traces that she'd ever passed that way.

PART THREE

CATASTROPHIC LOSS

CHAPTER THIRTY

"JESUS, A COUPLE PEOPLE ARE DOWN HERE in the ditch. I'm going down to check their vitals."

Shannon heard the voice as if it were echoing in a hollow cave. *Yes, I'm alive.* She tried to mouth the words, but no sounds escaped her lips. She didn't raise her head. She didn't raise even a finger. A figure in green-brown turnouts—a firefighter—appeared at her side.

He spoke into a radio Shannon couldn't see. "They're breathing. I need two stretchers over here. No burns visible. . . ."

Someone turned her gently over and slipped an oxygen mask over her face. Cool, clean oxygen filled her lungs. She looked up. An ambulance.

Soon the medics had loaded her into it, and it was heading for town.

Safe.

"Luke?" she managed to croak.

"Luke the guy you were holding in a death grip down in the gully? He's in another ambulance heading the same place as you. He can thank you later for hauling his ass in and out of the ditch. Right now, I need you to just close your eyes and relax."

Shannon did close her eyes, but then said, "My cat?"

"Oh boy. A cat now. I didn't see a cat. Did you get those scratches from a cat?"

Salesti?

Very faintly, Shannon heard its reply.

coming. narci and salesti coming home.

* * *

Back in the hospital, again, new waterproof casts with clean bandages beneath them, again. In bed, again. How she hated these places, no matter how nice the staff, no matter how cheerful the walls and hospital gowns, no matter how good the food . . . but really, when did *that* ever happen? She glanced at the clock again. 11:25 p.m.

Dr. B. had promised she would release her as soon as she managed to push an adequate amount of electrolytes and glucose into her system, possibly tomorrow morning. Shannon had not mentioned her extra guests, afraid she'd never get out of the hospital.

Shannon's throat hurt. Her lungs hurt. Her arm ached. Her ankle ached. Her ribs . . . Shannon quit thinking about it.

For now, she lay trapped in her bed, railings down, call button at the ready, another tube running from her good arm to a plastic bag. Which meant, essentially, that she had *no* good arm.

Tidak had kicked up a bellowing fuss when he regained consciousness, forcing Shannon to reimagine his cell as completely soundproof.

Essi and Roebor maintained an uneasy truce: Essi, wary that Roebor would in fact reveal himself as another Tidak in sheep's clothing, and Roebor, wary that Essi would make another escape attempt and abscond with the virus. Shannon had assured them that each could be counted on, but the tension in her Great Room had given her a dragonpanther-sized headache.

Roebor had exhibited a decidedly frosty attitude when he regained consciousness. He was sulking, it appeared, because she had not allowed him to defeat Tidak on his own.

"Really, you *had* already won, Roebor, given the injuries you'd inflicted. I merely sped up the process so we could leave, and good thing too. You saw how far the fire had advanced by the time we got out of Luke's head. Plus, I couldn't—we couldn't—bear to watch you sustain any more injuries. We're your friends, *for Odinssake*.

Roebor dipped his angular brows above his flashing eyes at Shannon's choice of the word "friends." But he only made an odd noise that sounded like *mmmp*. After a moment, he said, *So long as you recognize I had won.*

She had visited her guests for a while this evening, learning more about Essi's experiences on Riverworld, how the few remaining adult Seladorans and all the children had struggled in the early days, building new shelters against the heat of the suns, starving, exhausted. Awaiting the winter rains.

Shannon felt guilty over Essi's terrible struggles on Riverworld, as if she should have kept Essi on earth until Riverworld had revived. Ridiculous notion, of course, since Shannon would have died if she'd kept Essi on board—had nearly died anyway. And Essi had wanted to go home. Fortunately, life was improving there; Essi was proud of her part in that work.

Shannon learned, too, more about the strange dual nature of which Roebor and Tidak had spoken at the battle in Luke's Great Room: how the conflict between their highly refined intellects and primal instincts shaped his people and defined their battles; how Tidak had set himself against Roebor ever since they were children, growing more bitter and frustrated as time went on when he could never best his rival.

Eventually Essi and Roebor had wandered off to rest on their own.

Shannon worried about Salesti and Narci. Salesti had sounded weak back at the fire when it replied to Shannon's telepathic call. Dr. B., who had left the hospital after her evening rounds, had promised to take the back road next to the irrigation ditch to search for them. She would go as far as the authorities would allow to try to spot the small black cat.

Shannon had asked Essi to visit Dr. B. when next she could. Dr. B. always thrilled to the notion of extraterrestrials, and Shannon squeezed a great deal of mileage out of that obsession. Case in point—in exchange for Essi's promised visit, Dr. B swore that first thing in the morning she would find out what had happened to Luke.

Luke. He shouldn't have died at Tidak's hand, just because Shannon had been unable to keep him out of her alien troubles.

A harsh sob escaped her, and the sound itself seemed to release a river of tears. Shannon let them run and run, until she had tired herself so much she hadn't the energy to cry anymore. Yet, now that she wished for nothing so much as forgetful sleep, in her grief over Luke, her mind would not release her.

Perhaps he had not died. She couldn't be a hundred percent sure yet, could she?

She stared at the ceiling and studied cracks. She used her good hand, needle and tube and all, to tickle her face with the tip of her braid. She watched the clock: 12:29 p.m.

Sometime along about three in the morning, she finally drifted off again.

* * *

"No sign of Narci and her alien parasite," Dr. Bennett reported during morning rounds.

"Salesti isn't a parasite," Shannon said.

"Is she or is she not a foreign entity feeding off the nutritional system of the host?"

"When you put it like that, sure. But she's a friend. I mean you met Essi. The words Essi and parasite don't belong in the same sentence, right? And it's the same with Salesti."

"You evaded my question when I tried to find out how many aliens you currently have on board, but judging from the fact that you've lost weight since you arrived last night—and don't argue the point; your face has become distinctly more gaunt—I can deduce that you have quite a bit of company. Am I wrong?"

"No, you're not wrong. You want to say hello to Essi? She's back. But prepare yourself. She's grown."

"Of course I would like to say hello." Dr. B. stepped off the stool she'd been sitting on while typing away at the computer keyboard with notes on Shannon's case. She walked without hesitation to Shannon's side and placed her hand on Shannon's arm.

"Essi? Would you care to say hello? Totally up to you," Shannon said.

Shannon imaged a picture of Dr. Bennett to Essi. "Do you remember her?"

Essi, ever the shy one, hummed, nodded, smiled a little smile, traveled down Shannon's arm to Dr. B.'s hand, floated gently over, and allowed the doctor to visit with her and smell her wonderful perfume for about three minutes. Then, in a flash she raced back.

"Roebor? What about you? Want to say hello, one scientist to another?"

I am not an animal at an Earth petting zoo to be trotted out on cue to please the spectators. Absolutely not. I will not speak to this Earth woman.

"She went out looking for Narci last night. Spent hours searching the road as far as the wreck of my poor Bug, may it rest in peace. When she couldn't find them, she went over to my house to put out a mountain of food for Narci, to be ready when she does push through the cat door."

She befriends Shannon and Narci you are saying.

Yes.

Very well then. For three minutes, as Essi did, I shall tolerate the petting zoo.

Shannon laughed. "Thank you, Roebor. You're a decent guy, for a dragonpanther."

"Dragonpanther?" Dr. B. asked. "Who's Roebor?"

"You'll see. I'm about to bring him over. Close your eyes and imagine you're in your Great Room again. But keep your eyes closed."

Dr. B.'s Great Room featured sparkling white walls, a black glossy floor, and marble beams that stretched up and out of sight.

Shannon and Roebor arrived in due course. The dragonpanther, still peeved, paced back and forth as Shannon said, "Open your eyes."

Dr. B. squeaked at the sight of the giant, blue, panther-like creature with wings and eyes of fire. "Oh my god. Oh my god. Oh my god."

Roebor sighed and said, "Dr. Bennett. I am curious about this instrument you used on Shannon to take her temperature. It appeared that you merely ran it across her forehead. Now. The mechanism by which. . . ."

Shannon tuned out the specifics of the conversation. She had no business ferrying Roebor over. The energy required had sapped her completely, and she must still find the suds to take him back to her body. Too bad he didn't have the Seladoran skill of flowing between bodies by himself, a skill the lavender lightning had gifted to Shannon.

She lowered herself to the floor, which was incredibly clean and shiny and reflected her image back at her. She noted absently that Dr. Bennett had found her voice, and she and the dragonpanther had moved on to the topic of MRIs and CT scans, and who knew what. As advanced as Roebor's people might be, these innovations apparently had not yet evolved on FireWorld.

Oh, but now she overheard Roebor explaining a process that eradicated cancer cells in a completely painless and harmless way for the patient. As a result, cancers of every variety, no matter what the origin or cause, whether viral, genetic, environmental, or other, were diseases no longer to be feared on FireWorld, as easily treated as a cut on the knee. Impressive.

Soon Shannon became nauseous and pressed herself flat against the floor, placing her cheek to the cool surface.

So weak.

Shivers wracked her. Her head pounded, right behind her eyes, as if Thor's hammer were inflicting blow after blow to the optic nerve.

"Roebor," she said in a small, thin voice. "I'm sorry. I need to go back. I don't feel well. I can bring you back later to talk again, but . . . but please, can we go?" She feared it might be too late. They might be trapped here because Shannon could not summon the energy to take them home.

Roebor took one look at her, broke off his conversation in mid-sentence, gave Dr. Bennett a courteous nod, swept Shannon up in his giant paw, and said, *You apply the magic that gets us back; I'll apply the brute force.*

With that, he took off flying back the way they'd come. Shannon concentrated on guiding them, Roebor propelled them, and, to her surprise, it worked. As they left Dr. B.'s mind, Shannon could just make out the doctor's voice, saying, "Oh my god. Oh my god."

Even before Shannon and Roebor had settled back in Shannon's mind, Dr. Bennett had gone into action, ordering medications, calling for more glucose, administering a shot of some kind, and putting in a summons for a consulting cardiologist.

Shannon couldn't bring herself to work up any interest. Let them bustle about, let them patch her up. She had to rest. Just let her rest . . . she needed to rest. . . .

* * *

The sun beat through the western window of Shannon's room. Dust motes swam in the bright beam. The sky beyond looked yellow-white, as if all the blue had burned away. Shannon had stared at it for some minutes before she registered that afternoon light filled her room, that her gaze seemed frozen.

"Essi, you good?"

Essi hummed, but not too happily.

"Toss?"

Essi responded. *Not ssspeaking yet.*

"Roebor?"

I am fine. Much better than you. I thank you for allowing me an enlightening conversation with Dr. Bennett. But you should have alerted us earlier. You cannot push yourself so hard for our sakes. I am ashamed that I did not discern your distress and urge us to leave much sooner.

Shannon shrugged. "My fault entirely and not any great disaster. Although I don't think I'll be up for an encore very soon. Maybe I can ask some of your questions, Dr. Bennett can tell me the answers, and you can eavesdrop."

You shall not worry about that. Not today. But I have news. Dr. Bennett left during her lunch break and checked for Narci. Still no sign. And—

"Okay, let me just call for Salesti."

Salesti? Have you made it to my house yet?

No answer.

Shannon called for Narci.

No answer.

"Roebor, did Dr. Bennett say when she would be seeing us again?"

Yes. Evening rounds, approximately seven o' clock.

"Okay. If I happen to doze off around then, and she comes in, will you wake me right away?"

I have more news, D. Important news. I am not sure what I make of it.

"Okay. Hit me. What've you got?"

Hit you? Why would I hit you? Yes, you sometimes aggravate me, but one blow from me, even a gentle blow, would—

"'Hit me' is an expression. It means 'tell me,' hit me with the information. Do you see?"

Yes. Very strange, your language, because you never say what you mean. Everyone must learn two languages: the actual meaning of your words and the code words for the actual words. Why do you hide the real words, D? Every time you speak, do you test the one to whom you speak? Or do you test only me? Do you mean for me to fail? For I do fail this code of yours.

He sounded upset, which puzzled Shannon. "No, sorry if it seems that way, Roebor. We all speak this way all the time to everyone. For me, it's a lifetime habit. Not a test at all."

Roebor rumbled, but he stopped abruptly. *Forgive me, D. I have become distracted for the second time. The news."*

"Oh right, right. I'm the one who's distracted. What news?"

Dr. Bennett learned news of Luke. The doctors placed him on life support. She said he has fallen into a coma.

CHAPTER THIRTY-ONE

"BUT I DO NOT UNDERSTAND THIS," Roebor said. *"If Tidak has pushed Luke out into the ether, and Tidak has left the body, should not the body expire? Yet if Luke fled to a safe place, as you suggested, should not he regain consciousness, now that we've captured and removed Tidak, as Toss did?*

"Did Dr. Bennett have any theories?"

No. I observed that Dr. Bennett disapproved of Essi and me being on board. I did not think it wise to mention that you brought a second dragonpanther aboard, and a second Seladoran.

"Good thought. I don't know what Luke's coma means either. Luke may have buried himself so far in his subconscious to avoid Tidak that he can't find his way out. Or Tidak might have been able to throw out all Luke's important bits, and just left some automatic functions working. I just don't know. We'll have to go look."

Shannon pulled the intravenous feed out of her arm. A monitor above her head began beeping.

Wait, D.

As she had when Roebor took over her body to fight Tidak, Shannon experienced the strangest feeling that Roebor gently touched her. This time he stopped her hand and covered hers with his own.

Wait until Dr. Bennett comes. She can wheel you to Luke in one of these moving chairs, so that you will have the energy to search. If you try rushing to Luke now, you will have nothing left, just as you had nothing left when we visited Dr. Bennett. True?

"True." Shannon eased back against her pillows.

A nurse named Juju bustled in and clucked at the loose needle.

"I turned over in my sleep, and out it came," Shannon lied. "Sorry."

She tried for her sheepish face, and perhaps it worked, because Juju said, "It happens." She looked sternly at Shannon as she replaced the needle, and added, "But we don't want it happening too often, do we?"

"No we certainly don't," Shannon said. "Say, I think I'm allowed to have extra food. I'm hungry for a couple candy bars. Do you think I could wheedle someone into buying them for me?"

"I'll send one of our volunteers over," Juju said, as she changed out Shannon's glucose bag.

* * *

Shannon dozed fitfully. Something was nagging at her, but she couldn't quite pull it from her subconscious. One of her many worries. She'd forgotten something important, something that she must attend to. What?

She sank into a dream.

. . . .In the dream, she is flying on Roebor's back. Tucked at the base of his fine long neck where it connects to his spine are two indentations. Shannon can sit with a knee in each indentation as if on a slender, rounded rock, with her legs on either side, her knees resting on Roebor's back. She feels no discomfort, because she is also leaning slightly forward onto his neck, where she can rest her elbows as she grasps three-inch-long fur to steady herself. If she wants, she can lean all the way forward and rest her cheek on Roebor. She finds this perch surprisingly comfortable.

She peers out to the left and down past Roebor's neck. The wind whips in her face. Her braid stretches out behind her. Far out along the horizon she views a shining ocean. The entire surface of the water as far as Shannon can see burns with pale silver-blue fire. It's hard to estimate from this height, but the flames appear to shoot fifty feet above the surface of the ocean.

Islands dot the water. No large continents, just island after island. No wonder dragonpanthers evolved wings. The island over which Roebor is now flying looks to be one of the larger ones. At the edge of the sea, the island rises not to pleasant sandy beaches, but into swamps—dark, watery, grassy places where creatures slither from fallen logs into the water as Roebor's shadow passes overhead. The creatures remind Shannon of alligators, and yet Shannon counts too many legs, too many tails. Similar animals for similar niches?

Upland from the swamps, a high granite cliff rises, tracing the island down its long lee edge and out of sight around a curve. Rich river valleys filled with tree-covered forests lie above the cliffs, dotted with open meadows. These forests and meadows might exist on any mountain on Earth—if Shannon doesn't look too closely at the shapes of the trees or the unusual animals that show themselves now and then in a meadow, at the cliff edge, on an outcropping of rock.

Highest on the island, along its spine, sits a string of craggy peaks covered with caves, lakes, and dusty, rocky soil bereft of plant life. Roebor heads here.

He flaps down to a gentle landing. Shannon wants to meet his people.

But she squints at the landscape. Nothing moves. She sees forms dotting the clearing in front of the caves and slides down Roebor's wing to the ground. Nasty bugs with large pincers and six large eyes across their heads swarm over heaps of things that block the way to the caves. Some sort of prey for the tribe's food supply?

Shannon looks more closely.

No. Not prey. Dragonpanthers. Roebor's people. Scattered along the entire clearing for hundreds of yards. Dead. Skin rotting away, terrible blisters and deformities on heads, backs, wings, paws.

Roebor shakes his head, too late, too late. . . .

A dream, only a dream. *Please Odin*, not a premonition.

* * *

Shannon sat bolt upright in her bed, unsure at first of her location. *Oh right.* Hospital. Recovering. Luke. The virus.

After the near-fatal encounter with the fire west of town, Shannon hadn't thought once about the virus. But Essi had joined them now; they must accomplish the transfer of the virus from her to Roebor as soon as possible.

"Roebor, are you awake?"

Yes, D. I am watching for Dr. Bennett as you requested. She has not yet arrived, although I understand they're bringing your dinner now. You were dreaming. I saw your dream. How do you know the geography of my world?

"You saw my dream? How?"

It played here in the Great Room on all the walls. On the ceiling. On the floor. Very hard to miss.

"Holy Odin. And the details of your world were accurate?"

Precisely. Down to the sharp-eyed scissor fly. Unpleasant creatures attracted to carrion.

"But how could I know about them?"

Perhaps you have stolen theses facts from me.

Odin's eye. Sleep-stealing? "If I somehow became privy to your thoughts, I'm very sorry. I didn't mean to. I didn't even know I had."

A dragonpanther values his privacy, D. Lives have been forfeit for thefts much less important than thoughts. I know you did not intend it. But you must try to stay out of my mind.

"Yes. I will. Of course. But, Roebor, I must have dreamed of Riverworld to remind me how urgently we need to remove the virus from Essi so you can take it home. Or did you try to remove it from Essi while I slept? Did I dream about it because you've done it?"

No.

"Why not? Do you need some equipment you don't have? Some kind of medical tools?"

No. But I will need you sharp and focused to assist me. As of now you are neither.

"You need me? Why?"

"As matters have developed, I believe the virus extraction will require the two of us."

"And after you remove it from Essi, how will you carry the virus back to FireWorld without contaminating Earth?"

I believe that I can extract a section of Essi's brain that contains the virus. This section shall be so small she will not even feel it happening or notice its absence. Then I plan to cut a small bit of my skin and insert Essi's inside it.

"But when you flow back into your own body, won't you lose the virus?"

This will prove tricky. I have formed theories but have had no chance to carry out trial experiments. It saddens me that I cannot use my equipment.

"You have equipment? How did you get that?"

I believe you witnessed the ball of fire that deposited me on this planet at the UC. Roebor paused. Have I apologized for disrupting your facility? I am deeply regretful of this. At any rate, I carried the equipment in a shock-proof container approximately the size of one of your cars. It awaits my return to Alaska, but of course it's useless to me here.

"So should we do the extraction now? Get it over with?"

Let us wait until you have spoken to Dr. Bennett at seven o'clock. When your mind clears, you may better assist me.

* * *

Precisely at seven, Dr. B. walked briskly into Shannon's room. With the doctor's medical treatment, and a robust dinner under her belt, Shannon felt better than she had for several days. The physician sat at the computer and studied Shannon's latest lab reports.

"You're still in a world of hurt, Shannon. Being in here where I can modulate medications hourly from anywhere has helped prolong the inevitable, but you're still dying. Yet you seem so cavalier. Do you understand that I'm not joking? I'm not exaggerating. *You will die.* You must send your visitors home. Today would be preferable."

"I haven't even asked how we get you home, Roebor."

I will return to the precise place where I entered this planet, at the wreck of the Dickson Underwater Complex. I must arrive at the precise hour I have calculated so the rebounding worm hole will carry me back to Riverworld.

"What did he say?" Dr. B. asked. Shannon repeated his words.

"We need to get you that virus and get you on your way."

"Virus? What virus?" Dr. B. asked.

"A little nasty that could kill everyone on earth. Don't worry. We think we have it handled."

"You think?" Dr. B. sat down abruptly at the foot of Shannon's bed.

Shannon nodded. "Fingers crossed," she said.

But Shannon didn't want to pursue that discussion; she abruptly changed the subject. "Luke? He's here? He's alive?"

The physician shifted, stood, and sat carefully back down, as if by sitting just so, she might make her next words sound just so. "I'm not sure we can say he's alive in the sense you mean. He's on life support, because he can't breathe on his own. We have detected a brain wave functionality of an unusual kind. I've never observed anything like it. For one thing, it registers only very faintly, which may mean he will cease all function soon. But more importantly, we haven't successfully interpreted the pattern."

"What does it show?"

"We've found activity in only one area, a part of the brain we would not expect to function this way: the amygdala. The fear center of the brain."

Shannon's good hand tapped her bedcovers. "But that might make some kind of internal sense—as much as anything about about invaders to people's minds makes any sense. When Tidak entered Luke's mind, I yelled for Luke to hide somewhere deep in his subconscious, to build a room, lock the door, and keep Tidak out. So maybe Luke fled right to the center of his fears and shut himself off, surrounded by fear. Maybe Tidak wouldn't venture into such a place. Brilliant move from that perspective. But what if venturing into the amygdala, the fear center, has somehow paralyzed Luke with terror. What if he *can't* get out now?"

"That makes absolutely no sense from a medical perspective. But then neither does it make sense that I spent time inside my own head comparing scientific advancements with a dragon the size of Detroit. So if we want to test this theory of yours, what do we do?"

"You take me to Luke, and I try to reach him and bring him out."

CHAPTER THIRTY-TWO

DR. BENNETT WHEELED SHANNON UP a floor to the acute care wing where Luke lay inert in his hospital bed, looking more dead than alive. His thick black hair stuck out in some places and stuck to his head in others. His five o'clock shadow, always visible, had grown to a short unruly beard. His wonderful, honeyed complexion had paled, and, although he'd only been here a day, he looked haggard and impossibly thin. The staff had stitched up the gash on his forehead and wrapped it in gauze.

Shannon regarded him without moving for a moment. At the first glimpse of him, her emotional center had collapsed into grief and guilt. She had inflicted this on him. She had driven purposely into the front corner of his car on the driver's side to disorient Tidak long enough for her and her allies to come aboard. And in doing so, she'd injured him and plunged him into a coma.

Stop. If her grief over his condition, her horror at what she'd wrought overwhelmed her now, she'd never finish what she must do: locate him and bring him out.

Better to feel nothing, to be numb. And do her job.

He wears death like a winter coat, Shannon. Do not try to enter his mind.

Shannon maneuvered her wheelchair so that her right hand could reach over and touch his neck. She rested her index finger on the little indentation at the front base of the neck where it met the collar bone. She laid her head on his chest and listened a moment to the slow, steady beat of his heart.

"It will be all right, Roebor, I'll leave if nobody's home. Indy, come with me. And Luke, too, if you want. The rest of you wait here."

"Indy? Who's Indy? Do you mean to tell me you have more than just Essi and Roebor on board? And how could Luke be on board your mind? I thought he was lost in his own mind." Dr. B. asked.

"It's all right," Shannon said in a monotone. "Indy's always with me. She was my dog. She's dead now. I do, however, have Tidak on board and Toss, but hopefully not for long. And Luke has visited my mind, so he's always with me too, not the real Luke but more than a memory of him. His ghost, you might say."

As Dr. B. started what Shannon imagined would be a long tirade, Shannon slipped through her fingers, through Luke's neck, to his mind.

* * *

Shannon sought Luke's Great Room and called out for him. Her voice seemed to echo in a vast emptiness.

No response.

She cast her colors, his deep forest green seeking its like, Luke's essence.

She couldn't sense him anywhere.

"Up to you, Indy. Find Luke."

The ghost dog raced off, stopping every few minutes to raise her nose to the air. Back they charged into the red pulsing maze. The pulse had weakened considerably since yesterday; the red of the walls had faded to a grayish rose.

Indy traveled the same route through the maze that she'd taken yesterday and, just as she had then, she stopped short and sniffed in confusion in the middle of the same passageway. No doors, no openings, no intersections.

The haze ended at the spot too, as it had yesterday.

This time, however, Shannon did not give up the search so easily.

Think.

Assuming Tidak had not chosen this spot to push out Luke to die, Luke must have left the maze here to enter a different hiding spot in his mind. Since she could find no way to follow, he must have sealed off his exit without a trace. She examined the walls first, taking her time, running her fingers along them, pushing, testing, looking for the slightest crack or hole. Then the floor. Nothing. The ceiling proved the more difficult surface, situated some two and a half feet over her head. Too far—until she remembered that reality functioned differently here. She imagined herself lifting, floating upward, stretching out her legs and flipping horizontally onto her back, so that she could examine the ceiling just as she had the walls.

Still nothing.

Next, she tried imagining an axe, hoping it would appear in her hand, but no such luck: no axe. Apparently she could imagine herself in various ways but she couldn't manufacture artifacts.

The ghost Luke had stood silently regarding the area. "I would have gone through the wall, Shannon, built a new passage, one not located in this maze, and then covered up the opening as if it had never existed. Try to break through," he said, gesturing to the right.

How weird was this, hearing from ghost-Luke what the real Luke—who was the same but not—would do. He'd probably nailed it; nobody knew Luke better than Luke.

"Looks like this calls for stronger measures, Indy. Let's employ that thick skull of yours to bust up this maze." Shannon took a step back, and rushing forward, threw her shoulder into the wall. A small dent appeared where her now-throbbing shoulder had made contact. Luke followed, throwing his shoulder into the same space. Now the dent was a small hole. "You too, girl, with me," she said and rushed the wall again. This time the mastiff crashed into the wall like a battering ram and a large v-shaped rupture appeared where Indy's head had made contact. Shannon pried it upward to meet the hole Luke had made, until she could peer through.

Black nothingness.

"Good girl. Now let's try this side." Indy happily butted the opposite wall, and the three of them succeeding in pushing out an entire rectangle of red, pulsing matter. Shannon knelt to position herself for a better look through the resulting hole.

"This could be it. Good job, sweetheart."

"Are you talking to Indy, or me?" ghost-Luke asked, grinning.

"Both." Shannon smiled back, and then leaned into the hole.

Shannon ought to be looking right at the adjacent pathway of the maze beyond the wall; Shannon and Indy had been on the other side, just before they made a U-turn and Indy led them back down this pathway. But Luke had constructed a different reality here. On the other side of the wall Shannon could make out what appeared to be a hallway. Impossibly, it stretched off into the far distance.

Shannon and Luke tore away enough of the broken wall to allow them to crawl through.

"What do you think, Indy? Can you pick up Luke's scent? Luke, you'd better wait here, don't you think? Watch for Luke?" Ghost-Luke nodded.

The dog barked gleefully and took off once more. Shannon cast her colors and followed. Soon doors appeared along the hallway, but Indy didn't hesitate. She kept moving, Shannon right behind her.

The farther they progressed, the darker and colder it became. A dampness clung to the air, a thickness. Goosebumps appeared on Shannon's arms. She shivered, and the shivers continued.

A certainty formed in her mind that something immeasurably frightening lay in wait ahead in the dark. Scratching, scuffling sounds reverberated in the walls, behind doors, in the darkness that stretched in front of them.

Go back. Something terrible existed here, more terrible than anything she'd ever known.

Now Shannon was shivering so violently she couldn't move without putting a hand to the wall for support. But she didn't want to touch that wall, she didn't want to move forward: she wanted to run back the way she'd come and get out of this place.

Indy had moved in close to her legs, leaning against her, growling low in her throat, but she too remained where she stood. Then she backed up one step, another step.

That clinched it.

Shannon turned and ran.

With Indy at her heels, she fled all the way to the ragged opening in the maze wall.

She hesitated.

Wait, wait, wait. The amygdala. The fear center. That's where Indy had led them. That's what had frightened Shannon—and Indy—so badly. The very place where the brain generated fear. The memory of every fear that Luke had ever known might reside here; the primordial fears that men and women had entertained since they first walked erect might still exist here.

If Tidak had managed to find this place, once he hit that wall of terror, he must have turned back, just as they had.

Smart guy, Luke.

Now, could Shannon and Indy force their way past their fears to Luke? And if they could, could they face their fears yet a third time on their way back to the maze?

Only one way to find out.

"Stay with me, Indy," she said, turning from the maze wall, taking a big breath, and running full tilt back the way they'd come.

She would get as far as possible before the amygdala could slow her down.

She concentrated on running as hard as she could. She closed her mind to all other sensory input. *Run. Run. Run.*

Slowly the oppressive atmosphere of the hallway began to penetrate her awareness. The darkness. The noises. The sweat on her forehead. The hair on the back of her neck rising.

Run. Left foot, right foot, left. . . .

The shivering began again. The noises in the walls grew louder.

Right arm pump, left arm pump. . . .

A large shape up ahead, filling the entire hallway: pincers, tentacles, bug eyes, so many legs. . . .

Breathe in, breathe out, breathe in. . . .

. . . . Its mouth open; huge, sharp teeth, thick saliva dripping; moving, moving all those legs, coming toward her. . . .

Shannon concentrated so hard and her fright made her so rigid that she almost failed to notice that Indy was no longer trotting by her side. She stopped and dared to look back, taking her eyes off the undulating darkness ahead.

"Indy?"

The dog had stopped at a door indistinguishable from every door they'd passed. Shannon checked her haze. Yes, a forest green glow, shining through the small gap beneath the door.

Luke.

She tried the handle. It twisted. The door swung open. More darkness. Shannon and Indy slowly entered.

"Luke?"

The darkness blinded her. She couldn't find Indy and panicked. *There.* The dog brushed against her leg. She grabbed Indy's collar. "Can you find him, girl?"

Indy led Shannon off to the left. Her feet scuffed against a thick object. She bent down. A body. She let go of Indy's collar to feel the face attached to this body. The chin, the mouth, the nose, the hair.

Yes. Luke. Unconscious but breathing.

A small involuntary sob escaped Shannon's lips.

Taking in a big shuddering breath, she floated him up and guided him out the door.

But now the huge, slavering, insectile *thing* had passed Luke's door and had hunkered down between them and the maze wall. She could just make out its shadowy form in the black inkiness of the hallway.

Amygdala. Fear Center. Move.

"It's not real, right, Luke?" Shannon called out to the ghost Luke at the maze wall.

"I don't know," said ghost Luke. "I'm not sure."

"It's not real," Shannon said again.

Indy growled, louder this time, her eyes glued on the giant spidery shape ahead.

It was not real. It was a personification of all things fearful. It was not real.

CHAPTER THIRTY-THREE

SHANNON TOOK ONE STEP, THEN ANOTHER, guiding Luke's body. Indy hung back, whined, lifted a paw, as if beckoning Shannon away from the *thing* that stood between them and the maze. Shannon kept moving, slowly, one step at a time, her eye on that shape.

Indy hesitated, followed, and then inched out in front of Shannon.

Shannon honed in on the maze wall up ahead, grayish-red light shining weakly through the ragged hole that Shannon and Indy had broken open. But perhaps six feet in front of it, the *thing*, looking real enough in the dim light from the maze, looking . . . horrible . . . *It intended to kill them. Those legs would grab them, the pincers would hold them and haul them toward that cavernous mouth. Acid from the dripping mucus would burn them, immobilize them. Those long sharp teeth would rip them to pieces.*

Not real not real not real.

Shannon curled her arm down over Luke's waist as he floated stiffly beside her, like a football player tucking in the ball for a run up the sideline. She ran toward the *thing*. Indy stayed in front of her, barking and growling now, snapping her jaws.

Why didn't it disappear?

Indy and Shannon, with Luke in tow, reached the creature and the maze wall at the same time. Ghost Luke had climbed through to help them come back through the hole in the wall.

She could smell the creature now; a stinking, putrid smell that reminded Shannon of dead things. Suddenly, it thrust a claw at her with a sharp appendage at the end of one of its legs. A great slash appeared on her left arm, dripping blood. In the real world, this arm was in a cast, but in Luke's mind, her arm was free. The blood looked real enough.

It was real. In this place, the wound was real. She felt a terrible stinging and a throbbing pain. But, according to Salesti, nothing had happened to her actual arm.

Before Shannon could call her off, Indy ripped into the advancing creature. When the *thing* reared back in response, Shannon and ghost Luke gently and swiftly maneuvered Luke through the opening.

She turned, and shouted, "Luke, hurry. Indy, here, girl."

At that instant, the creature snatched ghost Indy with one of its long claws and pulled her in. The dog struggled and howled from the pain of the pincer around her chest. Indy snapped at the pincers but her jaws couldn't reach them. Two of the creature's legs lifted off the ground, one grasping Indy's body, the other her head.

"No," screamed Shannon. She looked around desperately for a weapon, anything she could use to attack the thing and make it drop Indy. Nothing in the dark hallway—but where they'd broken through the wall, *there,* a stout-looking length of red matter, jagged on both ends. She grabbed it and lunged toward the creature. But just as she approached close enough to jab the pincers with her stake, she heard a terrible snap and Indy went limp.

Shannon's vision turned red. She lifted the stake and swung down on the appendage with the claw giving it everything her rage could muster. Her blow landed squarely on one pincer. The creature hissed, dropped Indy and retreated a step from the pain, and Shannon stepped even closer to the hideous thing and stabbed at it, aiming for an eye. Made contact. This time it reared back and let out a high screech.

She felt ghost Luke's arms around her waist, pulling her back toward the opening in the wall. As they reached the wall, Luke pivoted and shoved her through. She fell to the floor and immediately scrambled to her feet.

"Come on, Luke, hurry."

She waited. Nothing but silence issued from behind the maze wall. She heard neither the monster, nor ghost Luke.

Shannon carefully pushed the unconscious Luke to the opposite wall of the maze and stuck her head back through the opening. From this safe vantage point, she detected none of the fear that had racked her only moments before. No creature loomed in the hallway. But also no body of ghost Indy. And no ghost Luke. They had all vanished together.

"Luke," she screamed.

But screaming didn't help. Ghost Luke, along with the body of ghost Indy, had disappeared, taken by the *thing.*

* * *

Salesti had warned her that they could die inside Luke's mind. Tidak or Roebor, or both, might have died if Shannon hadn't stopped their battle. But what had happened here? Her mind, growing more numb by the second, struggled to grasp the truth.

To ghost Indy, to ghost Luke, the creature had been real. *To Shannon it had seemed damn real too.* And in the fear center, perhaps it was real. Real enough to kill. Indy had sacrificed herself to save Shannon once again. Luke had survived, but the part of him that had resided in Shannon's mind, that which was more than memory, that had vanished. She couldn't call on a single trace of Luke in her mind now, unless the real Luke came on board again one day.

Indy. Completely gone.

Shannon bawled then. Loudly. She sat and wailed and didn't care about much of anything but her poor Indy.

After a time, the first overwhelming wave of her grief spent, she struggled slowly to her feet, picked up the unconscious Luke, and tried to remember her way out. After several false turns, retracing her steps, and choosing different paths, she made it back to Luke's Great Room.

She laid Luke down and sat with his head in her lap for a few minutes. He still didn't stir. But his breath pushed softly against Shannon's cheek when she placed it next to his face. He looked much less gaunt than the Luke whose body she had entered. He looked relaxed, asleep. She wouldn't wake him. Let him rest.

* * *

She traveled alone back through Luke's body, back through her fingers, into her own mind, and awakened with her cheek still on Luke's chest. She lifted her head. In that moment it weighed ten pounds.

"How are his vitals?" she asked Dr. B. in a scratchy voice.

"Better," Dr. B. said, "much better. Whatever you did, it seems to be working. He even looks better. But what's this?"

Dr. B. pointed to her arm cast. Injuries, Salesti had said, inside the mind would not appear on real bodies. Yet her cast was slashed nearly in two and blood seeped from the opening.

The insectile thing. Real enough.

"Again?"

"Again," she said, and explained what the insectile creature had done to her, Indy, and Luke. She touched Luke's face.

Dr. Bennett examined Shannon's new wound more carefully. "I don't like the look of this. Not only is the gash deep, but the edges look almost acid-burned. And I'm going to treat you with some powerful broad-spectrum antibacterial medications, just in case. In fact, let's get a blood sample right now and see what's in there."

Shannon nodded slightly. She didn't much care. She said, "You might try removing Luke from the breathing apparatus. I think he'll breathe on his own now."

"I'll arrange it."

"I need to eat."

"I'll arrange it."

* * *

I heard you tell the doctor about Indy and the Luke of your mind, Roebor said.

"I don't want to talk about it. Okay?"

Of course. I am very sorry, D. I know they meant much to you. It cannot be made right. I grieve for you, as you grieve for them.

"Thanks." Shannon sounded like a robot. Felt like one too. "I mean that. And by the way, what does the 'D.' mean? What happened to Daq?"

Ah. On my world, good friends often use the first letter of a name to refer to each other. I needn't use it if it offends you.

"I like it. Use it. Can I call you 'R.' then?"

If you wish to. I would be pleased.

"I will. Everyone all right here? Essi? Toss? You, R?"

All of us are fine. Do not worry over it, D.

* * *

Dr. B. returned Shannon to her room and treated the new wound. She applied yet another arm cast. Of more interest to Shannon, a double meal appeared. The doctor then proceeded out to the vending machines and returned with a bag of chips, three kinds of candy bars, a tube of hard candy, and a large slice of vanilla cake with raspberry cream frosting.

"Where did you get this?" Shannon asked, stabbing a large bite of cake with her fork.

"One of the receptionists had a birthday today. Goodies in the staff room. I'm going back for more and I'd like you to pace yourself, eat at reasonable intervals throughout the rest of tonight and tomorrow."

"Tomorrow? I thought you said yesterday I could go home today."

"Yesterday you hadn't made an excursion into the wilds of Luke's mind from which you've returned looking like a zombie. Yesterday I didn't know you were harboring a second dragonpanther, some entity named Toss, and a dog as well as Roebor—my god, Roebor!—and Essi. Anybody else?"

Shannon didn't correct her regarding Indy. No energy for that. "No, no one else for now. At some point Salesti will be back, but I hope to have offloaded the dragonpanthers by then," Shannon said dully. Yesterday she'd wanted to go home vey badly. At the moment she didn't much care. She looked down at her white sheets, where her good hand slid absently back and forth across her cast from fingers to elbow.

Dr. B. threw up her hands. "Sometimes I think you have a death wish."

Shannon looked up. "No, no death wish, doc. Too much to do."

"I want to hear about what happened in Luke's mind. Give me as much detail as you can remember," Dr. B. said.

* * *

Shannon consumed her double dinner while Dr. B. raided the staff room once more and supplied Shannon with snacks to last until the next day. At that time, Dr. B. said, she'd allow Shannon to go home, *if* she refrained from further adventures, and attempted nothing more strenuous that the chomping of baked goods.

Shannon called again for Salesti and, receiving no reply, fell into a restless sleep, but, to her surprise, no nightmares tormented her.

When she awoke, the hospital had darkened and quieted. The bleak heaviness of all that had happened descended on her immediately. She lay, staring at the ceiling, running her eye along that crack again, noticing a tiny spider web in the far corner. She shuddered. She'd never been a spider fan, but now she expected to develop a real phobia. There would be screaming and fainting at all eight-legged sightings henceforth.

She pushed the thought away. She needed to *do* something.

Fumbling in her bedsheets, she found the nurse's call button and pressed it.

"I want to go up to Luke's room," she announced to the nurse's assistant who came in answer to her call. "Dr. B. took me to his room earlier and allowed me to stay for quite a while. She said I could go again any time I wanted."

A tiny lie in a good cause.

Okay, a big selfish lie. So what?

"Luke Quintana up on Floor Five. He and I were in the same car accident," she added by way of explaining why she wanted to visit him.

That part rang true—they *had* experienced the same car accident—and if the nurse thought that meant they also experienced it in the same car, too bad, her mistake. A mistake Shannon wouldn't bother to correct.

The nurse's assistant, whose name tag read "Tulsa," promised to try to obtain permission. Luckily for Shannon, the resident now on duty acquiesced without consulting Dr. Bennett.

Tulsa and Shannon made desultory small talk on the ride up to Floor 5, but she didn't have the heart for it. Tulsa positioned Shannon next to Luke's bed so that she could watch his face.

At the moment he looked asleep. The breathing apparatus had been removed from his nose, but the glucose bag and attendant tubing remained. So. They'd tested his ability to breathe on his own and he'd succeeded. A step in the right direction.

Luke's color looked healthier to her, less sallow. The extreme gauntness had lessened. Yet Tulsa checked the computer screen which showed his chart, and learned that he hadn't regained consciousness.

Now, D., you promised the physician you would not go in again, Roebor said.

"No, I just promised I wouldn't overexert," Shannon replied.

Did she hear Essi chuckling?

Momentarily distracted, she asked, "Hey, I haven't heard much from Essi since I returned from Luke's mind. She hasn't contracted the virus, has she?"

She has not. The Seladorans seem a quiet people. She fears the moment we must make the extraction and so absents herself from my presence.

"We need to get that done, and I'm the holdup. As soon as we finish here, let's do it."

Very well. So you mean to go in then? Do not do it.

"Just to Luke's Great Room. Perfectly innocuous. Just to find out why he hasn't awakened."

Do not do it.

"Have to."

Do not.

To avoid further argument, Shannon laid her head on Luke's chest again, listened to the steady beat of his heart, then placed her hand on his hand and entered.

* * *

In his Great Room, Luke remained on the floor where Shannon had laid him. Nothing was moving in the room, and nothing indicated the terrors of the amygdala had followed him here. She listened; nothing but deep quiet. Casting the colors, she threw her haze into the far corners of the room and up toward the darkness above. She detected nothing.

Luke's tormentor had remained in the amygdala.

She knelt by Luke's side and gently shook him.

He opened his eyes.

"Luke. *Thank Odin.* Do you remember what happened? You're in the hospital now, with a big gash in your head. Concussion. And coma. Why can't you wake up?"

He looked at her, his eyes sad and haunted. He pulled himself off the floor and sat with his knees drawn up under his chin.

"I know what happened to your friends after they hosted the nasty variety of aliens. Death and insanity. Why would I leave here? I might try to hurt you. I can't let that happen. I'm staying here. Tell them to remove the glucose feed. I signed a 'do not resuscitate' order. 'Take no extraordinary measures,' it says. The Police Department has a copy."

"Look, Tidak disgusts me, but the aliens from before seemed much worse. Nothing could be as bad as them. You remember."

"Only good guys have occupied your head, cara. I hosted a cruel, sadistic, psychotic being, an altogether different experience. Forget his alien nature, which is mind-bending enough: Tidak is a psychopath, as alien to me as the brain of any human serial killer. I have never succeeded in wrapping my mind around what kind of mind could do the things I've seen serial killers do. And now I have been forced to wrap my mind around every nasty, nightmarish, frightening aspect of the dragonpanther. Where is he now? You dispersed him into the ether, I hope?"

Shannon had listened to Luke's description of harboring Tidak with a sinking heart.

"Um, actually, he's locked up tight in my mind right now. In a soundproof cage."

"My god, Shannon, you must get rid of him. Push him out. How did you end up with him?"

"Roebor, Juneau, Indy, Salesti and I came over to your mind to relieve you of his presence. Roebor fought a fierce battle with him, and eventually I knocked him out. We roped him up and tucked him away, so Roebor can put him back in his own body, and take him back to FireWorld."

"Do not keep him. Remove him. You have no idea what he's capable of. Psychopath. Remember that."

"Anyway, back to the problem at hand. If you wake up, you'll have all the support you need. We can get you through this."

"No you can't. You think I would take the smallest risk that I might hurt you? No. And believe me, having felt his hatred, his rage, his sadistic pleasure in hurting, and knowing I have a part of him with me now—his essence—I am a huge risk. I always will be." He closed his eyes again and would not look at her.

Shannon rubbed her lips with her thumb as she thought this newest dilemma through. Luke feared Tidak's psycho essence would cause him to act psychotically himself.

But. If she could find Tidak's essence and get rid of it, Luke should have nothing to fear, right?

If only Salesti were here. She might know more about this business. Shannon could go back to her own mind to consult with her ghost Salesti since the real Salesti was out in the world with Narci somewhere. It might think of something

But no. Shannon must learn to manage her skills herself.

"Wait here," she said.

First, find Tidak's essence. But where? She conjured the image of Tidak, everything she knew about him, her sense of him, her feel for him, and she cast the colors, a dull bronze streak burning brightest. *Scanning, scanning*—yes, his essence resided here, and she knew where.

She passed through Luke's maze, and opened a door to his powdered essence. Luke had begun to amass his own stockpiles now. Some of her own essence resided here, Roebor's, and a touch of ghost Juneau's and ghost Indy's, as well as

Tidak's dull bronze pile. More of Tidak than anyone else, since he'd been here the longest.

Now, what to do with it? She'd already learned she couldn't conjure up any solid objects like the axe she had wanted when she and Indy were searching for Luke—or like a box to put the powder in.

Think.

Ah. She could use this new skill Salesti had taught her with the wind: *if* it would work in the essence room. Risky. She might succeed only in scattering Tidak's essence all over Luke's mind, making matters much worse. She might scatter the essence of the others, and who knew what the effect of that might be.

But she could think of no other way.

Okay then, do it. She cast the colors into the room, then inhaled the haze. She created the air current, but more softly this time; she wasn't trying to knock down a pair of giant dragonpanthers; only to gather some powder. She now controlled a small, gentle wind.

Carefully envisioning the wind wrapping itself around Tidak's hill of dull bronze, creating a small whirlwind, she sent it forth and tightened the rotating wind, tighter, tighter, until the entire heap had been absorbed up into the whirlwind.

Careful, don't lose even a flake of Tidak's essence, hold it all in the rotating wind, hold, hold—

Shannon floated slowly out of the room of essence, casting the whirlwind before her. Through the maze, back to the Great Room, beyond the Great Room, down to Luke's chest she floated. At the very moment she would have crossed to her own hand, she instead cast the wind out into the air, and Tidak's essence with it.

. . . . Except for a small bit of the powder, a quarter teaspoonful, that had moved directly along the path where Luke's hand connected with Shannon's hand. That small bit of Tidak's essence dispersed within Shannon instead of out into the ether.

Loki's luck.

As for the essence she'd sent out into the air, she must be sure that it had dissipated: she watched the powder scatter, dispersed by the hospital's air conditioning, separating into single flecks of powder until the flecks disappeared completely. *Gone.*

Then she passed across into her own body. No sign of the quarter teaspoon of Tidak's odious powder; it had spread within her system.

What effect it would have on her, she had no idea. But it couldn't be good.

Returning to the Great Room, she smiled at Luke. "I sent Tidak's essence away. Without it here to influence you, you won't become crazy like my friends did. You won't be like Tidak. You'll just be you."

"Sent it away? How?"

Shannon explained.

"Not a trace left here?"

"Come on, I'll show you." Shannon took him to the room of essence and they combed the place for any slight hint of Tidak's dull bronze. Completely gone.

"And none of it passed to you?"

"Not a drop." Luke took his job of protecting Shannon at all costs very seriously. It would destroy him to learn she carried some of the dragon panther's unsavory essence because she'd helped him, and if Shannon had anything to do with it, he would never find out.

CHAPTER THIRTY-FOUR

SHANNON RETURNED TO HER OWN BODY from Luke's, but fought her first inclination to sit up right away. She continued to rest, eyes closed, hand over Luke's hand, ear pressed to his chest, comforted by the regular rhythm of his heart. When at last she stirred and sat up, he was gazing at her solemnly with those beautiful, soft brown eyes, partially shaded by thick, black eyelashes.

"You're awake," she said.

"I am."

"I'm glad."

"Me too."

She paused. Luke said nothing more. He wasn't smiling. *But why?*

Oh. The car crash. Of course.

As if following her thoughts, he said, "You nearly killed us both."

"Yes, I did. But I'd found Essi at the maintenance center. Inside a mouse." She checked to see if that bit of news brought out a small smile.

Nothing.

"Anyway, since Tidak wanted to kidnap her, and I wouldn't give her up, and I also feared he might've pushed you out, but if he hadn't, then we needed to get him away from you so he wouldn't, you know, damage you, and out on that gravel road I knew he'd catch up to my poor deceased Bug, RIP, so a little wreck to catch him by surprise seemed like a good idea—" *Odin's eye.* Would she ever be coherent around Luke?

"But *a car wreck.*"

"I just planned to stun and disorient him, so I could bring Roebor over to defeat him, which he did."

Luke returned to silence, regarding her. "A dangerous maneuver," he said after an uncomfortable minute. "You might have killed yourself in that little tin can you drive, and left Tidak to do his worst. I'd still be trapped in my own head."

"The little tin can I *drove.* The Bug is no more. It's true, it could've turned out badly, but I didn't have a lot of time to think of alternatives. And the point is that we succeeded in taking out Tidak. Literally"

"You did. And thank you. But yes, this could have turned out badly in so many ways. Almost every time I am with you, I experience events that could turn out badly in so many ways."

"Why didn't you bring this up . . ." Shannon glanced out the door and mouthed the rest of her thought: *in your mind when I was there?*

"I didn't think I was coming back, so it didn't matter.

A flash of anger all twisted up with hurt rippled through Shannon. "All right then. Nothing more to talk about."

She backed up her wheelchair, ineptly, too quickly, banging into Luke's bed. "Sorry," she said, and wheeled out the door as quickly as she could with one hand, which wasn't very quickly. Tears tore at her eyes. "Can someone help me here? I need to get back to my room."

* * *

He will get over his uncertainty, D. What he is really saying is not that you almost killed him but that you almost died. Tidak nearly destroyed him. He nearly lost his mind to his own fear center. Those realizations have shaken him. Do you understand? He needs to work through all these unsettling experiences. He needs time.

yesss, Essi said.

yes, said ghost Salesti

"Maybe," Shannon said, sniffling.

The nurse's aide Juju, a taciturn young fellow with a beautiful diamond stud in his nose and hair on only half his head, had wheeled her to her room, and she'd climbed back in bed, where she sat peeling an orange. "But on to another important matter. I think we now have the entire night ahead of us without interruption to get that virus out of Essi. I have a suggestion."

I am listening.

"Since we're doing this while you're both in my head, I can create a secure place for us to store the virus for safekeeping until we get you back to your body."

No, I think not, D. Too dangerous. If, in some way I have not anticipated, the virus escapes, your brain would be infected.

You would die. You would infect others. The plague would spread worldwide. I frankly do not know this planet or its inhabitants. But I do know you. I will not let harm come to you. Or the little dragonpanther Narci. So no. I will tuck the virus inside a fold in the skin on my chest, useful for carrying small items, much like the pocket your people wear on their clothing. That will suffice.

"Okay. Up to you. But the offer stands. I don't think the virus will escape. Your plan will work. I have confidence in you."

This pleases me, D. I am honored to have gained your confidence.

"So let's do it. How do we find an object so minuscule?"

Meet us in your Great Room and I will show you.

* * *

Shannon, Essi, Toss, and Roebor gathered in Shannon's Great Room.

Before leaving FireWorld, I made complex calculations regarding the location of the virus in Essi's brain, and I brought to Earth a highly sophisticated microscope with an ultra-high-power magnifying lens that I believed could locate the virus. Unfortunately, I left this equipment with my body off the Canadian coast. When I left FireWorld, I had no idea, of course, that I would be riding inside a human mind. Now that I am, I believe we can use the haze you cast to accomplish what my microscope would have.

"Back up. The virus has entered her *brain*? But how can we get the virus out without hurting her?"

We must shrink, of course. This ability is available to us in your mind, in the same way Juneau has the ability to float there in the same space where we are walking. We will shrink so much the virus becomes visible to us. At such a small size, we can remove the virus and pass through the brain without difficulty.

"Ah. Of course. We shrink so tiny we'll be walking around inside atoms or molecules. I knew that."

This is more of your high humor, is it not? You say you knew it, because you didn't know it? I fear I still don't understand the joke.

"No worries. It wasn't that funny. Explain the virus to me, send me some images, give me enough to focus my casting of the colors."

Roebor pictured the shape and dimensions of the virus, explained how it moved, how it reproduced, how it infected host cells. Soon Shannon had a decent enough grasp of the tiny germ to be able to cast her colors for it. They asked Essi to lie on the floor of the Great Room. She settled down, her head in Toss's lap, fear in her impossibly emerald, impossibly huge eyes, humming discordantly, like jazz at its most jarring. Toss took one of her hands, Shannon took the other. Essi gripped them both hard. Shannon murmured words of comfort; Essi nodded and closed her eyes. Shannon felt Essi's hand relax in hers. Her hum softened, mellowed.

* * *

Holy Odin. This scared the beejeebies out of Shannon. No wonder Essi felt nervous.

Shannon and Roebor made themselves comfortable while touching Essi, and flowed through her hand into her mind.

Essi's Great Room flowed like a crystal clear river, which came as no surprise to Shannon. Shannon and Roebor floated through the waters. She cast her colors, using a silvery orange for the color of the virus, a bright streak among her colors imbued with all that Shannon knew of the virus. She searched. Patiently. Carefully.

She found it.

The haze showed a black object about the size of a pea against the riverbank and well within it, the virus. She tapped Roebor on his shoulder as he swam next to her, and pointed. They approached and examined a dark and ragged hole: a small opening between Essi's constructed river of the mind and the physical structure of her brain.

"So does this mean we will now leave Essi's cognitive mind and enter her real brain?"

Roebor thought for a moment, the claw on the index toe of his left paw tapping the river bottom.

How shall I explain this to you? We exist now in a construct devised by Essi's mind. Within this construct are elements of the real brain. The real virus resides here, in a real location, but Essi has superimposed over this real location her understanding of its location and her attempt to convey that information to us in a way that we can understand. Do you see?

"Yes, I think so. We will be seeing a construct of Essi's making, but real elements, like the virus, will exist there?"

Roebor nodded. *Here's an example of why we need this construct to stand any chance of finding the virus—an atom is smaller than a wavelength of light; therefore light cannot bounce off the atom to show its interior to us. But in the construct, we will be able to see within the atom.*

"And the actual virus will be there?"

It will. We must go smaller now, D., much smaller.

Shannon inhaled a deep breath.

They imagined themselves shrinking; the pea-sized black hole soon matched Shannon's height, then it became a huge mansion, and finally it appeared like nighttime itself, stretching so far above them and to their left and right, it presented an overwhelming black expanse.

Shannon glanced at Roebor. "Good enough?"

He shook his head no. *Smaller. Keep your haze focused on the virus.*

They would surely get lost at such a minuscule size. Lost forever. Shannon's body turned as icy as it had the day she'd plunged into the Alaskan Sea. She hesitated.

But only for a moment.

She and Roebor must find the virus, for Earth, for FireWorld. Her lips tightened into a grim line; she concentrated on the colors she'd cast toward the distant virus and shrank again, smaller, and smaller still. At last Roebor nudged her with his paw and nodded. She stopped shrinking and looked around. She floated in place because blackness extended out in all directions as far as she could see, including below. She spotted objects in the distance that looked like bright planets. She reached out for the comforting touch of Roebor's neck.

He continued to shrink until he hovered, in comparison to Shannon, at about the height of a horse.

"A much better size, R. I only wish I had a saddle and bridle," she teased. She imaged these items for the dragon-panther to view, along with their use.

You'd never get the bit over my incisors, D. Not that you'd ever get the bridle over my head or the saddle on my back. Not while I had breath to fight it. He growled ominously, then smiled.

Shannon laughed. It felt good. How much had she laughed since that day Juneau had gone missing and Roebor had destroyed the UC? Not much.

"Just kidding, R. You're nobody's pet, nobody's property. But you do understand that plenty of people on this planet would love to make you their pet or property if they ever caught you, right?"

Yes, D. Your species harbors both compassionate people and people who understand nothing. Like my own world, I suppose. I do not plan to be captured.

Shannon's gaze followed the colors she'd cast. "We need to go this way. But will we be able to find our way back?"

Good work, D. Without the accuracy of your casting we could have missed the virus by dozens of molecules. As to finding our way back, I will use those distant objects—he pointed to the planet-like objects—*as markers by which to navigate, incorporating in my calculations their own movements relative to each other. I believe that, yes, we will retrace our route with reasonable accuracy.*

The two traveled along companionably for almost an hour, Roebor flying, Shannon catching a lift by grasping the fur on the back of his neck. The haze of colors stretched out before her.

* * *

So what do you do, D., when you are not saving world populations and young alien women?

Shannon laughed quietly. "The beluga whale Juneau and I work together as a team. On Earth, some zoos and entertainment parks hold whales and dolphins captive. I hope they'll soon be forced to shut down or alter their practices. I've pinned my hopes on a system where facilities allow the whales and dolphins to come and go as they like, and where some of them might choose to check in for food, for care, for interaction with the human teams, and where people still visit, to watch them and love them."

Roebor nodded. *Excellent, D.*

The two lapsed into silence again as they continued on their journey.

"Could it possibly be this far? The casting indicates it's still ahead, but I've never cast at such a great distance before, even when I cast for Essi all the way out to the maintenance center."

I had hoped we might spot the virus sooner, but great distances can separate objects at this level of microsystem. Your haze, I believe, still accurately leads us forward.

* * *

A few minutes later, as they moved along, Shannon said, "So, what I do, that's nothing compared to you—you're a leader on FireWorld, right? Are you like a king or a mayor or what?"

I am not sure to what you would compare leadership on my world to, D. Perhaps I can explain it this way: We are, above all, members of our birth clans. I am the leader of my clan. Clans join to form a Hill. Hills might be small, just a few clans, or very large, consisting of fifty or more clans. The space on the land on which a Hill lives largely determines the size of the Hill. I am the leader of my Hill. All the Hills on one island join to form, of course, an Island. I lead one of these Islands: the Island of Swords, the largest island on FireWorld, as you call it. I am called the First of the Island of Swords.

"And what do you call the leader of all the Islands?

In the entire history of the dragonpanthers, as you call us, we have never united as one people. I dream of our unity, and have fought for it ever since we discovered that other planetary systems contain living creatures, some of which are hostile. Our foolish inability to join in harmony has placed us at terrible risk, D., and so it will remain until we can unite and plan to meet the forces of the universe.

Roebor shook his head. *But the dual nature of my people has always led to war and division, never peace and unity. I may not achieve the unity of all dragonpanthers in my lifetime. It breaks my heart.*

"Earth hasn't ever had a worldwide government of humans, either. Too much distrust. Different world views. But you never know, R., you may yet make it happen," Shannon said, giving Roebor a little encouraging fur tug.

* * *

Forty-five minutes after that conversation, Shannon caught sight of the virus, straight ahead, and pointed at the pale orange ball with short spines protruding from points all over its surface. Roebor nodded.

As they approached, however, the virus, compared to their current size, loomed as big as a Ferris wheel. A giant nucleic acid molecule in a protein casing: It looked more like a prop from a sci-fi movie. *Invasion of Influenzilla.*

Shannon's expression darkened. All this shrinking and growing had begun to take a toll on her. "Don't tell me. Bigger."

Roebor nodded. With that, he started to grow and Shannon quickly followed.

Suddenly it occurred to Shannon that if she hurried she could beat Roebor to the right size, and even grow bigger than him. *Hah!* That would be a sweet reversal. She shot up.

When Roebor could grab the virus like a softball, he stopped enlarging, but Shannon, in her desire to beat Roebor, overshot and didn't stop growing until Roebor's back grazed her ankles.

"Who's the puny FireWorld thing now, R.?

You entertain yourself, D., but it's a dangerous game. At some point, if you outshoot me, this virus will be of a size to attack you. Remember, we are in a live host; a virus can invade here. And we know this virus to be aggressive.

The words had no sooner left his mouth than the virus wrenched itself from Roebor's grasp and flew upward, attracted by the nearest unprotected entry point, in this case Shannon's open mouth, and slid quickly in.

CHAPTER THIRTY-FIVE

THE VIRUS MOVED INTO HER THROAT before she could react.

Triple shitsky.

Although she immediately tried to hack it up—spitting, coughing, gagging—nothing dislodged it. She felt the bulge caused by the virus as it traveled past the back of her mouth, down her throat, and into her stomach. And there it seemed to lodge. Cold shivers crawled down her spine. Sure, if the virus was pill-sized to Shannon, it shouldn't be small enough to pass into her cells where viruses typically wrought their damage. But then, who knew what an alien virus could do?

Don't panic don't panic don't panic.

Do not panic, D., Roebor said, and not unkindly.

No roaring, no grumbling, no "I told you so." Shannon silently thanked him for that.

As far as we know, the virus is too large to negatively affect you in any way. He hesitated and then asked, *How do you feel?*

"Panicked. But otherwise no different."

Then let us return to Essi's River. Roebor grew to match her size.

"But when I must grow again?"

Let us meet that challenge when we come to it. In the mean-time, I will cogitate.

Mother of Odin. First, bits of Tidak's essence in her blood, now an alien killer virus in her system.

I shall not let you be harmed by this virus, D., I swear by the four moons.

Shannon took heart from Roebor's words, although she feared Roebor couldn't do much about it.

Roebor extrapolated their course of travel by studying first one and then another of the planet-like objects in the distance, and took off in the direction that Shannon, too, judged would lead them toward the opening to Essi's riverbank.

The planets off in the distance had not changed size appreciably, meaning they were still far away. "What are those things, R.?" she asked, pointing at the planets.

Constructs of electrons, protons, an occasional muon, I believe. I could not accurately measure our diminution, so I cannot be certain.

He cannot be certain. Right.

* * *

At their current size, Roebor and Shannon should have made good time. But the minutes passed slowly for Shannon.

After a while, she let loose of Roebor's fur to wipe sweat off her forehead. "It's getting so hot in here. Do you think Essi has a fever?" she asked, as she floated along behind Roebor's head.

Roebor stopped and turned to her. *The surroundings have not changed temperature, D.* He peered into her face, placed a paw gently against her entire face. *You're the one who has the fever, not Essi. You are flushed as well. Do you feel any aching in your muscles? Other symptoms?*

"Yes, to the aches, and I feel generally a little dicey, like with the flu—tired, upset tummy issues, but that could just be from all this moving through dark space and my metabolic issues, don't you think?" Shannon's nose began to run. She automatically tried to block it with the back of her hand, then swung her hand back to her side.

"Probably too soon to—"

Roebor grabbed her hand and held it high, forcing Shannon to look at it. The back of her hand ran red with blood.

* * *

Shannon stared at Roebor. The pale silver-blue fire in his eyes flickered wildly.

"This virus isn't anything like ebola, is it?" Shannon asked.

I do not know the disease ebola. But on other planets this virus causes massive internal bleeding, and at the end, bleeding from nose, mouth, eyes, everywhere.

Not unlike ebola. *That's all she wrote, then. The virus had infected her. She was a dead woman walking.*

For a minute or more they floated in the vast black expanse, their movements frozen, staring at each other.

All at once Roebor said, *I am going into your body to gather the virus and kill it. No time to talk about it. I must finish before the virus can multiply to such a degree I cannot stop it, and that point will occur shortly.*

"But—"

Before Shannon could say more, Roebor shrank so quickly he disappeared out of sight and left her alone in the immense darkness.

* * *

Shannon looked around. Blackness in all directions except for the planets—the electrons, protons, and occasional muons, as Roebor had explained, whatever a muon was. Not a sound penetrated the deep stillness.

Without Roebor, the sheer immensity of the emptiness overwhelmed her. *So lonely here.* She grabbed her braid, pulled it around and ran her hand down it for luck.

The urge to *do* something, anything, overpowered her. She started moving off in the direction it seemed they'd been going when she'd so foolishly decided to play games with Roebor. She shook her head in disgust at the memory; she'd tried so hard to cautiously follow his lead in this bizarre endeavor, so she wouldn't accidentally hurt Essi. Why in the world had she suddenly given in to the strange impulse to beat him at enlarging herself? The answer came to her immediately.

Tidak.

Of course. Tidak, who wanted to best Roebor at all costs, to beat him to the virus and prove himself the better scientist, to defeat him on the battlefield and prove himself the better dragonpanther. Just the small bit of Tidak's essence that had slipped into Shannon had given her the sudden competitive desire to grow bigger than Roebor, to make *him* the tiny one for a change.

Odin's eye. If she lived through this, a big *if* at the moment, she would have to stay vigilant to counter any impulses she'd inherited from that lowlife.

Not that pinpointing the cause of her woes helped her much now.

* * *

Time passed slowly.

Lonely, slow time.

No sound except her own breathing. Silence never sounded so cold. No scent, no stirring of faint breeze, no stimulus of any kind, except that she could still smell her own mysterious scent, hear her own voice, feel the soft smoothness of her braid.

In all that great expanse around her, there was no one. No one at all.

Would she pass her final moments alone in this emptiness as vast as eternity? A startling thought flitted across her mind: maybe she'd *already* died from the virus and this *was* eternity. But no. Stress and the overwhelming *nothingness* caused that kind of panic. She still drew breath; *by all the heroes of Valhalla, she was still alive.* For now.

The vast, dark silence pressed in on her, unbearably, painfully, as if she were an astronaut whose lifeline to the mothership had broken, leaving her to float off into black, empty space, alone with her thoughts until her oxygen ran out. And the darkness suffocated her, as if it were a living thing, surrounding her, engulfing her, consuming her.

Shannon shook off those thoughts. She also suffered from a different existential crisis, one easier to wrap her mind around: her energy was running out. She must eat again soon, or it would be a close race to determine whether the virus took her down her first, or her body gave out from the presence of her guests.

Her guests. *Odin's eye.* Essi and Toss. Roebor. They'd die with her if she didn't get out of here alive.

She must help herself. She must *do* something. She must act.

No.

She must do the hardest thing: wait, rest, conserve her energy, be ready when Roebor returned.

Okay, she could do *nothing* if she had to. She fidgeted. Probably she could.

She closed her eyes. *Better. She could pretend her surroundings were anything but interminable nothingness.* She imagined she was floating in the ocean, in a beautiful turquoise sea, warm and calm. She breathed deeply and slowly, six counts in, six counts out. Six in, six out. When her breathing became slow, deep, and steady, she concentrated on relaxing each muscle, beginning with her toes. Once she finished, she floated loosely, calmly, and began to count again. Six in, six out.

* * *

The blood was running steadily from her nose now. Roebor had not defeated the virus yet.

* * *

Weak. Getting weaker every minute. Hungry like she could her weight in ice cream.

Shannon could do this. She would not panic. She would not cry. Those actions wasted too much energy.

Do nothing.

Six breaths in, six out.

* * *

D.? Wake up! I have destroyed all the virus molecules except one. Why have you not regained consciousness? D., please!

Shannon stirred, her thoughts rushing outward. Roebor. He'd emerged. She'd moved deep within her mind. The deepest meditation she'd ever experienced. Her yoga instructor would've been proud. But Roebor had returned.

The virus? Yes, the virus had disappeared from her system; she could feel its absence. *Thank Odin.*

She opened her eyes. Roebor's fiery eyes peered down at her. He had gathered her in one great paw, tenderly curving his toes around her.

How did she feel? The aches had disappeared. She didn't feel uncomfortably hot anymore. She raised her fingers to her nose. No new bleeding.

But still tired. Still damn tired.

"How did you stop the virus?"

Fire, Roebor said.

Fire? Shannon pictured slightly singed blood vessels, smoky organs, perhaps the occasional ember still burning in her brain. She shut her imagination down.

"And you're okay? The virus didn't attacked you?"

I am fine, D.

"We need to return soon. I'm losing too much energy. But thank you! You saved my life. I owe you."

Roebor blinked, then blinked again. *You owe me nothing, D. This I did gladly for you. Come, let's go home.* He wrapped the one remaining virus, baseball-sized again, tightly in his paw. *You will keep a distance from me and at my back.*

"Not a problem." She floated down to Roebor's tail, as far from the virus as she could go, grabbed some fur, and held on.

* * *

After another hour, Roebor stopped again.

If my calculations are correct, we have now passed to just beyond the river wall. But we must take great care from this point, so as to not injure ourselves or Essi.

"Okay, but I don't quite understand how we'll wrap up the virus."

I must take a few atoms belonging to Essi and reinsert the virus. Then we must take a small piece of my skin, and insert Essi's atoms into a molecule of the skin.

"How could we possibly do that?"

One step at a time, D.

He began to grow but very slowly. Shannon followed suit. Very carefully. When he had grown so that the virus appeared about the size of a very small seed, he placed it on the pad of his paw and beckoned Shannon over. Shannon closed her mouth and pinched her nose; she would take no more chances.

Do you see this scar here at the tip of my pad? I'll wedge the virus right here. It will be there, although it will soon be impossible for us to see. I am counting on the balance of particles to keep it in place. You see?

Shannon nodded. *Not a bloody clue.*

Roebor grew again, but at an exceedingly slow pace. Shannon matched him, equally careful not to grow in any way that might harm Essi. When Roebor next stopped, Shannon looked around. More of the constructs of electrons and protons and that other thing dotted the landscape now, and they all looked tiny and close together. Shannon and Roebor had grown larger than single atoms.

Roebor reached out with his free paw, the one without the virus, and scooped a set of the atoms into his hand. He pressed this little mass right onto the virus. Pressed hard.

I hypothesize that in this place, comprised of both mind and matter, where the virus cannot penetrate into my skin, it will instead be drawn and trapped in one of these atoms, just as an atom trapped it back on Riverworld, when the virus randomly attacked Essi.

Shannon wanted to ask a million questions. She bit her tongue.

Now I must test this theory, which presents a dangerous point of the process for you. First try casting your haze at each of my paws. Can you find the virus?

Shannon cast the colors, and then looked at Roebor in alarm. "I'm not picking it up on either one. How could that be?"

I feared this would happen. My handling of the virus has interfered with your ability to discern it. To see it, you will have to be closer to the bundle of atoms where we hope the virus now resides. You must shrink until I can put you on my hand, and then you must shrink again until you can tell whether my paw is still cradling the virus, or whether it has been absorbed into the bundle, as we hope.

Stand as close as you can to this paw, which should now carry the cluster of atoms with the virus. I will shift you onto my paw when you have shrunk small enough. Go slowly.

"Are you sure this will work?"

No, Roebor said patiently, *but you will be safe if you take care. I trust you, D. Essi trusts you. You will not let us down.*

Easy for him to say.

CHAPTER THIRTY-SIX

SHAKING LIKE A LEAF, Shannon shrank again, smaller, smaller still. Roebor now looked like full-sized Roebor. Smaller she shrank. Now she could see only one giant paw and a furry leg stretching up and out of sight.

She stopped.

Roebor placed his paw beside her so that she could climb onto the pad. Although his fur should have made the climb easy, it took her a full fifteen minutes to make it to the top. There she collapsed from fatigue.

Can you proceed, D.? Did you locate the scar?

Shannon struggled to her feet.

"I'm moving. And I've found the scar."

She straggled along his paw pad toward his toes, and examined the scar. It looked from her height like a pale, rough-edged hill running toward the edge where his fur curled over the pad. At the edge, a groove separated pad and fur.

She cast her colors along the top of the hill. Nothing.

She walked down the length of the scar right to the very edge of the pad. She cast. No virus.

"Am I in the right place?"

Walk about five paces to your left. And then shrink again.

Shannon shivered. Doubts overwhelmed her. *Would she get lost? Would the virus attack her again?*

No matter. She had to do it. She clenched her fist and shrank again.

When the scar looked like a cliff, the top of which she could no longer see, and the edge of Roebor's pad looked like an abyss without bottom, she cast her colors. Cast with silvery orange as strong and bright as she could make it. Cast as far as she could. Left along the pad, right along the pad, down into the abyss. Up along the scar-cliff.

Nothing.

Just to be sure, she shrank one more time. Cast again in every direction. Hiked out to the abyss. Cast. Cliff, cast and rested. Walked along the cliff, over to the abyss, along the abyss, back to the cliff. Nothing.

Getting so, so tired.

She must head home. Had she looked hard enough? Cast far enough? Shrunk small enough? What if she missed it? She could easily fail. Fail Essi. Fail Roebor. Fail humanity. Maybe she should shrink one more time. Just one more. *Odin's eye, she hated to do it.*

She shrank as far as she dared. She might not have the energy to enlarge again if she shrank much more. She cast down into the abyss again.

Nothing. Of course noth—but wait—*there*—she saw it. A small dot of orange in her haze. Roebor must have pushed the virus deep into the crease between his pad and his fur. It couldn't remain there. She had to retrieve it. She would have to go down. But how?

Think. What had she learned from Salesti?

Okay. Not only could she shrink in a mind-space such as this, but she could float. Nothing prevented her from floating down to the virus except her own understanding of the laws of physics. She'd have to take care; if somehow she believed she'd fall, she would. And she could die here, just as Indy. . . .

Carefully, slowly, she floated over the abyss and imagined herself sinking. Down she floated until the little dot of the virus came into view. But only the light of her casting of the colors revealed its location. It remained too small. To reclaim it, she would have to shrink again.

Shrink again? *No!* Every fiber of her being objected. *She wouldn't make it. She'd die.*

So. Terror feels like this. She couldn't move. She could scarcely think. Some part of her brain, that part most concerned with self preservation, rejected the idea of shrinking again, here where no one could help her. Where, if she became too weak, she might never find a way out. Where, if the virus attacked her, she'd bleed to death. Where, if she ran out of energy, she'd die alone. She couldn't do it.

And yet.

How could she not? Everything depended on it. If Roebor returned to the real world with the virus lodged in his paw, it would surely escape and cause the destruction she must stop at all costs.

At all costs.

For a long moment Shannon stood still, capable of neither turning her back on the virus nor of shrinking down to claim it. She must find a way to make herself move.

She thought of her Indy. She'd lost the beloved dog completely and utterly this time. That loss hurt her almost more than she could bear. If she remained paralyzed with fear, she'd lose more of those she loved. She couldn't, wouldn't witness the loss of anyone else, not Luke, not Narci, Essi, or Salesti. Not Roebor.

Tidak, meh.

But the rest, no. If somebody had to bear the loss of *her*, too bad; *she* refused to grieve any more today. So shrink she would.

And so she shrank again, carefully, slowly, until she could locate the virus. *There.* The bundle of atoms Roebor had swiped from the periphery of Essi's mind-brain river wall construct had, as hoped, trapped the virus. Shannon shrank until she could grasp the bundle in her hand. She held onto it in a tight fist and floated up until she reached the pad of Roebor's paw.

She walked to what seemed to her the midpoint between the abyss and the cliff

"I found it, R. Deep within the crease between your paw pad and fur. The atom bundle absorbed it and now I'm holding it in my hand."

D! You've been quiet so long, I feared . . . Stay with it while I cut a patch of my skin so that we can place the atom bundle in a molecule of my skin.

Shannon handled the bundle with extreme care. She would take no chances that the virus might shake lose of its atomic wrapping and attack her again.

After a few minutes, an island dropped from the sky some distance away, and thudded with enough force to jar Shannon's teeth. *No, not an island, a piece of Roebor's skin. Ew.* She checked the virus: still deeply embedded in the atom bundle. She floated with the bundle over to the piece of skin to examine it. Along the skin, which looked like another cliffside, she faced lattice-like structures made of roundish objects, some small, like dome-shaped houses, some huge, like office towers dozens of stories high. Molecules?

Can you hear me D.?

Yes. Do you hear me?

I do. I am glad your telepathic link makes it possible for us to talk. Otherwise it would be scientifically impossible.

I hate it break it to you, but everything we're doing is scientifically impossible. It's the mind–brain connection working for us here. And who knows what else.

Indeed. Do you see a cross-section of my skin?

I believe I do. I think I'm looking at molecules of your skin cell wall. I think I can stash this bundle right in one of them if the bundle will penetrate. Do I need to cut a hole through a molecule or what?

Try simply pressing the bundle against a molecule to determine if it will pass through.

Shannon selected the closest molecule, one of the towering structures, and tried first at one point, then another. She pushed as hard as she could, given her food-deprived weakling status. No luck. She tried one of the smallest molecules. *Oh!* Shannon emitted a little gasp: The bundle had slipped right in.

It absorbed. It's inside, she told Roebor.

The island of skin disappeared from view, as if the sky had sucked it up with a straw.

Roebor must be tucking it away in the skin fold he mentioned.

Shannon began to grow again.

Abyss became valley. Cliff became hill. Valley became groove, hill became scar. She looked up. Roebor had lowered his head close to his paw and peered right at her. *Damn,* from this perspective, Roebor's eyes looked like volcanic eruptions of blue fire; his incisors looked like stalactites and stalagmites. Huge, sharp ones.

A small sigh escaped him when he caught sight of her. The sigh hit her like a brisk, warm wind. She fell backward with its impact and banged her head, although Roebor's paw pad allowed for a soft landing.

When she reached the appropriate size, they grew together to greater and greater size, until Roebor stopped them and again adjusted to horse-sized status compared to her, and they found themselves just in front of the pea-sized dark patch, floating in Essi's River.

"You have it safely tucked away?"

Yes, D. We have done it. Or rather, primarily you have done it. I can scarcely believe it. He gathered her up in a great hug.

She hugged him back. "I can't believe it either. And I can't believe we lived to tell the tale." Realizing she was still holding him around his great neck, she let him go, adding, "Let's get out of here and send you home."

Shannon couldn't help herself. Her relief at being safe, and in no more danger of becoming lost, her gratitude to Roebor for eradicating the virus within her, for devising the method of safely transporting Essi's virus off Earth, all welled up in her at once and she hugged the big brute around his neck yet again.

"Thank you, R., for everything."

* * *

They swam to Essi's Great Room, where the relieved faces of Essi and Toss revealed that they had been waiting with great anxiety.

After hugs all around, they sat in a foursome on the floor.

"You feel fine, right, Essi? No headache, no bloody noses or ears, right? No disruptions to your thoughts or ability to talk or move around?"

She hummed as if Hawaiian sun warmed each note. The vibrations of her humming in turn warmed Shannon to her very center.

Essi said, *toss watches over essi. essi fine. tell toss and essi how shannon and roebor find virus.* Toss had not yet spoken a word.

"Go ahead, R., but make it quick." She sat down at Essi's side.

While Roebor explained their journey with great detail, and cast the two of them as the bravest sort of heroes, Shannon studied her quietly humming little Essi. She chuckled at herself for still thinking of the alien child who had visited her only five years earlier as *her little Essi.* The Seladoran was neither little nor hers anymore. Shannon couldn't adjust to the fact that the five-year-old she'd come to love could possibly have grown into this beautiful young woman, even though the lavender skin, the wonderful green eyes, and the wispy silver-blond hair all belonged to her Essi.

As Shannon sat with the other three, these musings weighed heavily on her heart. She'd subconsciously come to think of Essi as the child she'd never had. And somewhere in the back of her mind, she'd expected that small child to return to her, love her, and be loved by her, over and over as the years passed. She'd expected, in some unacknowledged corner of her subconscious, that she would watch as Essi grew and changed. But Essi's transformation into womanhood had happened without her.

Nor had Essi arrived in the condition in which she'd arrived last time. Essi had just lost her mother to the aliens when she'd arrived five years earlier. She adopted Shannon as her surrogate mom so deeply that not long after she arrived, she transformed Shannon's eye and hair color overnight to those of her mother. And Shannon in turn protected and fought for her as a mother would.

But now Shannon watched Toss wrap his long slender arm around Essi's shoulder and lean toward her. She watched Essi respond by leaning into him, resting her head against his chest. Essi belonged to Toss now, as much as she could belong to anyone.

This was as it should be. Shannon and Essi would be reunited again one day; she felt sure of it. Maybe next time, she'd be Shannon's age and they could try out sisterhood for a short time. Shannon smiled.

She let Roebor finish his embellished tale and then, with apologies, told them she must return to her body for food. Without delay. More hugs all around, and then she returned to the real world.

* * *

When Shannon opened her eyes, she found Dr. Bennett sitting beside her bed.

"Dr. B. How long have you been here?" Shannon asked, trying to scoot up against her pillows.

Dr. Bennett, who'd been glaring at her cell phone, jumped at the sound of Shannon's voice. "You're awake! I've just been debating how long I dare let you sleep."

"I need to eat, and eat a ton," Shannon said. "What's the time?"

"You slept through the night and half the day, and now it's almost six."

Dr. B. dialed a number on her cell phone and soon arranged a veritable feast to be delivered by Uber Eats.

"I wanted desperately to wake you up to tell you that I looked through the photos the Humane Society posts online, and I'm pretty sure I found Narci. I talked to a representative down there and the cat's not doing well at all. If you promise—*promise*—me to take it easy, I'll complete the paperwork tonight to have you discharged early tomorrow, so you can go down and claim her. I asked them to just hold the cat for you, but they must follow the rules, apparently, and you, as the owner, must show up and sign the documents, or they just keep processing her as if I hadn't explained the whole situation. If I correctly understood the volunteer I talked to, she's scheduled to be euthanized tomorrow afternoon because she's sick, and they don't know what's wrong with her. But they will open the doors for you, even though it's Sunday."

CHAPTER THIRTY-SEVEN

"WE'RE OUT OF TIME all the way around, R.," Shannon said on Sunday morning, as she stood in front of the Ocean City Humane Society's front doors waiting for the staff to unlock them. "I have to send Essi and company home very soon or we're all goners. And you have to reach the portal up in Alaska on schedule. I think I'll charter a seaplane so we have at least a slim chance at that."

Agreed: we must act now.

True to her word, Dr. B. had signed the discharge papers. Even though the hospital's administrative offices had not yet opened, she personally escorted Shannon out of the facility and drove her to the nearest diner for a hearty breakfast.

"History repeats itself, Shannon," Dr. Bennett had said in her no-nonsense way, as Shannon finished up the last of her waffles. "You look terrible. As bad as the last time we hospitalized you for weeks and still nearly lost you. I ought not let you out of my sight."

"I feel as bad as I look. But you know as well as I do that I need to send everyone who's on board home, and *then* I'll take all the help you can give me. So, if you could drive me over to the Humane Society, I'll Uber from there, and you can get back to the business of medicine." *Odin's eye. Tired just from talking.* She said nothing more, except to ask if she could have Dr. B.'s remaining piece of French toast.

* * *

When the Humane Society finally opened, Shannon produced her driver's license, which matched the information the OCHS had received when they scanned the cat's chip. She also described her little, blue-eyed, black cat down to the tiny scar on her lip that she'd acquired in a scrape with a tom cat the winter before. The staff cautioned her to accept that she would be taking the cat home to die of an unspecified illness. But Shannon knew better; stuffing the cat with calories would probably turn the tide.

A sweet, young volunteer named Yishun showed them to a small room, and went off to fetch Narcissus.

As Shannon waited for Yishun to bring out Narci, she kept her eyes closed and slouched against the chair back. The door opened, she heard a scrabbling, and opened her eyes just in time to watch Narci struggle free of Yishun's arms, not shy about using her claws for leverage. With one leap the cat crossed the distance to Shannon's lap.

"Hello, my baby," Shannon murmured. As the cat purred and rubbed any part of Shannon she could reach, Shannon could feel the cat's bones beneath sagging skin. Her fur clumped in some spots, and bare skin showed in others where her fur had fallen out. Her dull, half-lidded eyes no longer gleamed. She meowed half-heartedly in a hoarse croak. If

Shannon hadn't arrived this morning, the HS might not have needed to euthanize her this afternoon.

Poor little dragonpanther, Roebor said. So this what Salesti's presence did to her system. And we now damage your system in the same way, D. I am sorry. Will Narcissus survive? Will they give her wings when she heals? Will you survive?

I'm hoping she'll be okay, R. I'm taking her straight to my vet. He'll do everything he can for her. But no, no wings. Her kind doesn't ever have wings.

Poor creatures. Only half evolved. Far in the future, long after you and I have passed, D., your little dragonpanther species will be winged.

"She was actually sleeping until about five minutes before you walked in the door," Yishun said. "She suddenly just woke up and started meowing. Now look at her. She's obviously really yours. How'd she get lost?"

"We were caught out in the Left Hand Campground fire," Shannon said.

The volunteer nodded. "The fire swept up a lot of pets. As bad as Narci looks, she's one of the lucky ones."

Narci curled up in her lap and lay very still. Shannon continued to hold her tight, but looked up to ask the volunteer what else she needed to do. Yishun had departed, apparently to give them a moment to reunite, and to put some antiseptic on the cat scratches Narci had inflicted.

"Come on back over to me, Salesti, Narci has carried you as long as she can."

Salesti raced back to Shannon's Great Room and Shannon spared just a moment to give her a hug, tiny wings and all, and left her in the middle of a welcoming huddle comprised of Essi, Toss, and Roebor.

Can Narci flow here too for a moment, D.? I should like to meet her.

"I should still say no, but, oh all right." Shannon checked with Narci by sending a series of images. Yes, Narci would go.

Shannon flowed over to the cat and brought her spirit back to Shannon's Great Room. Essi picked her up immediately and began to croon and pet her. Salesti flew in close and nuzzled her, cheek to cheek. Roebor craned his neck to catch a view of her in the little Seladoran huddle. Somehow, the silvery pale blue blaze of Roebor's eyes softened.

She is small compared to you, D. Yet I know a jet black dragonpanther who could be her father, so much do they look alike. Can you hold her up for me?

Shannon gently slipped Narci from Essi's arms into her own and, cuddling her close, moved over where Roebor could lie down and have a better look. He moved his face close to the cat.

Be well, little dragonpanther.

Narci lifted her own head and gave Roebor a long lick across his nose.

Roebor pulled back and laughed loud enough to rock the Seladorans and Shannon back on their feet.

"I should get her back to her body, R."

Roebor nodded and sighed.

Shannon kept Narci tucked in her lap while she finished signing the paperwork to spring the cat from incarceration.

Then she slipped Narci into the cardboard crate the staff had given her for transport and carried her carefully to the car.

Shannon Ubered directly to her vet where she explained that Narci needed nourishment due to her high metabolism issue and the recent trauma of escaping the fire. Dr. Tenpass soon had Narci on a sucrose drip and medication.

* * *

With a hug and tears, Shannon left her behind to urge her Uber driver to race on to the marina so she could find a seaplane pilot. Shannon's fatigue continued to grow. Fortunately, the charter office stood only a few yards from the street. Shannon made her way from door to desk to counter, using each to propel her to the next.

She explained that she wanted to fly to a Canadian bay she particularly yearned to visit for sentimental reasons, then she hoped to travel on up to the Dickson where she worked, and she needed to leave within the next few hours.

"You're the gal I saw on TV. The one who lost her clothes in that explosion in Alaska and got saved by the dolphin. Am I right?" said Squally Jones, a white-haired, deeply tanned, and wrinkled gentleman with eyebrows Shannon stared at in fascination. They grew as long as patches of grass.

I could curl up and take a nap in those eye mats, and no one would even know I was there, Roebor said.

Stop it, Shannon said, trying hard to lower her eyes to Squally's nose.

"Saved by the *whale,* yes, that's me," she said as brightly as she could muster. "Beluga whale."

"Nice perfume ya got on. Mind if I get a little closer to get a good whiff? The old sniffer isn't what it used to be." He leaned forward.

Shannon leaned back.

Roebor growled quietly.

Squally stepped gingerly away.

"Flying straight through except for gitting gas?"

"Yes, but you can get some shut-eye if you need to whenever we land."

"We can leave 'bout one. Gonna cost ya."

Shannon had no energy for haggling and soon had written the check demanded by Mr. Squally Jones. Good thing she had nowhere to spend most of her Dickson earnings these last five years up in Alaska, and she'd also made a killing at the White Wolf Casino here in Ocean City five years earlier, thanks to Essi. It still frosted Shannon to think about it: that old goat Tremaine had required her to cough up seed money for the Juneau Project to the tune of a million dollars, and she'd won that and a lot more at the casino before they booted her out. She could live off the proceeds comfortably for the rest of her life.

Shannon moved in wobbly fashion from the seaplane office to the boat berths to find the *Seatation*, so she could rest until departure time. Once on board, she poked around and found a large sack of sweet potato chips that they'd left behind in a small cubicle under the dining table. Lying on her bunk she munched the chips and asked Salesti, "Where's the portal to take you and your fellow Seladorans home? Has it arrived from Alaska yet? Or do we use the permaportal here?"

permaportal.

Shannon's heart sank. That meant she'd have to let Essi go before they boarded the seaplane. She'd hardly spent any time with little—with Essi. Any calm, uninterrupted time, anyway.

essi returnss, Essi said. *essi promiss.*

salesti helps remind essi.

"Okay, where's the portal? Do we walk or do I need to call another Uber driver?

Wait, D.—, Roebor began.

here. portal here. shannon climbs on deck and reaches out, salesti takes essi and toss home, Salesti said.

"How handy," Shannon said without enthusiasm. "I should do it now, or I won't have the energy left to get Roebor home. Oh—first I need to know where Tidak's body is. I forgot all about that. I suppose I should visit his lockup and find out where he stashed it when Toss took his spirit on board some poor earth creature," she added equally unenthusiastically.

Wait, D., I—, Roebor started again.

Essi said, *toss knows location of body. down coast. toss draws picture. toss shows shannon.*

"Excellent, Toss. But if I've got to run the boat down to him, we'd better get to it." Shannon wondered if she even had the energy to cast off the boat lines. Her ankle had been throbbing all morning. And the dizziness had increased.

"Stay put and rest. I can navigate. Just tell me where to go. And here." Luke appeared in the stairwell and tossed a carton of ice cream and a store-wrapped apple pie onto Shannon's bunk.

She sat up gingerly. "When did you leave the hospital?

"As soon as I heard you left. Now stay put."

"Wait! I thought—"

But he disappeared before she could say what she thought. She frowned and then smiled after him.

"R., what will happen when we put Tidak back in his body?" She asked.

As I have been trying to say, if Salesti is willing, we both will flow into Tidak's body together and fly him up to my body. Salesti can return to Shannon there, and I will tether Tidak and fly him to FireWorld. I have the chain and collar for that purpose hidden with my equipment. So you won't be sending Salesti to Riverworld yet, Shannon, if Salesti gives its okay.

salesti willing.

"You have a collar ready and waiting?"

Roebor shrugged. *I suspected Tidak would break the rules of my people here on Earth, and he has. I suspected I would need to take him home to receive justice. If he lived.*

"You'll be careful when you get near the UC—I mean what used to be the UC—right? As far as we know, they're still trying to find whatever caused the implosion, which is to say—you."

We shall not linger in the vicinity long enough for it to be a problem.

"Salesti, will the other portal stay with me when I fly back to Alaska?

portal with shannon always.

"Yes and why does the portal stay with me exactly, Salesti? Can you explain that to me?"

Salesti shrugged, as much as a tiny hummingbird kitten can shrug. *is what is.*

"It is what it is? Very enlightening."

shannon special.

"Special? I don't think so. Special how?"

But Salesti fell silent. Shannon conducted a quick check of the Great Room. No Salesti. "Where did she go?" Shannon asked Toss and Essi.

Toss shrugged, and Essi said, *toss and essi do not know. salesti wishes to be alone.*

"Coward," Shannon shouted into her mind.

Salesti remained out of sight.

* * *

Shannon ate the pie and carried the chocolate fudge ice cream up to the deck. She explained what area they were looking for based on Toss's drawing, and Luke took them out of the harbor, speeding south along the coast. She ate in silence. Luke concentrated on navigating. She appreciated how great he looked in his sunglasses, but he looked twice as great when he took them off to pull the binoculars to his eyes, and she could catch a glimpse of those big, bottomless browns.

"He's around here, Luke," she said, consulting the picture in her head provided by Toss.

"I've got him. On that outcropping of rocks," Luke said. He pulled the boat in as close as he could, but Shannon would still need to suit up and swim over to Tidak's body to send Roebor and Salesti over. Since she didn't need a wetsuit in these waters, the new waterproof arm and ankle casts should be okay. She put the ice cream down and started for the cabin.

"Finish the ice cream first," Luke said. "You need the energy."

Shannon finished it.

* * *

As Shannon swam sluggishly toward Tidak's body, she said, "Are you sure you can keep a lid on Tidak once he returns to his own body, R.?"

If to keep a lid on *means* to control, *I am sure, D. If he wants another fight, I shall oblige, but he has lost and he knows it.*

"Very good, R.! Your command of English idioms has improved."

Roebor snorted.

Shannon swam around the outcropping of rock to a cove hidden from the view of any watchers on the shore or the sea. Tidak had left his body completely out of the water, his head curled to his chest.

"All right. We'll meet you at Roebor's body to retrieve Salesti. Fly safe."

We may not have much time for farewells when Salesti returns to you, D. I will need to proceed out of the area as swiftly as possible. We should perhaps officially part here.

Roebor's words set off in Shannon a pang of—what? Of regret. Of sadness. Of the discovery that she would miss her giant traveling companion more than a little bit.

"I'm sorry to see you go, R." she said. "I'll miss you."

CHAPTER THIRTY-EIGHT

ROEBOR LAUGHED WITH A TINGE OF MELANCHOLY. *Who would have thought it: the dragonpanther and the puny earththing, becoming good friends.* He hesitated and added, *We are, I think, good friends?*

"Good friends," Shannon agreed. She'd entered her Great Room where Toss, Essi, Salesti, and Roebor waited with the bound and sulking Tidak. She floated to Roebor's face and planted a kiss on his left cheek. He wrapped his huge paw around Shannon and gave her a whole-body hug with it before gently letting her go.

Good-bye, Shannon Kendricks, earth woman.

"Good-bye Roebor, First of the Island of Swords," she said, smiling quietly.

Salesti grabbed one of Roebor's wings, Roebor grabbed the back of the injured Tidak none too gently with his four clawed paws, and they flowed away into Tidak's actual body.

Shannon turned her attention to the real world again. She swam as if in slow motion back to the boat, climbed up on the aft ladder, and wiped at the tears that had formed in her eyes.

Luke regarded her quietly.

"A sad good-bye then?"

Shannon didn't speak, just nodded.

As they watched, Tidak stirred and lifted his big head off the rock. He turned and regarded the *Seatation* with fiery eyes. Shannon's heart stopped. Had Tidak managed to gain control again?

But no. The dull bronze dragonpanther nodded once, shook the water from his back and flew off to the northwest, with Roebor in control, heading farther out to sea to avoid observation.

* * *

When they had returned to the dock, Shannon made her way to the bow of the *Seatation* to send Essi and Toss home.

"I'll miss you two," Shannon said. "Toss, I want to get to know you. I really do. And my little Essi—do you hate being called that? I'm afraid to me you'll always be my little Essi."

Toss had not yet spoken since his rescue from Tidak, but Essi said, *essi not minds.*

Luke joined her on the bow.

Shannon continued, "You're special to me, Essi, as special as they come. Visit me again soon, especially if you're not dragging aliens and other difficulties in your wake."

Essi pinned the most roguish of grins on her face, as if to say, *wait until you see what happens next time.*

"Really, no more aliens. I can't survive it. Literally."

"Toss and Essi are leaving?" Luke asked.

Shannon nodded mutely and asked Essi if she had spotted the portal.

yess. above Shannon. cast colors and shannon sees.

Oh right. She cast her multicolored haze up and out toward open water. Yes. A blazing yellow window, almost right above her.

"I don't see any portal," Luke said. "You see it?" Shannon nodded again.

"It's time, then," she said to Toss and Essi, blinking back her tears. "You two take care of each other. And good luck in the portal."

shannon not worries. this portal salesti makes. this portal safe.

Shannon lifted her hand toward the portal and Essi and Toss flowed up her hand. With a crackle and a momentary flash, the portal drew the two Seladorans in, and Shannon found herself alone inside her mind.

How strange. In just a short while she'd grown so very accustomed to her company. *Empty now. So empty.*

She should feel stronger, and yet her knees buckled and she started to fall. Luke caught her up in his arms, and said, "Easy, cara, let's go down to the cabin." He steadied her waist as she made her way along the side deck to the stern and down into the cabin, and eased her down on the bench by the dining table.

"You will miss little Essi. It must be hard to watch her go so soon."

Shannon nodded and then let out a little laugh, which contained within it a small sob, and she said, "I never had a chance to tell you: time passes more quickly on Riverworld, and its people age more quickly, too, so Essi has grown into a young woman in these last five years. I could hardly believe it." All at once Shannon broke down and cried hard, so hard she started hiccupping. She buried her face in Luke's shoulder and let the tears fall.

* * *

A half hour passed before Shannon's wellspring of grief subsided and she managed to say, "I've rented a seaplane to get back up to Roebor's body to pick up Salesti. Leaving at one o'clock. And we found Narci at the Humane Society. She's in bad shape. I dropped the poor baby at my vet's."

"Then we'd better get back to the charter office and let the pilot know he has gained another passenger. Good news about Narci."

"You sure you want to go, Luke? It's all over now but the last good-bye when I send Salesti home. You've been through a lot. You look as bad as I do. Maybe you need to stay home and rest."

"I'm not the only one who needs rest. Go below and snatch some shut-eye. I'll take care of the charter. When it's time, I'll return for you. And I'm sorry about what I said at the hospital. You did what you had to do, cara, I know that."

Shannon took his advice. She couldn't focus. Had trouble standing on her feet. That awful headache had returned, the one she remembered so well from the first time she'd nearly died after Essi and Salesti came on board. She folded onto her berth and closed her eyes. Within seconds she had fallen into a dreamless sleep.

The chimes of her cell phone woke her. Her head felt as if someone had stuffed her purple afghan in it. How long had she been asleep?

"Hello?" she said into the phone.

"Ms. Kendricks. Dr. Moon here. I have been trying to reach you for several days. Where have you been?"

Moon. Odin's eye, she'd totally spaced out his publicity plans. She glanced at her voice mail messages. Seven missed calls, all from Moon.

"Dr. Moon, I'm so glad you called. I'm . . . I'm about to board a seaplane." *True.* "I . . . uh, there's a beluga north of us and we're on our way to check on her—I mean to see if it's Juneau. I mean, who else would it be, right? But I haven't been in touch because I injured myself in a car accident when I became trapped in the Left Hand Campground Fire, and had to go to the hospital . . . again . . . and my cat Narci ran away and almost died in the fire, but I have her back now so . . . so that's why I haven't been in touch."

Moon remained silent for a beat. Shannon imagined him counting to ten. Or a hundred. He'd done it before on Shannon's account.

"All of my scheduled media interviews have been disrupted. We have lost any publicity momentum I had managed to build. You have acted completely irresponsibly. But for now the most important thing is Juneau. I want you to report back to me before the end of the day, do you understand?"

"Absolutely, Dr. Moon. We'll get the media thing straightened out, I promise."

"Yes, Ms. Kendricks, we will. If you wish to remain in the Dickson's employ, we will."

"Right, understood. Right."

"And Ms. Kendricks? I am glad that you escaped the fire. You have been through a great deal in these last weeks. Do not overtax yourself."

You haven't heard the half of it, Dr. Moon.

"I won't. I promise. And thank you."

Shannon clicked off the cell phone and turned over, falling back asleep with a long moment of regret for holding back the whole truth from Moon. Again.

* * *

Luke drove Shannon back to her house to grab her duffel and close the house for a few days. She said good-bye to the raven, which flew down and parked on her outstretched arm for several minutes, while Shannon explained that she wouldn't be gone nearly so long this time.

They returned to the dock and found the sea plane ready to go. Shannon looked down at Ocean City as they took off to find Roebor. The wildfire had come perilously close to the populated suburbs. She shuddered and looked away.

* * *

When at last the seaplane reached the isolated bay in which they'd hidden Roebor's body, Shannon changed into her dry suit, now modified to fit with her waterproof cast, and left Luke and the pilot discussing the finer points of the current overheated presidential campaign. She swam off "to explore," but made her way as quickly as her waning energy allowed to the spot where they'd left Roebor's body. She hoped fervently that nothing had happened to it in their absence.

The body not only still floated just where they'd left it, but Roebor currently inhabited it, and Tidak, in his real body, floated beside him.

"Roebor! You made it. And the virus?"

Roebor patted his chest pouch. *Safe and sound,* he said

"How did you transfer the virus from your essence to your real chest pocket?"

"When Salesti and I flowed from Tidak's body to mine, we placed Tidak's paw in my skin pouch and as we left Tidak's body and flowed into mine, I released the skin patch into my real pouch at the very moment we crossed before flowing to my mind. I do need you to cast the colors to see if it is there as it should be." He pointed to a wrinkle on the skin of his chest where his pouch lay hidden.

Shannon cast the colors into the pouch, with the orange of the virus burning most brightly, hoping fervently that she didn't need to shrink again.

"Yes." she said. "I can just detect it. It's there, but it's very small. Will you have any trouble getting it from your pouch into your lab?"

Roebor shook his head. I have instrumentation for that once I am back in my laboratory."

"How is Tidak doing?" Shannon eyed him warily. He looked harmless enough with a huge iron collar around his neck, anchored to an enormous heavy chain held by Roebor.

Do not worry, D., Tidak is ready to return to FireWorld. Right, Tidak? Tidak nodded slightly, a resentful frown on his face, but didn't speak.

"You ready to come back over, Salesti?" Shannon said, running a hand along Roebor's neck.

yes.

This is good-bye then, D. Perhaps we will meet again sometime.

Without waiting for a response, Roebor paused only long enough for Salesti to flow back to Shannon before he lifted off with Tidak in tow. Shannon had no time to replace her goggles over her eyes, and barely had time to take in a large breath, before their ascending bodies created a giant wave that washed over Shannon, lifting her and propelling her on the surf out in the bay.

Good-bye, Roebor. Good luck.

* * *

Before she returned to the plane, Shannon called out for Juneau.

Juneau? Can you hear me?

The image of the whale came back to her clearly. Juneau had heard her. Shannon explained they would meet at the Dickson.

How have you been?

The whale imaged that she was fine; content and free. She'd managed quite well without Shannon.

A pang of unease and sadness coursed through Shannon's veins.

Juneau then imaged that she would head north, and Shannon sighed and made for the plane. Every stroke she swam felt heavy and slow, as if she were dragging Roebor and Tidak in her wake.

* * *

When she returned to the seaplane, she found that Luke had maneuvered Squally around to the outer windows to look out to sea so that the rise of the dragonpanthers would take place behind their backs.

"I'm telling you, I saw a blue," Luke said to Squally as Shannon came around to the fuselage door, and Luke helped her in. "We saw a blue whale off to the west. Can you believe it?" Luke said to Shannon with a wink.

"*We* didn't see it, *you* saw it. I didn't see a thing. I think you been smoking too much crack."

"A blue? How wonderful. Maybe we'll catch sight of it if we swing that direction on our way north. I'm ready to go now."

"That's it? We came all the way out here to this little bay, which ain't no great shakes anyhow, if you ask me, just so you could swim around for fifteen minutes? Both you been smoking the crack, ain't yer?"

"I needed this sentimental stop, Squally. I left the body of a good friend here once. I had to return to say good-bye."

True.

Squally swiped his hat off his head and made his apologies.

Luke passed her a package of cinnamon raison bagels, and she eased back in her seat, ate the bagels, and dozed all the rest of the way to the Alaska Dickson.

* * *

As Squally deposited them in a small inflatable near the Dickson dock and taxied around to use the fuel pump, Shannon shivered. The temperature up here had dropped unseasonably.

It must be fifteen degrees colder than when they'd left just days earlier. She wished she had worn her winter parka. Dizziness struck her swiftly. She felt nauseous. A splitting headache descended. *She'd pushed herself too far.* Suddenly she swayed, grabbed Luke's arm, and said—*an absolute shocking all-time first*—"I need to go to the infirmary."

She promptly fainted.

* * *

When she regained consciousness, she saw a dark, solid gray sky, a lone seagull, and the back of the bald head of an infirmary medic who had a firm grasp on the front two handles of a stretcher to which they had securely strapped her. Upon further inspection, she saw Luke off to her left, striding along beside the stretcher, his countenance grim.

That *didn't bode well.*

Groggy. Light-headed.

How could a solid gray sky give off such a glare? Shannon eyes hurt. She closed them again.

* * *

When she next opened them, she found herself in familiar territory. The infirmary. Back again. *Odin's Eye. What a nightmare.* Her head, still spinning, made her feel as if she'd eaten a few too many marijuana brownies. She couldn't remember exactly how she'd come to be in this bed.

The infirmary. Hateful place . . . Had she actually *asked* to be brought here?

She looked up at her IV drip. *Oh, right.* She was dying.

Wasn't the first time, hopefully wouldn't be the last.

Something. She should do something about that. Shannon gave her head a tiny shake. She couldn't remember much at all.

shannon knows what to do. shannon returns salesti to riverworld. then shannon not dies. darkness comes, shannon goes to dock. portal there.

"Is this like a fever dream?" Shannon asked the empty room. She tried to place her left hand on her forehead but discovered a cast on her arm. She felt her brow with her right hand. "Doesn't feel like a fever."

But her head was throbbing as if Thor had dimpled the inside of her forehead with hammer dents. She found that the headache inflicted the least amount of pain when she kept her head very, very still.

shannon has no fever. shannon not dreams. salesti speaks to shannon. shannon visits great room. shannon sees.

"Great Room? What Great Room?"

A figured loomed in the doorway. The hall lights behind the figure contrasted with the dark of her room; she could only make out a silhouette.

Her body shivered. Her mind snapped into alert mode. Dr. Copper? She didn't want to run into Dr. Copper. She didn't recall the exact reason for that at the moment, but the thought came to her very clearly: *Do not talk to Dr. Copper; get help.*

Shannon slid her hand down and found her call button. Her finger hovered above it. "Dr. Copper?" she asked, her voice wavering.

CHAPTER THIRTY-NINE

"NO. DR. COPPER IS NO LONGER WITH US. He left under rather mysterious circumstances just after you sailed away, Ms. Kendricks," said the form in the doorway. "Will it be all right if I turn on the light over the sink here?" she asked, moving to the sink against the outside wall of the bathroom.

"Sure," said Shannon, although she regretted saying yes to the light the minute the visitor flipped the switch. The brightness stung her eyes and intensified her headache, which increased her dizziness threefold.

Still, she could tolerate anything if Dr. Copper had vanished. Shannon remembered him now, and she figured she knew why he'd vanished, too: because he worked for Homeland Security, same as Dakota.

Kota. Her good friend. So Shannon had thought. And the so-called friend had planned to steal Juneau and to set up Shannon and Luke on a fake drug bust. *How that hurt.*

Shannon remembered the days when she never let anyone get close to her. If no one came close; no one could hurt her. And she couldn't hurt them. Still, those days were over. She had learned to let people in, despite the occasional bad egg. Like Kota.

"My name is Dr. Killian. Kelly Killian. I don't believe we've had the pleasure." She put her hand over Shannon's right hand and sat on the edge of Shannon's hospital bed. She wore her light brown hair extremely short, wore her make up subtly, wore her smile with a sad, tired sincerity. "I've just been on the phone with Dr. Julia Bennett in Ocean City, California. I believe you two are well-acquainted. She notified the Dickson several days ago that she thought you planned to include us on your itinerary, and that if you did, you might need medical attention."

Dr. Killian grinned. "She turned out to be quite prescient. So I called her to be sure we understand your diagnosis and can treat you properly. I must say, Dr. Bennett did not provide me with an entirely clear picture about the underlying disorder that causes your metabolism to skyrocket out of control as it has. But fortunately, she has forwarded the records of the treatment that brought you back from the brink a few years ago. Do you recall that?"

Recall it? How could she forget it?

"Only too well, Dr. Kelly Killian. Luckily for me, though, I remained unconscious through much of it, so I don't have a lot to remember."

So tired. She couldn't speak more than two sentences without needing a nap to recover.

darkness comes, shannon sends salesti home.

Nausea erupted in Shannon's stomach and threatened to climb up her throat. Going out onto the dark pier to free the Seladoran would be a rough haul.

"Can you tell me the time?"

"Sure. It's now nearly five fifteen."

She couldn't get outside under the cover of dark to send Salesti home for hours yet. She would rest, and perhaps her head and stomach would calm down. Despite her nausea, Shannon knew she needed to replenish her energy.

"Am I allowed to eat real food?"

"You can eat." Dr. Killian bounced to her feet. "I'll go arrange for that right now."

"Excellent. Nice to meet you, Dr. Kelly Killian."

Dr. Killian stopped in the doorway. "That really is a lovely perfume you are wearing, Shannon. Ivy told me about it before I first came in to check on you. I thought she was engaging in hyperbole, but I know now she wasn't. Quite lovely." She stopped for a moment, contemplating Shannon's strange scent, before adding, "Oh, one more thing. A nice young man, very handsome, I might add, was hovering anxiously over you when you first came in, but I wanted you on absolute bed rest for a few hours, so I shooed him away. I promised to contact him if you regained consciousness and were allowed visitors. But you can decide who you want to visit and when. If you would rather he didn't come, just let me know. I will add that if you don't want him to return, you'll be breaking the hearts of half the staff on the floor."

Yeah, the number of hearts Luke broke just by existing irritated Shannon no end. "Luke can visit any time."

"The female staff of C Wing thanks you," she said and departed.

As soon as she disappeared, Shannon said, "Okay, I'm fully awake now, Salesti. Being scared right out of my hospital gown by the thought that Dr. Killian could be Copper has slapped me completely awake. I'll get you down to the portal if I have to crawl, my friend."

good. salesti has important job to do. must go.

So the little laid-back fuzzball had urgent matters to attend to. Who'd have thought? Shannon rested her head back on her pillow. Remaining upright took too much effort. Her neck already hurt from lifting her head. She *just might*, in fact, be forced to crawl to the dock.

She closed her eyes and returned to her Great Room.

* * *

"Salesti. Come walk with me. Or rather I'll walk, you buzz along."

Salesti's tinkling laugh followed in their wake. "I'll miss that laugh for sure, Salesti. It never fails to make me think of all the best things. Little children, sunshine, singing, rainbows, puppies, Luke."

salesti thinks shannon wishes to speak serious words?

"Yes. I want you to tell me the truth, Salesti. Why do I have to be the one to undertake these strange, terrifying, nearly-fatal missions? One of these times I won't make it back from the precipice of death, you know. You, and anybody else who's on board, will die with me."

truth. work of shannon very dangerous. but shannon brave. bravery most important thing. brave heart. open heart. heart that loves living things. and the other truth.

"What other truth?"

Salesti buzzed more loudly than Shannon had ever heard it buzz. As Shannon watched in astonishment, it turned in complete circles. It buzzed back and forth in a straight line. It landed on Shannon's shoulder with a thump.

"What's wrong, Salesti?"

salesti will say. salesti will say secret. fair to shannon to know.

And yet the little creature still buzzed as if unsure. Then it blurted out its words and buzzed away.

shannon more than human.

CHAPTER FORTY

IN HER GREAT ROOM, SHANNON STOOD PLANTED.

More than human?

Salesti couldn't say that kind of thing and then run away. Shannon called after her, "What do you mean I'm more than human? I'm only human. My bones break like I'm only human—she held up her cast; I starve like I'm only human."

Salesti stopped and buzzed back toward Shannon. *fair to say body of shannon human. but more given to shannon on day of birth. because of this, aliens find shannon. seladorans. dragonpanthers. so and so and so. but salesti never* makes *shannon help when aliens come. shannon helps because shannon does right thing. shannon does right thing even with tiny bit of tidak.*

"So you know about that. But look, Salesti, none of this makes sense to me. Given by whom? Given what?"

Salesti flew off, and when Shannon tried to follow, she disappeared right in front of Shannon's eyes.

"Hey, I own this mind. You can't just disappear in here unless I say.

But, in fact, Salesti had vanished.

* * *

Shannon's dinner arrived, and she vowed to eat it as slowly as she could, to make the time pass until the skies darkened enough for her to slip outside.

Her doctor returned just after the food trolley trundled in the door.

Shannon asked, "Dr. Kelly Killian, do you think I might sit in a wheelchair to eat, and leave all these tubes and wires off until I'm finished? I'll be fine while food's entering the system, right? And I'll stay where I can holler if I have any trouble. That way, I can maybe sit by that big window in the hallway and watch the sun go down when I'm finished?"

"I think we can accommodate that," Dr. Killian said, and carefully disengaged Shannon from her IV and monitors. Shannon stood on one wobbly leg just long enough to hop over to the wheelchair, which Dr. Killian slid toward her.

Good. She wouldn't have to crawl to the dock after all.

Despite her earnest intentions, Shannon's voracious appetite precluded a slow, decorous meal; she wolfed down every scrap in minutes. Then she hailed Ivy, who happened to be passing by her door, and asked if she might sit in front of the big window for a while. Ivy wheeled her out into the hall.

She contemplated the forest of evergreens that rose up quickly on the mountainside beyond the Dickson's clearing, and watched the sky turn peach, then pink, then lavender as the sun played off the cloud cover. Luke joined her at the window.

"Pull up a chair," she said.

Luke grabbed one from a small table situated farther up the hallway. He looked around and said in a quiet voice, "You need to send your last friend home as soon as possible. Where do we go to accomplish that?"

"Just down to the dock. I plan to slip out after dark, so nobody will notice."

"Rolling that wheelchair with one arm? No. I'll push you." He sat back and gazed out the window.

"I could do it if I had to," Shannon said.

"Yes, but you *don't* have to."

"Okay. As long as you understand I could do it."

"Cara, I am of the firm belief that you could do just about anything you put that clever, stubborn mind of yours to. I love that about you."

Wait. Did he just use the "L" word?

Be cool, be cool, be cool. "And you always seem to show up to make it easier for me. I love that about you."

Lame. Not *well played, cabbage head.* But at least she had worked in the "L" word.

"Yes. One of my best traits. I am dependable." Luke grinned.

A pair of doctors walked by, talking in hushed voices to one another, a set of charts clutched in the hands of one of them, the other pointing with animation at some entry on the paperwork.

After they'd passed, the conversation lagged.

Eventually Luke said, "What then? After Salesti has departed."

"I tell Moon—oh shoot; I've forgotten to call Moon. I'd better do it now. Hopefully he won't answer, and I can just leave him a voice mail message."

Shannon dialed Moon's cell phone. Unfortunately, he picked up after only two rings. She talked as fast as she could without taking a breath, so Moon couldn't yell at her.

"Dr. Moon. So glad I caught you. We've traveled all the way back up here to the Dickson, and as soon as we arrived, I had to be admitted to the infirmary again, so I need to stick pretty close to the medical center for a while, I'm afraid, but, anyway, Juneau is in fact up here in the vicinity and so, I'd like to keep her up here, if that's okay, because she clearly didn't like the southern waters, and I don't think it's a good idea to put her through a transport, and we can manage the public end of things from here, plus I shouldn't travel either, so what do you think?"

Moon sighed. As he often did in conversations with Shannon.

"I am relieved you have located Juneau. This news takes a great load off my mind. However, Shannon, Thomas Tremaine discovered her absence. And, it turns out our funding for rebuilding the underwater complex remains on very precarious grounds. As you know, I authorized certain activities to be initiated for the rebuild without financing in place. This has been discovered by Tremaine and certain board members, who are now calling for my ouster. It may only be a matter of days before I am gone and the Alaska Dickson closes for good."

In all the time Shannon had known Moon, she'd never picked up anything but strong, positive vibes about the Alaska Dickson, and Juneau and Shannon's project. Tonight Moon sounded utterly defeated.

"As soon as I'm back on my feet, we'll figure this out. I'm sure we can, Dr. Moon. Don't give up hope yet."

"Good night, Shannon," said Moon and clicked off before Shannon could say another word.

* * *

At midnight, Luke wheeled Shannon down the hallway. Her head throbbed in time to the creaky wheel on the front left corner of her wheelchair.

"I am going to take Shannon for a quick spin before she goes back to sleep," he said to the nurses at the central station, giving them the benefit of a wave and a wink as he passed by. No one protested, and a few seconds later, they rounded the corner of the infirmary's C Wing, heading for B Wing, in search of a door connecting the infirmary to the housing units on Q block. From there they proceeded through the housing units' hallways, out the back door to the parking lot, and from the parking lot to the dock.

Shannon checked the skies: not a rain cloud in sight. Dry weather would help her soldier through this last effort. However, the wind had picked up significantly. Shannon shivered in her hospital gown, even though she'd slipped on her sweat pants and Luke had tucked two blankets over her legs. They figured they couldn't get away with any more blankets or clothing if they wanted to convince the nurses they'd only set out for a hallway ride. The blankets flapped around Shannon's legs. Luke pulled off his leather jacket and draped it across Shannon, who placed her arms through the sleeves.

He tucked it in behind her and wrapped the blankets tightly against her legs.

"Better?"

Shannon nodded. "This shouldn't take long," she said, her teeth chattering. "Salesti, where exactly do we stop?"

shannon knows. cast the colors. seek flaming yellow.

Shannon cast the colors all along the sky above her head and down the pier, a bright orange-yellow band shining brightly within the multicolored haze.

"Got it," she said. "Out at the end of the main pier."

As they approached the end of the pier, Shannon watched a large rectangle of fire open above them, as if someone had painted over a swatch of dark purple sky with a fireplace hearth. Yellow flames leapt and danced behind the rectangle.

"Can you see it? I can't." Luke asked.

see? shannon finds.

Shannon's hands shook, and she didn't entirely blame the unseasonable evening chill. How could riding in a wheelchair tire her out so wretchedly?

"Ready to go?" she asked.

salesti tells shannon one more thing?

"You're about to tell me who infused me with specialness, I hope?"

no salesti not tells that secret.

"Why not?"

secret not mine to tell.

"Okay, now my head is exploding again. Thanks a heap for that little nugget. I think I'll send you home before you lay anything else on my tender psyche, okay? Oh, but I do have one question for you. Do all the worm holes go through Riverworld, and if they do, why does Roebor have to time his return, while the rest of you can leave when you like?"

most worm holes, as shannon names them, flow through riverworld, but not all. fireworld also center for worm holes. roebor comes to riverworld by fireworld portal and comes to earth by fireworld portal. portals from fireworld behave different, have cycles. very hard to travel.

"Got it. So are you ready to head out?"

salesti ready.

Shannon stood from her wheelchair, the wind whipping her braid and Luke's leather jacket. She extended her good arm as high as it would go. It shook so badly Luke grasped her wrist and held her hand firmly pointed skyward. Salesti flowed down from Shannon's Great Room, through her arm, through her fingers and upward, and then the flame caught it and sucked it into the portal.

And just like that Salesti vanished. From Shannon's Great Room, from Earth.

Love you, Salesti, Shannon said to the disappearing portal.

* * *

Shannon thumped down in the wheelchair heavily.

Now she really *had* sent them all away. She should be glad. Their departure meant her health would start to improve. Probably. Tidak would not harm Essi, and the virus would not harm Earth. Roebor would take the virus to FireWorld and find a cure for the disease taking out his people. Surely he would. Hopefully he would. Fingers crossed.

Yet joy did not overwhelm her. She would miss them—

"Uh-oh. Did you not say Roebor and Tidak had already gone home?" Luke said.

"I thought they had, why?"

"Look there, due west." He pointed out to sea. "Two dark shapes flying this way, with four light blue X-ray eyes lighting their path."

Shannon peered into the dark. "Roebor and Tidak, all right. They must just now be aiming for their underwater portal." She continued to watch the advancing forms, and then looked up at Luke in alarm. "Roebor is *chasing* Tidak, and Tidak's chain is hanging loose. Tidak has escaped."

CHAPTER FORTY-ONE

IN THE WATER FIFTY FEET OUT from where Shannon sat and Luke stood, a blue glow suddenly appeared.

"I can see the portal for Roebor and Tidak," Shannon said.

"Where?"

Shannon pointed and said, "just past the warning buoy, below the waterline about ten feet, there."

Luke shook his head. "I can't see it."

Tidak flew within a football field's distance of the blue glowing water and then turned to face Roebor.

Shannon grabbed Luke's hand. "Tidak means to stop Roebor from reaching the portal before it closes again. But Roebor's carrying the virus. We have to help him."

Shannon looked around, desperate for an idea. "We need a boat," she said, shouting to be heard in the rising wind. "Let's take the biggest one we can get."

"That one," Luke yelled back, pointing to the Dickson's flagship fifty-four-foot research boat berthed at the end of the pier. He pushed Shannon's wheelchair down the wooden planks at a full run. Shannon's head pounded with each bounce of the wheelchair. When they reached the boat, Shannon pushed to her feet with a surprising rush of adrenaline and began to clamber one-handed and one-footed up the ladder to the deck, fighting the wind with each step. At the same time Luke pulled the lines free from their mooring.

Her eyes stung from tears caused by the pounding in her head. The fingers of her hand on the arm encased in the cast clung to the ladder, while she used her other hand to pull herself up. Needles of wind pricked her fingers, and her ears rang, buffeted by the now roaring gusts of ocean and air intermingled.

Luke climbed up behind her.

The boat keys were in the ignition, as they usually were in all the boats here, since the public didn't have access to the marina. Shannon started the engines and pulled the boat out from its berth. She steered the boat toward Tidak, who hovered just above the water, the chain still dangling from his collar, as he waited to see from which direction Roebor would approach.

"If I can hook the chain," Luke shouted. "We should be able to attach it here," he pointed at one of the metal loops on the boat's railing, perhaps designed to hold fishing poles firmly in place.

"Go for it," Shannon shouted, slowing the boat as it neared Tidak. She glanced up. Roebor continued to close the distance between them.

Tidak turned his great head, and stared with those pale blue, flaming eyes directly at Shannon. The eyes squeezed into slits. His great tongue licked the side of his mouth. The hairs on the back of Shannon's neck rose in chilly formation.

He glanced up at the approaching Roebor, studied Luke and Shannon in the boat, then turned and aimed for land.

"Where's he going?" Luke shouted.

Shannon studied the shoreline. On the rocky beach, a pile of debris that staff had pulled up from the wreckage of the UC spilled out toward the forested mountain.

Shannon concentrated on Tidak's images. "He knows what we were planning, and now he's looking for a weapon," she said to Luke as the wind howled.

Tidak landed near the debris pile and grabbed quickly at one or two scraps, and as quickly discarded them. He tried unsuccessfully to untangle two of the larger slabs of wreckage. But in the next moment, he uncovered a long steel beam that had been twisted to a near point at one end. He lifted it in a giant paw, his expression grim, as he turned to face Roebor.

Roebor had begun a steep dive for Tidak's back while the bronze dragonpanther was searching the debris. He'd nearly overtaken Tidak when his enemy secured his weapon and turned with a roar, thrusting his makeshift spear toward Roebor's descending chest.

Shannon saw the weapon before Roebor could. She shouted, "Roebor, watch out." She pointed, her voice nearly lost in the wind.

Roebor slowed when he heard Shannon's warning. He spotted the spear, and jerked away, just as Tidak thrust for his heart. The spear dug deep into his upper chest, but missed his heart. Roebor flew on another twenty feet, but then fell heavily into the debris pile, purple-red blood flowing freely from his chest. He shuddered and lay still.

Shannon watched from the boat, horrified, too far away to be of any help. Tidak flew toward Roebor's unmoving body to strike again. But Roebor slowly lifted his great head and shook it, roared, pulled himself up to stand on all fours, and lifted a steel bar of his own from the debris pile, swinging it around to face Tidak.

Tidak hesitated, calculating the odds, then roared in frustration, threw his spear at Roebor, who easily blocked it with his steel bar. Tidak flew for the portal. As he pulled around to dive toward the underwater portal, he veered off course just enough to lunge straight for Shannon and Luke's boat.

Before Shannon could even shriek, he had thrust out a great furry paw and snatched her up. She read his images: He planned to take his revenge on her for his defeat, capture, and imprisonment, and thwart Roebor at the same time. He hovered above the tossing waves. His claws dug into her; she felt a gash open up on her good leg and the ankle cast break as a sharp nail pierced it; another gash to her ribs, her arm cast taking the brunt of one of the nails; a final gash along her shoulder.

She saw herself drowned in Tidak's grasp as he held her under water, or ripped in two by his powerful jaws. Or worse, traveling through the portal at his mercy.

Maybe not.

She'd allowed plenty of guests come on board her mind in recent days; now she'd go visiting herself. With no time to think through her options, she flowed through Tidak's paw, his arm, his broad chest, and into his Great Room, a gray misty place, full of rotting shapes, crumbling walls, fallen arches, a foul smell of decay. The sheer desolation of the place stopped her in her tracks.

As she gazed around, stunned, Tidak's inner consciousness flew down and attacked her, wrapping her in one great paw and lifting her to his mouth. She screamed. He would rip her in half. She could die in his Great Room; that lesson had been driven home to her very clearly. She struggled against his grip.

No good. What could she do now? Think!

She could waste no time. She decided in the split second available to her to try what she and Roebor had struggled so hard to avoid in Essi's mind.

She grew.

And grew. Larger and larger yet. Not carefully, as she had in Essi's mind, but recklessly and as fast as she could. Until she filled Tidak's Great Room. Until she burst through its roof.

Until his brain exploded.

His consciousness dissolved around her.

Just as she tried to gauge her next move, she lurched as his body plummeted into the sea.

Odin's eye. Not again. She shrank as quickly as she could and traveled as fast as she could, down through Tidak's chest, arm, and paw. Taking one big gulp of air, she flew back to her body.

With Tidak's mind destroyed, his grasp on Shannon had loosened, but the force of hitting the water tightened his fist as he plummeted downward.

Shannon struggled to free herself. His lifeless, fingerlike toes pressed tightly against her ribcage; she couldn't loosen them.

The cold water enveloped them. *Been here, done this.* It didn't feel any better this time around.

She would drown in Tidak's dead grasp.

* * *

Shaken by a great jolt, she looked up in time to see Roebor crashing into Tidak. The dead dragonpanther's fingers flew apart, and Shannon fell free, plunging farther into the ocean depths. But then Roebor's huge paw snatched her up. He bolted straight out of the water and she gasped and gasped again, trying to draw air into her desperate lungs.

She checked the portal. The blue glow appeared to be dimming.

"I'm good, Roebor, drop me. Get through the portal."

Roebor did drop her with one last glance, but only four feet onto the deck of the boat she and Luke had borrowed. Luke helped her to her feet, and helped her—mostly carried her—to the railing to urge Roebor on toward the portal before it closed.

Roebor, bleeding profusely from his chest, faltered, landing on the surface of the water. His great head jerked with the agony of the spear wound, and he emitted a low roar of pain.

Just then a submarine surfaced almost directly in front of them. Some sort of warning horn sounded as it surfaced, as if it might be arming its weaponry.

Shannon struggled to the comm center. "Ship to sub. I repeat ship to sub. Do you copy?" she said.

"USS *Perilous.* We copy. You are on a collision course with this sub. Turn hard to starboard. I repeat, turn hard to starboard."

"Copy, *Perilous.* Will do. Be advised that you are endangering a member of a protected species. Move forward. Repeat move forward."

The sub moved beyond the portal.

"It would be excellent if we could produce a beluga when they arrive to scream at us," Luke said.

"We might be able to."

Juneau, can you come to us?

The whale responded in the affirmative.

Shannon's heart lifted for the first time that night. "She's here, Luke."

Roebor came to life and struggled to move forward. He snagged Tidak's limp body, and swam as far as Shannon's boat. But as he descended down toward the portal, he lost his momentum.

Shannon pulled their boat hard to starboard; they missed the sub. She cut the engines, placing the boat between the sub and the portal.

Shannon knew what she must do, even as her entire body rebelled. "I have to help him, Luke."

"Shannon, no—"

Quickly, reluctantly, Shannon took a deep breath, and pushed herself over the railing of the boat and into the water once more. She surfaced and choked. The shock of hitting the frigid water had taken her breath away; she couldn't breathe. After a moment that seemed suspended in time, her lungs began to work again and she inhaled deeply. The sea lifted and fell in huge, choppy waves, she could rarely take in air without a mouthful of water.

Hurry.

She struggled forward until Roebor was drifting under-water just below her, then took a breath and dived. *Odin's eye, it was cold!* The wounds Tidak had inflicted throbbed and sent shocks of pain along her spine. *Getting weak.* She made it to Roebor. One look told her he'd lost consciousness. His blood was ribboning freely through the water, even as cold as it was.

It had worked with Tidak; she might as well venture on board once again. She entered his mind, and without hesitation, took over his motor functions. She grabbed her own inert body with one paw so that it stayed with the dragonpanther, covering her mouth with one huge furry finger to keep water out of her lungs, and then grabbed Tidak's body with the other and pushed hard for the portal. It wasn't far, which was a good thing, because only a few moments would elapse before her body suffocated. She must send Roebor home as quickly as she could.

The passage's light continued to dim, but it hadn't disappeared yet.

Come on. Push, push him as hard as he can go.

Her view of the portal grew larger as she approached, until she found herself right in front of it and . . . it began pulling Roebor, Tidak and her body into it!

Have to get away now!

She raced down Roebor's arm to his paw, took a deep breath before she left his gill-breathing body, and raced over into her own. She peered out immediately and saw that the three of them were inches from the pale blue light. From here, the light looked more like misty fog, and on the other side, FireWorld. She could make out the fiery ocean, snow-capped, lush green islands stretching out in a great arc . . . *mesmerizing. . . .*

She heard the blast of a ship's horn. *Luke.* She shook her head, blinking away the hypnotic view through the portal. She peeled Roebor's toes from her body, aided by the pull of the portal, which loosened the toes and dragged each one separately its way. She swam for the surface. *So weak. The pull—too strong. She had no energy left. Nothing to draw upon.* Behind her, the portal pulled her slowly back. She turned in time to watch Roebor's front legs, then his head, disappear into the portal. Soon she would follow him. She couldn't escape it.

Shannon couldn't hold her breath much longer. The crazy thought raced into her brain that her death by drowning must be preordained, and that she would find herself plunged into the water again and again, until the ocean depths at last triumphed.

Suddenly Luke appeared next to her, a rope attached to his waist, pulling her up, away from the portal, using one hand to hold her, one hand to pull them along the rope. He heaved her up onto the dock and pulled himself up behind her.

No watery grave today.

Breathing hard, she turned to watch the portal as the light disappeared, the blue glow subsided, and the sea became black once more.

"Will you be okay while I swim out to bring the boat back in?" He shouted above the wind.

Shannon, shivering so hard her teeth really did rattle, nodded. As she watched, Luke swam back to the boat along the rope, and then he edged the boat back into its berth. She heard him talking over the radio to the sub.

"I have lost sight of them, *Perilous*. Do you have eyes on them?"

"Negative, *Moonbeam*. They seem to have vanished. We're getting nothing on sonar."

"Thank you, *Perilous,* for making way for the whale. She's a special research animal, very valuable. Well done."

As if on cue, Juneau appeared at the side of the boat.

Shannon swayed where she stood and collapsed onto the wooden dock. Luke tied up the boat and found a blanket on board to wrap around Shannon. They sat for a moment on the dock waiting for the sub to send an unwelcoming party their way. But the sub had disappeared below the waves, and they could spot no sign of it. It had disappeared as quickly as it had appeared.

* * *

The Dickson crews had ceased their around-the-clock search efforts, and the damaged facility had become such a ghost town that no one was standing at the pier to berate them over their unauthorized use of the *Moonbeam* or to confer over the gigantic flying objects that had crashed into the sea. No one had seen a thing.

Shannon's head throbbed so painfully that she leaned over the side of the dock and threw up. When Luke retraced his steps, pushing Shannon back to the infirmary, he moved slowly and gently.

Luke helped Shannon into a dry nightgown and back into bed, and Ivy reattached her IV and monitors and cleaned her wounds. She said a doctor would be along shortly to reset her casts and stitch up the gashes. Shannon stared at her body; she'd bear deep scars from this night, from this whole terrible misadventure.

And how many times had they redone the casts now? Shannon had lost count.

Luke tenderly took her hand. "What happened, *cara?* How did you escape Tidak?"

"I . . . I essentially blew his brains out from the inside," Shannon said, the horror of it only now sinking in. "*Mother of Odin,* Luke, I'm a monster."

Luke brushed a wet lock of Shannon's hair from her face and tenderly kissed her forehead.

"No, cara. He planned to keep Roebor from the portal, kill you, and then escape at the last minute. You saved yourself. You helped Roebor to go home and take the virus with him. You escaped the only way you knew how." He wrapped Shannon's slender cold hand in his two large warm ones.

Shannon knew she would have nightmares about this night for the rest of her life. But she said, "Thanks, Luke, you're the best," Her eyes grew heavy. "You know what I really love best about you?" she murmured, already half asleep. "Everything."

As Shannon drifted off, she thanked *Odin* that her entire virus–Roebor–Tidak–Essi–Salesti–Juneau nightmare had finally—finally!—ended.

Except that the doctor woke her five short minutes later to sew her up and re-do the casts.

* * *

Shannon had slept only an hour or so when someone shook her hard and didn't let up. She peered out through sleep-heavy eyes. A form hovered directly over her in the dark. She opened her mouth to scream and scrambled for the nurse's call button. A hand clamped over her mouth.

Shannon reached up and grasped a hunk of hair, yanking it with all the pitiful strength she could muster.

"Ow! Let go. Don't scream, Shanny. It's me," Dakota whispered. "Sorry I had to scare you. I need to talk to you right now, and nobody can know I'm here. If I let go, can we talk?"

Shannon relaxed and nodded. Kota lifted her hand and let it hover for a moment, as if in readiness, should Shannon decide to shout after all. Shannon scooted up into a sitting position.

"How did you get your hair wet?" Kota asked. "You'll catch cold."

Shannon choked up a rueful laugh. "A cold would be the least of my problems. It's a long story. I fell in the ocean tonight, and then drifted off before I could dry it. Can you hand me a towel from the bathroom?"

"Let me," Kota said. She unbraided Shannon's hair and ran her fingers through it to loosen it, dried it with Shannon's hair dryer, found a brush in Shannon's duffel, and braided it. And all the while she explained to Shannon why she had come.

"How could you possibly fall in the ocean from your hospital bed?" she asked.

"Never mind that. I thought you'd be long gone by now, your plan to grab Juneau and me for your espionage work having gone bust," Shannon said, her voice shaking.

"So you caught on to me. How did I give myself away?"

"Oh, I guess I became convinced when you threw the drugs out from the side of the boat where you couldn't be seen and yet they claimed to have seen you throw it. But there were a lot of little things."

"Damn! I hoped you wouldn't notice that. It was a stupid plan anyway. I told them it wouldn't work. But I gotta tell you, when you came up with that five pack of beer, my jaw nearly hit the floor. That was priceless."

"You could have ruined our lives, Kota. Not that funny. So I assume your bosses have given up now?"

"No! That's why I'm here. Juneau is still in danger. And keep your voice down," Kota whispered.

Much more quietly, Shannon said, "Juneau is still in danger? How?"

"Copper wants to dissect her brain to find out what makes her tick."

CHAPTER FORTY-TWO

"DISSECT HER BRAIN? That's mad scientist crazy. He can't tell anything about Juneau by dissecting her brain. Who would give him permission for that? Why doesn't he just take a DNA sample?"

"I already took a DNA sample. Remember? When we cut that small tissue sample to check her immunities? Copper couldn't find anything, but he doesn't know enough about genome sequencing. He has this wacked-out theory that her brain has evolved in some way ordinary cetacean brains haven't, that he can lay out the brains side by side, Juneau's and ordinary ones, and demonstrate the difference. Then he thinks we can genetically engineer the brains of other cetaceans, more pliable and easygoing than our Juneau, to match her characteristics."

"But that's so far from the truth, it's ridiculous."

"Copper sees fame and dollar signs with Juneau. It's made him blind. He easily swayed our supervisor who is a weak man. That jerk figured it might pan out and if it didn't, nothing lost—that's all Juneau meant to *him*," she said with a heavy dose of disdain. "And, I think he's a little afraid of Copper. Afraid to tell him no. Copper was delta force before he left to go to med school. I think that duty made him a little twitchy, brought out his sadistic side. Anyway, they've been searching for Juneau ever since word reached them that you'd lost her on the way to Ocean City. And now she's back here, and the sub saw her tonight. Our man on the sub sent a sighting report straight to my boss. A ship capable of netting her and putting her in a water-filled hold set out from Juneau hours ago. They could arrive at any time. You've got to get her out of here."

"Why should I trust you?" Shannon asked, a great deal more bitterly than she intended. "I considered you my friend, Kota."

"I *am* your friend. What do you think I'm doing here, risking my whole career? I'm telling you to send her away, not asking you to send her toward a trap. I don't need to know where she goes, what route she takes, nada."

Shannon stood up, weaved back and forth, and sat down again.

Shannon must warn Juneau to stay away. She tried calling her.

Her headache returned with a vengeance. The room seemed to be closing in on her. *No good. Her telepathic skills were too weak.*

"I have to get out in the fresh air. I can't concentrate. Let's go back down to the dock, and I'll try to reach Juneau from there. She may still be close by," she said, removing her IV paraphernalia once again. "And yes, I can reach her. Don't ask, because I will not elaborate."

"Hah," Kota said. "I knew it."

As soon as Shannon loosened her monitors, nurse Ivy appeared and placed her hands on her hips. Shannon said, "Just have to use the bathroom. Gonna be a while. I'll buzz as soon as I'm back in bed."

"I'll help her," Kota chimed in.

"I don't even know what *you* are doing in here," Ivy said to Kota, her arms moving to cross over her wide chest, "and as for you," she said to Shannon, "I saw that dinner they wheeled in here. No wonder you need the restroom. Call if you need me." With that she departed, throwing an extra scowl Kota's way. Kota scowled back.

Shannon swung her legs over the edge of the bed and waited for a bout of dizziness to pass. It did not. Doing her best to ignore the spinning, she stumble-hopped to her duffel, which Luke had left for her in a corner. Her heavy jacket looked rumpled and smelled of salt water, but it would do. She sank into the armchair by her bag to pull a sock and shoe onto her good foot.

"Here, sit in the wheelchair, sweetie. I'll steer."

As they passed the nurses' station to smuggle Shannon out yet again, Kota waived an identification badge at Ivy, who was reading a paperback and munching on soda crackers, and said, "Homeland Security. Just need to interview this witness. Have her back to you in no time."

They passed into the residential block, retracing the route Luke and Shannon had taken earlier.

Renewing their earlier conversation, Kota said, "I will admit that on paper, it seemed okay to me to secretly spy on you and Juneau, determine if you were a team HS could use. And

I will even admit that on paper—and that's the key, Shan—on paper, I would've been okay with swiping Juneau, because we knew that then you'd work with us, too.

"But I got to know you. I got to know Juneau. I know you and Juneau have formed an extraordinary bond that we won't ever be able to replicate with any other cetacean–human team.

"I never once put any of that in my reports. In fact, my reports were so vanilla, I almost got yanked from the project. Fortunately for me, and for you and Juneau, my cohort Copper ran up against a brick wall trying to figure out the nature of your bond, even when he had you right under his eyeballs in here."

"Thanks for that, then," Shannon said. And meant it.

"Yeah, but don't thank me yet, because the downside of those vanilla reports was that Copper concluded Juneau alone accounted for your extraordinary progress, and that he didn't need you at all. He just needed to make Juneau disappear from the Dickson. When she actually did disappear down the coast, he thought he had the perfect opportunity to take her. But the more our team talked it over, the more I convinced them that Juneau's disappearance made her a poor candidate for our espionage work, because she couldn't be counted on; she's too stubborn and independent minded."

"And we like that, right?"

Kota shook her head. "Wrong. Because that's when Copper hatched his brilliant idea that if we couldn't count on Juneau to perform in the espionage project, he might as well open her up, and check out what's under her hood. I think he's truly a psychotic, Shanny. Something is very wrong with him."

Shannon nodded. She'd sensed it all along.

"I argued my ass blue trying to talk my boss out of it, but couldn't make any headway. He's very old school. You know the type: 'We love having women around and all, but the big boys make the decisions.' He essentially patted me on the head and told me to take some vacation to cool off. So I did, and came straight here to warn you.

"But I got here just in time to see Juneau show up right where Copper can get his hands on her. I wouldn't put it past him to kidnap you, and try to force you to call Juneau to his vessel."

"Why did you risk coming here, Kota?"

"Two reasons. First you and Juneau both kind of grew on me. I didn't anticipate becoming good friends with the targets. I looked at you two, and I hated myself. Except for my pink triangle. I love that."

Okay, Kota could still make Shannon laugh.

"Second, I could live with a little strong-arming in a good cause, but dissection? My lord no, and after I decided Copper had gone off the deep end, I bailed. He's got it in his head that this would be Nobel caliber work, and so he wants Juneau very badly. He hasn't thought rationally in weeks, although he was putting up a good front at the infirmary until we sailed off with Juneau."

After she finished, the women continued the wheelchair trip in silence until they reached the dock. No sign of Juneau.

The sharp wind had continued unabated. "What caused these cold temperatures up here all of a sudden?" Shannon asked.

"Yeah, I don't know. Strange weather patterns. The locals say it's been happening more this year. Are you sure we can't do this from inside the building?" Kota asked, also shivering. She wore only a light corduroy jacket. "I knew there was something I liked about California."

"You can run back inside until I'm done if you want, but I just can't concentrate in there. I think it's because I'm so weak right now. Thanks for coming out here with me."

Kota nodded, wrapping her arms around herself. "If you can stand it, I can stand it."

Shannon gathered herself to urge Juneau to leave the area, but she hesitated. If she sent the whale away now, she wouldn't see her beautiful bright eyes for a long time. Her heart sank at the thought. But Juneau's safety depended on it.

She called out for the beluga, who appeared in front of them moments later. Shannon moved down onto her knees from the wheelchair, touched Juneau's lovely, rubbery head, and sent images to explain the situation to her.

We've encountered some real trouble here. People want to chase you in a boat to capture and . . . kill you. You must leave here now and get as far away as you can. Go north. Find other belugas to mix with, so these men don't spot you alone. No time to waste. Go now. It may . . . it may be a long time.

Juneau emitted a bleak call, forlorn and lonely-sounding. Shannon understood. The whale had known human companionship for her entire adult life, and Shannon's attentions for over a decade.

She floated with her head raised for a moment, then dipped below the waves and disappeared.

Shannon almost reached out with her mind to call Juneau back, for the comfort of contact with her, for one moment more.

But no. She would leave Juneau alone. Free to find her own way. Free.

And just like that, in the snap of two fingers, Shannon's close companion for fifteen years vanished from her life.

* * *

"It's done," Shannon said. Her cheeks were wet, but she didn't bother to wipe them dry.

So many good-byes.

"Good. Now we need to get *you* out of sight."

Shannon hesitated. She'd be a sitting duck in the infirmary if Copper came after her. But where could she hide? "Do you know if anyone is using your apartment?" she asked Kota.

"No idea."

"Let's go find out."

Once they reached Kota's apartment, three doors down from Shannon's own place, Kota knocked. No one answered. Kota unlocked the door and wheeled Shannon in.

"Nobody's been in here since I took off for Ocean City. Look, here's my green-and-pink-striped socks, and here's my—well, never mind. No one from HS knows I'm up here, as far as I know, so they shouldn't look here for you. Let's get you to the couch."

Shannon sank onto the eggplant purple cushions and curled into a ball.

Her Juneau had left. But she was safe. *Safe.*

Shanon sat up.

"Thanks for warning us, Kota, or Juneau might've been captured while I slept without a clue in the infirmary. But I don't want to ruin your career. You can transfer out of Copper's outfit, right? Do research on some more humane project?"

"Oh believe me, my transfer applications are already in. That's what I spent my entire mini-vacation at the Marriott doing once we landed in Ocean City, right up until Copper knocked on my motel door and informed me of the new plan. I argued with him for over an hour, Shanny, but I got a big fat nowhere, so I told him I wanted to go home to New Mexico to finish my vacation, and I'd report to Hawaii in two weeks. That's where we're based. So as long as none of them spot me up here, I'm good."

"Then we need to get you out of Alaska. How'd you get here?"

Kota shrugged. "Took a plane to Juneau. Found a guy who planned to drive over this way, and I hitched a ride. He left me in the village, and I hitched another ride with a nice older lady who was coming out here to visit her husband, who's in the infirmary after acute appendicitis surgery. Easy peasy. And I already have my ride out. Sweet old guy named Squally Jones. Bush pilot. He leaves tomorrow afternoon.

Although technically, since it's now after midnight, that's this afternoon."

"Good. Why don't you get some shut-eye then? I have to make some phone calls, and then I'll try to get some sleep too. If I could borrow a pillow and a blanket, I'll be peachy right here on the couch. Do you have anything to eat by any chance?"

Kota made a face. "A bit of a problem, but I'll check what's still here."

She rifled through the cupboards and checked the refrigerator. "You have a choice between steamable broccoli, and canned black beans," Kota said from the kitchen.

"Both," Shannon called back to her.

Shannon first called Moon and told him much of what Kota had told her, Copper's plans, the search for Juneau, her fears for her own safety. She didn't mention Kota's presence, and she didn't say that she'd sent Juneau far north to safer waters.

"But how do you know all this, Shannon?" Moon asked her. She'd placed the call on speaker, and glanced up sharply at Kota, who'd curled up in a bright red love seat opposite Shannon's couch to listen to the conversation.

"I . . . I still had Kota's spare key in my duffel. She lives just three doors down from me in Q block, and, as far as I know, she's still down in Ocean City. So I thought I would hide here instead of my apartment, in case Copper looks for me at my place. I'm here now. I found a boatload of documents here, and pieced all this together."

Once again, the full Pinocchio. Shame, shame, Shannon.

She raised her eyebrows at Kota. *Good enough?*

Kota thought it over and nodded, then nodded again more firmly.

"I have many connections in Washington DC. I will begin making phone calls immediately. This mission of Copper's will be terminated now. I can promise you that. The proper officials will be notified, as well as Dickson security officers. You stay where you are and wait until you hear further from me."

"Thank you, Dr. Moon. I'm sorry I'm so much trouble."

"Not at all, Shannon. I become fearfully bored with my model employees. You give my job the zest I yearn for." He clicked off.

Shannon held the phone in her hand for a moment and looked at Kota.

"Moon just gave you a compliment. Or not," Kota said laughing. "Moving on, let me guess. Luke followed you all the way back up here again, and he's next on your list of phone calls."

Shannon nodded.

"I'll get your blanket and pillow then, and leave you to it. He's welcome, as long as I don't wake up with a knife in my forehead."

* * *

Luke arrived five minutes after Shannon called. He'd crossed over from the Visitors Block, where he'd taken a room when he first arrived at the Dickson. Before the disaster, the Visitor's Block had housed various visiting scientists, dignitaries, donors, tourists, and the newest employees. Now it was virtually deserted.

Shannon's snack had given her enough energy to unlock the door for Luke when he knocked, but as she tried to maneuver along the hallway back to the living room, clinging to the wall for balance, and trying to stay off the injured ankle, he uttered an impatient sigh, and picked her up, depositing her neatly on Kota's couch, and handing her a bag of onion rings he'd brought along. Shannon didn't have the energy to spare for objections.

"I know," Luke said anyway, "You could have done it yourself."

Shannon began the story of what had happened since he last saw her, but, after she explained Kota's part, he interrupted. "She's here now?" His face darkened, grim and unhappy. Shannon had rarely seen that kind of simmering anger in him. But he nodded for her to continue.

When she'd finished, he said, "It sounds like Copper's operation has gone off the rails. Moon should be able to put an end to the official HSD support behind him, but I don't think Copper can be trusted even then, if he's obsessed with Juneau. Where do you think Copper went after Kota last talked to him?"

"I wish he boarded the boat that's out searching for Juneau. He must know, though, that he has about zero chance of finding her without my help. That's what has me spooked."

Shannon started to speak again, but lost her train of thought. *So damn tired.* Her eyes grew heavy. Luke fell silent, watching her as she slipped into a deep sleep.

* * *

She awoke to the sounds of Luke and Kota arguing in the kitchen. She shook her head, trying to clear her thoughts.

"I'm having second thoughts about this apartment as a safe spot," Luke was saying. "You worked with Copper, so he probably knows where you live, right?"

"Yes," Kota said, "but it's been almost three and half hours since Shannon talked to Moon. Maybe HSD has already pulled the plug—"

"If Copper's as crazy as you two think, I don't want him anywhere near Shannon, even if he no longer has federal backing. And he knows you and Shannon were friends right? He might figure she'd hide here. I think she should move."

Kota sighed and threw up her hands. "Okay, but where?"

"Hey, you guys," Shannon said sleepily. "I heard you, and you're right, Luke. I'm thinking we can find an empty place easily in the Visitors' Block. Let's break into a random room, and hunker down until we hear from Moon."

"Good. I'll check the hall," Luke said.

"I'll pack a few things," Kota said.

Soon Luke was wheeling Shannon briskly down Q Block toward V Block, Kota bringing up the rear. They pressed on into one of the interior halls until Shannon signaled for Luke to stop. "This one looks as good as any. Your own room is nowhere around here, right?"

"Right. I'm a floor up and over in the opposite wing." He slipped a small packet of tools out of his pocket. "A safe distance."

"Lock picking tools?"

"The things you learn waiting with felons in custody before court," he said, and winked at her. "I brought them along when you called, in case you'd locked Kota's door and were too weak to answer."

He fiddled for a short moment and swung the door open, then pushed Shannon's wheelchair in. Kota followed.

Shannon suddenly sensed the haze forming at the door behind them and she turned.

"Luke, somebody—"

Before Kota could close the door behind them, someone pushed it hard from the hallway and rushed in.

Not again.

Kota stumbled forward, tipped the wheelchair on its side, spilled Shannon onto the hallway tile, and fell against the hallway wall, crying out with pain when her elbow slammed the wall. Luke tripped on Shannon and banged into the wall near the kitchen entrance. The logjam halted the entry of the unknown person long enough for Shannon to push herself up, and turn to identify the intruder.

Copper. A gun pointed directly at Luke, who had quickly stepped back into the middle of the hall, directly between Copper—and his gun—and Shannon.

A gun? How had this struggle over Juneau turned into an armed conflict? She couldn't comprehend it.

"Shannon, get out the back door."

"Stay, Kendricks," Copper said, leveling the gun at Luke.

As if she'd leave Luke.

"You're coming with me or I will put a big hole in the forehead of your boyfriend here."

Surely he was bluffing.

Copper took a step toward Luke. He didn't look like a man who was bluffing. Unwarranted fury pushed his mouth into a small, tight line; his eyes, bloodshot and unnaturally bright, radiated conviction.

He seemed to have forgotten Kota altogether, perhaps thinking she would still be on his side, perhaps dismissing her as inconsequential. She very slowly reached into her jacket pocket and pulled out her gun.

Shannon, who had considered pushing to her feet, froze where she was. "You don't need a gun, Dr. Copper. Let's just talk about this."

"I didn't think I'd need a gun either, but thanks to that bastard Moon, it seems it's the only way I can get my hands on what I want. Thanks to him, my government career is in the garbage can. This is my only chance to get the whale. Now do you come with me, or shall I shoot him? Don't think I won't. War in Iraq. Plenty of practice. Sanctioned and un-sanctioned." He pushed the gun forward another few inches.

"Leave him alone. I'll go with you."

"That's kidnapping, Jim. Wouldn't be approved by Homeland Security, I'm sure. Put the gun down and let's figure this out."

"Step over there." Copper waived his gun toward the opening to the living room.

Luke hesitated, then moved slowly toward the living room.

As Shannon watched out of the corner of her eye, Kota pulled herself onto her knees as quietly as she could, now a foot closer to the door than Copper, who had slowly stepped forward. Years of field work observing wildlife without alarming the subjects served Kota well now.

"As I said, I'm no longer with HSD," Copper said and stepped forward again to shepherd them all into the living room. "Thanks to Moon. But it's better this way anyway. Too many restrictions, too much delay and ethical B.S. I'm on my own now, and the rewards from my research will be mine—and the people who hide me and fund me. You," he said, waving the gun at Shannon. "On your feet."

He wouldn't leave Luke alive. Or Shannon. Crazy as that seemed—*Copper had taken the Hippocratic oath, for Odinssake*—Shannon felt the truth of it in her bones. He'd have to get rid of their bodies to take his shot at fame and fortune, but with a big, lonely ocean just outside the door, that wouldn't be so hard. Her vision faded. Another premonition. She heard Luke's voice, the words muffled, followed by a gun shot. She smelled blood. Lots of it. Then an echo of her own voice screaming. As suddenly as the darkness had come, it lifted. She stared in horror at Copper's gun; he was about to shoot Luke. She glanced at Kota.

Kota took aim at Copper. Shannon spoke to draw his attention away from her friend.

"Dr. Copper, Juneau doesn't possess the kind of brain anomalies you think she does," Shannon said. "We've forged a strong bond because we've worked together for so long, that's all."

"You may believe that; I don't. She's different from other belugas, and I'll uncover the difference and exploit it. I'll clone her if I have to. I plan to have a squadron of whales and dolphins that the world will pay handsomely to get their hands on."

He's lost it.

"Drop your gun, Doctor, I am locked and loaded," Kota said.

Copper started to speak, and slowly turned, his gun held loosely, as if complying with her directive. "Kota. Whose side are you on?" But instead of dropping the gun, he suddenly ducked and fired.

Kota, hit, fired wildly, missing Copper. Shannon felt a sting in her arm. She looked down. A small round hole had penetrated her arm cast twice, once going into her arm, once coming out and entering her rib cage. There it seemed to have lodged.

Kota fell back against the wall and sank slowly down. Blood streaked the wall behind her. She looked at Shannon. *Sorry,* she mouthed.

Copper jerked his gun back toward Shannon and Luke.

When Copper had turned to Kota, Luke had moved quickly to Shannon, and had tried to pull her back behind the living room wall. But the exchange between Kota and Copper had happened too quickly. When he saw Copper level the gun at them again, he quickly lifted his hands.

Shannon stared in horror at Kota's slumped figure. She hardly registered her own gunshot wound.

"Stand up, you bitch. I'm not going to ask you again."

"Okay, I'm trying. I've been shot. It's hard. . . ." Shannon scrambled on her good hand and knees toward Copper. *She must stop him.*

Think!

She continued to scrabble toward him, pretending to try to rise. "Can you give me a hand?"

"Stop right there. Use the wall if you need help," Copper said.

By that time, she'd nearly reached his leg. In one motion, she lunged for it, pulled it toward her, and bit down as hard as she could on the side of his calf. She ended up with a mouthful of slacks and sock, but she'd hit flesh.

Copper yelped and fell back against the door, his gun swinging up and away. But he recovered quickly, as he had before. As he stabilized, he leveled the gun at Shannon. "You bitch."

While Copper was preoccupied with Shannon, Luke pulled his own gun from his back waistband.

"Copper," Luke said, yelling to pull the doctor's attention away from Shannon.

Copper's gun swung back toward Luke.

Before Shannon could make another move, two gunshots rang out in the confined space of the hallway. She splayed herself against the floor and waited for another round. Perhaps a bullet in her back. If her premonition had come true, she'd welcome a bullet. For a few moments, she could hear nothing but a sound like rushing wind on the far side of a thick window in her ears.

Nothing.

No more shots, no grunts or groans, no movement of any kind that she could detect. She struggled onto her knees.

Her eyes flew automatically to Luke. He'd been hit in the chest.

CHAPTER FORTY-THREE

LUKE HAD BEEN HIT IN THE CHEST, and was bleeding copiously. His eyes were closed. She scrambled over to him and laid her face against his. *Faintest breath; did she only imagine it?* She felt for his pulse. Yes, she detected a pulse. Barely.

Where had she tucked her cell phone? *Here.* Her hands shaking, blood dripping from her cast, from her torso, the phone slipping in her fingers, she called for medical help, begging them to hurry. She tore off her sock with her good hand, and pressed it to Luke's chest.

Hang on Luke, just hang on.

She figured Copper was incapacitated, or she'd be dead, or he'd be calling her names, or ordering her around. Just to be sure, she gave him a cursory glance. His figure lay motionless, gun on the floor by his hand. *Good.*

And Kota?

Shannon peered down the short hallway toward her friend. A huge pool of blood surrounded her. She still slumped awkwardly, her eyes open but unseeing. No. Not Kota, *please Odin*, not Kota.

She used the wheelchair, still jammed against the wall nearest the kitchen, to push herself up. Then she limped to her friend and knelt beside her. "Kota?" Shannon whispered, shaking her gently. "Kota?" Kota didn't move, didn't respond. Shannon pulled close.

Breathing? Nothing.

Pulse? Nothing.

A rage surged up within her.

Copper.

Copper had done this.

She would kill him. She limped back to Luke and searched frantically for his gun. She would kill the bastard for what he'd just done, for what he'd planned to do to Juneau. Even as a small rational voice in her head whispered that she was channeling Tidak's irrational rage, not her own, she searched until she found Luke's gun where it had fallen by his leg.

She turned.

"You bastard," she said, holding the gun in two shaking hands.

But unlike Luke, Copper stared at her with lifeless, pale gray eyes. The bullet Luke fired had hit the dead center of Copper's forehead. Luke had made sure he couldn't hurt Shannon, wouldn't hurt Juneau.

She screamed in rage. Copper couldn't be dead. She wanted to be the one to kill him. For hurting Luke, maybe fatally, for killing Kota, she had to be the one. She had the right. To do it. For Luke and Kota.

The gun shook in her hand. She aimed for his chest, to mark him just as he'd marked Luke. She let the rage wash over her, wave after wave, until the heat in her brain nearly burst it apart. She aimed.

All her onboard friends had left her. Salesti, Essi, Toss, Roebor.

Shannon must act alone.

But of course, they remained with her too. Their essence. More than memory, though less than the real thing. She sensed them, then, at that moment of utter rage, soothing her, touching her shoulder, her arms, her back, murmuring quiet words, surrounding her with the wonderful spicy unknown scent that made her think of everything good.

Her rage subsided.

The gun slid from her hand.

* * *

A crowd had gathered at the source of the gun shots.

Shannon could hear them talking in low, excited voices. She watched Kota's blood oozing across the hall floor and escaping under the door.

She heard someone ask what had happened.

"We heard four gun shots, *bam bam* and then some shouting and *bam bam*," said a short Polynesian woman in a bright orange bathrobe just visible through the two-inch gap between the nearly-closed door and the wall. "But the door won't open. It's blocked. We called security."

Someone tried the door again. Shannon watched its progress stop at Kota's body, blocked by her weight and by her corduroy jacket, pink of course, which was caught under the bottom edge of the door. Kota in turn was blocked by Copper. Wheelchair. Shannon. Luke.

Shannon could have moved Kota enough to allow the spectators entry. She considered it. But she stayed where she huddled, leaning her back against the hallway wall, Luke's head in her lap.

"I'm going around the back," someone said. "Tell the medics when they arrive that I'll break in if I have to."

Shannon could unlock the back patio sliding glass door for them. She thought about it. She stayed put. With Luke.

After a few moments, Shannon heard glass shattering in the living room, the sliding glass door opening, footsteps across the living room carpet.

Voices. Footsteps. Dr. Killian kneeling beside her.

"Shannon? Can you hear me? Can you understand me? We need you to let go of Luke now so Dr. Quirin can attend to him. I need you to come with me to the infirmary. Can you do that?"

Shannon shook her head no. She didn't want to let Luke go.

"I'll give her a tranquilizer. She's in shock. And her pre-existing condition had already compromised her health. Just give it a moment."

Shannon wanted to protest. She thought about it. But in the end, she just blacked out.

CHAPTER FORTY-FOUR

SHANNON AWOKE TO TYPICAL SOUNDS OF MORNING in the hospital. Breakfast trays clattering down the hall, early visitors talking with the nurses at the central station, doctors beginning morning rounds by knocking on doors and asking if their patients were awake—and of course thereby awakening them—an occasional boisterous laugh that Shannon somehow resented. The nurses had closed her curtains, but bright Alaskan summer light filtered through above the curtain rod, down the crack that separated the two curtain panels, across the edges where curtain met windowsill. Shannon stared at the streaks of light. *Bleak.* As if the sun were fighting valiantly but futilely for entrance. A useless struggle.

A totally dark room would have given her more comfort.

Mind so fuzzy. She noted her newest arm cast—the previous one hadn't even lasted the night—and felt the bandage on her torso where a bullet had penetrated a small distance into her side. Right. Kota had shot her when. . . .

She jolted upright with the shock of remembering: *Luke.* She pressed the nurses' call button. *Had Luke survived?*

Nurse Shed—*Great Odin; she knew too many nurses by sight now*—peeped his head in the door.

"You're awake. I'll let Dr. Killian know."

"Wait, please. I need to know about Luke Quintana. Is he alive? Please, Shed."

Shed stepped into the room, shutting the door behind him. "I'm not supposed to talk about any other patient with you, but I can tell you this much; he's alive and expected to live. He lost a lot of blood and the bullet made a mess of his shoulder, so he'll need several surgeries when he's stronger. But he's alive." With that, Shed slipped out the door.

An injury that probably has ended his career as a police officer, a career he took such pride in. Shannon's fault. The weight of her guilt pressed her down into the bed.

But he'd survived. Thank Odin, he'd survived.

Shannon's chest suddenly felt much too small to contain her lungs; she couldn't breathe; her lungs had no space to expand. *Luke had lived.* Nothing else mattered; no space in her chest existed for anything but that immense knowledge. *Luke had not died.*

As Shannon struggled to take a breath, the door opened and Dr. Killian entered. She started to speak but caught sight of Shannon's pale face, which had perhaps begun to take on a bluish tinge from a lack of air. The physician reached her side in an instant.

"Shannon, can you speak to me? What's wrong?"

Shannon flapped her hands in the air, helplessly, and closed her eyes. She pictured Luke, not as she'd last seen him, bloodied and crumpled to the floor, but well and smiling in that way he had of crinkling his eyes up and grinning broadly, putting his whole face into the happiness effort. Luke. Suddenly her chest expanded and she inhaled deeply, gasping in a large breath.

"Are you all right?" Dr. Killian asked, watching her closely.

Shannon nodded. "Sorry, I woke up reliving the moment Copper came after me and shot Kota and Luke." She wouldn't let the doc know Shed had spilled the beans. "How is he?"

"He's recovering. You may be able to visit him later, if he's up to it. Lord knows half the female staff has found a reason to go check on him, so I don't see why you shouldn't have your shot. Now, let's have a look at how you're doing."

Dr. Killian proceeded to ask her about the events of the night before, and when Shannon dutifully and falsely told her that Copper had chased her off the pier into the water before being run off by Luke, only to return later with his gun, Dr. Killian put her back to bed on a glucose drip for precautionary purposes.

* * *

For once in her life, Shannon didn't mind cocooning in her blankets in the still, dim room. It gave her time to think.

About how she seemed to live in a new reality now, about the inevitability of aliens, the inevitability of her death.

About Kota, and before her, her friend Andy. Becky.

About Luke, how he had tried more than once to stay away, how she'd allowed him to come back each time. How he'd nearly died. What had he said after coming out of his coma?

Almost every time I am with you, I experience events that could turn out badly in so many ways.

Indeed.

* * *

Two days later, she asked Dr. Killian if she could visit Luke. The doctor at first refused to allow it; Shannon's body was still much too weak, the bullet injuries unhealed, her gashes being carefully watched for infection, her organs damaged, her entire system strangely depleted. She still needed intensive treatment. But Shannon promised she'd do exactly what Dr. Killian wanted if she would allow just this one visit.

So Dr. Killian relented and arranged for a big breakfast to be carted in. Shannon extracted herself from the glucose drip, and slowly and shakily showered. She dressed in sweats from her quarters that marvelously didn't smell like they'd been marinating in shrimp brine. She ate ravenously and asked for seconds and thirds, and then she borrowed a wheelchair and Ivy, so she could venture out in search of Luke.

When she entered his room, she saw that he was sleeping. She pulled up beside him. *How refreshing to be the one on this side of the hospital bed for a change.* She studied his face, his hands for a long time. She wanted to remember each precious detail of them.

At length he opened his eyes and smiled at the sight of her.

She smiled back, but she couldn't seem to put much warmth into it.

What had Becky advised her five years and a lifetime ago?

Let them down gently. . . . but cold. That's the way to clear them off.

"What's wrong?" he asked.

"Luke, I'll say this quickly, or I won't be able to say it all: You must stay away from me for now, and I must stay away from you. It has nothing to do with how I feel about you or how I think you feel about me, and everything to do with telepathy and aliens and body-killing visitations. Those things loom too large right now. If I can, I'll find you some day, but in the meantime, don't put your life on hold." With that, she took his big square hand in her good hand and brought it to her cheek. She held it there, memorizing its cool softness, the gentle way he curled his fingers around hers. She would remember the feel of him always.

Luke didn't speak. He didn't need to. Shannon didn't meet his eyes after she had spoken. She didn't want to witness the relief that might flicker across his face, or the hurt, although she suspected both had made an appearance.

She placed his hand gently down on the bedcovers and struggled to turn her wheelchair and leave.

"Shannon—" Luke began. But Shannon didn't stop to listen. She didn't dare.

CHAPTER FORTY-FIVE

DR. MOON ARRANGED SHANNON'S AIRLIFT DOWN TO CALIFORNIA for further treatment once Dr. Killian had stabilized her.

Eight weeks later, Dr. B. released Shannon from the rehabilitation wing of St. James Hospital in Ocean City. She'd rid herself of her casts, finally, *thank Odin*—her bones healed quickly once her alien guests had departed, once her casts remained dry and puncture-free for an extended period of time, and once she managed to stay off her ankle. The scars—from the UC debris, the *thing's pincer,* Tidak's claws, Kota's bullet—had left unmistakable, deep marks on her, but the surgeons had done a good job with the stitches and she harbored hopes of escaping the Frankenstein look. Her limp had disappeared, the bruises and cuts had healed—all the physical wounds had mended.

The emotional wounds would require more time.

* * *

Settled at home, Shannon often felt as if she'd left her actual body behind in Alaska. She thought like a ghost; she moved like a ghost; she must be a ghost. Shannon would have scolded herself for such a hang-dog perspective, but she couldn't muster the energy.

True, she didn't eat like a ghost.

* * *

Shannon missed Kota. She missed Luke. She missed Essi, too, and Salesti, but they had a world to rebuild, new lives to begin. She missed Juneau.

But Shannon had found plenty of time during her hospital stay to contemplate Copper's thwarted plans for Juneau. Other people, both in this country and in far less hospitable ones, could cook up many uses for a pair like Juneau and Shannon. She must keep Juneau from such people at all costs.

For the foreseeable future, such people might try to keep an eye on Shannon in hopes of getting their hands on the whale. Juneau would fare much better in the pod of belugas she'd adopted in Alaska. And she was socializing very well. That was all that mattered.

Juneau would receive no medical care out in the wilds; no human companionship of the kind she'd become accustomed to after the SQ had captured her. But she would be free.

* * *

Narci had recovered in due course under the excellent care of her vet, and had stayed on in his deluxe cat lodging wing during the two months of Shannon's recovery. When Narci returned home, Shannon waited with great hopes for the cat to communicate again as she had in Alaska, but independent little blue-eyed Narci had apparently decided to keep her own counsel once more.

* * *

The day after Shannon reopened her house and brought Narci home, the raven reappeared on the back patio when Shannon brought a broom out to sweep up the accumulation of leaves that had gathered in her long absence.

"Hey, bird," Shannon said, allowing the bird to perch on her shoulder.

"Hey, bird," the bird replied.

A short burst of surprised laughter escaped from Shannon's lips.

She really ought to name the little guy.

* * *

A submarine had documented the occurrence of the same phenomenon that had caused the UC destruction, only in reverse: the sub recorded two immense objects flying down from the sky, detouring briefly to the shore, then plunging into the sea and disappearing exactly where they had first appeared days earlier. No official explanation had been forthcoming.

Shannon read with no small amount of glee that the government had labeled much of the information from these observations classified, and neither the press nor the investigating Senate subcommittees succeeded in obtaining them, not even the mention of a strange interaction between the sub and a Dickson boat identified as the *Moonbeam*. Dickson officials professed no knowledge of any activity by that boat on the night in question. Dickson staff determined that a single blanket had disappeared from the *Moonbeam's* inventory on that date, and the crew had discovered a small quantity of unexplained seawater on deck the day after the incident, but the Dickson declined to mention these small anomalies to HSD, as they seemed to bear no relationship to the alleged interaction.

* * *

Dr. Moon had visited Shannon several times while she was recovering in rehab, and kept her abreast of developments at the Dickson, where the troubles stemming from the collapse of the Underwater Complex in Alaska continued.

He had thus far escaped dismissal from the Dickson, which was welcome news to Shannon.

The insurance carriers eventually agreed with Moon, based on the government's documentation of unidentified objects at the site, that the UC destruction event seemed to have been an extraordinary one-off and unlikely to happen again. Even so, they preferred that the Dickson relocate a few miles up the coast to another property that had been on the market for some time and could be obtained for a reasonable price. However, the owners of the site had never developed roads, docks, or amenities, nor had they leveled any land for building. The start-up costs at that location would therefore be enormous.

Moon had been forced to concede that, in any event, rising sea levels due to melting ice to the north would have required major modifications to the original Dickson site at some time in the future. This knowledge could be folded into the building plans for site two. However, again, the further up the mountainside they built the new site, Moon explained, the more costly it would prove.

For these reasons, as Moon repeatedly impressed upon Shannon, the largest obstacle to any such rebuild remained the funding. To his credit, he never once asked Shannon if she would participate in a new public relations campaign. Perhaps he could tell by looking at her that the death of Dakota Quartermark, the shooting of Luke Quintana, and the disappearance of Juneau after Copper had tried to capture her had well and truly knocked the stuffing right out of Shannon.

Of course, Juneau had not actually disappeared, since Shannon could still contact her telepathically, and did so on occasion. But to do so more often didn't prove healthy for either of them.

Losing Kota, letting go of the whale—and of Luke—had, indeed, knocked the stuffing right out of her.

Because of Juneau's disappearance, even if the Dickson could get back up and running, Moon made plans to feature other whales and dolphins, trained to respond to their human handlers, who would gradually give the cetaceans freedom while encouraging continuing contacts with their people and the facility. Shannon and Juneau had started the ball rolling;

if the funding could be found, Shannon's dream would still be fulfilled.

Funding.

Therein lay the problem.

* * *

Shannon had curled up in bed one night not long after she came home from the hospital, Narci nestled into the curve at her waist. She pulled her braid forward over her shoulder so that she could lie back against her pillows, as she sipped an ice cold orange juice and contemplated the thorny subject of funding.

She'd just finished talking to Dr. Moon on the phone about a battle raging between two factions of the Dickson's board of directors.

One faction, led by Thomas Tremaine, remained dead set against any attempt to reconstruct the advanced research facility up in Alaska, and that faction especially objected to an Underwater Complex. For that matter, those board members opposed reconstruction of a research center similar to the Alaska Dickson anywhere.

The other faction, led by Ambika Chidambaram, fought hard for the center to be recreated in Alaska, and, if Alaska proved impossible, then here at Ocean City, where its first test subjects would not consist of belugas, which did not thrive in southern waters, but rather any number of captive dolphin species who could live quite successfully off the coast of California when they were set free.

Moon put his money on Ambika. But, Moon had cautioned Shannon yet again, even if the board voted to resurrect the project in some form in some place, it wouldn't matter much if they couldn't fund it.

As Shannon was mulling over this struggle, Narci sprang up and charged down the stairs, into the kitchen, and out the cat door, which Shannon could just hear bang behind her.

What—?

She threw on her long-sleeved, blue-and-black-plaid flannel shirt over her white cotton pajamas, and followed the cat out onto her back patio.

As Shannon shut the kitchen door behind her, Narci jumped onto the sturdy cedar picnic table, and stared upward at something Shannon couldn't see. But she had a suspicion. She cast her colors. A flash of lightning, a ball of rose red light—and Narci shook her head, as if a fly had landed in her ear. That could mean only one thing. Salesti had arrived for a visit.

Shannon laid her hand gently on Narci's back.

"Over you come, Salesti, let's not overtax Narcissus now that she's recovered." And with that, the little hummingbird-kitten flowed through Shannon to her mind. Shannon sat down at the picnic table, laid her head on its warm surface, and joined Salesti in her Great Room. She hugged the tiny buzzing dynamo, who backed away to shake out her wings and landed on Shannon's shoulder.

shannon watches portal. package coming.

"Package? How could a package pass through the portal? *package comes.*

Shannon watched the portal, and a few seconds later a package the size of her overstuffed bed pillow fell from the sky. Shannon tried to catch it as it came down, but it slipped through her hands and thumped onto the picnic table.

eek. shannon not lets gift break.

"Sorry, small one. What have you brought?"

Salesti buzzed. *open package. gift from salesti and roebor. for underwater building roebor destroyed.*

"A donation! To help with the rebuild. That's so kind of you two. I'll be sure it gets delivered."

shannon opens package now, Salesti insisted.

"Well all right then."

The package's wrapping consisted of some sort of pink-ish, shimmery, liquidy material that looked as if it shouldn't even hold together. But it bound whatever it held inside quite effectively. Shannon had no idea how to open it.

shannon pulls edges here and here, Salesti said, grabbing the "edges" that Shannon could not make out, and peeling the substance away. Inside, she found an enormous, leather-like bag, made of a soft, white material with a thin sheen of fuzz on it. At the top, a strip of the same material fastened it shut.

"Neat bag."

from world of roebor. wait. stop. shannon and salesti go inside, in light, and see better.

Shannon shrugged. "Okay by me." She picked up the bag and headed for the kitchen, Narci tagging along at her heels.

She loosened the closure and spilled the contents onto the kitchen table, which sat under the bright kitchen chandelier.

Shannon blinked. For a moment she merely gazed at the glittering objects before her, stunned.

"Are these diamonds? *Holy Odin*, look at the size of them," Shannon said. "Salesti, some of these look bigger than the Hope Diamond." Most of the diamonds also looked perfectly translucent and colorless, although a few sparkled in blue, red, purple and black.

highest quality. roebor finds. roebor finds as many as shannon needs to rebuild underwater building.

Shannon picked them up, one after the other, to watch the sparkling facets catch the overhead light. "I can't get over the size of these hummers."

salesti not stays now. goes home. roebor finds more when shannon needs.

"Salesti, I don't even know what to say. If these bring in as much as I hope they will, you and Roebor might single-handedly reconstruct an entire new Dickson."

Shannon planted a big kiss on Salesti's forehead. The miniature creature buzzed loudly, either from irritation or pleasure.

"Definitely the best thing to happen to me in a long time. Will you tell Roebor he's made a puny earththing very happy?"

salesti tells roebor. before salesti goes, look at slit in bag. shannon sees?

Shannon peered inside the bag. At first the bag looked smooth, but when she ran her hand around the fabric just below the opening, she touched a flap that had blended in perfectly. She slid her hand inside and pulled out a silver arm cuff set with perfectly matched, oval cut, intensely green diamonds.

"I've never seen anything so beautiful."

The green of the gems appeared slightly lighter than the green of an emerald; perhaps more like . . . like. . . .

yes, color of eyes of shannon.

"Hey, you're supposed to stay out of my head, small one."

salesti makes lucky guess.

"Uh-huh, sure. But anyway, this will be the icing on the cake to solve the funding issue."

no, shannon, bracelet for shannon only. from roebor.

"For me? Oh, I don't know. I didn't do anything to deserve this. I don't think I should take it."

shannon only sends roebor home alive through portal unconscious. and shannon saves earth from virus. without shannon, roebor dead, tidak alive, no antidote for roebor's people. roebor wants shannon to have bracelet. salesti not takes bracelet back. anyway, dragonpanthers not value gems. not wear bracelets. shannon keeps.

"Tell Roebor I will keep it then, and I'll think of him every time I look at it. I just wish I had something this valuable to give him.

shannon gives friendship says roebor. enough. salesti goes now.

Shannon carried Salesti back outside to the picnic table, climbed onto the bench and lifted her hand toward the stars. The portal flashed again, and Salesti flowed through Shannon's outstretched hand and away, and the portal disappeared.

Shannon and Narci stood alone in the evening quiet. Shannon looked down at the cat.

"This calls for a celebration; tuna for you, chocolate éclairs for me. Agreed?"

Narci, silent as ever, bee-lined for the kitchen.

When Shannon returned to the house, she picked up her phone.

"Dr. Moon? I think I've found a way to at least begin to pay for the Dickson rebuild. Can you come over?"

* * *

Moon arrived at Shannon's house exactly twenty-three minutes later, even though midnight had come and gone, a clear measure of his desperation for funding.

Shannon brought him a cup of his favorite tea, and said, "So I heard a rumor that the Dickson board is now leaning toward situating the Underwater Complex down here instead of Alaska. True?"

"Such a suggestion has been placed on the table. Some board members lean that way. We have contracted a feasibility study for a site here, just as we have contracted one for the alternative site in Alaska, now that the government has confiscated our current property. As you know, I am a great proponent of a facility in Alaska, so that if we can replicate your venture with Juneau using other cetaceans, we might entice the bigger whales in for care, study, and public viewing. Humpbacks, fins. Even blues someday perhaps. Something different from that which can be accomplished in the rest of the country, where many will wish to emulate our model in warmer waters if we succeed."

"did you say the government has confiscated our site?"

"The Department of Homeland Security has now given way to the air force in terms of the branch of government most interfering with our site. The government made no official statement, of course, but it appears they have termed the object that destroyed the UC an 'unidentified alien object.' They believe it landed on earth at that spot. They also think it returned to the exact same spot to escape from earth. The air force has cordoned off the entire area, and has started negotiations with the Foundation to purchase the site. It appears they wish to be ready when the alien object next chooses to visit Earth." Moon shook his head. "At least the forced sale of the property will provide us with some funding."

Shannon gathered from the skepticism dripping off his every word that he didn't buy the government's theory. *And yet they're right on the nose for a change, Moon. Right on the nose.*

"So wherever we build, we're starting from scratch," she said.

"Quite so." Moon quieted for a moment then brightened as he added, "At least one good thing has come from all this mad talk of alien invaders. Our insurers inform us that since one well-defined point of alien ingress and egress has been identified, if we do not rebuild at that site, we can be reinsured at substantially the same rates."

"Great, and I think I can help on the site funding." Shannon left Moon sitting with his tea and fetched the white bag from the kitchen. She moved everything off her coffee table and carefully shook out the bag's contents.

Moon jumped to his feet and sat quickly back down again. He popped up again and reached for a gem to study it more closely before pausing. "May I?"

Shannon nodded.

A half hour later, Moon took his leave of Shannon, secreting in his pocket a quart-sized zip lock sandwich bag filled with eight of her gems. These he planned to send with four trusted agents on special trips to Chicago, Antwerp, London and Hong Kong. But as he left, Shannon grabbed his arm and spoke solemnly. "I have one more thing to say, Dr. Moon. My diamonds come with conditions." She owed Moon this for all the trouble she'd caused him.

Moon paled and took a step toward the doorjamb, as if to brace himself.

"First, if the feasibility study turns out at all favorable, the Alaska site must be selected, not Ocean City. And second, Thomas Tremaine must resign from the board."

Moon's shoulders relaxed and he grinned. "I shall inform the board at my earliest convenience, Ms. Kendricks. And thank you."

* * *

Shannon spent the days waiting for news from the diamond markets largely curled on her couch under her softest pale blue afghan. She started, but did not quite finish two urban fantasies, a futuristic dystopian novel, and a suspense thriller.

Moon called her six days later with the news: the buyers judged the gems as nearly perfect as they'd ever seen: they had fetched astronomical prices. This meant the remaining gems could be sold gradually over time to pay off the loan the Dickson should now easily obtain with a large cash down payment from the first set of diamonds.

They were back in business.

CHAPTER FORTY-SIX

THE CALIFORNIA SUMMER GAVE WAY to the California winter. In Ocean City, that meant cooler, though pleasant, daytime temperatures, a great deal more fog and rain. Crisper nights.

Shannon failed to notice.

The money from the first eight diamonds had worked its magic: the new research center would be built, Underwater Complex and all, in Alaska, only five miles from the current site. Work would begin as soon as spring returned to the North Country. Shannon made plans to join the project team when the new facilities could accommodate them; in perhaps another five or six years, as the new site would require more preparation and construction than the current one had.

Shannon devoted many hours to the committees that met to draw up plans to make the new facilities even better than the now-abandoned site. She helped update biologists, scientists, and other staff from the destroyed facility as the new plans took shape.

Strictly speaking, Moon needn't have involved Shannon in the work on the new Dickson Center in Alaska. Other than the skills that gave her a bond with Juneau, she possessed no special training for designing new facilities or caring for whales. He included her because of her jewels, certainly, although he appeared to value her input too, and perhaps he still hoped that someday Juneau might return to the team.

And perhaps Shannon would allow it, if the whale consented, and if all outside interest in Juneau died away completely.

She'd made no other plans to fill the time before Moon finished the facility. Or, more accurately, to the outside world, her plan appeared to be to rest and recuperate.

In fact, she was learning as much as she could about her abilities, honing and refining them, corralling them when necessary. But she did not enter people's minds; there she drew the line.

Twice a month she also visited the institution for the criminally insane where the authorities continued to hold her friend Becky in confinement. Becky still refused to see her. But Shannon kept at it. One day she would break through to her friend. She wrote Becky urgent notes: Having figured out how to remove the essence of Tidak from Luke's mind, she couldn't wait to remove the essence of the ancient alien, and Old Salty, from Becky's mind. Being rid of them wouldn't cure her nightmares, but it would erase the perverse, swampy, predatory, killing instincts that haunted her now. Being rid of them would surely improve her chances of recovery. She could do this much for her friend, even if Becky's suffering had irrevocably severed their friendship. So far, however, she returned Shannon's letters unopened.

* * *

Spring arrived, warmer than usual, as seemed to happen more and more these last few years. The winter had been dry, and fears of wildfire rose again. Shannon rarely traveled outside the city limits, and absolutely refused to do so if the slightest chance of fire existed.

Shannon came down to the marina occasionally to join Dickson researchers on sea excursions. She especially liked venturing out on the *Seatation* or the *Moonbeam*, her sentimental favorites.

And she assiduously avoided events where she thought she might run into Luke. She couldn't bear to catch sight of him while having to keep her distance. Long ago, she and Becky had talked about such situations, too: doing the kindest thing could be the hardest thing.

* * *

One night, Shannon had settled into bed, Narci tucked under her arm, her cooler on the floor next to her, stocked with snacks and drinks, in the event she awoke too weak to make it to the kitchen. She opened one of the novels that she'd left stacked in the living room—one of the many she had started over the past months, but never managed to finish. She'd made a vow that she would read this pleasant little tale of elves and demons through to the end.

Howeve, having improved her ability to predict when someone would visit her, she soon picked up the warning haze out in the back yard by the picnic table. That would be Salesti.

Instead of heading down, she waited to see when Narci would sense its arrival. Five minutes passed. Ten. Suddenly Narci jumped off the bed and ran to the bedroom door. She looked back at Shannon.

Salesti, she imaged.

Shannon grinned at her improvement in sensing an arrival. *But wow. Narci had spoken up at last. And what was with Salesti and these midnight visits?*

Shannon tugged down her old University T-shirt with the holes in both shoulders, hitched up her black running shorts that hadn't seen a run in some years, and flew down to the picnic table.

Salesti arrived in due course, and flowed to Shannon's outstretched hand. Shannon eased down on the picnic bench, closed her eyes, and sent herself into her Great Room to greet the little fuzz ball.

After hugs, Salesti wasted no time with small talk.

roebor in trouble. shannon must help.

"How? How can I help? Is he here in Ocean City?"

fireworld. shannon comes with salesti.

"But I would have to leave my body behind, right?"

no, body comes with Shannon.

"Narci would have to go. I can't leave her. Um, you'd want to go, would you, Narci?"

Narci imaged, *I go.*

Oh, salesti not knows. Salesti buzzed at length, then hesitated only a second more before saying, *okay, yes, narci goes. but goes now. shannon and narci go now.*

Salesti expected her to decide with a snap of her fingers to go off through a portal to a world where the seas burned with blue fire and gigantic dragonpanthers ruled the cliffs?

"You mean I have to decide right now? Like right this minute? I can't sleep on it? Chew it over for a couple days, get my affairs in order, all that?"

now.

The very idea of such a leap scared the beejeebies out of her.

No. She wouldn't go.

And yet, what could happen?

She could die.

And so what? She had grown accustomed to living with the possibility of death that visited her every so often along with her alien friends and enemies. She'd even grown used to having the beejeebies scared out of her once in a while.

Still, she hadn't recovered from this last alien visit. She was dreaming if she thought she possessed the strength, the confidence, the bravery to help Roebor. What if she failed him?

She remembered Roebor then: the first time she'd seen him, so utterly impossible and magnificent; their little quarrels; their journey to secure the virus; their sad farewell.

At that moment, a certainty wrapped itself around her like a warm quilt on a cold bed. She pulled her braid over her right shoulder, ran her hands down it softly, and nodded slowly. Her belief that she was a shadow of her strongest self didn't matter. Her fear that she might lose him didn't matter. A simpler question lay at the heart of the matter: her friend was in trouble and he needed her help; would she give him everything she had?

* * *

Dr. Moon, who had dropped by every few weeks or so to update Shannon on the progress of the Dickson project, knocked on her door ten days later. When no one answered, he pulled out his cell and called Shannon's number. He'd become increasingly worried about her pallor, her gauntness, her sadness. And because of those worries, when no one answered, he called the police.

An hour later, Detectives Luke Quintana and Londell Taney, along with Dr. Moon, searched Shannon's house and found no sign of her or her cat. Her purse still lay unzipped where it had been tossed on the hall table, along with her car keys and her sunglasses. Dishes, washed and shiny, evidence of her last prodigious meal, were stacked high in the dish drainer, long since dry. Only the refrigerator revealed signs of a hasty departure: the milk had turned, the romaine had wilted, the bananas had gone soft and brown. On the kitchen table sat an envelope. Luke picked it up. It was addressed to Dr. Julia Bennett. It said:

THIS WILL EXPLAIN EVERYTHING

The End

Thank you for reading! It would mean so much to me and future readers if you were to leave a review.

Watch for the third and final novel of the

POWER RISING TRILOGY, POWER STABILIZED, available in 2021.

Want updates? Go to AuthorCathyParker.com to subscribe to my newsletter.

ABOUT THE AUTHOR

Like her protagonist Shannon Kendricks, Cathy Parker is an attorney, She volunteered as a zoo keeper's aide for eight years and did have a very special beluga buddy, Mauyak. As to encounters with alien children, she is not saying. She was also a radio and print journalist and once was the 'Jill of all trades' for a small satellite paper in Wyoming. She did everything from taking to the photos to writing the articles and op-ed pieces to helping with layout and hauling the newspapers through blizzards once a week. As a result, she saw lambs being born and went on a cattle drive and ate her first (and last) Rocky Mountain Oyster. She has seen mountain gorillas in the wild in Rwanda and orangutans in Borneo and even rocked an orphaned baby orangutan to sleep on her chest. She has volunteered with a chimpanzee sanctuary for former research subjects. So you can see where her heart lies. Currently she is happy at home with her black brindle mastiff and her black cat. All similarities between her cat and Narcissus are purely and probably coincidental. And she only wishes she could eat like Shannon Kendricks.

You can find her at her website, AuthorCathyParker.com.

www.ingramcontent.com/pod-product-compliance
Lightning Source LLC
Chambersburg PA
CBHW060609100726
47907CB00006B/1549